To those who told stories —

that led us to our dreams.

Contents

Terminology	VIII
Prologue	IX
1. Skin	1
2. MindSpace	14
3. Cy	23
4. That's Fine	27
5. The Arena	31
6. Forbidden Fruit	46
7. Chen's Kitchen	53
8. The Meeting	68
9. Platinum Pantry	78
10. This Was a Mistake	85
11. Big Dog	94
12. The Estate	96
13. Marston Mansion	110
14. You've Changed	118
15. Old Crow	129
16. Eagle	136
17. A Shaman &...	139
18. Distraction	146

19.	Katelina Chen	148
20.	Psy(Cy)chometry	157
21.	Sometimes it's Okay	163
22.	Mr Mayor	167
23.	Man of the People	172
24.	Surveillance	184
25.	Hermit	187
26.	A Message	193
27.	Almost	195
28.	Constellation	199
29.	The Present	203
30.	The Story of the Villager	209
31.	Legendary Name	212
32.	Coming of Age	216
33.	Infinisphere	228
34.	A new friend and an old	236
35.	Change	247
36.	Flight	249
37.	An Ocean of Shattered Glass	251
38.	When We First Met	260
39.	The Warrior	273
40.	Dreams	276
41.	It Felt Different	278
42.	The Wizard's Tower	283
43.	Part of the Truth	289
44.	You'll make it	296
45.	The President	297
46.	And so it Begins	299

47.	Ojo	302
48.	The Anti	304
49.	The First Wave	310
50.	Rain	313
51.	Water	315
52.	Brothers	317
53.	Home	319
54.	Seer	322
55.	A Battle on The Rooftops	324
56.	Dog Eat Dog World	331
57.	The Silver Officer	335
58.	A Chat	345
59.	Nathanael	350
60.	The Next Wave	364
61.	Platform	367
62.	Kitchen to the Rescue	371
63.	Blackjack	374
64.	The 4th	386
65.	All the Best Attacks Have Names	389
66.	The End	399
67.	Ascension	402
68.	Black Box	423
69.	Dream	446
70.	Hero	450
71.	Mother	452
72.	As We Enter a New Chapter	457
Epilogue		460
Afterword		461

CLASS	GREATER SELF	POWER	PLANE OF INFLUENCE	WORLD MATERIAL
Sentien	Mind	Sen	Metaphysical	Logic
Shaman	Soul	Mana	Spiritual	Ether
Seer	Body	Aura	Astral	Energy

We're going to tell you a story.

You may wonder at this point who 'We' are.

But it's too soon for that information to make itself known to you.

One must experience a story in the order it's being told.

Otherwise you miss things.

1

S<u>KIN</u>

There's a time in the morning, a little bit after dawn, where the briskness of night is all but alleviated by the first glimmers of sun. The air isn't cold, but cool. Just cool enough to blow a cloud of vapour in the wake of one's steps.

There were times, on a morning such as this, where the moon gave a dim presence in the clear sky. But on this day, a little bit after dawn, neither of Areth's two moons were in sight. The dawn was the sun's domain, after all. And if Jimoh had chosen to emulate these moons on this particular morning by not venturing into a place he did not belong, perhaps it might have begun far less eventful than it would turn out to be.

The early morning, a little bit after dawn, wasn't the time to be wandering around unfamiliar places, especially when one might then be considered unfamiliar to that place.

But, there Jimoh was. A young Eruban boy whose presence was unwelcome in the place he found himself in. There was something about this part of the district. It was... brighter... than the rest. It had well-maintained high-rise buildings. The structure of how everything was laid out was an organised aesthetic. A sort of uniformity born from the distinguished mind of a perfectionist. Nobody could tell you who designed this particular part of the district, but they would all speculate that whoever it was, they played no part in designing the rest.

The eastern side of West District was where most of the Irians lived. And the Irians got the best of everything. Everyone knew that. Including Jimoh. But he was young, inquisitive, and somewhat adventurous. He wanted to see what the difference was between them. Between the Irians and the 'others', as many of them said with contemptuous tones. They said 'others' because the Irians were but one skin amongst three, and sometimes, distinguishing the other two from one another proved too arduous a task.

But other times, the need to distinguish was delivered with a ferocity that might make one wish they'd settled for 'others.'

How strange a thing it is to categorise only some under the slur of 'others', when in reality, everyone is an 'other' to one another, are they not?

The Erubans were the darkest of the three skins. They were called Erubans if one was being polite. Darkies if not.

But Irians – whether you called them Irians or lightskins - the two were equivocal in value. It was difficult to put the same tone of disgust on a word when one stood on the continent of those they wished to insult. And ultimately, that was where this sense of superiority that some Irians had, came from. This was their land, their home. The Erubans and the Orenians were guests. Unwelcome ones, apparently.

That was why this part of the district was unfamiliar to Jimoh. He wasn't welcome there. And the thing about trespassing somewhere you weren't welcome, was that trouble would nearly always find its way to you.

Alex was in her apartment, finishing her morning routine before work.

She was Eruban, too. Not quite the same dark tone as Jimoh, but not nearly light enough to be considered anything but Eruban.

She had a relatively average build, and amongst a crowd of Erubans, might not stand out. An average looking person by all accounts. But she stood out in the place she lived like the moons did in the night. It was the contrast of an environment that truly showed how beautiful something was.

She was just about ready to leave. The morning should have begun as all mornings did. Uneventful.

But, call it fate, or perhaps destiny, or just some random event picked out of a hat of possibilities, this morning had trouble written into it. All because a young boy decided to walk somewhere he didn't belong.

She heard the commotion from outside her window. Multiple voices interrupted each other so the words couldn't be discerned. But she recognised them. She'd encountered them so often in the past.

She peaked out of her window – as many of the neighbours did – to see a bunch of the local Irian boys surrounding a young Eruban boy.

This was the first time this Eruban boy had been seen round these parts, but not the first time Alex had seen him. She knew of him from elsewhere, though it was a one-sided relationship. When Alex would head down in just a few moments, that would be the first time he'd lay eyes on her.

But certain things would transpire before that.

The difference between skin and culture was nature and nurture; born with one and learned the other. There was no question who the Irian children learned their superiority complex from.

The boys formed a circle around Jimoh and began to push him around, laughing and jeering as they did so. Alex noticed more neighbours peering out of their own windows, even heard a few chuckles. Of course they wouldn't mask their satisfaction.

She knew, too, that nobody was going to help. That would fall on her.

She left her apartment and sped down the stairs. The situation couldn't escalate much further in the minute it would take her to reach them, could it?

It could, and it did.

She heard a loud clang just as she reached the door.

A tremor then pulsed in her chest. She really hoped what she thought happened hadn't actually happened, but the likelihood was that it had. And that meant even more trouble.

She opened the door to exactly what she feared.

It wasn't his fault. They had attacked him, after all. He was only defending himself.

That didn't matter. The neighbours certainly wouldn't see it that way.

The police might not, either.

7 Irian boys had surrounded Jimoh, but all of them now found themselves on the floor, clutching at scrapes and grazes. But it wasn't

their grounded positions that was of the most concern. It was their proximity. They were so far from him now.

What had happened?

Alex knew exactly what happened. Jimoh had pushed them.

No, a push would imply a physical action. What Jimoh had done wasn't physical at all.

He hadn't pushed, so much as he'd *pushed*. An action performed not with the body, but with the mind, bound by far less restrictions and capable of achieving much greater results.

The greater the results, the more dire the consequences.

The neighbours would have seen what he'd done. No doubt they would have reported it to the police right away.

Alex stepped onto the street. Examining the boys, she noted minor injuries, which at the very least meant this wasn't the worst case scenario. *He really did push them far,* she thought. Even she was impressed. At merely 8 years old, his mind shouldn't be strong enough to *push* seven boys at once. But perhaps Alex, very much like the Irians did, was forgetting that Erubans specialised in functions that imitated physical acts of power. How else would they survive the harsh lands of their home continent?

They'd underestimated him, and he showed them why that was a mistake.

But if only he'd held out just a little bit longer. Alex could have resolved the situation without things escalating as they had. But it was too late now. The consequences would be arriving soon, and Alex needed to figure out how to deal with them.

She marched over to Jimoh.

The first thing she saw was the anger in his face. Understandable. Nobody liked getting picked on. But Jimoh was young. He still had much emotional development to go through, and an emotion like anger, which had such a great impact on one's mental state, was a dangerous thing.

She bent down to his level and put a gentle touch to his cheek, followed by a whisper in his ear of, 'It's okay.' This seemed to settle him just a little bit. Enough for him to not attempt another function, anyway.

Not that he could.

Impressive as his *push* had been, it had drained him mentally. He wouldn't be performing another.

In a situation like this, someone in Alex's position may ask Jimoh where his parents were, allowing him to roam the streets as he did. But Alex knew exactly where his parents were, and they were in no situation to monitor Jimoh's comings and goings.

So Alex didn't ask about his parents, or his brother whom she also knew of. She simply said, 'You mustn't be reckless. These situations can land you in trouble. And you know what happens when you get into trouble?'

He knew all too well. It was only within the last year that his parents had a run in with the law and got taken away. Away to a place nobody knew.

Those who got taken were never seen again. Everyone knew that.

Jimoh and his brother were as good as orphans.

He nodded. Far too angry to speak.

Alex's attention was drawn to her peripheral vision.

The police had arrived, punctual as always.

'Don't say anything. I'll handle this,' she said.

She took a breath of relief as the officers approached. By some stroke of luck, the ones that responded happened to be people she was familiar with. Things just might work out in her favour.

Officer Dodds approached the scene of the reported crime.

He greeted Alex familiarly.

She reciprocated, and extended the greeting to his two apprentice officers.

His son, Maxwell Dodds, and his son's best friend, Bolu.

It was uncommon for Erubans to have second names. That was more of an Irian thing. Orenian, too.

It must have been somewhat strange for the neighbours. To have put in a call to the police and have an Eruban be one of the responders.

No matter. Officer Dodds was there, and he was one of the most respected officers in the district. He would make sure justice was served.

That was what they all thought, anyway.

But the mentality of Dodds wasn't quite the same as other Irians. He had experiences of old that had taught him differently. Made him see the world with a wider scope. He wasn't the man people thought him to be.

He was much better.

Alex knew that. She'd experienced first-hand his open-mindedness. That was why she had confidence that this altercation may not end as badly as it perhaps could.

But that wouldn't stop it from escalating just a little bit.

The boys Jimoh had attacked were locals, known to most of the neighbours who witnessed the encounter. So it wasn't long before some of their parents showed up in the street. And parents, being what they are, were furious.

Good thing Dodds was already there. It was a shuddering thought to think what might have happened to Jimoh should the parents have taken matters into their own hands.

That would have been an even more troublesome thing for Alex to deal with.

Dodds recalled the account of the numerous reports he'd gotten about an Eruban boy attacking several Irians.

The multiple reports saying the same thing, alongside the scene of the event itself, gave it a lot of credibility. Things didn't look good for Jimoh.

But Alex gave her own account of events. After all, none of the locals would have ever admitted that their kids were picking on Jimoh first, and that his retaliation was in self defence, even if a bit excessive.

'Are you seriously going to listen to her over us?' said one of the mothers, gripping her child closely to her.

The shift in tone partway through her sentence wasn't lost on anyone. It was something of an ability to turn a simple pronoun into some form of slur. Alex could feel the disgust that manifested within that single word.

"Her!"

Dodds might have handled the situation differently up until that point, but now, he wouldn't give them the satisfaction.

'Well, one surefire way to solve this would be to look through the memories of everyone involved, Dodd's said. 'But that requires permissions, which involves preliminary investigations, and can be quite invasive on the minds of those undergoing it. I imagine you wouldn't want such a stressful experience befalling your children? Not to mention what I might find?'

Dodds was an experienced officer. He knew how to read the body language and expressions of those he questioned, or interrogated. So when he saw the nervous reactions that they all had to his suggestion, but noticed both Alex and Jimoh remained calm, he knew something was amiss.

Things didn't go down the way the locals had initially reported. He was sure of that.

'Youngsters get into scuffles every now and then,' Dodds said. 'Even these two have their scraps, and some would call them grown men,' nodding to Max and Bolu. 'I'm sure a situation like this can be resolved with an apology.'

An apology. Yes. Good. That was a suitable outcome for Alex.

She'd been standing between Jimoh and other boys, but now she stepped aside, opening up a line of communication for them.

She saw the locals all staring at Jimoh, waiting for his apology. It must have been quite intimidating, to be looked down on like that.

Alex thought to encourage him along.

'Go on, Jimoh,' she said with the sweetest voice.

'Go on, what?' he asked with a completely deferential tone.

She was confused for a moment. Had he missed the conversation?

He hadn't. That wasn't what was happening.

Everyone was waiting for Jimoh to apologise, but Jimoh was waiting for them.

Alex understood. They had come for him first. They should apologise first. She believed that. But this wasn't just about who was right or wrong. This was about resolving the situation as peacefully as possible. And when it was the one against the many, well, the one usually lost.

'Apologise for hurting my son, you little...'

The mother didn't finish that sentence. It would be improper. Especially in front of the police.

'He should apologise,' said Jimoh.

How outrageous, the locals thought. *The audacity of this child!*

Dodds could see the rising tensions. So he said to Jimoh, 'Now son...'

But Jimoh sent him the most ferocious of looks. Pure, unadulterated anger. 'I'm not your son!'

Dodds knew that was his mistake. And he knew, then, that apologies weren't an option for either side. So he did the only other thing he thought he could.

Facing the locals, he took off his hat, brought it down to his chest with a bow, and said, 'On behalf of the West District Police Department, I apologise for the situation that transpired here. I hope you can find it within yourselves to forgive and move on. This situation needn't escalate further. I'll see to it that the young man is escorted back home safely.'

Where he belongs, they thought.

It wasn't the preferred outcome, nor was it a satisfactory one, but, it was Officer Dodds, and if for nothing other than the respect they had for him, they would comply with his request. After all, no point having the day ruined by such trivial events. Certainly not because of an Eruban.

The parents left with their children, not missing the opportunity to give sideways glances to Alex, which she met an unwavering expression of her own dissatisfaction with their presence. It had been a while since she'd been affronted like that. They tended to steer clear of her.

And it was a good thing they did. The bad side of Alex was a place one didn't want to find themselves. Or they might soon have their world collapse on them.

An unexpected start to the morning, but all things considered, it could have been a lot worse.

The remaining issue was Dodds convincing Jimoh to allow him to be escorted home. Another problem whose solution seemed to turn up out of nowhere.

They all heard it at the same time. The voice of a man calling Jimoh's name.

It was yet another voice known not only to Alex, but Bolu, too.

Jimoh's brother, Chuks, came running down the street.

'Don't you say anything, Jimoh!' He shouted.

He was with them in just a few seconds.

'Don't talk to them, Jimoh,' he said again, looking straight at Officer Dodds. He didn't even notice Alex standing there, who, in any other circumstance, would have caught his eye at first glance, and held his gaze in the moments proceeding.

But not this time. He took hold of Jimoh, tucking him into himself protectively. He had that same look on his face that Jimoh had. That look of burning hatred.

They were brothers. They had suffered the same loss. So their hatred was the same. Except, where Jimoh only knew his parents had been taken by police, Chuks knew exactly who the arresting officer was.

There was a reason Officer Dodds was revered by the community. He had the second highest number of arrests in the district, most of whom were Eruban.

And he remembered Chuks, too, but hadn't known he'd had a brother. So even though Jimoh didn't know it was Dodds who'd arrested his parents, Dodds still accepted that look he'd been given. Because whether or not Jimoh's parents were good or bad, right or wrong, just or unjust, heroes, villains, or something in between, they were still his parents. He would hate anybody who took them away from him.

There was nothing left for Dodds to say now that Chuks turned up.

He gestured a goodbye to Alex and took his leave.

Max and Bolu would shortly follow, but both were holding a respective gaze. Bolu's eyes were locked in a visual conflict with Chuks. There was a history there, and not a good one.

There was a history between Alex and Max, too. But that was a story for another time.

Bolu and Max turned to leave.

Chuks waited until they were well away before saying anything.

Then, to Jimoh. 'What have I said about going off on your own? You don't listen!'

'I wasn't doing anything!' Jimoh defended.

'This is Irian territory!' Chuks snapped back. 'It doesn't matter if you're doing anything.' Then he looked at Alex. 'Who are you?'

Again, in another situation, he would have been jaw-droppingly dazzled by her. But here, now, under these circumstances, he didn't know if she was friend or foe.

Or something in between.

'Just a concerned observer,' Alex said. Then she smiled at Jimoh and went on her own way.

'Wait...' Chuks called out to her.

But she waved her hand in dismissal, shouting at him that she was late for work, and there was nothing more to be said on the matter.

And that was the start to what should have been a normal day. Slightly troublesome, but easily resolved. Although, the story of conflict between Irian and Eruban wouldn't end there.

That was but a trickle of the impending storm. The aftermath of which would spell a new dawn in the city of New Heart. And long withheld secrets would come to light.

2

MindSpace

There weren't many who remembered the old city. MindSpace, the organisation responsible for the city's technological revolution, was its singular greatest power, and it championed the transition of Old Heart into New so phenomenally, that the old city became all but a lost memory.

Alex Arrived at the West District branch of MindSpace via travel station. They were the primary means of transport in this city. A network of interconnected pathways that altered the meta of space. An hour of travel by any other means was reduced to a matter of seconds. They called it warping.

That made being late for work all the more unacceptable, which Alex found herself to be on this occasion. She knew she'd get an earful as soon as she stepped in.

Once she was in the lobby of the building, she took a few more steps forward and then disappeared from sight.

She reappeared a few floors up, where her office was.

No, that wasn't warping.

Warping required an unrestricted path to follow. You couldn't warp through walls and ceilings, or any other type of obstruction.

What Alex utilised was something unavailable to the general public, and tended to only be found in building's like MindSpace, allowing its personnel to utilise a more advanced means of traversing space. Teleportation.

Like her supervisor, who was there, waiting, ready. Alex prepared herself to be scolded, but it never came.

'I need you straight in, Alex,' said May. 'We've got a big one. Fred and Rachel have been at it all morning.'

A big one. They hadn't had one of those in a while.

A big one certainly did warrant a few hours of work. A few more if Fred was the one tasked with dealing with it.

He wasn't the most competent of employees. Not recently, anyway.

Alex, on the other hand, shone like no other. She was the golden girl. The star of the office. Would-be permanent employee of the month, if they did such a thing.

Much to the dissatisfaction of many who worked there, Alex was the best diver in the West District branch of MindSpace.

She exchanged obligatory niceties with May, taking advantage of the urgency of the situation to move past the fact she was late.

She entered the bullpen of 40 or so workers. Most of whom were mid dive.

Taking a seat at her cubicle, she put on her interactive goggles. A device manufactured from Rethium which gave divers administrative access to the network. It was a necessary requirement for carrying out the work they did.

They were called divers because they submerged themselves into the subconscious of their clients. Deep into the expansive ocean of thought they called the mind. But, diving was simply the surface of their responsibilities. It may also be accurate to call them mind surgeons. Tasked with removing the mental tumours that developed from unchecked use of the network.

It was how virtual reality worked. Your mind immersed itself into the realities of others, and when it left, it took part of the reality with it. It was like a memory. The way the mind is able to recollect past events is due to remnants of those experiences laying dormant, waiting to be called upon. But what the mind retained from being in the network held much greater weight than a simple memory. It carried fragments of the reality it had experienced, and those fragments didn't simply fade away. They banded together over time, until eventually, they formed something called a clutter.

As soon as Alex entered the client's mind space, and stood before the clutter she was tasked with removing, her first thought was, 'Wow. It really is a big one.'

This clutter was an amalgamation of all sorts of things that had no business being together. It was a monstrosity. The personification of randomness.

Think of any number of things in this world. Animals, insects, plants, earth, wind and fire, foods, fabrics, art, books, and all forms and variations of all things in the infinity of possibilities. Take all of those individual items of existence and stack them atop one another.

That was a clutter.

And because it was made of different things from different places, its meta wasn't definitive. It changed with every piece that made up its whole. A large mass of multiple problems, each one needing its own solution.

Rachel was the first to notice Alex. 'Reinforcements have arrived!'

Hearing this, Fred turned around, too.

Reinforcements indeed, but not the type he wanted.

Alex wasn't particularly liked by her colleagues, but none bore as deep a hatred for her as Fred.

And none held her with as great admiration as Rachel.

'We're handling it,' Fred said.

'I don't think the client wants to spend the whole day bedridden because it took us too long to clear her mind,' Alex retorted. Which was only meant to be an insult to Fred's abilities, not Rachel's.

'Shouldn't have let it get so big then, should she?' He replied.

He wasn't wrong. Clients were advised to get their minds cleared regularly for this very reason. Large clutters were too problematic.

But Fred had this natural ability to instantly annoy Alex any time he opened his mouth. There was just something about the way he spoke. A distinct lack of care. And she'd bet she could guess why.

Clients maintained some degree of anonymity when their minds were being cleared, but certain things could be determined about them from the clutters they manifested.

Clutters were formed from remnants of what users experienced within the MindSpace Network. Naturally, there was specific content that attracted a certain type of person. Or a certain skin of person.

Much of the content within this client's mind suggested an Eruban woman, and whilst they couldn't be certain of that, it didn't stop them from making the presumption.

The reason behind Fred's uncaring tone towards the client was the same as his reason for his animosity towards Alex.

He was amongst the subculture of Irians that held the belief that they were the superior skin, and the Erubans in particular, by any account, were savages, masquerading as civilised.

It made his blood boil that he had to work with one.

Even more so that she was, without question, better at the job.

She got to work quickly.

Alex, Rachel, Fred; everyone that worked at MindSpace, and most people who lived in this city, were Sentiens. Sentiens had the ability to directly apply the metaphysical nature of their minds to the metaphysical nature of the world, thus, changing the state of the world itself. What most never developed an understanding of, was that the metaphysical - or meta - was composed of logic, and logic was something you couldn't perceive. Not unless you had the interactive goggles. Or... (well, we're not there yet)

Here, in the virtual, the meta was all there was. Nothing here existed in a physical or spiritual capacity. It was just information.

Clutters were an amassment of random pieces of information that came together. And in order to remove a clutter, one simply needed to apply the opposing meta. Anti-meta.

It was the yes to the no. The left to the right. Right to the wrong. To counteract a step forward, one simply needed to take an equal step backwards, and that was the simplicity of getting rid of clutters. You just needed to know how to structure its anti.

But what was the opposite of a fox? Or of the colour green? Was the opposite of a cloudy day a clear sky? Or did they simply exist as two options that were mutually exclusive? Mutual exclusivity didn't necessarily mean the opposite. In truth, it didn't matter. One didn't need to know what the conceptual opposite of a fox was. One simply needed to be able to perceive the logic that gave the fox its meaning, and then, reverse it. Create its anti, to take it from something, to nothing. That was what the goggles were for. They allowed divers to visualise the structures of meta that defined all things within the network. It was then left to divers to construct the anti, and fuel it with enough sen to neutralise it.

Sen was to the mind as strength was to the body. Where the body used strength to enact change in the physical world, the mind used sen to enact change in the meta. And the soul... we're not at that part of the story yet, either.

It was impressive. Both the network, and what Alex was achieving. Little by little the massive clutter was losing itself, until eventually, a little became a lot.

Where Fred and Rachel had noticeable intervals of space between each wave of anti, Alex's utilisation of the ability was fluid. It was a mystery amongst those in the office how it was that her mind could decipher meta so quickly. But the people in the office didn't know Alex, not her real self. Not the version of her that struggled with so much greater a burden in the past. If they had known, perhaps they'd realise how easy this truly was.

Half an hour. In half an hour, Alex had cleared as much of the clutter as Fred and Rachel combined, and they'd had a 2-hour head start. It's not that they were necessarily bad at their jobs, Alex was just that much better.

So why was Fred incompetent? His attitude aside, he made mistakes from time to time.

Like now.

Seeing Alex work always frustrated him. One needed to be level headed when diving, but Fred allowed his emotions to get the better of him at times. And when they did, he'd miscalculate.

The anti required to remove a clutter needed to be nearly exact. The allowed margin of error was minimal.

If you got the structure wrong, or used too little or too much sen, the clutter could splinter into smaller fragments. Or the anti could become unstable, and instead of neutralising the clutter, would damage the client's mind.

That was something divers needed to constantly be cautious of. They were within someone's mind space. Everything they did there had the potential to affect it in some way.

That was why divers were so important. It wasn't just the individuals themselves. It was the resources at their disposal. The goggles they wore had been programmed to allow them to navigate a client's mind safely. Without them – without the safety precautions they had in place – unrestricted access to someone's mind space was a very dangerous position to be in. A person's mind had a natural way of defending itself from whatever it might consider a threat.

In Fred's blind rage, he'd misstructured his next wave, and the piece of the clutter he'd targeted fragmented off. This wouldn't cause any direct damage on its own, but each piece now needed to be dealt with individually, which was a more difficult task than dealing with the whole.

'Damn it!' He muffled his voice, but it didn't matter. Alex had already seen what happened.

'Get yourself together, Fred!'

'I don't need you to tell me that!' He scowled back at her. So much spite in his tone.

Never mind dealing with the fragments individually. He'd release one big wave and take care of them together.

Alex anticipated this. Surely he wasn't serious? As if the situation wasn't bad enough already. She couldn't allow it.

The moment Fred released his wave, she released her own. An anti to his anti. The two clashed and neutralised each other

Fred looked up to her in bewilderment. Perhaps it was his rage, or perhaps his disbelief, but what occurred next seemed to happen in slow motion for him. He saw Alex raise her hand, form a wave of anti, and then throw it at him.

Have you ever witnessed a ball heading straight for you? Your mind deciphering what was about to happen but your body unable to respond? That was what this was like. He knew what she was doing. He knew it was coming, but his body - his virtual one - couldn't do anything to stop it. And the last thing he saw before being forced out of the network was that look. That look Alex had as she stood there above him. The look of superiority that only Irians should have.

He hated that look.

'You really shouldn't have done that,' Rachel said to Alex.

'He was becoming a liability,' she replied.

'I know. But that wasn't your call to make. You're not a supervisor.'

There was a certain tone with those last words. A sort of accusation. Alex knew what she was referring to. And Rachel was right. She really shouldn't have done that. She overstepped her position. That, alongside her being late that morning... there was a conversation to be had later.

Alex could hear the voice of her best friend echoing in her mind, 'I'll burn that bridge when I get to it.' She had work to finish.

Back in the real, Fred threw off his goggles and stormed over to Alex's cubicle. He was intercepted by May, who was by no means a friend to Alex, but couldn't allow Fred to interfere with her body mid-dive.

'Did you see what she did?' He yelled.

'I did, and she'll pay for it,' she replied. 'Just let her finish first. We'll take care of this later. Okay?'

They shared a look. There was more being said than what was actually said. Things that others mustn't hear.

Things that would be discovered when later came.

3

Cy

Chuks and Jimoh arrived back at the south of the district. Eruban territory.

The architecture was entirely different to the east side. The buildings weren't glamorous, and consisted of more low-rise with less open space between. It looked cramped by comparison. But, somehow, there was more life to it. More evidence of 'we were here'. This was the place Chuks and Jimoh called home.

They came upon a building titled "Workshop". Upon entry, they were greeted by a woman of notably dark skin, even for an Eruban. Darker than Alex by a few shades. And she was decorated, too. Black ink had been etched under her eyes to make the appearance of... tears?

'Chuks, Jimoh. You look parched,' she said. A wave of her hand drew water from a large basin into two glasses she had on the counter.

They drank more out of courtesy than thirst.

She waited until they finished before asking, 'What brings you here today?'

'I need to see Cy, if he's available,' Chuks said. 'We had a little trouble this morning.'

She looked between the two of them, nodding her head gently.

'He's just round back. I'll let him know you're coming.'

'Thanks, Mara,' said Chuks, guiding Jimoh to the back.

They walked through a rather ominous hallway. It was eerily silent. The only light that came through was from the entrance, and grew dimmer the further down they went, which somehow made the corridor seem longer than it was. It was almost daunting.

They reached the door at the end and Chuks knocked gently. He'd need to wait for permission to enter. It was about 30 seconds before the go-ahead came.

He and Jimoh entered, and right away were met with:

'You've interrupted me at a vital time, Chuks. I hope it's important.'

Cy was sitting alone in an empty room. It was dark. Not pitch, but barely visible. Only partially illuminated now by the light from the hallway.

He was the darker side of Eruban, too. And his skin seemed dim in tone, but that might have just been the lighting. He was a tall but slender man. Reasonably built by way of muscle definition, but not quite enough to be considered muscular. His most noticeable feature was the somewhat permanent expression of seriousness he had on his face. As if one would never catch him smiling. Which, if you asked anyone, they'd swear he never did.

'We had a run in with the police this morning,' Chuks said.

'And who, between the two of you, was the perpetrator in this, "run in"?'

Chuks hesitated to answer, which Cy understood would only happen if he was covering for his little brother.

Cy looked at Jimoh.

'Jimoh, I need you to show me what happened this morning. I'm going to try and access your mind. You just need to relax and let me in. Okay?'

Jimoh nodded.

He felt it immediately. It was like a tap on the head. The sensation without the physical pressure.

The mind itself had a natural defence against other people accessing it. It could be broken through, but that brought about its own set of issues to overcome.

Cy could now visualise Jimoh's thoughts. He asked him to recollect the events of earlier that day. He saw everything quite quickly. Jimoh patrolling through the streets of the eastside. His altercation with the locals. The young woman who came to his aid. Officer Dodds.

He left Jimoh's mind.

'Well I can't fault you for defending yourself,' he said, 'But you've been warned extensively about delving into other territories. And for that, you owe your brother an apology.'

Jimoh did apologise, to both of them.

'Is it all good, then?' Chuks asked. He was wondering if this encounter spelt any more trouble than it immediately presented.

'It should be,' Cy replied. 'Dodd's won't investigate that particular issue any further. We should be able to carry on as planned.'

Chuks was relieved. He thanked Cy, and then apologised again. 'I'm supposed to watch him, so it's my fault this happened.'

And Cy said to him with a calm voice, 'Remember, it takes a village. The responsibility for raising Jimoh lies with all of us. When he acts out, it's a sign that we all need to do better.'

Chuks nodded, and even mustered the start of what might be considered a smile. There was nothing left to discuss so he excused himself.

Basking once again in the darkness of the room, Cy felt a sort of uneasiness about him. There were things in this world that were coincidence, and things that were far too coincidental to be coincidence. Seeing Alex in Jimoh's memories, he couldn't quite decide which of the two categories their encounter fell into. Why was it now, on this particular week, that Jimoh should find himself being rescued by an Eruban woman Cy had never seen before?

Perhaps it was something. Perhaps nothing. Time would tell. And though Cy was a particularly patient man, this mystery would play on his mind with an urgency he didn't usually experience. He wanted an answer to his question.

Who was she?

4

THAT'S FINE

May's office.

It took another hour, but Alex and Rachel finally got the clutter cleared. What awaited Alex was something even more troublesome. A conversation with May. And to make matters worse, Fred was there, too.

'You know you were in the wrong,' May said. 'You don't have authorization to kick people out of clients' minds. Just because you have the ability, doesn't mean you should.'

That was a lecture Alex didn't need or want to hear from the likes of May. Alex was well aware that just because you could do something, didn't mean you should. Choosing not to use one's ability to take advantage of others was a core principle of discipline. One she'd learned a long time ago.

Not to mention how laughable it was that she was being scolded for doing something the supervisor would have been required to do.

'He was a threat to the client's mind,' Alex defended. 'I made the right decision, whether I was authorised to or not.'

That was a level of insubordination that wouldn't go unpunished.

'Regardless of if it was the right decision,' May said with a stern voice, 'it wasn't your decision to make. You acted outside of company protocols. What if you had structured your anti incorrectly? How much more detrimental would that have been? Only supervisors have access to the program that can lift employees from a dive. We have these measures in place for a reason. Going rogue and issuing your own function was reckless, and I can't let that slide.'

'I wouldn't consider my course of action reckless,' Alex responded. 'Certainly not by comparison.'

She sent an accusing look towards Fred. She didn't even try to be subtle about it. Perhaps she should have kept it internal, but she didn't think to do that either. She was firm and audacious with her stance, which was never a situation that ended well.

And Fred? Well he didn't take too kindly to being given that look. This wasn't his reprisal, it was hers.

You could see the physical strain he exerted from holding himself back. How he wanted to wrap his hands around her neck and squeeze with all his might. It was a loud statement when a Sentien resorted to physical acts of aggression as opposed to meta. But his hatred burned so passionately it couldn't help but be expressed in physical form.

But he was lucky. Lucky that he'd held himself back. Nothing good would ever come from him laying a finger on Alex.

'*Calm down!*' May thought to him.

That wasn't all she said. She reassured him of certain things. Certain things that mustn't be made privy to others. How naive of them, in a city where infiltrating the minds of others was a professional practice, that they thought their own minds would be safe. It was a foolish mistake to assume nobody was ever listening.

A foolish mistake to think Alex wasn't. Or perhaps, the mistake was to assume that she couldn't.

She could. But she'd learned a long time ago that she had to be responsible with her abilities.

When you read someone's mind, you become responsible for their thoughts.

Someone told her that once, and that had been enough for her to learn the lesson. She'd been careful ever since.

But she couldn't help it if certain items of information made their way to her by other means. And when they did, responsibility or not, she had to act on them.

She'd become lost in thought for a while. May had said a few more things, but by the time she snapped out of it, she couldn't recollect a word of what it was.

'You're doing it again, Alex!'

'Hmm?' was Alex's response.

'Wandering off!' May exclaimed. 'Every time you get that blank expression on your face I know you're not listening to a word I say. It's rude and disrespectful and I've had enough!'

Alex had that blank expression on her face quite regularly. It happened when she needed to focus on something internally. One of those interesting items of information had just made its way to her.

'I said I'm putting you on administrative leave, Alex.'

Alex was listening now. She looked curiously between May and Fred. The deviousness of the two. Were they really planning what they were planning? How laughable. And Alex did laugh.

May and Fred thought she was laughing at her suspension, which was also amusing. They looked at each other, confused. It wasn't the response they were expecting, though technically, she hadn't even responded yet.

Then she finally said, 'That's fine.'

'What?' May asked, even more confused.

'I said it's fine,' Alex repeated. 'Actually, you might as well make it permanent.'

The shock factor seemed to grow more and more.

'Now Alex,' May said, 'I know you like to show people how in control you are, but this isn't one of those situations where one upping me is going to be beneficial for you. I'll give you the opportunity to retract what you just said.'

And grovel at your feet? Yeah you'd like that, Alex thought.

'I mean it,' was Alex's immediate response. 'Tell people I quit. Tell them you fired me. Whatever makes you sleep better.'

May's eyes flared up. 'Your insubordination has gone too far, Alex!'

Alex raised her hand, gesturing May to silence. 'I don't work for you anymore,' she said. 'Insubordination is no longer a word that applies.' Then she got up from her seat. 'Fred. A displeasure as always. I'll see myself out.' She gave them both one last contemptuous look, and then left, expecting - knowing - that she would see both of them very, very soon.

5

THE ARENA

With her work day cut short, Alex decided to take advantage of her new-found free time. A quick message over The Network, followed by a warp journey and a minute's walk home found her back in her bedroom.

She removed unnecessary clothing and lay down.

Divers accessed The Network as administrators through interactive goggles, but regular citizens accessed the Network as users through their coders.

The Network was the foundation of everything that went on in this city. All the programs its citizens had access to, the warp paths, the various functions that made the city run as the futuristic utopia it was; all of that meta was contained within the Network. Without it, New Heart wouldn't be what it was.

The Network could be used for general on-the-go purposes, but its most common use was the fully immersive virtual reality that could be utilised from the comfort of one's home. A fantastical world of endless possibilities, limited only by the imagination of its users.

And how fantastical it was.

Alex couldn't help, whenever she entered The Network, to gaze up into its artificial sky and read the words printed above.

I Dream of Touching Stars.

Sometimes I lie, under the night sky,
And stretch out my hand.

When the light of a star reaches us,
Does it ever find its way back?

Do stars see their reflections in
The eyes of those who gaze upon them?

Are they warm to feel?
Do they taste sweet, or bitter?
Do they crackle, like flames?
Or shimmer, like lights?

Do they scent the emptiness of space,
Like candles in a dark room?

Is anything we think of stars true
In places other than our own minds?
I don't think so.

So I dream of touching stars.
Because only in my dreams
Can stars be touched.

-W.O

Navigating The Network wasn't too dissimilar to travelling in the real. It just had less restrictions. One's feet didn't touch the ground, because there was no ground. There was no specific verb to describe the action of movement one undertook. They didn't run, or fly, or swim, they just moved. From one point of space to another. What differed was the speed at which they did so. Whether they wished to slowly explore the many wonders around them, or reach a far away destination instantaneously, they could perform the action whenever or wherever they chose. As Alex did now.

The world she went to was called The Arena, which was a popular destination for several reasons.

Of the 200 days in an Areth year, 199 of them were dedicated to free use of The Arena and all it had to offer. And the one day that differed from the rest? That was the most celebrated day in this city.

It was a regular meeting spot for Alex and the two people she frequented it with.

The Arena was a rather unique world within the Network. It didn't necessarily exist as one whole, but rather multiple overlapping layers of programming which users could choose to access. The various maps available were said to be reminiscent of places in the real, though most of New Heart either had no experience of the outside world, or had been closed off from it for too long to remember what it was like.

Even if they did remember, who was to say the world they knew was the same world now? New Heart alone was evidence of how much things could change in the span of 25 years.

Alex entered a map called Coliseum, a place where users engaged in gladiator-style combat. That particular combat art originated from one of the Southern Kingdoms, or so they said.

There were multiple battles taking place at this time of day, each of them occupying a pocket space within the Coliseum's coding. That was the thing about a virtual network. It was all information, so creating 'smaller' spaces with exactly the same meta as 'larger' spaces was relatively easy.

Then there were the markets. Licensed stalls made for the purpose of selling goods that could enhance one's virtual experience. And in the case of The Arena, where one could obtain programs that weren't permitted for use anywhere else. These were how a lot of New Hearters made a living, by selling programs they'd either created, or had rights to sell as a third party. She walked past many stalls until she came across one that was titled 'MARSTON'S', which was a place all-too familiar to anyone who entered The Arena. It had a reputation as the most expensive shop in the markets, but equally the place to get the best merchandise. You spent a premium, but you got what you paid for. The shop itself was managed by an automated avatar, which was an expensive program to run. You could tell, most of the time, who the upper-class were. But even amongst that crowd, the Marstons were in another league.

Alex only ever browsed what was on display, never bought. She looked at items to gain inspiration. When she told anyone this, they asked if she was a smith - a general term for someone who created - which she would tell them she wasn't. And without a doubt, they would be confused as to what inspiration someone who wasn't a smith might derive from simply looking at items. But there were different types of sights. Or rather, different means of perception. There were things one could only see when observing with something other than their eyes.

Reality – virtual or real – was composed of many layers; multiple planes of existence converging at a single point to create the world they knew. Within that reality were an ever growing number of individuals who could see beyond what was immediately shown to them. The perception of what existed behind the physical world.

Alex could see things otherwise unseen, but now wasn't the time for that. The person she'd come to meet was here.

His name was Daniel, though nobody could tell. Both he, and Alex, took on avatars that took away all of their real-world features. Everyone on the MindSpace Network was represented by an avatar of some sort. All manner of imaginary things that couldn't possibly exist in the real. But in a virtual reality where they made the rules, things that couldn't possibly be real were the norm.

There were categories for the type of avatar you could choose. Humanoid, fae, plantae, spirit, ethereal! The most recent was a word nobody in this city had ever heard before.

Astral.

How was it that words came about? They were simply a metaphysical means of identifying aspects of the world in a way that could be relayed and understood. They had no definitive value, did they?

And what did Astral even mean?

Where stars gathered. That was the description given. But what did it actually mean?

Both their silhouettes were a black canvas with stars twinkling inside an endless space. An ethereal glow surrounding them. Astral. There was more to that word than any of them knew.

Daniel gave a gentle wave as Alex approached. 'I have a room,' he said, opening up a door that led to a pocket space. Alex followed him through it and it closed up behind them. They would be able to have a private conversation here. Unlike the pocket spaces Alex had passed along the way, this one wasn't public.

They could watch whatever public pocket spaces they wanted from that room. Have conversations that nobody else was privy to. Or do whatever else people might do when they were alone.

This wasn't that type of meeting. They didn't have that sort of relationship.

'Day off?' Daniel asked.

'No,' Alex said. 'I got fired today.'

'Oh. I'm sorry to hear that.'

'Don't be. Technically I left, but I was suspended before that, so, fired.'

'Still a shame,' he said with sympathy. 'You loved that job.'

'I liked the work,' she corrected. 'I don't need the job to keep on doing it.'

'To keep on doing it legally, you do.'

'Well they haven't caught me yet.'

Daniel smiled. Not that she could see since his astral form was absent of facial features. 'So you'll just keep clearing people's minds until...?'

'Until I get out of the city, I suppose.'

He smiled again. 'So are you taking the test this year?' There was something gleeful about the way he expressed himself just then. This wasn't the regular excitement someone got when their friend told them they were taking the test. This was different.

'No,' Alex said. 'I'm not taking the test. There are other ways out of the city.'

'Hmmm,' Daniel mumbled with concern. 'Do all of your plans involve breaking the law?'

'Is it a problem if they do?'

'Well yes,' he said as a matter of fact. 'It's the law.'

Her tone shifted when she asked, 'Is it right just because it's the law?'

'I'm not sure if it's right or wrong, ' he said. 'Whether you're justified or not, the consequences of your actions are the same. Why risk the trouble?'

'Some things are just worth the risk. Can we ever truly claim to be ourselves if we consciously go against our ideals to conform to those of others? That's what laws are, aren't they? The ideals of other people just like you and I. Isn't following the law just an admission that their ideals are greater than mine?'

'Are you saying they're not?'

'I'm saying I owe it to myself to find my own truth. We all do. And I know mine won't be found in this city. I also know that you agree with me.'

'Hmm,' again. But this time it was an acknowledgement. 'Well, however it is you plan to leave the city, I hope our journeys align at some point. It's a vast world out there.'

Alex then understood that gleefulness he'd displayed earlier. 'You're taking the test?'

He nodded.

'That's great! It's about time! Why the decision?'

He couldn't quite make it out in a way that was specific to what he was thinking, but, 'It just feels like something out there is calling me.'

That was a feeling Alex knew all too well. 'Where would you go first?' She asked.

'Dunno. I don't know where there is to go. I'll definitely visit where I was born.'

'You mentioned that before,' said Alex, intrigued. 'The Southern Kingdoms?'

He nodded, and said in turn, 'The land of knights and alchemy, according to my grandfather.'

'And druids,' Alex said under her breath.

'Sorry?' Daniel hadn't quite heard.

'Nothing. Just remembering something I read once.'

Something that perhaps shouldn't be shared so casually. She did that from time to time. Absently said something that wasn't supposed to fall on open ears. Knowledge was a very powerful tool for Sentiens. You couldn't use a function if you didn't understand its meta - unless you cheated - so knowing things was important. And there are things that must only be known by those supposed to know them.

A casual slip of the tongue of such 'things' could bear grave consequences. The world, as Alex would eventually find out, tended to be very unforgiving.

Then she said, 'I don't suppose you taking the test has something to do with chasing after a certain someone?'

'Someone?' he asked. Then it dawned on him. 'Oh. You mean Reena.'

Yes, Reena. 'It just seems too coincidental that you decide to take the test a year after she became an ambassador. You always spoke so highly of her, so, I thought maybe... she's influenced your decision somehow.'

Alex's choice of words weren't overlooked. 'Spoke,' past tense. As in, it had been a while since he'd mentioned her, and he hadn't even realised.

Reena. A name he'd not heard for some time, nor a person he'd heard from since... well, since she left the city. That's what ambassadors did. Leave the city in representation of MindSpace, and the government - as if the two were separate entities. The exact nature of their role was unknown to most. The only definitive information that was shared throughout the city was that ambassadors were the keepers of absolute order. Their word was law. Defying them was, well, that was a mistake one never really got the opportunity to make. They spent so little time in the city. Most of them, anyway.

Reena. That was a name that meant something in New Heart.

'Maybe,' Daniel said. Maybe his decision was influenced by her to some degree. Like the idea of her was constantly in the back of his mind, steering his courses of action in a way that would, what? Impress her? But she wasn't there to impress. And there was no certainty whatsoever that she might return.

Reena. A name that meant something. Especially to Daniel.

'Sorry,' Alex said, noticing the sombre nature of his 'maybe'. She wouldn't bring her up again.

'You've always sort of reminded me of her, you know?' Daniel said. 'She's a whole development stage ahead of you, and obviously has a lot more experience from being out of the city, but you're the two smartest people I've ever met. Maybe that's why I haven't thought of her recently. You filled the void. But, I guess filling the void doesn't mean much if you're replacing ruby with sapphire. They shine differently. It'll never be the same. Maybe I am chasing after her, maybe not. I guess I'll have my answer once I take the test.'

'Do you think you can do it? Become an ambassador?'

'I know I will.'

Alex scoffed. 'How audacious.'

Daniel shrugged. 'That's how the story plays out in my head. I see myself exploring the world beyond the city. Doing good for the people I come across. Making a difference that matters. I see it so clearly in my mind. How can I doubt something that I live so vividly every day?'

'There's a difference between the world within your head and the world without.'

'A story told by yourself, and a story told by others,' he said.

'What?' Alex asked, confused. He'd never said something like that before, and there was something about that particular sequence of words that seemed uncanny. As if she'd heard something like it before.

'Just something I remember from a book,' Daniel replied.

'But you don't read.'

Daniel was offended by how quickly she'd blurted out that response. But she was correct, Daniel wasn't much of a reader. 'True,' he said. 'I didn't actually read the book. It was the first sentence. "The difference between the world within your head and the world without, is a story told by yourself, and a story told by others."'

How curious. 'What's the book?'

He couldn't remember. 'It was a present from my coming of age ceremony. The guy who gave me my coder gave me the book and asked if it's something I might enjoy. I read the first line and gave it back. I was even less of a reader back then than I am now.'

'Well you were only 10,' Alex defended him. 'Still, that was 18 years ago. You can't remember the book but you remember the first sentence?'

'He gave me the book with the first page opened. And it was the only sentence on the page.'

The only sentence on the page. Alex had encountered that sort of book before, but the first sentence she remembered was vastly different.

'And the man?' she asked.

Daniel shrugged again. 'Never saw him before then, haven't seen him since. All I know is he must be an ambassador of some kind.'

'Name?' Alex asked immediately.

'Never told.'

'Can you remember how he looked?'

There was a pause. Daniel couldn't remember exactly. And not remembering exactly meant it wouldn't be worth him sharing the image with her. All he could tell her definitively was, 'He was hybrid. Eruban and Irian.'

This time it was Alex who paused. She was organising the information in her mind. So many curiosities lay within these revelations. Only government officials had the authority to present coders during a coming of age. Bolu aside, Alex had never heard of anybody working for the government who wasn't Irian. But to hold a great enough position to have presented Daniel Marston – the Daniel Marston – with his first coder... who was he? And was the book he'd gifted Daniel the same that had been gifted to her all those years ago?

You may wonder, if the books were the same, then surely Alex would be familiar with the words? But this was a book which changed its contents based on the reader.

The Book of Things That Must Only Be Known By Those Supposed to Know Them.

'What's gotten you so curious?' Daniel asked.

What could she tell him? He'd denied the book. His awareness of its existence didn't stretch beyond that one sentence. He'd been worthy of receiving it before, but was he worthy of knowing it now? It wasn't for Alex to say.

'Nothing,' she told him. And in a completely different tone, 'It's rude to reject gifts, you know.'

Daniel laughed. 'I know. Won't happen again.' And then he, too, in a different tone, 'Everything changes after this week. Whatever journeys we find ourselves on, I hope we'll still be able to meet like this from time to time.' Outside. In the real, and beyond the boundaries of the city they'd lived in for as long as they could remember.

Alex liked to imagine that she hadn't lived in the city her whole life. That sometime before she became aware of her existence she might have been elsewhere. Born in a place different to the ceiling she first gazed upon. A place different to the doorstep where she was found. Another place she might call home, and hopefully, one day visit.

Yes, a great adventure awaited outside of the city. She just needed to make it there first. 'Same,' she said.

They spoke a bit more about various things. In particular about the most recent episode of Lore that was aired some days ago.

'We finally get to meet the Warrior next episode,' he said. 'I was surprised by the trailer, though.'

Alex questioned.

'The words that were said,' Daniel continued, 'I swear I said the exact thing when I was a kid.'

Alex didn't pay too close attention to Lore. She was more interested in learning about the world than in works of fiction. But she did, as tradition, watch Lore with her best friend, and did in fact remember those words that were spoken. And she looked at Daniel and laughed.

'What kid says something like that?'

'I swear!' he defended. 'I know it was a long time ago, and I can't even remember why I said them, but they just sounded so familiar. I said it. I promise you, I said it.'

Alex believed him. In so far as she believed he believed what he was saying, even if the reality of it didn't seem credible. It just seemed very far-fetched that a child would say something like that.

But then again, it was Daniel.

And it wouldn't be until a little later that the memory of when he'd spoken those words would clarify itself in his mind. And that clarity would come to the realisation that the day he'd spoken those words, was the same day this enigma of a man had given him that book.

'Oh,' Daniel said suddenly. 'There is one thing. He had a long black coat on. It had 501 printed on it.'

6

FORBIDDEN FRUIT

The Arena was just one of the worlds that catered to the escapism the Network offered. In another part of the virtual space, less accessible to the younger population of the city, wanderers may stumble upon the world of Forbidden Fruit, where every unrelenting fantasy could be satiated in the most lustful of ways.

There was something very dangerous about allowing people to be their pure – or impure – unadulterated selves. A person who was wholly themselves was a terrifying person indeed.

And yet, here, people were themselves, but not themselves. They were masked. Hidden behind virtual avatars that allowed them to maintain anonymity. And that was what Forbidden Fruit was about. When the truth from within came out, the truth from without went in. The two things were never really supposed to meet.

You see, a forbidden fruit must never be tasted. Was it sweet, or sour? Did it fulfil one's need to quench thirst, or satisfy hunger? It was a question that should never be answered. And that was the purpose behind the world and its name. Nothing that occurred in this world was real. They weren't the real bodies of those who underwent the activities. Whatever taste a biter had of an apple , they could never truly know if that flavour, that satisfaction, that otherwise unobtainable pleasure was true to the nature of its reality. It was, by all accounts, a place where fantasies were birthed, but short-lived.

Alex found herself standing before House of Red. A large neon glow made it stand out within the area's architecture.

World traffic wasn't too intense at this time of the day. The perfect time for Alex to pay a visit. There were benefits to being jobless.

She was greeted by her patron as soon as she entered. *Odd*, she thought. She was sure she hadn't mentioned she'd be stopping by.

But stood in front of her was Mistress Cherry (to her professional associates). But to Alex, just Cherry. Childhood friend. Something of a big sister growing up.

True to her name, Mistress Cherry had ruby red lips. Two cherries floated a fixed distance from her avatar, never straying from their orbit. She used them as a prop as much as an accessory. There was something biters seemed to love about a woman wrapping her lips around small bits of fruit, twirling it around her tongue as if teasing them in an illustrious kiss. When she would eat one, another would take its place. An endless seduction of red. Even Alex was somewhat mesmerised by the aesthetic of it all.

The rest of her outfit was red, too, with some streaks of black here and there, which only served to accentuate the voluptuous nature of her appearance. A fork-tailed whip was wrapped up in her hands. One had to come across just a little bit dangerous when dealing with another's pleasures. She came forward, put a hand to one of Alex's cheeks, and kissed the other, leaving a red imprint of her lips.

'Now you know you can't be in here without a little bit of red,' Cherry said.

'Didn't want to miss out on the greeting,' Alex replied.

'There's always greetings for you, hunn.' Then she smiled. 'I see you work quickly as always.'

In the brief exchange that they had, Alex had cleared Cherry's mind. That was the reason she went to Forbidden Fruit. The apples interacted with so many biters that their minds formed clutters more frequently than the average citizen. This was what she'd meant when she said she didn't need the job to keep doing the work. She didn't need the interactive goggles, and she didn't need to work for Mind-Space. She was a diver in her own right.

'Come,' Cherry continued, 'let's chat.'

Alex found herself in one of Cherry's pleasure rooms. One of many within the building. Each of them had a replica of herself. Programs created from her persona which imitated her behaviour, acting as she would in any given situation. Even now she was entertaining a few other guests.

A world of short-lived fantasies.

'Day off?' Cherry asked.

'You're the second person to ask me that today?' Alex replied with a laugh.

'Second?' Cherry feigned shock and offence. 'And here I thought I'd always be your first choice. Who're you cheating on me with?'

'A very handsome man, I'm sure you'd think.'

A very handsome man. Cherry muttered it to herself in contemplation. 'Oh! Him? Handsome indeed. Have things transpired between you two? It's been so long since you and...'

Alex didn't let her finish. 'Let's not bring up the irrelevancies of the past,' she said. 'And no, nothing has transpired between us, nor will it ever. Our relationship isn't like that. He's like an older sibling. Like you.'

'Oh, he is older, isn't he?' Cherry said with something of a mischievous smile. 'Perhaps you need to introduce your big sister to your big brother.'

'Saying it like that makes it sound incestuous,' Alex pointed out.

'Oh you know what I mean!' Cherry protested.

She did, but Cherry was easy to tease, and Alex took the opportunity when it presented itself.

'I'm sure you'll both be introduced someday.' Then on a separate note, 'I'm going to the orphanage tomorrow.'

'Oh,' Cherry chippered up. 'How's everyone doing?'

'Good, last time I checked. I'll update you again after tomorrow. You should really visit.'

Cherry gave a wry smile. 'I don't think I'd really be welcome there anymore, given what I now do.' She was sitting on the bed and Alex went to join her. She placed her head on Alex's lap and let herself be stroked.

'There's nothing wrong with what you do,' Alex said. 'It's a tough world out here. You're just doing what you have to do to get by. Like everyone else.'

'Hah,' Cherry laughed. 'Not like everyone else.'

Alex misspoke. Not everyone was just 'getting by'. Some were very privileged. Born with some advantage or other than made their lives significantly easier by comparison.

Daniel had been one such person not too long ago.

'You should come see me in the real, soon. As nice as it is to see your silhouette, I miss your pretty face.' Cherry looked up to the featureless Alex, looking for some expression of acknowledgment.

'I'll come by soon.'

'Please do!' She sounded desperate. 'Big Dog aside, there aren't too many friendly faces around. And things have been stirring up recently.'

'Things?'

Cherry shook her head, trying to wave it off as if it were nothing. 'Just issues with Rado. He's been acting out.'

Ah, Rado. A name well known

'Why don't you leave?' Alex asked.

Cherry let out a frustrated breath. 'A debt of gratitude I suppose.'

New Heart was supposed to be a utopia. That was the idea behind it, and its selling point. Perhaps it was in other districts. But in the West District, where things were different – for some reason – the conflicts of everyday life seemed to catch up with the culture. There were street gangs, all engaged in an idealistic battle over territory and status. Producing and selling their unique strains of herb, a psychedelic plant which gave a different sort of escapist fantasy to what you'd find in the network. When it came to that, it was very easy to get roped into a whole other life than what the city intended. That was the road Cherry was headed towards, and the Madame saved her from it.

Alex didn't really see it that way. But this was Cherry's decision. If she was going to leave, ever, it had to be a choice she made herself, and one she believed was right.

'I'd better get to work,' Alex said.

Cherry sighed again. 'I guess you should,' she said reluctantly, forcing herself up from Alex's lap. She gave Alex a hug, kissing the unmarked cheek in a much longer show of affection than the greeting earlier. When she pulled away she kissed the tips of her fingers and then put them to Alex's non-existent lips. 'You'll come see me?' she asked.

Alex nodded.

'Promise?' she insisted.

'Promise,' Alex agreed.

Cherry smiled. 'Okay. You be safe.'

'And you.'

They hugged once again before Cherry finally let her go.

Alex did her rounds with the other apples.

When she finally finished, she came back to the real. There was plenty of time to spare before the evening's affairs. Time Alex would use to further prepare herself for what was to come. A not-quite-once-in-a-lifetime, but certainly once-in-a-while opportunity.

One way or another, she was getting out of the city.

She accessed her *Space*. A program built into coders which acted as a storage unit, giving the user their own personal pocket space to keep... well, anything they wanted. If it could exist in real space, it could exist in their personal space. The trade off was that they had to carry the weight in some form. Whether they carried it with their mind via telekinesis or some other ability, or simply bore the force of the weight with their bodies, it had to be carried. For that reason, the quantity people carried with them tended not to be too great.

Alex personally didn't carry much, but there was one thing she always had with her. She hadn't brought it out in a while. She didn't need to. The information it gave could be accessed straight from her mind. It wasn't a book she needed to read. But after that conversation with Daniel, she felt like holding it in her hands again after so long. Perhaps, because she wanted to try and convince herself that showing the book to Daniel was a good idea.

She knew it wasn't. It wasn't for her to divulge. Whoever this man was that had given it to him, perhaps he had authorisation to share it. After all, she had received her book from someone as well, and she was overdue a visit with them. That, and a conversation that had been postponed for far too long. She needed answers. Answers the book decided it wouldn't give her.

Because she didn't need to know? Or perhaps because it was something she needed to find out herself?

That was the nature of the book that decided what information to give to you and when.

The book that told her what conflict was going to be heading her way later that day.

The Book of Things That Must Only Be Known By Those Supposed to Know Them.

7

Chen's Kitchen

One never really saw a pitch black sky on Areth. The stars were plentiful and luminous, scattered across the veil of the night. And Areth's two moons were in their crescent phases; drawn into the night sky as though one came first and the other was simply mirrored. And had they been a bit closer and more in line, they could come to make a full circle. How peculiar a sight that would be. Two crescent moons coming together to create a full moon that wasn't full.

There would be no moons at all the following day. A rare occurrence.

With the night came a bawling street culture. It wasn't exactly a celebration, but to one who'd never experienced it, that might be the only way to describe it. In the centre of West District was what one might call a street food market, which prompted all of the various subcultures in the district to come together and enjoy the culinary expertise of artisans who'd dedicated themselves to the craft of good food. And when people enjoyed food as much as they did here, one might be forced to call it a celebration.

Within this bustling food market was an open-air restaurant called Chen's Kitchen, which offered the brilliant cuisines of Oren, perhaps the most wide-ranged variations of foods amongst the three continents. It was run by One Armed Chen, as the locals called him, and his daughter, Katelina Chen.

Having come to Iria at a young age, and being half Irian herself, her name, Katelina, would get shortened to Kate. And she, having been accustomed to the Orenian vernacular due to her father, couldn't pronounce Kate Chen the way Irians pronounced it. And said it in such a way that Kate Chen came to sound like Kitchen. And so that was what people called her. Kitchen.

The restaurant was a very lively place. It had to be. The Chens gave a cooking experience that couldn't be found anywhere else.

Satisfying one's hunger cravings was a much simpler task in this city than in others. There were programs that transmuted the very air into nutrients and put them straight into your body. Or you could transmute a meal and enjoy all the flavours as traditionally achieved across all forms of life. Even many of the street vendors didn't actually cook, but simply used programs to create their unique flavour combinations. Cooking wasn't something you really needed to do in this city. Not unless you were a Shaman.

But because it didn't need to be done, it was rarely done, and that was what made the Chens so popular. They still did things the old way. With metal pans and utensils, water and oil, salt, pepper and all manner of herbs and spices. Different sauces that nobody could tell you how they made because they kept those secrets to themselves. And most importantly, the crutch upon which all forms of cooking stood on, fire.

There was no cooking without fire.

They cooked right in front of you. You could see everything they did, and it was astonishing the way they coordinated themselves. Truly a magnificent sight to behold. And there, with a front-row seat to the action, was Alex, admiring the work of her best friend.

The meeting of Alex and Kitchen, and everything they'd been through since, was a story in itself. And if you were to describe what type of story it was, you'd call it one of discovery. Discovery of oneself, and of friendship, and love.

There were those that spoke of soulmates. That person who completed your life in such a way that no-one else could. Those that spoke of soulmates often referred to someone with whom they shared some romantic engagement.

Alex and Kitchen were amongst those who spoke of soulmates, but there was nothing romantic about their relationship. No, their love for each other was the purer kind. The type that wasn't based on conditions or reciprocation. They would give their entire selves to the other willingly, and perhaps, that, in truth, was what soul mates really were.

Perhaps it was because of that, that no matter how often Alex came here, she was forever amazed at the fluidity with which Kitchen moved. She darted around the space with an efficiency and grace that made you question if this could be considered work. It was like a stroll through the park for her. She was small, and nimble, and it worked in her favour.

Whereas her father didn't move around much at all. He did less of the physical work and concentrated on the meta. Where Kitchen cooked manually, One Armed Chen used functions. Various instructions given to telekinetic forces that acted like extra pairs of hands.

In the physical world, there were only two in that kitchen. But in the greater conceptual world, the world that Sentiens could perceive, the meta; in that world, there could be as many in that kitchen as Chen wanted.

The magnificent display of skill wasn't the only reason Chen's Kitchen was so popular. There was another thing that piqued people's curiosity. A topic which many stories had been developed around. Many theories had spread across the district about exactly why, how, and when it happened. But Chen never spoke a word about it to anyone. A story nobody knew, so they made up their own. And the story always began with the same question.

'Do you know how Mr Chen lost his arm?'

Even Kitchen didn't know. It had been the norm growing up. For as long as she could remember, he didn't have his right arm. It wasn't until she really became aware of her own body that she questioned why he was different. And yet, with that curiosity, not once did she ever ask him the question. She couldn't say why. The curiosities of children rarely ever remained as such. But there was something within her. An instinct, perhaps, which gave her a natural aversion to the topic. So in her 22 years of life, not once did she ask her father how he lost his arm. And it didn't matter. All that mattered was this. Cooking together. Smiling and laughing together. The metal, the salt and the fire. All that mattered was the kitchen.

Alex had been lost in admiration of the two when a drink was presented to her. A quick glance to her right saw a familiar face from her past, distant and recent. Maxwell Dodds, currently a trainee police officer, formerly her boyfriend.

He was the pretty-boy type. Blonde hair, blue eyes, tall and relatively muscular. And he was known around these parts, not least because of the accomplishments of his father. He was someone who'd had eyes on him nearly his whole life, and upon whom a great weight was placed. And then, amidst all that, living in a district where tensions between skins was an everyday occurrence, he decided to be with an Eruban. The eyes continued to be on him after that.

He had been something good in a rather messed up world.

'I have one, thanks.' Alex said.

'You don't want another?' he asked.

'I'm not sure I want what comes with it,' she retorted.

'You don't even know what it is.'

'Hence the uncertainty.'

They entered a very brief stare contest. He pulled away first, laughing at the situation. 'I see you haven't changed.'

'Categorically, no,' she replied. 'Just become a better version of myself. You?'

'Have I changed?'

She nodded and carried the motion into another sip of her drink.

Max didn't say it out loud, but there was something admiringly attractive about the way she performed things with such fluidity. It was one of the things that drew him to her in the first place.

Alex had been a tough nut to crack. She didn't swoon after him like the other girls, but didn't play hard to get either. Their attraction for each other had been mutual and she wasn't afraid to acknowledge it.

'Well, I'd like to think I've also become a better version of myself,' Max said. 'But who's to say?'

You, Alex thought. If anybody was to know if he had grown as a person it should have been him. She moved on from the thought. 'So how've you been, then?'

'Good. Yeah, good. Just working, yanno. Almost a full-fledged officer'

'That's good.'

They shared another period of locked eyes. He didn't turn away this time. 'I've missed you.'

There it was.

'Oh yeah?' Alex asked, sceptical. 'Did you realise that before or after you saw me this morning?'

He laughed. 'I actually thought you might have been avoiding me, I hadn't seen you in so long.'

She really hadn't put that much thought into it. Their lack of crossing paths until now was a coincidence. And if not coincidence, it wasn't of her own doing.

He locked onto her eyes again. They were brown, and bright, and beautiful, and dangerous, and he found it sexy in a way that frustrated him all the more.

'I have missed you,' he said again. 'There hasn't been anyone like you since.'

Uh oh.

'Oh,' she said with a sharp curiosity. 'How many times have you tried?'

He realised his mistake, and his frustration turned into nervousness. 'Just two,' he said.

Two? In almost a year?

Lies.

Max didn't know that Alex could read minds. It wasn't an ability one really came across within the streets of West District. And unless someone created it themselves, or purchased it from the black market, only officers had a program for it. And even then, they needed special permission for its use.

Alex could create a program for it if she wanted to, but even without one, it was just something she could do. So when he'd said "two", she'd read in his mind that he'd thought about 8 different women he'd been with since her. And that was just the ones he thought about at that moment. There was every possibility there were more.

'You?' he asked.

'None.'

Max would have had no way of knowing if this was the truth, but Alex didn't need to lie. There really hadn't been anyone since him.

'So I'm your first and last?'

'As it stands, yes.'

He was happy to know that. She could tell even without reading his mind.

'I still don't understand what went wrong,' he said.

She'd explained everything to him back then; the reason she was breaking up with him. Maybe he'd just forgotten, or maybe he hadn't and still just couldn't accept it. She would clarify it one more time.

'Nothing went wrong, Max. Our relationship was good, and we were both happy at the time and I'll admit that to anyone that asks. And at the end of it all, you hadn't actually done anything wrong. But whatever feelings I'd had during, whatever happiness I obtained from being with you, it just wasn't there anymore. Relationships end, and that's okay. There doesn't always have to be something wrong and it doesn't always have to be on bad terms. What we had just ran its course, that's all.'

He was contemplating this, but even then, he didn't understand how or why it happened.

'Staying with you would have been dishonest,' she added.

'And honesty is the only thing two people ever owe each other?' he said, to quote the words she had said back then.

'Exactly.'

'Okay,' he said. 'So be honest with me now. What was it that made you stop loving me?'

That word made her flinch internally. Loving him? Had she ever claimed to do so? It wasn't that she was afraid of the word or the commitment that came with it, she just wasn't sure it accurately described her feelings for him. Perhaps she had claimed to love him back then, and perhaps she'd meant it within the capacity of her understanding at the time, but now that she was older, and wiser, she knew that love was not what that was. 'Like,' and 'lust,' maybe, and a genuine affection for him. But love? No. Love was what she felt for Kitchen. A genuine, whole-hearted want for her happiness, and the willingness to make sacrifices to ensure it.

However strong her feelings for Max had been, they never compared to that level of closeness. If they had, perhaps she would have told him that she could read minds, or that she could do other things that nobody would ever suspect from an Eruban girl in West District. But she hadn't. She'd never told anyone what she was really capable of. No one apart from the Chens.

'You just weren't what I wanted anymore,' she said.

'So then what do you want?' he swiftly replied.

That was an easy question. She knew exactly what she wanted. It was something that pertained not just to what she wanted out of a relationship, but out of life. And there was something within her that compelled the seeking out of this one thing. 'Truth,' she said. 'I want truth in a world full of lies.' She looked straight at him, her eyes sharp and accusing. 'And liars.'

He felt a pang in his throat. Was she referring to him specifically? Did she know about the other women? 'I'm not sure there's anyone who fits that criteria,' he said foolishly, as though admitting his own guilt.

Alex smiled for the first time since he'd joined her, though it was more of a belittling smirk. 'Well, Max, that's exactly why it can't be you. You think too small. And I've got much bigger dreams.'

That one really hit home. Of everything she'd said to him the first time when they broke up, she hadn't said anything like that. Maybe those were the word's he'd needed. The words that spelled out that things were really over.

'Okay, I get it,' he said. 'You've moved on, there's nothing here anymore, I accept that. But we're adults. We don't have to be in a relationship to have a little bit of fun now, do we?'

'No, we don't.'

'So,' he said, smiling in a way that enticed the other women. 'How about it then?'

'No thanks.'

'Why not?' he asked with genuine surprise.

'Because, Max, I just don't want to. And that's all the reason you should need to stop asking.'

This was a critical moment. What would the son of the district's most famed officer do in the face of rejection? The answer was, nothing. He just gave one of those little sombre smiles. The ones one gave when they accepted something, even though it dissatisfied them.

'Okay,' he said in a much gentler voice. And just before he turned away, in a voice as genuine as any could muster, he said, 'Good luck with your dreams.'

And Alex, appreciating that, reciprocated, 'Good luck with the test.'

Which he thanked her for, and then walked away. And before your mind ventures into the possibility of what might come next between these two, that was actually the end of their story.

Kitchen finished her shift some hours later, freshened up, and then joined Alex. Mr Chen was managing the rest of the evening alone now that the big wave had ended. He fixed up some dinner for them.

'So what did Max want?' Kitchen asked, taking a big swig of her own drink.

'To rekindle,'

'Aaah,' Kitchen said, half in understanding and half out of satisfaction for quenching her thirst. 'Still got all the pretty boys coming after you.'

'You can have them.'

'Hah! Like any of them are brave enough to approach me. Especially here.'

'You'd just reject them anyway.'

'Yes. But I can't reject them if they don't approach me. There's no satisfaction in that.'

'I don't think you get how this works, Kitchen. The satisfaction comes sometime after you say yes.'

'Oh I know how that works,' Kitchen said with raised eyebrows. 'But I'd just like to have the option of saying "no" to someone. Yanno?'

She'd closed her eyes during this little narrative, and through the permanent link that Alex and Kitchen shared between their minds, Alex sent her a message. Upon seeing it, Kitchen opened her eyes and gave Alex a lovingly vicious look. 'Crazy people hate being called crazy, you know.'

'Then you must be reeeaaal mad right now.'

'Furious. Hotter than an oven.'

'Yes you are,' Alex said flirtatiously.

Kitchen had just attempted to take another sip and almost choked from restraining a laugh, resorting to holding her mouth shut.

'So attractive,' Alex said jestingly.

'Right?' said Kitchen. 'I mean who doesn't want a piece of dribble girl.'

Alex took Kitchen's hand, the one she hadn't covered her mouth with. 'So you'd like the satisfaction of rejecting someone?'

Kitchen gave Alex a look of concern.

Alex took Kitchen's hand up to her lips and made her move, progressing up her arm with each word separated by a kiss:

'Will,' kiss hand, 'you,' kiss wrist, 'come,' kiss forearm, 'home,' kiss elbow, 'with,' kiss upper arm, 'me,' kiss shoulder, and then finally, whispered into her ear, 'tonight?'

Kitchen thought with certainty that Alex was going to kiss her ear then, or perhaps, in her vivid imagination, that she might do one of those other things people did in their private moments. She anticipated it, waited for it even. The suspense of what was to come sent a shiver down her whole body. But it didn't come. Kitchen felt Alex move away from her, and having closed her eyes briefly, she opened them now and looked dead into Alex's. They were just close enough to feel each other's breath, except Kitchen forgot to breathe. Then Alex pulled away.

'You feel better?' she asked.

Kitchen finally exhaled. 'Mmhmm,' she nodded.

'Good,' Alex said, very content.

A few quick inhalations and Kitchen finally caught her breath. 'You play too much, you depecate fool.' "Depecate" was a word that didn't really mean anything.

'Oh come on,' Alex defended. 'That was fun.'

'Yeah, it was. Most fun I've had in a while. Hence my problem.'

'Nothing stops you from meeting guys yourself. It's not like your dad will actually stop you.'

'No I know. But you decided to go celibate, and as your best friend I'm contractually obliged to join you.' She rewarded herself another large round of her drink, polishing it off in a few seconds.

'I don't think that's actually a thing.'

'It is. It's written into the world's meta.'

'And I haven't gone celibate. I'm just not wasting time on something pointless.'

Kitchen looked at Alex like she was a crazy person. 'Since when did sex become pointless?' The alcohol she'd so swiftly drank must have gone straight to her head because she said this just loud enough for the immediate people around her to hear, and Alex dove her head into a face palm, trying to avoid the curious looks that came her way.

When the looks returned to their own business, Alex edged closer to Kitchen and whispered, 'Since not being able to find someone worthwhile to have it with.'

Kitchen gave Alex a very gentle caress on her cheek. 'Well it's their loss.' The caress had been a distraction. She took Alex's drink and physically persuaded her to polish it off. 'I've ordered some more so drink up!'

This was Kitchen. The enabler. And the feeder.

'So, is tonight the night you tell me you're taking the test or do I have to wait another year?'

Alex put down her glass and coyly looked away.

'Seriously,' Kitchen continued, 'what are you waiting for?'

Alex knew exactly what she was waiting for, but she couldn't tell Kitchen. Not because she didn't want to, but because she'd been persuaded to silence. Kitchen was best not knowing what Alex got up to in her free time.

'It's just not how this story goes,' Alex said.

Kitchen scoffed. 'You're starting to sound like my dad.'

Yes. He's the person she'd first heard it from.

Their drinks came at just that moment. Great timing.

Even though Alex kept the truth about why she wasn't taking the test secret, there was something she needed to know. Something that would be important if she had been taking the test.

'When I do take the test... would you take it with me?'

Kitchen laughed. 'What do I need to take the test for? I'm a chef. I don't need rank to be a chef.'

'I know, but, if after I take the test I were to become an ambassador,' she thought of Reena, now, 'I'd have the opportunity to leave the city, and... well, it would be lonely without you.'

Kitchen understood now. Alex wasn't asking her to take the test. Alex was asking if she would leave the city with her. She knew of Alex's dream. She knew a step towards achieving it was to work for the government. But she'd always been so excited by the thought of it that she never considered the reality of her being left behind. If Alex left the city, for who knew how long, she'd be without a best friend.

Oh. The weight of the question dawned on her now. She'd never been in a situation like this before. Having to choose between the two most important people to her. Her father, or her best friend?

Alex and Kitchen didn't share everything through their mental link, but Kitchen hadn't hidden how she was feeling, so Alex knew what was going through her head. She put a hand on her best friend and comforted her. It wasn't a question she needed to answer. Not yet.

But the time would come. All things going to plan, of course.

Planning was such a curious little endeavour. No matter how many times you ran a sequence of events through your head, in reality, they rarely went the way you expected. But that was the difference between the world within and the world without. There were vastly different degrees of control between the two. It was often overlooked, or outright unknown, that the outer world had a will of its own, and it didn't very much like it when that will was opposed.

The world would always attempt to correct itself.

8

THE MEETING

There was a community gathering at the local centre in Eruban territory. It was a large building. Plenty of open space with a high ceiling. On nights like this, when the warm air of the day transitions to the cold chill of night, condensation may appear on such a ceiling. And after some time, those within may find themselves subject to the odd droplet of water or two. That phenomenon could be explained by science.

When rain poured to the land from the clouds, that could be explained by science, too.

So how would one, scientifically, explain the phenomenon of water falling not from the clouds, but from one such high ceiling?

It was an odd thing to experience for the first time. There were no clouds in the room. No water sprinkling system. The ceiling was bare, and was certainly absent of any water-conjuring devices. Yet, the droplets came in their hundreds, or thousands, or whatever order of magnitude it was that rain fell.

That was the ceiling of the community centre.

But down below, on the floor, dancing around in an organised chaos, were the Erubans.

Organised because there was rhythm to it.

Chaos because they hadn't mastered it yet. They were still learning the dance. The dance that called forth rain.

And at the centre of it all, teaching them, was Mara. Ojo'Mara.

She communicated with them telepathically. It was easy to show them the movements that way. Easier to get them to visualise their own selves. Being able to visualise oneself was important. It helped solidify your position in the world. This was only the first step, though.

The Dance of Ojo not only called forth rain, but through its fluid movements, the practitioners of it could control the flow of water, and further mastery allowed them to alter its properties.

She taught them basic movements first. Like creating a stream, which they all performed individually.

Then they combined their small streams into a large one that encompassed the group.

The rhythm of the dance was designed so that those who performed it together would be synchronised. Just like how a singular body of water may have multiple currents flowing through it, the dance brought the many that performed it together as one. Multiple tiny raindrops coming together to create something far more formidable.

It had been months since they'd begun learning it. Progress was steady, but they'd come far. They'd spent many weeks before that learning how to pray. Something the women took to with a greater degree of success than the men.

The steady stream of water exploded like a crashing wave. It was an explosion of expansion rather than dispersion. More water surrounded them. And as they increased the pace of their dance, the ferocity of the water became more and more intense.

Mara projected various shapes into their minds, instructing them to create them with the water.

They were basic shapes to start with. Various types of prisms.

Then it went to figures. Statues that seemed to have been formed from hammer and chisel. The intricacy of their detail was astonishing. But that was Mara. They may have formed the figures, but they did so under her direction. She was the one with the image, the vision. They were mere vessels of enactment. They issued the functions, but the meta had already been determined.

That was until one of them lost focus. They lost the rhythm of their dance, which would usually only take away their involvement in the water it produced. But that was the trouble with many becoming one. A single element failing could affect the nature of all.

The water exploded, and this time it was uncontrolled.

When logic delved into chaos, the resulting effect on the world was often unpredictable. Often dangerous.

It very well could have been on this occasion, but Mara took over. As one who was teaching the dance, she was an expert in the abilities it gave. Controlling water was second nature to her. She took the entire mass of water and separated it into ten smaller bodies, then transferred them into ten gourds that surrounded their communal circle.

She knew who it was that had defected, too.

'You panicked,' she said to him in a calm but stern voice.

It would have been fine if he'd simply allowed the breaking of his rhythm. There would have been no adverse effects in that. But in his mind's state of panic, he functioned chaos into the whole system, causing it to fall apart.

'I'm not built to dance around like a little girl,' he replied with his rustic voice. It matched his brutish demeanour.

Silence in the room.

The rain had stopped now, so his voice had echoed.

Cy was there. He didn't partake in the dance. He observed. And did other things within his mind. Things the rest didn't need to concern themselves with. But his attention was brought back out to the real when he heard the words that were just spoken.

It wasn't the words he had issue with. It was the tone and to whom they were addressed.

He shared a look with Mara.

Yes, they both understood each other's intentions. Now was the time.

'The Dance of Ojo is a celebration of one of nature's most powerful forces,' she said. 'It invigorates and empowers us. If you don't understand its value, you needn't be here.'

'Empowers us?' The man scoffed. 'I'm sure the Irians will think we're extremely powerful once we've finished getting them wet!' His voice had gotten progressively louder. It echoed in such a way that you could still hear it, even after it had disappeared.

Mara smiled. 'A demonstration, then?'

The man understood immediately. That was a challenge. One he'd willingly accept.

He *strengthened* himself first.

Strengthening was a basic skill amongst Arethians, but varied in necessity depending on one's residence.

It was an absolute necessity for the Erubans. The harsh climate of their continent; the great beasts they had to hunt; the sheer power of the land and those who resided in it. Strengthening was a basic necessity of life, so the Erubans were particularly good at it.

It enhanced all physical attributes. Strength, speed, endurance, durability. Allowed the body to handle more than it could in its base state.

The man closed the distance between them near instantly. His fists were clenched, his path was decided, and he was sure to strike true.

Mara responded to his assault in good time. She shifted from a front-facing to side-facing position. Not much of a change. His swing was still set on the same course, but a torrent of water emerged from his peripheral, too quick for him to react.

It encased his fist and carried it along its trajectory, causing him to miss, and almost lose balance from the force of the motion.

The water had emerged from one of the gourds and lost itself into another.

The man regained his balance and scouted the area around him.

There were ten gourds, and he was in the middle of them.

So that's how it is!

Well, two could play that game.

But he wouldn't use water. No. Not that feeble element.

Earth. A solid hard hitter.

He *lifted* a panel from the ground and *threw* it at her.

She swung both her arms, producing a torrent of water from both sides. They intercepted the panel mid-air, completely neutralising its momentum. It spun in place briefly before falling to the ground.

'Is defend all you can do?' he yelled. And then he yelled again. Not from anger, but pain.

He'd taken a blow to the face. Another torrent of water, swift and sharp like a whip.

Had his body not been *strengthened*... Well, these were strikes that could tear flesh.

He recoiled back from it, but she struck him again from both sides in a pincer attack. He spun in the air, but managed to stick a landing, even with how disoriented he was.

In his moment of vulnerability, Mara formed a body of water around his head, and altered its properties to retain a higher tension and viscosity.

He clawed at it, but it flowed freely around his hands. Every attempt he made to scatter it was futile, and he was running out of oxygen.

He tried *ripping* it off. Or *bursting* it. Any function that would free him from this prism, but his powers were inferior to Mara's. The water had been empowered to a level greater than anything he could muster. He was at her mercy.

He fell to the ground. His body writhed in agony.

It was a shock to the system, to be suddenly cut off from air. To be in that state of panic where you didn't know if your eyes would open to the light once again.

"When we get them wet," he'd said.

How easy it was to forget how dangerous water could be.

Had Mara carried on much longer, he'd have died. But that wasn't the purpose of this demonstration.

She released the tension of the water. A puddle dispersed around him. His heavy gasps echoed throughout the hall.

Everyone was silent. It may have seemed cruel, but it could have been worse. It could have been a permanent end. And it was necessary. To show, and for them to know the severity of what they were trying to accomplish.

There was purpose to this, after all. The dance performed by the men. The women who had been learning the true act of prayer. And Cy, who never took part in the dance but was left to his own devices. Each was but an element to a greater plan. An event of grandiose nature.

Everyone had to play their part, or not play at all. There was no space for gaps in the structure.

Mara began to pace around.

The man, Eme, had managed to regulate his breathing. You could barely hear him now.

Then Mara said, 'Water is merely the foundation of much greater things. It can be life, but also death. Sanctuary, or catastrophe. It's one of the most fundamental and dominant forces in this world. It must be feared, and respected. Admired, and revered. Only then can you use it in its truest nature. That is the basis of the Dance of Ojo. The reason my ancestors were conquerors wherever they ventured. If you can harness even a fraction of that power, you'll be a force to be reckoned with. You'll be able to take back that which was taken from you. That is the point of this, is it not?'

It was a requirement to remind them why they were doing this. To motivate them into taking this seriously.

The Rank Test was just a week away by this point. They needed to be ready. All the pain, struggle and sacrifice. It would mean nothing if they didn't succeed.

They needed to be ready.

Cy needed them to be ready. They were integral to his plan.

The women with their prayers.

The men with the dance.

Everything factored into him having the power he needed to see this through to the end.

And he would see it through. One way or another, this would end.

And a new story would begin.

But in the story they lived now, this was about the time when trouble manifested. Officer Dodds entered the centre, and Bolu was with him.

Cy sent over a quick glance to Chuks and Jimoh. Chuks returned the look, but Jimoh's eyes were fixated on Dodds.

Dodds took a few moments to scour the room. Beside him, Bolu kept his attention strictly forwards. He knew the looks he would be getting from all directions. He knew it best not to engage them in any way. He knew he wasn't welcome here.

Dodds was someone the Erubans tended to stay away from. They avoided eye contact. Shifted themselves away as he approached. It was only Cy who kept his eyes fixated on him.

Dodds met the challenge. He approached Cy with a very casual walk. 'I take it you're the man in charge?'

'Just a community enjoying each other's company,' Cy replied. 'Nobody's in charge here. I must say you're an unfamiliar face around these parts. Officer...'

Dodds laughed. As if anyone in West District didn't know who he was. Cy was playing a game, and Dodds was all for it. 'I heard the streets have been a bit quieter recently,' he said. 'Figured I'd come up and check for myself. So many gangs, so much violence. It's good to see you getting along. I guess police presence really has made a difference.'

'You'd certainly like to take credit for something like that.'

Dodds gave a little shrug. 'Unless there are some other variables you'd like to educate me on, I'd say police arrests and the decline of gang violence have a pretty causal relationship. Less troublemakers on the street means less trouble on the street, doesn't it?'

'It depends what street you're on.'

'I'm on yours. And it's unusually quiet.'

There was an accusation somewhere there. But the lack of anything concrete was akin to the lack of specificity with which he could claim to know exactly what it was that was going on. As authoritarian a state this city was, there were still restrictions to what the police could do. It was odd.

'That's not my concern,' Cy said.

'Isn't it? My concern is the safety of the citizens,' he said whilst walking away. 'Dark, fair, light. Irian, Orenian, Eruban. As long as they're in New Heart, they're my concern. And being that we're a community, they should be all of your concerns, too. It's imperative that we protect ourselves.' He was back with Bolu now. He scoured the room one more time, and then looked back at Cy. 'Even from each other.'

The room was dead silent. Maybe it was the humidity from all the water, but the air felt dense. It was that instinct, that feeling that you had when something was about to happen.

Something did. But it wasn't what anyone could have predicted.

The silence had been broken by the pitter patter of footsteps coming from the hallway. The rhythm was familiar enough for some to know what it was before it peaked its head through the arch.

A dog.

It sauntered into the hall, pacing itself slowly as it intuitively stared everyone down. Everyone knew this dog. Everyone knew where this dog had come from. Everyone knew whatever conflict may have been pending, it needed to be squashed there and then. The presence of the dog demanded it.

'Curious,' Dodds said, staring into the dog's eyes, knowing that gaze was being received elsewhere. Then he turned back to Cy. 'Until we meet again.' He and Bolu took their leave. Potential conflict averted.

The dog left with them. It exchanged glances with Cy briefly. A reminder that somewhere in the district, "he" was watching. Which coincidentally reminded Cy that "she" was watching, too. and he needed to be sure that neither of them were giving information to people they shouldn't.

He'd have to pay them both a visit.

9

Platinum Pantry

Central District. The place that boasted the tallest buildings in New Heart's skyline. At its centre was MindSpace HQ, seen even from the outskirts of the city.

It was common practice in cityscapes to associate the size of the buildings with the affluence of the area. And in a world where the power of the mind could be exchanged into currency, the Central District was home to some of the most mentally superior in this city.

The sky was covered with the shroud of night, and someone had poked holes through its fabric so that light could peak through. At some point, for some reason, someone decided to name those holes in the night sky, stars. They were plentiful, and somehow unaffected by the glare of unnatural light that coursed through the district.

The streets were busy, too. Much more footfall than West District saw. But that was the difference between the two echelons of this society. There wasn't much in West District that piqued its residents fancy enough to not immerse themselves in the network. Whereas in Central, the things they could get up to out in the open made The Network a bit less fantastical by comparison. It was like two completely separate worlds, kept apart - not connected - by a bridge, and a warp path.

But that was what it was ultimately like for all five districts. Each was vastly different to the others. Separated by a bridge over water, connected by warp paths almost nobody could use.

Somewhere in the heart of Central was a bar; Platinum Pantry. A place for the elite amongst the elite... And those foolish enough to spend the majority of their daily Credits for the simple pleasure of feeling its atmosphere.

This may have been the most affluent district, but even high society had its classes, and not everyone could afford the vast luxuries this district had to offer.

Hence the name, Platinum Pantry. Not Bronze Bar, Silver Social, or Gold Gamble, which were all bars with their own target social market. No, Platinum Pantry. The place where the people who were known went, and those who wanted to be known would eventually start to go.

As always, the venue was full. Being mentally elite in this city gave the ability to enjoy its benefits with nothing more than one's natural sen value. And so much of the clientele found themselves having nothing greater to do with their time than come here.

The bar was built with Rethium - the same material that made coders. With full connection to the programming of The Network, from within these walls, one could experience everything this city had to offer.

The difference was, in Platinum Pantry, everything was real. The pleasures that West District experienced only as fantasy, those in Central could experience as reality. And when people found themselves armed with the ability and freedom to manifest their dreams, the events that subsequently transpired revealed the best, at times, but more often the worst of human nature.

Absolute freedom was a very dangerous thing to have.

There were multiple cliques in the bar, varying from all sorts of ages.

Elite families often gathered together here, discussing the various nuances and intricacies of the city. And engaging in certain illicit activities they couldn't do elsewhere.

The younger crowd, the newer generation who had only ever known New Heart, had slightly different attitudes. The way they approached the world was shaped by the fact they didn't know much of it. Born into a city of virtual reality, and having never left, their views on how the world worked was slightly askew from those who had knowledge of what things were like before.

It was as if the younger generation lived without fear of consequence. Because even though within this elite establishment, everything they experienced was real, there were protocols in place that stopped the real from ever really being dangerous.

Danger was often the accepted consequence of adventure. Yet as adventurous and explorative as they might find themselves to be, danger would never meet them along their journey. And perhaps, there were some who would say that that reality in itself, was the most fantastical of all things in this city. Because if reality existed in a state of balance, then action and consequence went hand in hand. Taking one of those things away resulted in a reality that didn't seem entirely real, because it wasn't. Actions have consequences. That's just the way the world works.

This world is different.

Within this bar full of people who were known or wanted to be known, was a member of one of the more economically prestigious families in Central. The Jewelz.

'So what exactly is it your family is so famous for?' said a girl next to him.

Viktor replied, 'We're alchemists. Although I've not quite followed in the family trade, I do know a few tricks.'

He took off his coder, proving what he was about to do was the result of his mental prowess alone. It was a common trait in the city for the younger generation to have spent so much time using commands from coders, that they didn't spend enough time developing their natural ability to use functions. Such that it became a rarity when someone did.

Viktor took *hold* of the cocktail in the girl's glass. After *identifying* the individual components that made up the mixture, he *separated* them. A clear liquid, an orange one, and a pale transparent green. Then he *formed* them into individual shapes. A circle, a square, and a triangle. And then, *evaporated* the clear liquid, kept the orange as it was, and *froze* the green. The frozen green triangle became engulfed by the orange cube, which was surrounded by an opaque mist. Each of the three components took on the three main states of matter, and were recombined into what some might describe as art, purely for the fact it bore some degree of artistic aesthetic.

'Alchemists have full control over matter,' Viktor said. 'We can create anything.'

The girl, and many around them, were impressed. Even with commands, performing something with such specificity wasn't a common ability found in these parts.

'So I've not seen you here before,' Viktor continued. 'My guess...' he eyed her up and down briefly. 'You had your birthday recently. You're in your four... no! Fifth development stage, and had a bit of a spike in your sen capacity, so suddenly, you can afford to be in a place like this.'

She was impressed. 'I guess you don't have that silver coder for nothing,' she said.

'They don't let just anyone become an officer, let alone a silver one. I think you'll find I'm quite impressive in many ways.'

There was a smug look of achievement on Viktor's face, which might have been attributed to him 'sealing the deal' as the phrase goes, but anyone who knew Viktor could attest that he had one expression, and that was it. Being smug was how he went about his everyday life, and there weren't many who could tell him otherwise.

But amongst those who could, one of them happened to be walking by, and it was no coincidence.

How could it be, when this person was privy to anything and everything that occurred within the multitude of spaces occupied within this building. Such was the benefit of being the establishment's owner.

'Spreading misinformation again, eh, Viktor?' said the man.

There was a bit of a stir amongst those in the vicinity. You see, everyone knew who this man was, because whilst the Jewelz were well known in this city, none held a greater title of prestige than the Marston's. And standing before them, was RJ, the first Grandson of the prestigious Richard Marston, a man credited with being one of those responsible for the revolutionization of Old Heart into New. And that wasn't the only thing the family was known for.

'You see the trouble with learning something from a guy like Viktor,' RJ began, 'is that he knows so little of it himself, that the idea of him teaching it is laughable. That little party trick he just did wasn't alchemy. Not in the pure sense.'

Viktor maintained his smug expression, if for no reason other than to save face. Then he said, 'He's right. I didn't want to bore you with the specifics, but as I've been called out...'

'Yes, as you've been called out, why not let someone who knows what they're talking about step in. You see, sweetheart,' he took the girl by her chin, 'Alchemy isn't an ability, it's a practice, and it follows three principles. The first, and most basic, is smithing, which is what Mr. Jewelz here just performed. It's simply the art of reshaping an object.

'After that is transmutation, which lets you transform one substance into another. That's a bit beyond the capabilities of Viktor and his family. And last, is enchantment, which is the application of unnatural properties. When you combine those three principles to a certain degree, that's considered true alchemy.' He slid his hand down to her wrist, wrapping it around her coder. 'These, the building you currently find yourself in, that's alchemy. What Viktor did is child's play, and is no more worthy of your amazement than if he'd stripped off his clothes and danced around like a savage Outlander.' Then he leaned over and whispered into her ear, 'if you want to see something really impressive, you should come with me.'

The girl, as most of them tended to be, was awe-stricken by RJ's presence. There wasn't anyone in this city whom you might benefit from knowing quite as much as him. It was an ambition amongst almost all of the social elites to be considered amongst his clique.

If not for the fact that he and Viktor had an unspoken rivalry between them, perhaps they, too, would be more amicably acquainted. But they weren't, which made what Viktor said next an unsurprising rebuttal.

'Well, smithing isn't really my strong suit. My real value lies elsewhere.' He made a point of showing his silver coder. 'How's your cousin, RJ? Haven't seen him in a while.'

Everyone around them went silent, because everyone knew the situation with RJ's cousin, and knew it wasn't a topic someone brought up so haphazardly. Furthermore, RJ wasn't known for controlling his temper. But he didn't erupt on this occasion. He just smiled, and said to Viktor, 'Enjoy your evening, Officer Jewelz,' before taking his leave, either forgetting, or simply no longer being interested in taking the girl with him.

10

THIS WAS A MISTAKE

Alex's night at Chen's had come to an end, but the evening wasn't over yet. The virtual world was calling her back.

She entered The Network as soon as she got home. There was a world she routinely visited. She spent so much time there, that one could simply lie in wait, and be confident that eventually she would show up.

But for the obscene amount of time that she spent there, most of the city didn't even know it existed. In the city that had opened the doors to the future of technology, what this world represented could be considered outdated. There wasn't as great a need for it as there used to be.

But perhaps those who didn't see the value of the world, weren't worthy of the knowledge held within it. The world known as The Library.

This was a world of storytellers, and teachers, and discovery, and philosophy. Of the knowers, the thinkers, and, the dreamers.

In The Library you could find people's truths, recorded and stored for others to learn, and adopt, or challenge. This was like an armoury for Sentiens. How greatly one could improve themselves if they only took the time to learn.

But life in New Heart was full of so many other activities. Things that were more entertaining than reading a book. Things that distracted one from how they might otherwise develop. It was a thinning of the herd, as they say. Only those who sought the knowledge within The Library were worthy of it.

There are things that must only be known by those supposed to know them. And Alex, for as long as she could remember, always had a compulsion to know things. She craved knowledge in whatever form it took. Discovering The Library was one of the most significant events of her life.

It was a book in this world that gave Alex her limited knowledge of druids. Knowledge she planned to expand on with real-world experience someday. It also taught her a lot about sen, and the history of the world, and the various different cultures and ways of life. It showed her that there were places in the world where you would go to learn certain things. That the metaphysical nature of one city differed completely to that of another.

If you wanted to learn something in particular, your best chance of doing so was to go to the place where it was most known. The place, potentially, where the practice of that thing began. That was all the more reason to be adventurous. There wasn't a single place in this world that wasn't worth visiting, because you could find there what you may not find elsewhere.

Which was both the benefit and the crux of this world. There were countless books catalogued into The Library's database. Books that existed somewhere in the real, whose information had been uploaded to the network. It was a curious thing, how anybody could put whatever information they wanted into this world; share the knowledge from any book. Yet there was one book in particular that you couldn't find in The Library. A book that only existed in the real, which gave knowledge only to those worthy of having it.

The book that told Alex what was going to be happening tonight.

There was something bigger going on here. A story larger than any individual character within had the scope to perceive. But that was how great stories were made. The eventual crossing of multiple paths. The stories of many, forming to become the story of one. Yes, big things were coming to New Heart, and they were coming soon.

It was the 19th hour. Alex arrived at The Library right on schedule. But not for reading. The Library had a community that suggested recommended reads. Sometimes they were advertised on flyers, but other times, representatives handed them to you directly.

The recommended read on this occasion was a book titled Wasteland. Just recently finished.

There were multiple types of books you could find in The Library. It all depended on how the author programmed them. Some books were read. Some were voiced with audio. Some opened up a holographic sequence. But the most prestigious of books were the ones that swallowed you up. They transported you to a whole other world in the MindSpace network. You didn't interact with the world – though with some books you could – but rather viewed it from the perspective of a third-person observer. You experienced the story as though you lived it, but didn't have any effect on how it was told. That was what this world, Wasteland, was. An immersive but not interactive experience.

Alex accepted the book and allowed herself to be swallowed by it.

She found herself in an environment true to its name. A wasteland. There were hills and cliffs far off within her scope of the horizon, but other than that, it was a dry and desolate area. One might wonder exactly what kind of story was going to be told here. One who didn't have prior knowledge of what this world was made for.

But Alex did. It was something The Book told her. A warning of what was coming. It was times like these where Alex questioned why she didn't read people's minds as often as she'd like. Had she read the minds of Fred and May earlier, she wouldn't have needed to be told about what was going on tonight. She wouldn't have run the risk of being caught off guard.

What might have happened if this warning hadn't been given to her? She'd had The Book many years and she still didn't know exactly what the criteria was for how it decided what information to give. Or even how it got its information in the first place. It was a curious thing.

This world, Wasteland, had been created by Fred and May, and a few other friends they had who were programmers. They were hiding in a different layer of the world's coding. A separate intersection of space that someone on Alex's layer couldn't perceive. They watched her, preparing themselves for their attack. It was going to be a humbling experience.

How foolish and ill-prepared they were.

They knew of Alex only within a professional capacity. A genius diver. Perhaps if they'd known Alex was a programmer in her own right; perhaps if they'd known she could *see* them, now just as they could see her; perhaps if they'd known exactly who, or what it was they were dealing with, they'd have eliminated the whole idea of their plan before it had even fully manifested as a thought. But they didn't know. They had no idea. And in the moments that would follow, they would realise with undeniable certainty that this...

This was a mistake.

They stood behind Alex in their hidden layer. 7 of them in total. Alex turned around and looked May in the eye.

May gasped. It was a shock, but there was no way Alex knew she was there. This was a coincidence, right?

But then Alex stretched out her hand and issued a function.

May, and her party, saw and heard the crack at the same time. The very fabric of this virtual reality had been broken. The crack started in front of them, and made its way all around to their exterior, trapping them within a dome of broken space. Like they'd been standing in a glass house and someone was throwing stones. Soon it would collapse.

They heard the sound of shattered glass as they were taken out of their hidden layer of space and brought into the same plane as Alex. They stood there, shocked and bewildered.

How could she do something like that? You needed administrative rights in order to access the higher layer of coding where they hid. Alex shouldn't have been able to do that. She shouldn't...

But she did. And so here they were. Face to face.

'H-how did you...?' May couldn't even finish her sentence. She was riddled with disbelief. But her disbelief very quickly turned to anger. A blinding rage. Had she maintained her composure, she might have drawn intelligent conclusions. She might have recoiled from her intended course of action. But, taken over by the feelings of spite she had for Alex, she carried on as intended.

It was possible, if you knew how, to cause direct mental damage to a person through the network. An illegal activity, of course, but that was why they had created Wasteland. It was more difficult to monitor and regulate this sort of thing when it occurred in a private space. The world they had created could be destroyed in a moment, eliminating evidence of what had occurred. And had their plan to attack Alex from within the hidden layer succeeded, Alex would have had no memorable recollection of who had attacked her. It was the best way to get away with the crime.

If only they hadn't chosen Alex as their target.

May got the program ready. She and Fred had been working on it for a while. Its meta was designed to directly interfere with the mind's ability to function. A tragic thing to occur to someone who lived in New Heart, and a heinous crime for the one who committed it.

May issued the command, but as soon as she did, the space in front of her glitched. There was only one thing that caused a glitch in virtual space.

When logic delved into chaos.

The metaphysical was what defined the nature of all things. It was made up of logic, just as the physical was made up of matter. It was what kept all forms of reality in a state of balance. It existed by compiling rules together to tell the world how to behave. Logic, existed in a state of order.

Chaos did not. Chaos was free and unpredictable. It didn't have a definitive structure. It didn't separate reality into individual identifiable features. No. Chaos was random. It took away form and stability, causing things to fall apart.

This wasn't like destroying clutters where a very specific logical structure of equal and opposite nature was needed to remove it safely. No, this was like trying to fell a building. All you needed to do was remove the stability of its foundations, and the building would collapse on itself. And that was what Alex did.

She didn't need to destroy the entirety of May's program. Just a critical element of it. That one strand of logic that kept it stable. When she'd gotten rid of that, what was left of its structure fell into chaos, and that chaos appeared as a glitch.

But May wouldn't let that be the end. She issued the command again. As did Fred, and the rest of their group whom they'd shared the program with. But each command they used resulted in a glitch. Alex foiled every single one of them.

They couldn't believe what was happening before their eyes. How could someone be this capable? Especially someone from the West District. Especially an Eruban! They were supposed to be the savages. The unintelligent. The primitive and most basic amongst the 3 skins. So why... Why was she so capable?

This was one of those times where the answer was so straightforward it became easy to overlook. May, and Fred, and others like them, never took the time to consider that perhaps, just maybe, their assessment of what an Eruban was, was wrong. That they were just as capable of the application of intelligence that Irians were so proud of.

If only they knew.

They kept at it for a short while, eventually realising one by one that this wasn't going to go as they'd planned. Fred and May were the last to stop. They still couldn't understand what was going on.

And they knew Alex. They knew her face and general demeanour. So even though she was in her astral form, they could see the image of her through the expressionless silhouette. They could see that neutral face she always had. Those eyes that they knew looked down on them, almost as if with pity. Like they were some tiny pups, trying to climb a great step for the first time. Not realising, not acknowledging, that it was simply beyond their reach. And that Alex, magnificent as she was, stood many of these steps away from them.

'How did you know?' May cried out.

Alex said nothing. May wasn't worthy of knowing about The Book. All May got was the blankness of Alex's astral gaze

'Who are you?'

That was a good question. And the truth was, Alex didn't really know. She didn't have parents to tell her where she was from. All she had was the story of how she'd been left at the steps of an orphanage with a note that had her name written on it.

Who was she? She raised up her hand and said, 'The destroyer of worlds.'

And then there it was again. The cracks in space. The sound of broken glass. But this time, the cracks spread all the way to the horizon, and further on, right to the edges of this artificial world. And just like that, the world known as Wasteland crumbled to pieces.

They were all forced back into The Library. Not Alex, though. She was nowhere to be seen. Nor would they see her again.

There weren't many people in the world who could claim to have ever witnessed a calamity. Worlds on MindSpace were built around a source code. It was like the foundation of a building, everything else rested on it. Getting rid of a world would usually be a case of deleting the source code, and the rest of the world would follow. But that wasn't what Alex had done, and she'd made a point of showing them just how serious and capable she was.

Alex hadn't broken down that world through its source code. She'd destroyed it in its entirety, and made it look effortless. How much sen did someone have to use to pull off a feat like that? How much focus and strain would a function like that place on the mind?

She shouldn't be able to do that! May kept telling herself. And yet, she witnessed it first hand. She looked to her accomplices. They were all speechless. They couldn't fathom the sheer magnitude of what they'd witnessed. But it was only May and Fred who recognised the true error of their ways.

How patient had Alex been with them all this time? How many opportunities did she have to perhaps do to them what they attempted to do to her? This really was a mistake, because they asked a question they didn't want answered. Uncovered a truth that was meant to be kept secret.

Tonight, they met the true Alex.

Destroyer of worlds.

11

Big Dog

There was one brothel in West District. In this city where any fantasy could be explored over The Network, the need to satisfy physical pleasure was significantly less than you'd find outside of the city.

But there were those who wanted the real thing, and others who needed it. Those who wanted it enjoyed the dangers of what consequences might arise. Those who needed it...

Sentiens weren't the only ones who occupied this world. There were Shamans, too. And they didn't deal with the meta. They dealt with the spiritual. Their souls could perceive the world's ether just as their bodies could perceive the world's matter.

It was all to do with the various aspects of self. Humans, curious beings that they are, are a combination of mind, body, and soul. But those three components don't necessarily exist in equal parts. Whichever of them was greater, that became the Greater Self.

Shaman couldn't utilise sen, so they couldn't access The Network. The entire world of MindSpace was lost to them, alongside all of its pleasures. So they did things the old way. Grew their own food. Performed tasks physically. And shared their bodies with each other in the real. There was something else they could share, too. But that's another story.

The Shaman lived a separate life to Sentiens in the district. They had their own quarter, and generally didn't intermingle with Sentiens for reasons other than trade. There weren't many Sentiens who could tell you the names of more than 5 Shaman in the district. And yet, there was one Shaman in particular who everyone knew in some capacity. Whether they'd met him in person, or simply heard of him, he was as big a name in West District as Mr Chen, but not for the same reasons.

His name was not known through fame, but notoriety. The man whom everyone knew as one of the gang leaders that ruled the streets of West district. And whether or not he had a real name wasn't something anyone could tell you.

He was simply known as Big Dog.

12

THE ESTATE

The next afternoon, Alex took a visit to her childhood home. An orphanage in a little estate that lay just between the outskirts of the centre and north-west sides of the district.

There were dogs on almost every street. Some stood stationary on corners. Others took to high buildings to gain good vantage points. Between them, they had eyes on everything, and passed that information on to each other in whatever way it was that animals of this type communicated.

Alex came upon the house she'd grown up in. Years had passed since she laid her head there. Even more for Cherry. But Cherry hadn't been back since, and Alex visited from time to time.

Sister Mabel, the orphanage's House Mother, saw Alex approach from the window, and even past the warped image through the sun-kissed glass, Alex could see that heart-warming smile. It stretched cheek to cheek, and like a pond disturbed by a thrown stone, dimples and wrinkles rippled further towards her ears. She hurried to the door, rushing out to meet Alex who'd just come through the gates.

'Oh, child! How wonderful to see you,' she said, grabbing Alex by the cheeks and proceeding to inspect her. She pressed against her shoulders, arms, waist and stomach intrusively. 'You're looking well. Though you always were one to take care of yourself.'

'You say that every time you see me, Sister. And my visits aren't far enough apart for you to be so surprised that my physique hasn't changed.'

'Oh but this visit has been after a greater period of time than the last was to the previous. Plus, it is very easy to carry on treading down a path after the first step has been taken. One must be vigilant in observing these things. And I recall, observing these things for you was my role until not so long ago.'

Alex took Sister Mabel's hands between hers and held them warmingly. 'Enough years have passed since then. I'm not a child you need to take care of anymore.'

'Perhaps not,' Mabel agreed. 'But whether you are my child, or my friend, the care is the same.'

Alex sighed, relieving herself from her position in the back and forth, conceding victory to Mabel. 'You always were so quick with a response.'

'And you picked up the sharp tongue rather well. So much so it caused me trouble on one occasion or another.'

'We'll just call that one of the many gifts you've given me.'

The two smiled. They went about this ceremony in some form or other whenever they met, and just as with any other tradition, it meant everything to them that it be kept.

'Come now,' said Mabel. 'The children will be excited to see you.'

She escorted Alex inside and through the halls, right down to the playroom. The children screamed at the sight of her, running and tackling her to the ground (she allowed herself to be felled). With hugs, kisses and fist bumps, she greeted every one of them, and within that time, shifted some of her focus to clearing their minds of any clutters.

She spent a decent amount of time with them, entertaining their naturally childish endeavours, ones she'd very much grown out of. But one thing that brought Alex joy was seeing joy in others, and none were as pure and innocent as that of a child.

Play time eventually ended and the children had other matters that needed attendance for the day, which left Alex to spend some quality time with Sister Mabel.

'Fancy a game?' Mabel asked.

'Always.'

The two became cosy at a table with tea, biscuits, and a game of Chappel. It featured a 10x10 playing board with opposing sides of beige and burgundy. Each player had 20 pieces. 10 Slingers, 2 Riflemen, 2 Heavies, 2 Bombers, 2 Snipers, 1 Gunsmith, and 1 Lord. The aim of the game was to catch the opponent's lord.

Mabel had taught Alex to play. It was one of the few things that anyone could claim was a shared interest with her. Alex took to it quite well, being as intelligent as she was. It wasn't long at all before she began defeating Mabel on a regular basis, though Mabel was self-professed to not be particularly good at it.

The game was well underway. Mabel had claimed a few of Alex's pieces, and Alex the same, but that meant very little in a game of

Chappel. It was the type of game where losing pieces was often part of the strategy.

'So what's new?' asked Mabel. 'You seem troubled.'

Alex gave out a little laugh. 'I'm sure you must be reading my mind,' she said.

'You know I don't have that ability.'

'Yet you always know when something is wrong.'

Mabel made a move on one of Alex's riflemen. Not the most valuable piece, but not the least either. 'You know, dear, our ability to change the world with our minds doesn't excuse us from experiencing it with the rest of our faculties. Call it intuition, or instinct, or perhaps even just guesswork. When the mind fails, you must be able to rely on other things.'

She wasn't wrong, but those words had yet to be as meaningful to Alex as Mabel might hope. She was far too capable to find herself in situations that her Greater Mind couldn't handle.

'I did something yesterday.' she said.

'Something you shouldn't have done?' Mabel asked.

'Something I didn't want to do, but needed to, maybe...' It was an irregular occurrence for Alex to be uncertain about something.

'You needed to do it, yet it still weighs on you?'

'That. And...'

Mabel took the second rifleman.

'Aaaaand?' she asked.

'You told me once, "When you read someone's mind, you become responsible for their thoughts". Well this time I didn't read anyone's mind, but the information got to me anyway. But I'm wondering, now, what if it hadn't? What if I'd remained in the dark, and the thing that could have happened, happened? I can't help but wonder if the fact that I can read people's minds so easily, gives me a responsibility to do so.'

Mabel smiled. 'You've grown,' she said.

Alex didn't understand what she meant. How was that the appropriate response to her dilemma?

'You're finally understanding the meaning behind those words, dear child. To be responsible for someone's thoughts doesn't mean not to read them. It simply means, you must be ready to bear the burden of whatever you discover. To know the inner, deepest, darkest desires of everyone around you, is to take yourself from definitive reality, to obscure possibility. You become aware of all the things people *might* do, but may ultimately choose not to. To have to contemplate something with so much uncertainty can drive one mad.'

Oh. That made sense.

'So I just have to be prepared to act on someone's thoughts to justify reading them?' Alex said.

Mabel shook her head. 'Whether you read someone's mind or not, you're not necessarily responsible for their actions. Simply knowing something bad is going to happen, doesn't make you responsible for preventing it.'

Hearing this came as a shock to Alex. 'But you've always said we have a responsibility to be good within ourselves, and to expect it from others.'

'Yes,' Mabel said callously. 'I taught that to all of you as children because that was all the morality an innocent child needs to know. But, as you delve into adulthood, you begin to see the world differently. You realise good and bad, right and wrong, justice and injustice, they're not so black and white. There's more to any situation than we see at first glance. And there's a natural order to things. A balance of fortune and misfortune. We'd have no understanding of what it is to be good if we didn't equally have knowledge of what it is to be bad. And our understanding of those two things doesn't necessarily translate into reality. The shepherd and the sheep will see the father fox as a villain, but to his mate and cubs at home, he's the hero keeping them nourished. The misfortune of one is the fortune of another. What is bad in your eyes, in the grand scheme of things, may be the best thing to happen to the world. What I'm trying to say in so many words is, it's for you to decide your own morality and how you choose to apply it. What matters when making a choice is that you make the one you can live with. Should you or shouldn't you read people's minds? That's for you and you alone to decide, so long as you can bear the burden of the knowledge you obtain. Sometimes bearing a burden requires it to be done in silence.'

There was a moment of clarity there. Alex understood things now in much greater depth than she had before. This was the first time Mabel expanded on the life lessons she'd taught Alex in the past. And Alex wondered, what more was there to the infinite wisdom of the woman who raised her?

She made her next move. Attacking with her sniper, she hit one of Mabel's bombs, which was something of a double edged sword in Chappel, as its setting off caused the removal of any piece within a certain radius, indiscriminate of ally or opposition. Mabel had both riflemen and a heavy within this vicinity, and the heavy was a valuable piece to lose. That, alongside a few slingers, placed Alex back in the lead, all in a single turn.

'Goodness me,' Mabel said. 'You orchestrated that.'

'You got too distracted, Sister.'

'You're just too good at this game Alex. Should you find yourself in West Iria someday, as I'm sure you will, you'll find the people there are a much worthier challenge.' And that was the shift in conversation that led to Alex revealing the true purpose of her visit. Yes, the events of the night before were serious enough to consult Mabel over, but that wasn't why she'd decided to come here today. It was the events of earlier that day which gave Alex reason to think that now was the time she and Mabel had a conversation she'd been putting off for a long time.

Alex accessed her *Space* and pulled out The Book. She put it on the table in front of Mabel and waited for a reaction.

Mabel looked at The Book, and then looked at Alex, and waited. There was a looming silence for a while. Something was in the air, but it wasn't tense. They were both waiting for the other to show them something that would determine how this conversation would go.

Alex broke first.

'You still remember this, right?'

'I do.'

Alex swallowed nothing. She knew the question she wanted to ask, but for some reason, this time, she felt as though she weren't ready for the answer. But she asked anyway, 'Who did you get it from?'

Mabel smiled in a way that was familiar to Alex. It was the smile she gave whenever Alex said or did something that surprised her in a good way. 'So you're finally ready,' she said.

Finally? 'What made me not be ready before?'

Because Alex had asked before, but Mabel never told her. But this time, this time she said, 'Every time you enquired about this book in the past, you asked me where I got it from, not who I got it from. I could never give you the answer until you asked the right question. And even now, the fact that you've asked the question as you have, tells me on some level, you know the answer.'

'A hybrid man in a long black coat, with the number "501" printed on the front?'

'And the back,' Mabel added. 'Their numbers are printed on the front and back.'

'"Their"?'

Mabel smiled again. 'In due time, dear child.'

Of course. Alex knew why Mabel had kept the information pertaining to this line of enquiry secret all these years. But she was finally getting some answers, and wanted as many as Mabel was allowed to give. She pushed The Book towards her. The book whose cover was matte black, with no writing to tell what book it was.

Mabel knew what Alex wanted, and she obliged. She opened The Book.

'What do you see?' Alex asked.

And again, Mabel smiled. 'Nothing.'

That wasn't a lie. To Mabel, no matter how many pages she flicked through, all she saw was white. No words were printed on the page. It was a continuity of blank canvases. And then Mabel began to laugh. 'After all these years, even knowing the things I know, still, this book doesn't speak to me. I guess that's just how my story goes.'

'What are the things you know?' Alex asked immediately.

Mabel still looked within the book, but still there was nothing. Not even a warning? Because it knew she would never say the things she shouldn't. But, Mabel had a feeling that this might be one of the last times she would sit down with Alex like this. That this story of secrecy was reaching a turning point, and in the chapters that followed, there would be many revelations. Mabel would never reveal the things she couldn't, but here, now, she would tell Alex all of the things she could.

'I know who created the book. I know the name of the book, even if the book itself doesn't reveal it to me. I know its purpose, and some of the intentions of those who created it.' She paused, and gazed deep into Alex's eyes. 'I know that the book is only given to those who can offer it information as valuable as it gives, and there aren't many who qualify for that status. I know - I have known from the day I found you at my doorstep - that you are special, Alex. In more ways than you know. And I regret that I can't be of greater service to you than that. But dear girl, after all these years, you're finally closer to the answers you seek.'

Yes, closer. The hybrid man. The numbered coat. The implication that there were many of them. And the idea that Alex had something to add? But what could she possibly add to The Book which taught her more about the world than anything else? What secrets might she possess that would be of value to The Book of Things That Must Only be Known by Those Supposed to Know Them? She had more questions, now. But they weren't for Mabel to answer.

Alex thanked Mabel for finally telling her.

'You're welcome,' she said. 'Though I now have a question for you, dear girl.'

'Anything.'

'Ever since you could string together coherent sentences, you've been the most inquisitive person I've ever known. You have this thirst for knowledge I've not seen in anyone for quite some time. All the people I've met who are like you have all had something driving them. A reason for obtaining the knowledge they sought. Tell me, Alex. What is it that motivates you to know everything? For what purpose do you seek this world's truth?'

Alex had been asked variations of that question in the past, but only ever in fleeting conversation. Never had she been asked with such a conviction of curiosity as Mabel had just now. And in truth, Alex wasn't entirely sure why. Wanting to know things was all she'd ever known. It was a compulsion, on some level. Some innate desire to see the world as it was, and not merely as it (or others) tried to make it out to be. Alex wanted to sieve through all the lies and know the truth, absolutely, and in its entirety.

Alex didn't necessarily have an answer to Mabel's question, but there was something she'd come to realise over the years. She asked Mabel, 'Do you know why I don't read fiction?'

'Because you're too concerned with what's real to trouble yourself with what's not?'

'Almost. You see the difference between fiction and non-fiction is whether or not you know if the words on the page are true. So "fiction" itself is automatically a lie, and non-fiction is fiction, up until the point where I can verify the information for myself. I've read so many books about the world outside of this city, but until I experience those things first-hand, they might as well just be another story someone's told. Until I see it for myself, the world outside of this city might not even exist. Everything we read that we ourselves don't know, is fiction.'

Mabel did one of those smiles again. 'It truly is a wonderful thing discovering how your mind works. But I wonder, Alex, is your experience of something really what determines whether or not it's real?'

'Well if I experience it, then it must be real, surely?'

'Really?' Mabel asked with a near conniving tone. 'I have met men who could reach into the depths of your mind and project your wildest fantasies. You could see, hear, touch, smell, and taste your own thoughts with as lucid a clarity as you and I have, sitting across this table, talking as we are. If it's possible to experience one's thoughts so vividly, how can we claim that the worlds within our minds are any less real than the world without?'

Again, something Alex had never really considered before. But Mabel was right. They were Sentiens. They had the power to define the reality they lived in. If what was considered real was based purely on one's ability to perceive it, Sentiens could create that perception as vividly as the world itself.

What was real and unreal?

Perhaps Alex was right, too. That until you verified it for yourself, even that which is stated to be fact, may be nothing more than fiction.

But, the reason "why not" was the same as the reason "why". Because they were Sentien. Because the realities they created were subject to them having the power to create them. Because in the end, when whatever ability they had to define their reality ended-

'Because when all is said and done,' Alex said, 'this is the reality we all come back to.'

Sen ran out, minds crashed, lives ended; and everything they did ended with them. No matter how vivid a reality one creates, in the end, the world restored things back to how they should be. That was the bottom line.

And there it was again, that look that Mabel gave whenever Alex said something that shocked her. But this was more pronounced than Alex had ever seen. It was almost as if - no! - it was that Mabel was on the verge of tears. And there was a proud look on her face. And Alex equally had no idea of what she'd done or said to elicit that reaction, nor what to do in response to it. One thing that was certain, was that at least one last time, it was nice to see Mabel look at her so proudly.

They packed up the game. Alex would have to leave soon. There was more to accomplish that day. But not before mentioning Cherry.

'Goodness, Cherry!' Sister Mabel said. 'Truly a soul I've not seen in quite a while. How I wish she would visit.'

'She thinks you disapprove of what she does.'

Sister Mabel laughed and shook her head. 'Not disapproval, child. Concern. They're not always treated well, those girls. People can be rough. It can be damaging, you know, that sort of thing. Affects the mind, body and soul. We are never truly ourselves unless all three are in harmony.'

There was more truth in this than Mabel knew.

'Well,' said Alex, 'I do my best to take care of her mind. Her body and soul... well.'

'There is salvation from all that ails us. One must simply look in the right place. Or perhaps, to the right people. Now, onto the next order of business.'

Alex knew this was coming and had hoped to avoid the conversation, but there was never any escaping it. Not with Sister Mabel.

'The Rank Test is in a few days. I don't suppose you're here to tell me you're participating this time?'

Alex's smile gave it all away. It was one of those "I've been caught out" smiles. Riddled with guilt and disappointment.

'Oh, how long will you wait, child?'

'It's just not the right time yet,' Alex defended.

'And when will it be?' Mabel asked sternly.

'Next time.'

'What's the difference between then and now?'

Well for one, a revolution was supposed to be happening, though Mabel wasn't privy to that knowledge.

'You remember that other thing I told you?' Mabel asked.

Mabel had told her many things over the years. It was difficult to pinpoint which she referred to in this instance.

'You are a caged bird, Alex. You dream of venturing the vast sky. But you will never be allowed that adventure, until you first prove you can fly. The test is your chance to prove yourself. How else do you plan to leave this city?'

That was an answer Alex couldn't give her. Her plan to leave the city had nothing to do with taking the test.

'You just need to trust that I know what I'm doing,' Alex said.

Mabel, knowing Alex the way she did, knew that those words carried an assurance with them, and doubly meant that Mabel needn't inquire further into Alex's intentions. She'd learned a long time ago that Alex was the type to handle her business her own way. And one way or another it always got handled.

'Okay,' she said, gently. Then she smiled again.

With their game of Chapel finished, the two polished off their tea and biscuits. If everything went to plan, Alex would be leaving the city sooner than Mabel thought.

13

MARSTON MANSION

There's a rather oxymoronic situation that often occurs with families, where one might find themselves both admired and detested by certain individuals within a group of people. It was this understanding which gave Daniel pause to ponder for a moment if it was even worth getting out of bed.

Alas, the admiration got the better of him.

Stepping out of his apartment put him right into the hustling streets of Central District. He'd not been there for very long, just under a year. And it seemed now he was only just becoming accustomed to the rather subtle symmetry of its architecture. Or perhaps, it wasn't so much the symmetry, but that everything now seemed so familiar to him that it all just appeared the same.

A warp path took him to the south side of the district. It was a hillside landscape here. Much more greenery, and much less congested. Though it lacked the cityscape's symmetry, this little countryside had a much greater familiarity to Daniel than his current abode.

Atop this hillside range, one - should they be so fortunate - would stumble upon the Marston Estate. Home to the wealthiest family in New Heart, headed by Richard Marston Snr, the man publicly accredited with being responsible for the city's tech revolution.

The Marston Estate stretched for about half a mile in both length and width. Most of it was open land, intended to provide future houses for generations to come. For now, there were only about ten buildings, and one of them was the main family mansion. A large complex that could comfortably house the entirety of the Marston extended family, and a personal project of pride for Richard Marston himself.

It was just short of a year since Daniel no longer called this great estate his home. Not that he'd ever felt in place there, anyway. Whatever one might consider the Marston's code of honour, Daniel certainly never adopted it. His honour, his pride, lay elsewhere.

A stroll through the Estate gave rise to reminiscent memories. It had only been a year, but a lot could happen in a year.

The entire world could change in a year.

The houses to the outskirts of the estate were empty. Not enough family members yet. But as Daniel walked to the centre, where the main mansion was, he walked past the homes of his aunties, and thought of the somewhat fond memories he'd had there in his younger years. Yes, he and RJ used to play in the gardens. They were the pride of the family.

Richard Snr would place the entire future of the Marston family on their shoulders, and whilst one would take on that burden happily, the other would shy away from it entirely.

No doubts as to who did what.

It was an unfortunate reality to look upon fond memories and know that those past events had no place in the present or future. Daniel would never play in the gardens with RJ again, that much he was certain of. It was very unfortunate indeed, to be so detached, so unbearably opposite from someone that you now considered them an enemy, when, so many years ago, they were your first, closest, and truest friend. But that was the thing about growing up. People inevitably became their true selves, and friendship, as powerful a sentiment as it may be, couldn't compete with truth.

So on this day, almost a year since he'd last set foot on the Marston estate, Daniel Marston entered the main mansion not as a family member, but as a guest. Or perhaps, even, a stranger.

He was greeted by Garth, the mansion's head butler. More of a security guard, really. There were memories there, too. Memories of Garth addressing Daniel and RJ as 'Young Master'. And memories of the two of them tag teaming against Garth in their combat training, which Daniel excelled at, whilst RJ reserved his talents for more mentally stimulating activities. Between the two of them, they satisfied the duo of the scholar and the warrior. A combination that featured in many stories told on Areth. Their story was short lived.

'Daniel,' Garth said to him.

It was Master Daniel a year ago, he thought to himself.

Daniel greeted him back and enquired as to his well-being.

'Well,' was Garth's response. He'd always been a man of action and not words, but even this was a greater degree of verbal reluctance than Daniel was used to. No doubt Garth was under orders to take away any form of respect associated with the Marston name from his mannerisms when addressing Daniel. This was what it meant to no longer be part of the family.

Daniel didn't hold it against him. Above all else, Garth was loyal to the family, and that was something worth admiring.

Daniel greeted a few more of the mansion staff as he made his way to the main hall where the party was taking place. He took a deep breath before entering. Seeing everyone's faces after so long would be an ordeal of sorts. Especially with the expressions he imagined they'd have. Daniel was sure only one person would be happy to see him that day, and thankfully, that was the only person who mattered.

The first thing he saw when he opened the door was a banner, reading, 'Happy Birthday, Annabelle', and the number '10' was propped up in various different coloured balloons.

A 10th birthday was an important one in this city. Arethians became aware of their Greater Self around the time of their 5th birthday, entering their first development period. In New Heart, this was when they'd be given their first coder, allowing them restricted access to The Network. Their tenth birthday signified the mental maturity required to be given unrestricted access – bar places like Forbidden Fruit – which was when they received their permanent coders. They'd enter their 2nd development stage around this time, and would continue to evolve roughly every five years until their 50th.

The Marston's made a ceremony of it. The children didn't go to the local council like others did. No. Richard Marston couldn't have his family engaging in the same activities of others. His family was special.

Daniel was one of the last guests to arrive. So many eyes fixated on him as he made his way through the hall. *The prodigal son returns.*

Yes, he returns, but not for any of them. Just one. Well, two, actually. His mother, bound by the will of her father, couldn't openly express her love for her son. But the love was there, that much he knew.

But the only person who could really express their true feelings was little Annabelle, who was still young enough to be offered the privilege of innocence. *That would change today.* In the eyes of society she was considered mentally mature, and those were the same eyes that Richard viewed her with. Her days as a child would swiftly come to an end. So at least, before that, Daniel would make sure she could enjoy this day to its fullest.

He ignored the looks of everyone around him and went straight towards her.

When she saw him, the long year they'd spent apart was all but forgotten. She jumped on him, and in the moments of their embrace, everything else in the world seemed lost. And that was it. That unadulterated innocence. How much of a tragedy would it be to see that tainted by the obscured Marston ideology? Something would have to change if there was to be any hope of her turning out differently to the rest of the grandchildren. Hopefully, if anything, turn out like Daniel.

Unlikely. Not with Richard around. He was the head of the family after all, and had no intention of allowing anyone else to dictate what a Marston should be. He'd worked too hard and sacrificed too much to allow that.

Daniel put Annabelle back to the ground and very subtly placed a note in her hand, the contents of which was to remain between the two of them. 'This is your present,' he whispered into her ear, and she smiled giddily. She had no idea what it was or would be, but she and Daniel had exchanged notes many times in the past, and each time the note was simply a conveying of information. Information which led to something spectacular. So that was what she was excited for. The spectacular thing that the note pointed towards. It would be something the two of them would share much later, away from prying eyes. This would have to be it, for now. She'd wished to see him, so he was permitted to attend the party, but now that that condition had been satisfied, Daniel was no longer welcome.

He caught his grandfather's eyes. Yes, he could see even now the blatant disappointment. It was best he did leave, before his presence brought about something troublesome. He pulled away from Annabelle, caressing her cheek before letting her go. And that was the end of the niceties associated with visiting his family. All that was left now were the looks of disdain that would follow him on his way out.

But that was an event that would have to take a pause for a moment, because now was the time.

The guests were alerted that the Coming of Age Ceremony was about to take place. Every Marston grandchild had their permanent coder delivered by someone of high ranking in the government. A person widely recognised by the community. Whether they be a mayor, a top executive at MindSpace, or an ambassador. As long as they were someone looked up to by the community, Richard would be pleased. Unless...

Daniel was overcome by a feeling of uneasiness. The guests had all gathered around to create a straight path from the entrance of the hall to the little throne where Annabelle sat. A carpet of violet materialised down the path and music began to play. Majestic and elegant. Powerful, like a Marston. When Daniel saw the carpet, his heart skipped a beat. It was familiar. Reminiscent. A trademark colour of a certain person he knew. But he didn't have time to properly organise his thoughts.

The door to the hall opened, and the person who walked through it was someone nobody ever expected to see.

It was no secret that Richard Marston bore an unnatural and unexplained distaste towards women, so that was the first surprise.

The second surprise; she hadn't been in the city for a year.

Ambassadors had the important task of recruiting new people to come to the city, spending little time in the city themselves.

So nobody expected her when she walked through those doors. Elegant, beautiful, powerful.

Oh the memories that came rushing back at the sight of her. Memories of the Rank Test from a year ago where she gave a show never before seen.

But for Daniel, there was so much more there than just that. Beyond the acknowledgement of how formidable a person she was, there was friendship. Love, even, in whatever forms it took.

It didn't dawn on him at this point to question what string of fate it was that caused the two of them to be in this unlikely place at that moment in time. But surely, someone, or something (from a place somewhere that's not here) was pulling strings. Because this crossroad would be an important one further down the line. A great story that would be told in the years to come. A story that began with a name.

The hall welcomed her with a great round of applause.

The beauty. The hero. The legend.

Reena Bordeaux.

14

You've Changed

Daniel's body forgot to breathe for a moment. The shock of seeing Reena was greater for him than anyone else. He remembered it so clearly. That last goodbye, told as if it may indeed be the last. That once she ventured out into the wider world, there may be nothing to bring her back to this fair city. But, here she was, at Annabelle's Coming of Age Ceremony. Not quite who Daniel would have hoped she'd come back for, but nevertheless, this was Reena!

She seemed to not notice him as she walked down her violet carpet. He wondered if that was true. It was easy for Sentiens to use functions which expanded their perceptions. Reena may very well have known the presence of everyone who was in that hall from the moment she arrived. She didn't need to see them, when she could *see* them. But in that reality, she'd have known Daniel was there and chosen not to acknowledge him. Not a glance. Not even a message sent directly to his mind.

No, stop it! He had to tell himself. It was natural to allow one's thoughts to wander uncontrollably when met with such an unexpected and shocking reality. It was vital to regain composure in such situations. Whether she knew he was there or not, it was up to him to approach her later.

For now, he would enjoy the spectacle of a performance she put on. The carpet untangled itself as she walked through it, and each string came together into new forms. Birds, of various species and sizes, fluttering around Reena like puppets led by string. And they sang, too. Which might be an odd thing to consider. A fabric bird singing like a real one. But sound was just a combination of frequencies and pitches. An easy thing to control if one understood the meta behind it. Well, perhaps not easy, not generally. But for Reena, yes. As simple a task as breathing.

A few of the birds perched themselves around Annabelle's head. Intertwined by the strings that guided them, they formed a sort of crown. A princess of nature was made. And as Reena approached Annabelle, then, the entirety of the carpet, now reconfigured into these living-but-not-living figures, they all came together, spiralling into an epicentre like water in a maelstrom. And they... compressed? They seemed to disappear as they bunched together. What was once a long and dazzling carpet was now a ring of sorts. The fabric was no longer soft, or fluid, but hard, stable, and metal.

Aah, yes, this was Annabelle's coder. Formed by... magic? There were very few who even knew of the word "magic" let alone knew of its existence or put it into any form of practice. It was an art known by few, and practised by fewer, Reena notwithstanding. But this hadn't been magic. This had been a much more commonly known skill. The transformation of one substance into another.

Alchemy.

Everyone in the hall knew coders were made through alchemy, but most of their knowledge ended there. They didn't know the true essence of an alchemist, or of the three principles of alchemy, or of Mothers, or even what Rethium and Arethium actually were. Their knowledge of the way the world really worked was so limited, they couldn't possibly fathom the true brilliance of what Reena had performed in front of them. Whether she'd transmuted it beforehand, or created the coder there and then, each was a brilliant feat in its own right.

Annabelle stretched out her hand and Reena placed the coder around her wrist.

'For the princess,' Reena said. Her voice was soft. Smooth. Like velvet.

Annabelle smiled gleefully. Whoever orchestrated this had done so perfectly. Aside from Daniel, Reena was the person Annabelle looked up to the most.

Richard Marston didn't share their sentiments. Reena didn't need to look at him to know how disgusted he was. Someone would be getting an earful later.

There was one more aspect of the Coming of Age Ceremony that needed to be completed. Now that Annabelle had her first permanent coder, she needed to use her first command.

'I've made something special for you,' Reena said. Then she stepped back and gave Annabelle the stage.

Commands were just functions already programmed into coders. Even if the person using the command didn't quite understand the meta behind it, as long as their mind could bear the burden, they were able to use it. A mind with the basic intelligence of a ten year old couldn't be expected to use functions of particular complexity. Commands made it possible.

Some moments passed while Annabelle adjusted to the coder. It was an odd experience having information just come into your head from an external source. Being able to access the massive MindSpace network was overwhelming at first.

But when it finally happened, it was more dazzling than any of them would have imagined it to be. It wasn't anything overly extravagant. A simple message that displayed itself for about 10 seconds. Light gathered from every corner of the room, forming an illumination of pink neon just above Annabelle's head. The light formed the figure of a little girl, and the little girl danced around the ballroom, leaving sparkles in her wake. This was a familiar image. There was a world in MindSpace where you could see something very similar.

With a final twirl in the centre of the ballroom, the little girl of pink neon danced herself away.

And that was it. Light returned to where it was supposed to be, and the room lit up further with a big round of applause, for both Annabelle and Reena.

Annabelle ran up to Reena and hugged her. It wasn't because Renna had made her look so impressive in front of everyone. It was because pink was her favourite colour, and Reena remembered. She really was still an innocent child.

The hug was cut short by Richard. Reena's purpose had been served, and Annabelle had gifts to receive from other guests.

'Such a pleasure to have you back, Reena,' Richard said to her. It was a wonder why he'd make the effort to say words that were so insincere. Under normal circumstances, he wouldn't. But even he had to give Reena some degree of respect. Knowing full well whose daughter she was.

'A short but vital visit,' she responded.

When Richard and Annabelle left her, she was swarmed by many of the other guests, each bombarding her with questions of her experiences outside of the city. Questions she wasn't permitted – nor wanted – to answer.

Daniel observed her as she was surrounded by the love of the Central District elite. He remembered a time when he was viewed with so much regard. It wasn't even that long ago. He might have felt a pang of envy had he not noticed Reena glance over at him briefly. It could have been an accident, but he was sure of what he saw. She hadn't just looked in his general direction, or looked past him to someone else. Their eyes made contact. And brief as that moment was, even the shortest moments contained their own infinity. And many, many things could be conveyed in such a time.

The message came not long after.

'Meet me outside.'

Reena had sent that to him, which prompted him to take his leave. He waited out in the foyer for all of a minute before she appeared next to him. And just as with any encounter, seeing someone from afar bore no comparison to being right up close. So close as to see the multi-coloured speckled pattern within her eyes. The point where the paleness of her cheeks transformed into a touch of rose lips. The shades of light violet that ran streaks through her otherwise silver hair. And her scent. Yes, that essence of flowers that was like walking through a garden on a sunny day, with just the right amount of clouds to make the sky look like art on a blue canvas. Reena was a presence to behold, and none did so with as great a vigour and purity of intent as Daniel.

Being face to face with her so suddenly, all he could do in response to her presence was utter her name, 'Reena,' in as whispered and absent a tone as he could unconsciously muster. He must have heard it in his own head like an echo. As though he were deep in some vivid dream and someone on the outside was calling his own name, resonating it through the reality of his inner mind. A reality that existed purely for her. Yes, this was that Reena, in the flesh.

Reality was truly a cruel mistress. Because here, now, Daniel had no notion, thought, or instinct of what to do next. His cloudy blue sky was now a blank canvas, waiting for someone to paint it.

That someone wasn't Reena.

'Well isn't this a fanciful reunion,' said RJ, looking down at them from the next floor.

Then he appeared in front of them suddenly. Teleportation, the same used in MindSpace branches. A perk of being a Marston.

'Reena,' he continued, 'did you see the look on my granddad's face when you came in? Priceless!' he laughed to himself. 'I don't know what your dad was thinking, sending you. He knows how my grandfather feels about women.'

'RJ!' Daniel snapped.

RJ smirked. 'Standing up for your childhood crush are you? Bit late to play the big man, don't you think? And here you two are having a secret rendezvous. Honestly, Reena, what do you see in this loser? He's just a deadbeat with the intellectual capacity of a commoner. Not worth our time.'

Reena sighed. 'I see you haven't changed, RJ. You still talk too damn much.'

RJ chuckled. Then he went serious. 'There's a limit to how insolent you can be when you're in someone else's home. Don't forget your place, Bordeaux.'

"Bordeaux". A name which held no historical significance on this continent. Unlike "Marston".

Reena ignored him. 'Come, Daniel. We can talk elsewhere.'

She walked to the door to leave. But just before opening it, turned back to RJ and said, 'I'm very well aware of my place and role in this story, RJ. Be prepared for the day you find out yours. You might be disappointed.'

RJ grinded his teeth and spat out at her. 'WENCH!' And attempted to *grab* hold of her, but she *teleported* herself and Daniel out of there before he could. She always had been a few steps ahead of him, even when they were kids.

Not much had changed.

Reena and Daniel appeared outside of the Marston estate.

'Let's walk,' she said, and began doing so without any clear indication of where they were going.

They exchanged all the usual niceties of how they were and how they'd been, which Reena very much considered useless small talk, but entertained that Daniel was a bit flustered on what to say. But then he asked her what she was doing back, and she said, 'My dad called me back.'

'For Annabelle's Coming of Age?' he asked.

'That, and some other business.'

'Official business you can't talk about, no doubt.'

She gave him a look confirming his assumption.

'How long are you back for?'

'Until my business is concluded, I suppose.'

'Well I hope it's for a week, at least.'

She looked at him curiously.

He smiled. He was giddy. He'd told so few people of this, and was happy that he was getting the opportunity to tell Reena before it occurred. 'I'm taking the Rank Test.' He wasn't sure what sort of reaction he was expecting from her, if any reaction at all. Reena wasn't the type to show if she was surprised or excited by something. Not that she ever really got surprised or excited. But the way she looked at him after he'd told her was familiar, in both that he'd often seen her give that look in the past, and that it was the same overlooking expression that Alex sometimes had. That gaze that seemed as though they weren't looking at you, but through you.

'You're making that face again,' he said. 'It's funny. I met someone this last year who does the exact same thing.'

This caught her attention, and for all that's been said about her lack of ability to be surprised, this time, she was.

'Met where?' she asked.

'Over The Network. She lives in West District.'

Even more shocking. The conversation may have continued down that path had Daniel not gone off on a tangent.

'Are you caught up with Lore?' he asked her with a sudden energy.

'Not from this last year,' she said.

'You need to!' he implored. 'This week... we're finally going to meet The Warrior!'

The Warrior.

Still, she looked at him curiously. She was processing things in her mind. There was a lot about this brief encounter that revealed things to her that were pertinent to her reason for being back. And with everything she'd heard in this short period of time, and seeing what she'd seen when she *looked* at Daniel, she had a pretty good guess of why. There was a conversation she needed to have to be sure. In the meantime, she needed to be careful with what she did, and in particular, what she said. *There are things that must only be known by those supposed to know them.* And she had a well of information that couldn't be shared with others.

But the time would come. And it would come sooner than people thought. For now, though, all she could say to Daniel in response to the person she saw now compared to the memory of who he was before she left the city, was:

'You've changed.'

'How so?'

'You're more mature. Less childlike. You seem to be taking life more seriously.' But that wasn't even what she'd been referring to. There was something else about Daniel that was different. Something even he wasn't aware of. It was difficult to notice the differences in oneself as they occurred over time. Sometimes one needs the perspective of an observer. Someone who could only compare the 'you' of now to the 'you' of however long ago. And, perhaps more importantly, was capable of seeing what that difference was.

'Well, I suppose that's true,' he replied. 'I have bigger goals now.'

An important thing to have.

Reena didn't say anything after that, so Daniel started a new conversation.

'What else are you doing while you're here?'

'I'm heading to the lab now. Apparently we have some interesting guests.'

'Guests?' he asked, confused. 'Interesting how?'

'That's for me to find out.'

'And for me to never know, I suppose.' He remembered what she'd always say to him when they were younger.

There are things that must only be known by those supposed to know them. He remembered that, and then, in some wave of epiphany, remembered something else. His mind had done that thing where it connected two things together to make sense of something it never understood before. What Reena had said now, and a conversation he'd recently had with Alex. He could remember it clearly now. That book. Those words.

His grandfather had said the same thing on occasion. He'd never really thought much of it until Reena said it time and time again. Those exact words, verbatim. And then, in the last year, Alex had said it to him, too. That was far too coincidental to be coincidence. He wondered if these secrets they kept were of the same nature. If this book he'd been offered once was the book they'd all read. What might he know if he'd accepted the book all that time ago?

It was very easy to imagine what other possibilities of life one might have had they made different choices at various points in time, and think they'd have found themselves in a better situation as a result. But sometimes, even if they didn't realise at the time, the decisions they'd made were exactly what would set their life on the course it needed to be. Was Daniel right to have rejected the book way back when? Who was to say.

'Not never,' Reena said. 'Sooner than you think.' Then she stopped, because they were at a travel station, which was purely for Daniel's benefit. Having an ambassador's coder meant Reena could access warp pathways from anywhere.

'I'll be seeing you,' she said, and *Warped* out of there quicker than he could even respond.

'Nice seeing you, too, Reena,' he said out into the air. He thought then that not much had changed. She was still as abrupt and focussed as ever. The question that remained was, what would Daniel do with the rest of his afternoon?

15

OLD CROW

As Alex left the orphanage, a murder of crows circled the skies above her.

She was being summoned.

A warp path took her to the west side of the district, the Shaman Quarter. Life here was very different to every other part of the city. It was said, if you wanted to know what life was like outside of New Heart, go to the Shaman Quarter. Shaman didn't interact with the world's meta. They couldn't use functions or commands. They had a stricter burden of obedience to natural laws than Sentiens did. But they still had their ways of breaking them.

Aside from purchasing a Shaman's unique strain of herb, Sentiens didn't find much reason to come to this part of the district. But Alex visited from time to time. She wasn't overly familiar with Shaman as a whole, but over the years had become well acquainted with two, and one of them was requesting her presence.

She came upon a rundown shack. A graffiti sign named it "Old Crow's," with many of the aforementioned birds stood atop its roof. One of them had its eyes fixated on Alex, and when her eyes met it, it shook its head vigorously. A rather curious thing for a crow to do.

But this crow was special, and the vigorous shaking of its head was a message.

She had been summoned, but she couldn't enter. Not yet.

Alex understood. There was someone in there she shouldn't see. No, that wasn't the case. It was someone who shouldn't see her.

She went to the back of the building and *looked* through the wall. Peering into the shop, she saw Cy was in there, talking to the shack's owner, Old Crow. He was one of the only other Sentiens who visited this place. So very few knew how valuable Old Crow was. Though, even Alex and Cy had no idea how deep her knowledge and sphere of influence ran. For as much information as she gave, she, too, had her secrets.

Alex was about to listen in on their conversation but saw that Cy was leaving. She'd have to go in and ask Old Crow herself.

She waited a while for Cy to leave via warp path. He was the cautious kind, and very perceptive. If she wasn't careful, he'd spot her. But she'd become quite good at keeping under the radar over the years.

She entered once he'd left, and was met with the soft but croaky voice of Old Crow in her very consistent greeting.

'Hello, dear.' Old Crow's physical presence in the world seemed that of someone at the end of their journey. There was a calmness to her. The sort of calm when something came to an end. Like the fizzling out of heavy rain, leaving a landscape that glistened from the rays of a setting sun. The approaching night after a stormy day. That sort of calm.

Alex greeted her. 'Something I can help you with today?' There were many things Sentiens could do in the city that Shaman couldn't, and even more things Alex could do. Alex traded favours with Old Crow for information.

'Not today. I'm not in need of anything. I simply brought you here to tell you he's been asking about you.'

'Within the capacity of?'

'He knows what you look like, and where you live. Information he took from that boy, Jimoh. He doesn't know your name, of course. Nor does he know about our relationship. I told him nothing, but thought perhaps you'd like to know you're on his radar.'

It was something worth knowing. Alex's plans relied on her maintaining total anonymity. She couldn't have eyes on her constantly.

'Come, dearest,' said Old Crow. 'Let me take a good look at you.'

A good look? As if Old Crow hadn't seen her enough times in the many years they'd done business together. But Alex obliged. She came in closer and had her face almost seized within Old Crow's palms. But it was gentle. Her cheeks were being caressed lovingly.

Alex could have read Old Crow's mind to know exactly what was going through it at that time, but she wouldn't do that. Business or otherwise, They'd developed some bonds of friendship. There was trust between them. Old Crow had told Alex many stories over the years, and whether those were true or otherwise, the contents of them proved valuable in some form or other. So Alex simply asked, 'What's going on?'

'I want to remember you exactly as you are. Your kind and gentle face. The touch of your soul. I want to remember them.'

Then Alex realised. Old Crow was indeed old. Not so old as to have no life left in her, but certainly old enough to be considered to have 'lived'. She must have some recognition that the end could come at any abrupt moment. 'You never did tell me your story,' Alex said.

Many stories she'd told, but never her own.

'Oh child, I'm not sure it's mine to tell. Oftentimes, the stories we call our own, are meant to be told by others. Perhaps he will tell you once I'm gone.'

'He?' Alex asked curiously.

'He whose name you do not know,' she replied.

'How do you...' she fumbled, and was cut off.

Old Crow gestured her to silence. 'Hush, child. That is a question I can't answer, so you're best not to ask. You must follow this story in the order it's being told, otherwise, you might miss things.'

That was the first time Alex heard Old Crow speak like that. How uncoincidentally coincidental that she chose now of all times to mention the man whom Alex had been curious about for so long. And what was it Old Crow had just said?

You must follow this story in the order it's being told.

But what exactly was this story? Who was telling it? And what was Alex's role in it?

Why did Old Crow and Sister Mabel seem to know about it whilst Alex remained in the dark?

And then another question, which Alex felt she might know the answer to. Who else knew what story this was? A very obvious name came to Alex's mind.

He whose name you do not know. It echoed in her head. The mystery of the man who gifted her that book, and had attempted to give it to Daniel all those years ago. A man whose very existence hadn't even been mentioned since then, yet, in the space of a day, had been referred to by three different people.

Alex may have been unfamiliar with fiction, but she understood enough to know that an event like this was a turning point, and something major was coming.

Something major *was* coming. The Rank Test. The revolution. And Alex's plan, all on the same day.

But what if there was something else? Something more? What if there was another story being told?

There are things that must only be known by those supposed to know them.

Well, Alex was clearly supposed to know something. Otherwise, why introduce her to the concept in the first place? So many questions. So many mysteries. So many secrets.

So many potential adventures.

'So what happens next?' Alex asked.

'You simply need to carry on down the path you've chosen, dearest. I don't know exactly where it leads, but I guarantee it will surprise you.'

'Okay,' Alex accepted. She went to take her leave, but before she did, 'I'll want to hear your story someday,' Alex said.

'You will, dearest. You will.'

Old Crow waited for Alex to leave before she added:

'Even if I'm not the one to tell it.'

Annabelle's party concluded all of its formal events, and the children were being left to play. A luxury that Annabelle may no longer be awarded once the day reaches its end.

Richard Marston had retired to his quarters momentarily to enjoy a cigar, one of his few guilty pleasures. He stared out of the window as he smoked it. A crow was perched on one of the trees in the back garden, and though it was at a distance that he couldn't see clearly using his usual sight, it seemed as though this crow was staring right at him. He might have given it pause for concern, if for just a moment, he'd associated the crow with some distant memory of an event long ago. But Richard Marston didn't allow such trifling things to take up space within his mind. So this crow, too, would be forgotten. But all too quickly, it, and the crows of his past, would resurface. And by then, it would be too late.

The MindSpace Tower. The most important building in the city. The pinnacle of representation of what New Heart was and would come to be. A place of mystery, inaccessible to most, yet, there, now, it housed two special guests. And over the course of time that these guests had been there, they'd frequently seen a crow circling round their living quarters.

It was there again now. Watching, waiting. But this time, its reconnaissance was cut short. A crow wasn't an unusual thing to see in the city. They were everywhere, after all. But an eagle! You didn't get those in this part of the continent. So the crow, unaware of its surroundings other than its direct line of sight, was surprised to see itself encompassed by a great shadow. Such that when it turned around to see this great and majestic eagle hovering above it, the crow, in a moment of panic, faded out of existence.

Strange.

That's not something crows do.

16

Eagle

An Eagle had soared the skies of New Heart that day.

There would be many who swore they'd seen it. But nobody who hadn't seen it would believe them, because everyone knew eagles didn't fly over this city.

But this one did.

It flew right to the most western part of the western district where it happened upon many murders of crows, and with its sharp eagle-sight, it observed what was happening down below.

It observed a man coming out of a shop, and then a woman stepping in. But they weren't its points of interest. They weren't who it had been looking for. Its interest was in the store owner. And as it hovered, high in the sky, beyond anybody's immediate perception, it waited, until eventually, the woman who went in, came out.

Shortly after that, the store owner came out and looked up, right at the eagle. As did many of the crows.

The store owner smiled at the eagle, and then went back inside.

The eagle, turning to head back to whence it came, spotted another point of interest, and swept down to meet it.

Atop a rooftop was a dog, which, too, looked up at the eagle, and continued to do so even as it descended.

It landed in a gust of wind, blowing up dust and leaves.

Up close, now, it seemed abnormally large in size, even considering the dog was merely a pup.

The two approached, greeting one another, beak to snout.

It was a prolonged greeting, full of what could only be described as affection. As though they were long lost companions, meeting one another again for the first time. And yet, in this exchange, there was no barking or screeching, nor any other characteristics one might often attribute to a canine or a bird. In fact, their encounter seemed of a sophisticated civility. Almost human-like.

It was an unexpected encounter, but a welcome one. And with it having achieved as much as it could given the limitations of the participants, the eagle once again leapt up in flight.

Its wings were loud and violent as it picked up momentum, and seeing it then, even having never seen an eagle before, one might think it flew faster than was naturally possible.

It returned to its place of origin in Central District, where it would disperse back into the mana that animated it. Mana that, once within a certain range, would be resupplied to the Shaman. And that was one of the curious things about this city at present.

In this city, MindSpace wasn't just the cause of the tech revolution, it was the foundation of the city itself, and also its government. It was MindSpace which made the laws under which all within the city abided. MindSpace which made the laws that only permitted Shaman to live in West District.

You wouldn't find a Shaman roaming the streets of Central District, so why was there one at MindSpace HQ?

17

A Shaman &...

N'Adina felt the mana return to her. She didn't need it. She had plenty left to spare, but recycling used mana was good practice.

She was in some sort of chamber. A large empty room that was clinical in how clean and bright it was. A blank canvas. Something upon which any creation could manifest. There were similar rooms in every district, though this one was special. The other rooms were direct links to The Network, used when a large group of people needed access under a controlled environment. Like during the Rank Test.

But those rooms only brought the consciousness of those in the room to The Network. They didn't bring things from The Network into the room.

N'Adina being a Shaman wasn't the only thing that violated this city's laws. She was Eruban, too. And the Erubans, like Shamans, only lived in West District. Yet here she was. In the most important place in the city. But she wasn't like any Eruban you'd find here.

A maze-like structure of dusk-blue ink coursed all around her body. Even her hair, which was plaited into long braids, had streaks of blue woven through it. And she wasn't dressed as was customary to Iria, either. This continent's cold climate called for a much heavier attire than that of her homeland. Yet, she wore traditionally light and soft lace materials. Her arms were fully exposed. Her garment only covered to just above her knees, and even then, they were loose-fitting. They were clothes designed to give full range of movement. Another requirement of her homeland.

Standing on one side of the room, she awaited the manifestations that would soon appear.

They emerged inversely to how the eagle had dispersed. Fading into existence until they were undeniably real. Their forms were horrid and monstrous, because that was what they were. Clutters in the virtual, monsters in the real.

There were two of them. They were large, bulky and horrible things, as most clutters were.

Not the worst thing N'Adina had come face to face with.

It was a short moment between them fully materialising and lunging themselves at her. Their hulking frames consequenced heavy-footed steps that shook the room.

The first one came in from her left and swung at her with sharp claws. It was fast for how big it was, but not so quick as to prevent N'Adina from tracking its movement. She let the monster's claw come in close, dodging at the last second. In the second that came immediately after, the other monster was upon her. With both arms stretched out, it attempted a grab. And this turned into one of those cliché moments where someone very small going up against something very large may find themselves in a position to crawl under them. And in the monster's open-bodied attempt to grapple her, N'Adina did just that.

She'd gotten behind both of them, now, and first, struck a heavy kick to the second monster's knee, causing it to keel over. The kick had such force behind it, the monster's knee dislocated, and the very ground which she'd used to steady herself had crumbled beneath her feet.

It was an odd sight, seeing something comparatively small be so physically dominant. But that was the thing about Arethians. Their size and overall physical makeup did very little to suggest the feats of strength they could accomplish. Both classes, Sentien and Shaman, could amplify their physical abilities through various means. But between the two, a Shaman could accomplish it with greater ease and fluidity of application. Their powers were just better suited for that sort of thing.

She jumped onto the felled monster, readjusted her footing, then propelled herself into the other. Again, bones cracked when she struck it clean in the face. Then, maintaining her momentum, took it by its arm, somersaulted it over herself with a great swing, and threw it into its companion.

With a broken knee and a compressed skull, the monsters dematerialised. Two more took their place, the room fixed itself, and the process began again.

In an adjoining room was Q. If Eruban's were identified from their dark skin, then he was as Eruban as they came. But unlike N'Adina, no ink decorated his ebony skin. No, not ebony. His skin was dark, but not dull. In fact, there was a glow about him. Something transcendent and... astral. As though he were sculpted not from something as mundane as clay, but as deeply dark and glamorous as obsidian.

He stood in the centre of his room. He was much taller than N'Adina, and while her hair was long, braided, and black with blue streaks. His was short, almost completely shaven, and it was white.

White?

Not totally uncommon. It was easy for a Sentien to change the colour of their hair. A simple function to perform.

Clutters emerged around him, too. A different sort to the ones N'Adina battled with. They were small, like birds, but had features more like insects of some kind. Wasps, perhaps, swarming all around him like a hive.

Q didn't have the muscle definition N'Adina had. He didn't have much of a dominating presence at all. Take away his height and his white hair – and his otherworldly glow that you couldn't really perceive – and he was an overlooked average. But he was the epitome of what Arethian's were. Much, much more than just the eye could see.

Q's simulation began, and as soon as it did, the room became dark.

The room became dark, because Q stole the light. He gathered it from all corners. Every individual light particle – photons, they were called – and formed them into a shining orb above him. It was like a candle in a dark, empty room. It shone bright enough to see, but not enough to illuminate anything around it. All of its radiance was contained.

Amidst this, the flying clutters around Q became barely visible. But he didn't need to see them, not with his eyes. He could feel them. The flow of their energy. The way their presence in the physical world altered air currents. His body could detect the most miniscule of changes in this enclosed environment. He didn't need to see with his eyes.

His hands began to dance around his sides. You couldn't tell what he was doing just by observing. One needed an unnatural ability to see patterns to understand what he did. Not simply dancing his fingers in random fashion, but tracing paths. The paths taken by the clutters.

And then, then he scattered the light. The light which was no longer just light, but had been altered in its properties. Multiple tiny particles reminiscent of fireflies shot out in straight lines like lasers. And those lasers pierced through any clutters they came in contact with, leaving clean, cauterised wounds in their wake. And when the lasers reached the walls, they ricocheted off them, returning upon themselves to burn through more clutters, and then hit the walls, ceiling, floor, and do it all again.

It was like standing in a room of mirrors. Beams of light piercing all around.

A light show of catastrophe to those trapped within. So little time had passed between the clutters' formation and total annihilation. And Q, who remained calm and collected amidst the mayhem, might only be described by this image as psychotic. And perhaps there was truth in that.

Beyond the virtual chambers, in the control room, October was analysing his new data. His slick, laid-back hair, and rectangular glasses fit the mad scientist archetype perfectly. And whilst one may give credence to that notion based on the fact that he was responsible for the existence of clutters in the real, he wasn't mad at all. October Jenson, one of the founders of MindSpace. His attention was momentarily interrupted by the arrival of an unexpected guest.

Lilith was beside him, another founder. She turned around and smiled at who it was. 'Reena!' She ran and embraced her, then kissed her repeatedly all over her face, which Reena met with protests of disgust, but allowed to continue because, well, this was her mother.

'How are you, dear,' Lilith asked.

'I'll be better when you stop smothering me.'

Lilith pulled away but remained in contact. 'Just like your father,' she said. 'I didn't know he was calling you back.'

'He wanted me to give Annabelle her Coming of Age coder.'

'Oh,' Lilith laughed. 'Richard must have been furious.'

Reena smiled. 'He was.'

'Marvellous. How long are you here?'

'The week.'

Lilith pondered. 'So you're here for the Rank Test.'

'Yes,' Reena huffed. 'I wanted to talk to you about that. The timing is uncoincidentally coincidental. I think dad is making—'

She was cut off. 'Careful, Reena. He's listening.'

'*Who?*' Reena then thought to her mother, assuming whoever it was couldn't invade their thoughts. And she was right. Q's depth of perception didn't extend to the mental plane.

He introduced himself by throwing his voice into the room. Reena heard it as clear as if he were standing next to her, even though there was an entire wall between them, designed to completely separate the room for outside interference.

Reena *looked* through the wall at Q, and then looked at him in a way that very few people could. She saw the very meta that defined his existence. Every structure of logic, infinite that they were.

Recognising logic was like understanding a language. Letters came together to form words, and those words had meaning. They identified aspects of reality. But when one encountered a word they'd never seen before, they needed someone, or something, to define that word for them.

Observing the logic that defined Q was like discovering a new language. She didn't even know how to begin trying to define it.

'What is he?' she asked before she'd even realised.

And her mother told her.

18

Distraction

Bolu had seen the eagle that day. He'd just happened to look up at the time it was flying back to Central District. But Bolu wasn't the curious type. He didn't even question the presence of an eagle in the city's air space. He saw it, and then looked away.

There was a group of children not far ahead of him. He'd catch up to them in about a minute at his current pace. They'd seen the eagle, too. And be it their young age allowing space for curiosity within their minds, they followed the eagle as it continued making its way east. They trailed it even to the point where they couldn't make out its form and it existed purely as a dot in the sky. But the time it took the eagle to go from clear to imperceptible was enough time for Bolu to walk up towards them undetected, unintentional as it was.

The children began walking in the same direction as Bolu, just ahead of him, and completely unaware of his presence. They continued the conversation they were having before they got distracted.

Bolu wasn't an eavesdropper, but they spoke loudly and freely enough for him to hear everything they said. And Bolu took from this conversation some vital information that tore him up on the inside, because now that he knew it, he had to report it. And no doubt, the people that already considered him a sellout would find some new word, more severe in accusatory nature, to call him.

Bolu loved his people, and hated the discrimination directed towards them. But Bolu also loved the idea of there being good in the world. And justice. And right and wrong. And it was his belief, his wholehearted belief, that the police were an organisation that represented justice, and goodness, and righteousness. Even if there were those within it who didn't quite fit into that mould.

He believed further, that if what he'd heard was correct, that leaving it alone would be more detrimental to the city than reporting it. Internal struggle aside, he had to do what he thought was right.

He slipped away from the children, having never been perceived by them throughout their conversation.

The children would never know what happened that day. They'd never ponder how their actions might have had different consequences if any of them had looked back at any point. Or if they'd never let Bolu get that close to them in the first place; had they not allowed themselves to be distracted by the eagle.

Perhaps those realities existed in some other versions of this story. But in the version, Bolu was on his way to give a report to Officer Dodds, to tell him about a conversation he'd overheard between some Eruban children.

Something about a secret meeting held over The Network,

19

Katelina Chen

Chen's Kitchen didn't open its shack during the day, but offered a delivery service instead.

'152 orders today,' Chen said as Kitchen loaded everything into her *Space*. The quantity of mass a person's *Space* could hold was dependent on their ability to carry it. It was typically used simultaneously with a form of telepathy, bearing the weight of the load with the mind, rather than the body.

The Chens' had clients all over the district, but most of the deliveries were for the north side, where the Orenians lived.

152 orders. Each one weighed a kilogram.

Kitchen had two strict rules she had to follow when making deliveries. First, she had to bear the weight of them without using functions or commands. Second, she couldn't use travel stations.

The humans of Areth weren't genetically built to carry such a load for prolonged periods of time. Without the benefits of their Greater Self, a woman as petite as Kitchen shouldn't be capable of such a feat. But there was more to this race than just the ability of a Greater Mind or Greater Soul. There were Greater Bodies, too.

152kg of weight. It was heavy, yes. But not that heavy. Not for Kitchen.

Everything was part of her training.

If you live like everyone else, you'll grow to be soft. That was what her father always told her. It wasn't out of a disdain for others, but rather an acknowledgement of who - *what* - Kitchen was. She wasn't like everyone else. She couldn't live like everyone else. In order to become her greatest and truest self, the life she lived had to be different.

She set off immediately, leaping through alleys and hopping onto rooftops. If she was going to take the scenic route, she wanted the scenic route! Running through the streets didn't offer the true aesthetic of the district's architecture, and as long as she didn't go too high into its airspace - the warp pathways existed above the city - there wasn't really an issue. There was no law against running on top of buildings.

Kitchen made her drops one by one. Customers will have paid an initial deposit for their orders, and once confirmation had been made that they'd received them, their *Banks* would release the remaining funds. In the entire district, Chen's Kitchen had the most profitable trade, despite it equally having some of the cheapest prices.

It was about an hour before Kitchen made it to the north of the district, and she'd only done 30 drops. She could never quite escape stopping to have a quick chat with the customers, and that slowed her down to operating at less than half of her would-be efficiency. But she didn't mind so much. She had the entire afternoon. Plus, the rest of her deliveries were more tightly packed together, the intervals between each would rapidly decrease.

She was about ten drops in before she noticed the company of an unruly group of men. No, she'd noticed them before, but couldn't be certain they were following her. Now she'd removed all doubt. And they'd multiplied in number.

She waited.

It wasn't long before they realised they'd been spotted. No use hiding anymore.

4...6...10...15! 15 of them, though only a few revealed themselves.

The one that spoke to her was very quick to the point. 'Our boss wants to talk to you.'

Kitchen recognised them. There were gangs in this city, all trying to claim as much territory as they could, whilst simultaneously protecting what they had. The men before her now; they were members of the leading Orenian gang. Rather notorious for the ferocity with which they operated.

Kitchen finally answered, 'Sure. But after my drops.'

'Now!' he insisted.

Don't beat them up, Kitchen. Don't. Beat. Them. up! She had to tell herself. *What would Alex do? Turn invisible and walk away. But you can't turn invisible, Kitchen!*

It then dawned on her that she probably could turn invisible. Just not the same way Alex did. But she was curious to know what the leader of northside wanted to speak to her about. So she repeated, 'After my deliveries. If I have to repeat myself again, someone's going to get hurt.' She looked him dead in the eye.

More of them came out from their corners now.

'So that's how it's going to be,' she huffed. But then, the man she'd been speaking to raised his hand.

'Boss says it's okay. But I'll be accompanying you, if you don't mind.'

'I mind very much, actually. But you'll follow me anyway, so I guess that's that. Try to keep up.'

She disappeared from sight after she said that, but the man caught on to her pretty quickly. She was on the next rooftop. He watched her disappear again and reappear on the next rooftop over. She continued doing this between houses, taking only a few steps between each, vanishing, and then appearing.

Keep up, she'd said. Well, he seemed to have no trouble with that at all, because in a similar fashion to her, he, too, dotted in and out of reality.

It wasn't teleportation or warping. It was *skipping*. When a Sentien cheated, they forced the outcome of a function without understanding the meta. The mind took a random path of logic to get there. It was rarely used; a social taboo, actually. Cheating was hardly ever worth the stress it placed on the mind. But there were specific forms of cheating, refined over the years into practical application.

Skipping, was an infamous Orenian artform, operated in various ways into their combat arts.

The Orenian continent's history had more internal conflicts than that of Eruba or Iria. With so many wars occurring, the Orenians became particularly adept at the stylistic side of hand to hand combat. *Skipping*, made them that much more of a force to be reckoned with.

Observing a *skip* was like following someone's movements with opened and closed eyes in one second intervals. The period spent with eyes closed would cause a displacement of events. The space that person travelled within that time wasn't visually perceived, but the mind knows that space must have been traversed in some way, and subsequently fills in that gap.

A Sentien's ability to *skip* was based around the same concept. Instead of moving through space physically, the mind filled in the gap and caused the body to appear wherever the mind stopped.

Anybody watching from their windows, or the streets, would see a group of Orenians coming in and out of reality, reappearing some metres ahead of where they'd disappeared from. And they would see that the men, supposedly chasing after the girl, were struggling to keep up with her.

Kitchen's *skips* were fluid. She performed them consecutively with a minimal interval between each. It was almost instinctive. Whereas even the best of the crew that were following her needed time to plan their route and destination, and to let their minds recover from the continuous function use. This carried on for an hour until she made her final drop.

When they'd caught up to her at the end, all of them had sweated right through their clothes. Meanwhile, Kitchen didn't so much as expel a heavy breath. She was in perfect condition. Which made it all the more annoying when she said, 'Your boss is at your hideout, right? I'll meet you there.' And left for the destination without them.

They swore vengeance on her for the trouble she'd put them through.

A very foolish oath to make to oneself.

At the hideout, Kitchen's hands were tied behind her back.

What's this supposed to do? She thought to herself. But it wasn't until she was inside that she realised its significance. Inside, surrounded by the gang members, she found herself subjected to a *blocking* program.

Her sen was being suppressed.

Blocking programs weren't something the public was supposed to have. You needed a special licence, and those were only given to certain organisations. The existence of one here meant these guys were familiar with the city's black market.

They obviously knew the threat Kitchen posed, so restricting her ability to use functions was a smart move.

If they'd known more about her, they might have realised how foolish a move it really was.

She sat down in front of their gang leader. A man named Lido. His second in command was his younger brother, Rado. Technically they both ran the gang together, but if you asked anyone who the shot caller was, Lido was the name you always heard. But as much as they respected Lido, they feared Rado. He was reckless, chaotic and unruly. Lido was the only person who could keep him in check.

'You comfortable, princess?' Lido said to her.

'Princess?' she said back with disgust.

'Aren't all little girls princesses?'

'Little!'

Kitchen had a superiority complex about her height. She was shorter than most people.

'Apparently not,' Lido said. 'Princesses don't do deliveries, do they?'

Kitchen met the rhetorical question with a real one. 'What do you want?'

There was a reaction amongst the gang members. It was a well known rule amongst the Orenians, you don't talk to Lido like that. What would he do now that Kitchen just had?

Nothing.

He answered her question very calmly, actually. 'A sit-down with your old man. Been trying to organise one for a while, but he pays me no mind. Guess he likes darkies and lighties more than his own people.' Lido scoffed. 'But look who I'm talking to. His half breed daughter. Where *is* your mother?'

Oh, so not nothing. Lido decided to get personal. And if his plan was to push Kitchen's buttons, he did so with complete success.

And Kitchen was a straightforward, speak-her-mind, rather bashful sort of person. So she answered his question immediately with, 'Around my neck, you depecate fool!'

Silence. It was the type of response nobody would have ever guessed a person to give. For how outlandish and ridiculous it was, she'd said it with so much confidence.

'Around your neck?' Lido repeated, too astonished to even take note of the fact he'd been called a depecate fool.

'That's right! This necklace is my mother. Depecate fool!'

This time the insult landed, but he had to keep his cool. And seeing her necklace, now, he was perhaps the only person knowledgeable enough to realise the error in Kitchen's understanding of what her necklace was. But he didn't care enough to correct her.

'You think holding me hostage will convince my dad to sit down with you?' she asked.

Lido pointed at her with a snap of his fingers. 'Key word, "Hostage." One of my guys is on his way to persuade your dad to meet with us now. The question is what state he finds his daughter in when he gets here.'

Oh, so that was it. Well, Kitchen heard everything she needed to.

They'd tied her hands earlier by bending a metal pole around them. With her sen being blocked off, there was no way she could get herself out.

It came as a shock when she stood up from the ground and the sound of metal rang. If they hadn't seen it, they wouldn't have believed it. The pole that they'd cuffed her with had been unwound.

But how? They were still blocking her sen. And just in case, Lido had his *Radar* active the whole time. If she'd used any sort of function, he'd know. But she hadn't, so, 'How?' he asked.

'I had to melt it a bit cos it was quite rough. But it slid right off after I did.'

Melt? Yes. Further inspection showed the inside was deformed. The otherwise smooth and perfectly round pole had waves from where its metal had melted and resolidified.

But she hadn't used a function, so, 'How?' Lido asked again.

She didn't answer his question. 'You might as well call off your guy cos my dad was never going to come here. You've entirely overestimated yourself, and completely underestimated me.'

No! Lido thought. 'You're telling me you took off that cuff with body heat and brute strength? Without the use of your sen? Tell me how!'

Yes, tell them how, Kate*l*ina.

She turned to him. There was a ferocity in her eyes. She wanted more than anything to cave in the heads of everyone there. But she couldn't do that. There were laws. But more importantly, there were rules. Per her father's teaching, she couldn't let her temper get the better of her. In the absence of violence, words would have to suffice.

'I'm Katelina Chen. I'm built different.'

20

Psy(Cy)chometry

Cy had been in the vicinity of Chen's Kitchen when he'd seen the member of Lido's gang show up. He was familiar enough with their activities to know there would be a benefit to reading his mind, and so he had.

Cy sat in front of Mr Chen and Big Dog, now, filling them in about what he'd overheard.

'Apparently they kidnapped your daughter in order to coerce you into a meeting with them,' he said. 'But she escaped. That's the overall gist of it.'

'Do you know if she hurt any of them?' Chen asked.

'They didn't say.'

'No matter. I expect she'll be returning soon.' Chen poured them all some tea. The room was empty other than the three of them. The windows had been blacked out to stop anybody from looking in, and a *wall* was in place to stop those who might eavesdrop by other means.

Cy was usually a get-down-to-business type of guy, but he began the conversation of this day with tangents. 'You're very protective of your daughter,' he said.

'Aren't all parents protective of their children?' Chen retorted with a smile.

'Perhaps,' Cy responded. 'But it's different with you. You're not protecting "her from," you're protecting "from her." Because of what she can do?'

Chen was surprised. He hadn't expected Cy to approach that topic so directly. Cy knew things, and Chen knew things, and they both knew each other knew things. But people who knew things had to be careful when discussing with each other what they knew.

There are things that must only be known by those supposed to know them.

A phrase known all too well by all participants of this conversation.

'It's true that Katelina poses a threat when she doesn't control herself,' Chen said, 'but that's why I've been so thorough with teaching her to be disciplined. All that aside, you seem to be taking many measures to avoid the topic you came here to discuss. Sensitive in nature as it is.'

'So you're aware of what we've been doing?' Cy asked.

'Big Dog has kept me informed of various things.'

Cy looked at Big Dog, now. 'Naturally. I've always wondered what the extent of your relationship is. The two of you are very... other. You're not like the rest of the people in West District. I have to wonder if your being here serves a specific purpose.'

'Don't we all serve a specific purpose?' Chen asked him.

'I'd say many of us have an unspecified purpose in the grand scheme of things. What's done by one could just as easily be done by another.'

'But not you,' Big Dog interjected. 'Who else in the district could hope to achieve what you're on the verge of accomplishing?'

Cy looked between the two of them suggestively, and Big Dog burst out in laughter. 'No,' Big Dog said. 'Not us. There isn't a person in this city right now who could do what you've done.'

Cy met this compliment doubtfully as he shook his head. 'I haven't done it yet. The revolution—'

'We don't talk of the revolution,' Chen said. 'Albeit, an impressive feat to raise people under a common goal, it in itself is not so uncommon. What we're talking about is far more impressive.'

Cy was still confused. This revolution was the pinnacle of his life at this point. Aside from Mara, it was everything he lived for. What could he have already done that was considered even greater?

'Regardless,' Chen continued, 'time is short. What did you come to discuss?'

He reluctantly moved on. 'As I'm sure you know, my primary ability is psychometry. What you might not know is, it's not just an ability. It's my affinity.' He waited for a reaction that didn't come. 'So you did know. Of course. Regardless, it's that psychometry that lets me know you two are cut from a different cloth to the rest of us. You're the two most powerful people in the district, yet you live such humble and simple lifestyles. I know there are reasons for this, even if I don't know what those reasons are. But—'

He hesitated. How exactly was it that one asked for help? Cy wasn't used to this. He was always the one helping others. He was the problem solver. The fixer. The anything-you-needed-him-to-be guy. The one in whom people put their trust. And here he was, having to trust others.

'I'm here to beg for your help.'

'With what aspect?' Chen asked.

That was a little bit soothing. It wasn't a straight no, which meant there was hope, somewhere.

'You've always made this part of the district a neutral area. No gang conflicts. No fights. Everyone in the district respects you. I hoped this might be a place of refuge for my people, when the time comes.'

'You know what you're asking, young man?'

'I do.'

'It won't be other civilians after your people on this day. It will be the police.'

Cy swallowed nothing. 'I know.'

'You understand the weight of your request?'

'I do.'

'And yet you ask it of me anyway.'

Cy swallowed again. But then he said confidently, 'Like I said, everyone in the district respects you. Including the police. Including Blackjack, and the mayor. I'm hoping you won't have to lift a finger. That your name alone will be enough. But if it's not enough, if they still come, and Mara is unable to intervene, then yes, I ask that you do whatever it takes to protect my people. I'll bear the weight of whatever happens.'

'Do you think you'll be able to carry that burden, young man?'

Cy looked at Chen curiously, then. The way he'd phrased that question had seemed odd. As if Chen intervening in the affairs to come bore greater weight than he realised. As if there were more - and there was - to this story than he knew.

'Like I said, whatever it takes.' That was Cy's response. And within that, Chen knew that he meant his words. That was all he really needed to know.

'Your people will be safe here. Of that you can be certain.'

Cy wasn't very good at expressing emotion. Certainly not positive ones. But his always serious demeanour had been humbled for this encounter. And though he couldn't bring himself to show joy through any expression, there was no doubt that there was gratitude in his eyes. The protection of his people was a vital aspect of his plan succeeding. He was relying on Chen more than he cared to admit.

And Big Dog?

Cy turned to him.

'Don't worry,' Big Dog said. 'The Pack has your back. Your people at home will be safe, too.' Yes, because it wasn't the entire Eruban community that was taking part in the revolution. There were those who refused. Those who simply weren't able. Cy couldn't bear the idea of them falling prey to an opportunist while there was nobody there to protect them. He would take his own measures against that reality, but just in case, it was good to have Big Dog on his side.

'You both have my whole gratitude,' Cy said, bowing his head once again. It was a practice found in certain parts of the world. Usually carried out in the presence of royalty, or those akin to it. Which exclaimed either the level of regard that Cy had for the two of them, or the degree to which he was willing to humble himself in order to guarantee the safety of his people. Or perhaps, even, a mixture of the two.

There was much more Cy would have wanted to discuss with them at this time. They both had a well of knowledge and experience to draw from that would benefit him. But time was of the essence. He still had things to prepare. Loose ends to tie up. That conversation would have to wait until another day.

Chen had one more thing to say to him though. A parting gift, of sorts. Presented in the form of what Cy could only determine was some sort of metaphor. Or riddle.

'You can't outsmart The Wizard.'

Everyone in New Heart had heard that particular phrase on numerous occasions. Either from the story from which it was taken, or from those who chose to use it idiomatically, due to its real-world application.

You can't outsmart The Wizard. It referred to a person's intelligence being so great that one should never think themselves capable of challenging them.

Cy didn't even bother asking, because he knew they couldn't answer. This was one of those need-to-know situations, and the answer wouldn't come to Cy so easily. The answer to the question:

Who, in this scenario, is The Wizard?

21

Sometimes it's Okay

Alex had made her way to Chen's after leaving Old Crow's. She knew Cy was going to be there; she'd read his mind in their near encounter earlier.

Alongside the *wall* Chen had put up, he also had his sen zone active.

The mind itself was its own personal world. A place of infinite size, contained within an imaginary space. When a Sentien used functions, they applied the meta of their mind to the outside world in an active state, in order to redefine it, thus, changing it. But it was possible, for those who were capable, to not only apply the meta of their mind, but to expand the meta of their mental world in a passive state. It wasn't a function in itself, but it made using functions within that space easier, because they no longer had to overcome the world's meta. It also meant that for others to use functions, they had to first overwhelm the meta of that person's mind. That was a sen zone.

Mr Chen's sen zone covered such a wide area, even standing on the other side of the street from Chen's Kitchen, Alex still found herself within it. He knew she was there, so attempting to eavesdrop on their conversation was pointless. She'd have to wait.

During this time, she sent a *message* to Kitchen, enquiring when she'd be finished with her deliveries. A few back and forths got Alex up to speed with the encounter she'd had with Lido's men.

'*Idiots*,' Alex said once she'd heard the full story.

'*Depecate fools*!' Kitchen agreed. She jumped down from a rooftop shortly after, joining Alex in her wait for the meeting at Chen's Kitchen to end.

The blackout screen on the windows finally lifted, revealing Mr Chen and Big Dog waving at them from inside.

Cy came out of the restaurant and saw the two of them across the street. He paid them no mind at first. But then he did a double take. He recognised Kitchen as Chen's daughter, but she wasn't what had caught his eye. It was this girl with dark, golden-brown hair, whom he'd never seen on his side of the district, nor ever on the few occasions he'd visited Chen's Kitchen prior to this. But, just once, a mere day ago, he'd first caught a glimpse of her in Jimoh's memories.

He stopped in his tracks, and had he waited any longer than he had to approach Alex, might have been accused of staring in a perverted manner. But somehow the same couldn't be said for the fact that not once did he break eye contact whilst approaching her.

Alex felt herself drop into a state of panic. It was only earlier that day that Old Crow had warned her about his inquiries, but didn't think enough of his ability that he might actually know what she looked like. An oversight on her part.

Cy bowed his head and greeted Kitchen. She returned the bow, not knowing how to address him for lack of a name.

Then he said to Alex, 'Forgive the boldness of my approach. I have reason to believe you helped out a young man with whom I bear some responsibility, in the early morning of yesterday.'

'Y- yes,' Alex stuttered over the words, still caught off guard.

Cy stretched out his hand. 'Allow me to offer my thanks. I understand the situation was quelled over more smoothly due to your interference. You have my gratitude.'

'Oh... yes... um, well, that's okay. Always happy to help the children, ahahaha.' This wasn't her being caught off guard. This was an act. She looked coyly at Cy's outstretched hand and made a statement of somewhat retreating herself into a closed posture, smiling awkwardly at his gesture of gratitude.

Cy retracted his hand immediately. 'Forgive me. I forget the discomforts of being approached by a stranger.' He bowed to her. 'Thank you again.' And then took his leave.

'*What was that about?*' Kitchen asked her.

That was about self-preservation. Alex knew all about Cy's psychometry. If meta was the information that defined the state of the world, psychometry gave him that information freely. Cy's affinity was the power to understand everything he perceived. He didn't have to touch something in order for it to work, but the ability was at its most potent during physical contact. Alex did a perfectly good job of hiding the secrets of her own body from this distance, but had she taken his hand, there was every possibility he would have discovered something he shouldn't.

She was just a few days away from executing her plan. Now wasn't the time for people to be taking an unwanted interest in her.

'Well you played that off nicely,' Kitchen said after Alex explained it to her. Because Kitchen knew the secrets of Alex's body, too. And that was another one of those curious things as to why, amongst all the people in the district, did two people whose very existence deviated from the norm, should somehow find themselves so inextricably tied to one another?

There were many mysteries in New Heart. And the thing about mysteries was that however great or old they were, someone, somewhere knew the truth.

Alex and Kitchen crossed over to the two people who knew more than they'd ever let on, but were duty bound to never disclose what those things were. Because this wasn't a story that revealed its true self from the get-go.

No.

This was a story of things that must only be known by those supposed to know them. And however much someone thought they knew, there was always more - so much more - they had to discover. That's just the way these stories are told.

22

MR MAYOR

'The mayor will see you now.'

Those were the words Dodds had been waiting half an hour to hear. For the fact they lived in a city where communication between two parties could happen instantaneously, it was frustrating to have to meet with the mayor in person. But Dodds understood. The protocols in place were designed to protect the mayor from dangers in The Network. His office was laced with a *blocking* program that you needed special permission to be exempt from. When discussing anything in the office of a government official, you did so at the mercy of their hand.

As it should be, he would always say.

Dodds entered the mayor's office. Unsurprisingly, Blackjack was in there with him.

Blackjack was an ambassador, like Reena. But unlike Reena, and other ambassadors, he didn't venture out of the city. He was the singular greatest enforcer of the law in West District.

He was tall, reasonably built, and clad in an all black military officer's uniform. A style of fashion one didn't really find in this city. He was the type one might call handsome, if his face wasn't so stern.

His demeanour wasn't too dissimilar to Cy's. You never really saw him smile.

The mayor, on the other hand - old and gluttonous man that he was - smiled all the time, except for occasions like this where an officer dared to come to him with a problem. He didn't much like solving problems. Ordinarily he wouldn't even take a meeting with an officer.

Blackjack and Dodds exchanged a nod. There was a mutual respect between the two. One was the most respected officer in the district. The other, the most feared.

'What is it now, Dodds?' the mayor asked, as though his time were being wasted.

Dodds would have no issue hurrying up with his information and request. He didn't see eye to eye with the mayor on certain matters, and found himself preferring to avoid any interaction with him at all when possible. This matter was too important.

Dodds told the mayor what Bolu had told him. 'The Erubans are holding secret meetings.'

'So?' was the mayor's immediate response. 'The more time they spend on The Network the less they spend on the streets. I say, encourage them.'

'Trouble is, Sir,' Dodds continued, 'I've run diagnostics on network traffic. The only worlds that reflect a mass gathering of Erubans implied by the information are hardly worthy of being kept secret. And they're worlds that are completely open to the public. They don't tie in at all to the information I received.'

'And where did this information come from?' asked the mayor.

Dodds Hesitated. 'My apprentice.'

'Your son, or the darky?'

Dodds wasn't surprised by the mayor's use of the word, but was surprised by the fact he even knew of Bolu's existence. He tended not to have that level of interest.

'Bolu, yes,' Dodds corrected him.

'And how did he get the information?'

'He overheard a conversation.'

'A conversation, huh?' The mayor scoffed. 'Has it occurred to you, Dodds, that you might be being duped? Or perhaps you'd prefer the word bamboozled, since you're so fond of those savages?

'The fact you even entertain the idea of that boy becoming an officer is bad enough,' the Mayor continued, 'but to come to me with a request based on information you've obtained from him... Perhaps you're not as smart as you've been given credit for? If you can't find the alleged "secret" meeting, then the reasonable conclusion is that it doesn't exist, and discipline must be carried out against the boy who has wilfully wasted government time!'

This was the mayor. Leader of the district in name, but truthfully, leader of the cultural divide between the Irian Sentiens and, well, everyone else. Even the Shaman in the district, despite most being Irian themselves, were seen as second class.

What class of citizen would he attribute to an Eruban Shaman, one might wonder? What degree of slur did he use for the only 2 Eruban Shaman in the district?

It was a mystery to some why a man like that should be appointed to lead the only multi-skin district in the entire city.

There was no democracy in this city. It was authoritarian, through and through. All decisions were at the government's discretion, so the mayor, as inhumane as he might seem at times, was there because they wanted him there. But for what purpose?

Dodds was amongst those who wanted to know why. It just seemed... odd.

'Bolu is a good young man,' he said. 'He's kind, and he works hard, and above all, he has integrity. He believes in the value of the police. So much so, he's willing to let his own community see him as an enemy, just so he can uphold his own personal sense of justice. If he tells me there's something going on, I'll believe him, until I'm shown irrevocable evidence otherwise.'

Dodds found himself caught in a pincer stare by both the mayor and Blackjack, but the message in both their eyes was different. The mayor was taken aback. He wasn't used to people speaking to him so firmly. Not people under him, anyway.

When Blackjack turned his gaze to the mayor, Dodds managed to take note of his raised eyebrow. What did that mean?

He assumed it was good, because the mayor said, 'You have a good reputation, Dodds. The people like you, and you're the most influential officer in the district.' He sighed. 'Because it's you, I'll grant you permission on this occasion, if only to satiate your curiosity. But be discreet! If this ends up being nothing, I don't want any blowback. Not when the annual meeting with the president is just a few days away. I don't need anything adverse coming up.'

Blackjack gave the mayor another look. It was more subtle this time. Dodds missed it.

The mayor caught Blackjack's glance and could feel his body beginning to perspire. He'd misspoke. The meeting the mayors had with the president wasn't supposed to be public knowledge, even amongst officers.

'Go on now,' the mayor said, trying to move past his slip of the tongue.

Dodds thanked them. He wasn't sure he'd be leaving with the permission he'd come to ask for, but now that he had it, he felt a tight pang in his chest. He knew what he had to do, but was afraid of what he might find. And from there developed an uncertainty of what, should he find something that shouldn't be there, he was going to do next.

23

Man of the People

The Rank Test was the most celebrated event in New Heart. Once a year, citizens had the opportunity to prove themselves within an official capacity. Showing off their mastery of commands, or even their own unique proficiencies at executing functions; it was a day of flashy and spectacular displays of power.

The test was 4 days away, and The Arena experienced its highest concentration of network traffic in the year. Most of the city's populace was engaged in the test in some way. Whether they were unranked, practising to obtain rank. Ranked, aiming at higher status. Or simply those who wanted to watch the spectacle that would unfold. Most of the people in The Arena now weren't taking part in any combat sequences, but were there to show love and support to those who were preparing for the test.

This was the place to go if you wanted to gain some form of recognition in this city.

It was mid afternoon and Alex and Kitchen were in The Arena now. Neither of them were taking the test, and Alex in particular didn't have much of an interest in taking part in combat sequences. She mostly just watched Kitchen blow off steam when she came here. But on this day, both of them, alongside many others, were there to see someone in particular.

Daniel Marston, the man upon whom many put their hopes and dreams. Born into riches, but with an equal, if not greater, sense of humility. He was famous not only due to his Marston name, or the fact he was the metaphoric black sheep of the family, but due to the impressive feats of power he displayed when he came to The Arena. For so long people wondered, and asked, and urged him to take the test. And whilst his motivations may have been unknown to most, at last, he was fulfilling what was many of their dreams.

The man upon whom people put their trust. Adored by the community.

The way people saw you was important.

The way you saw *yourself* was important, too. The combination of the two had the potential to define the very reality one found themselves in. Perhaps, even, the power to tell their own story.

Alex and Kitchen had been invited to a private room. Daniel was there, and he'd foregone his astral form for his regular appearance. It was important, when preparing for the test, for people to see you as you were, and not some virtual avatar designed for anonymity.

In front of Daniel was an avatar that did take on the appearance of an astral, which wasn't an option available to the average citizen. You had to be of a certain calibre to utilise the meta, "Where stars gather."

Their name was Niche, because it was the collective virtual avatar used by a group of programmers who found themselves not quite fitting in with the rest of the city. The programs they made were obscure, structured very illogically at times, and couldn't really be understood by anyone who either wasn't exceptionally intelligent, or not abstract enough in their thinking to apply their own interpretation to the meta being utilised. Niche found that their programs could never be efficiently used by the average citizen, and any business prospects, or calls to fame, were highly unlikely. A program had to be widely used in order for its creator to get any sort of recognition.

That changed when they introduced themselves to Daniel. It wasn't that he had the intelligence to use their programs effectively. Nor was it that he was particularly creative or abstract in his thinking (not back then, anyway). They'd surmised (with some degree of truth) that it was Daniel's lineage, and inherited superior mind that allowed him to completely overcome the obstacles manifested by the complexity of Niche's programs.

The relationship between the input of sen into a function, and the output of its effect on the world, wasn't wholly linear. Yes, the more you understood the meta of a function, the greater its effect would be. After all, you couldn't perform an action with the mind if the mind itself didn't understand what it was doing. That was the primary obstacle Sentiens faced. But it was possible to bypass this. It was possible to forego the process of understanding, and land straight on the conclusion. That was cheating.

But even when cheating, a function had to follow a path of logic in order to reach its conclusion, and when cheating, the path it took was random. That was why it was generally an ineffective way of using functions. The way it got to its conclusion didn't make sense, and the mind needed things to make sense.

But people like Daniel, they had the mental power to bear the burden of cheating without suffering its adverse effects. Perhaps that was the reason for his success? *It wasn't.* But regardless, Daniel was very good at cheating, because he didn't need to understand the process, he just needed to know the outcome.

One didn't need to understand the biological imperative related to the action of bending down and picking up a stone. The knowledge of how the muscles, bones, blood, and oxygen, and every other miniscule variable that took place for a single movement to occur, wasn't a necessary requirement for one to bend over, and pick up the stone. Simply knowing that you *could* do it, was all one needed *to* do it. That was what cheating was. Knowing - *believing* - in one's ability to do something, despite any obstacles that may get in their way. It was rare to find someone with such freedom of mind.

It was said, within rather secluded circles, that those who cheated, brought chaos into the world.

It was known in those same circles that chaos was the enemy of logic.

Whether or not that was true remained to be seen. As far as Niche was concerned, Daniel was the most valuable person in that city. He was the one who brought their programs to life; their dreams into reality.

Daniel and Niche became aware of Alex and Kitchen. They greeted one another, with Kitchen going through Niche's latest programs to give herself a preview of what was to come. Niche liked Kitchen, because though it wasn't as great a proficiency as Daniel, she could cheat into using their programs, too.

Alex and Daniel had a private word whilst the two of them were busy. 'How was the party?'

'The usual sort,' Daniel replied. 'Still going, I think. I told Annabelle to message me once she has time alone so I can show her her present. I'll let you know how it goes.'

'Please do.'

A short exchange of other pleasantries occurred, and then Daniel went into a map.

He'd been briefed on the new programs Niche had created. Their most complicated to date, they said. Even the mention of the word "complicated" didn't phase Daniel at all. It didn't really mean anything to him, other than that they had put a lot of work into making the programs and he needed to show them it was worthwhile. If anything, it made his execution of the commands that much greater.

The map he entered was called Cityscape, which seemed not too dissimilar in design to Central district, boasting multiple high-rise buildings. It was night, but the sky was absent of any stars. The buildings all looked black amidst this pitch landscape, but the artificial light of this city gave a dazzling contrast. Neon lights of all different colours shone from multiple directions. The city was black, but illuminated. It was unnatural - entirely so, given this virtual world - but even the unnatural could be incredibly beautiful, if the right mind combined its intellect with passion and care.

There was a noticeable symmetry between buildings, but the wide array of lights gave it the aesthetic it may otherwise be lacking. It was a beautiful place, said to be inspired by a real city, somewhere on the continent of Iria. Daniel wondered, if that were the case, if the virtual personas found on this map were reminiscent of the types of people you'd find in the real city.

In the map of Cityscape, one didn't encounter people who utilised coders, but rather, people whose bodies had been artificially augmented by Rethium.

The combat sequence began as soon as Daniel entered the map, and within a few seconds of standing amidst the hauntingly large buildings, he was struck by a ray of light.

Well, almost struck. He knew it was coming, even before he'd seen it. He'd activated his *Radar* as soon as he'd entered. He was getting information on enemy locations, alongside any functions or other forms of assault they might use. So the first shot of light came and missed, as he'd *bent* its trajectory.

His *Radar* told him another was coming.

Straight ahead, appearing from behind one of the buildings, came a figure clad in black military uniform, augmented with various bits of machinery all around their body, and holding a large gun.

It was a photon rifle, which shot out beams of light whose meta had been altered to mimic the physical properties of a metal bullet, whilst additionally increasing the application of heat which light naturally exhibited. In being struck by one of these beams, one would find their skin both pierced through, and completely cauterised. It was a lethal weapon, and this was a map where you went if you really wanted to test your combat skills.

They fired another shot. They weren't as fast as light - No, that would be ridiculous. Taking on the physical properties of metal made it interact with the world in the same way. It had weight, and mass, of some sort, and was slowed down by the air. But still faster than a real bullet.

There was no usual sound of gunfire either - not that the citizens of New heart were familiar with gunfire. - Just the click from the trigger being pulled, after which what seemed to be a long, straight beam of yellow light went straight for Daniel.

His *Radar* had given him the same anticipation of it as before, so he was ready. But he wouldn't avoid it this time. No, this would be a perfect test for one of the new programs. A very simple one.

Reflect.

A self explanatory application. It wasn't limited to light-based attacks, but it was most effective against them. And why stop there? *Reflect* would only send the ray of light back where it came, by which point the persona that fired it would have disappeared behind another building. It would be a wasted opportunity.

What would be judged during the Rank Test was one's ability to use functions and commands to effectively take care of a situation. This was the perfect opportunity to show exactly what that meant.

The fundamental difference between functions and commands was that functions were structured in real time, whilst commands were pre-made programs. But functions, ultimately, were easy to adapt. It was difficult to alter a command when one didn't know the process by which it was made. Adding a function onto a command was possible, but where coders really excelled was their ability to help their users fuse different commands together. A process called compounding. Daniel was particularly good at it.

He used *Radar* to locate the position of every persona currently spawned on the map. He ran the result through a *Kaleidoscope* program, which he compounded onto his *Reflect*, splitting the singular beam of light into multiple different rays, and giving each of them *Tracking*. All of those commands were applied in an instant, and the shot of light was reflected up into the air, scattered into 15 other rays, and each ray took a streamline path to one of the personas, piercing right through them.

Had this been in the real, they'd be dead. That was how lethal those gunshots were.

That was how lethal Daniel, and others like him, could be. The purpose of the Rank Test, of The Arena, was to train New Hearters to be able to do things like that. To have their own unique way of tackling conflict, as many places in the world did. This was, after all, the only place that used coders.

It was a city with its own story.

Death on The Network wasn't like death in the real. The personas didn't bleed blood, but data. Tiny, miniscule specs of light that faded the further away they got from the body. And when they'd lost too much, their entire bodies dissipated like tiny fireworks..

Up in the booth, Alex was going through a roster of the different programs Daniel had been given. Like:

The Piercing Spears of Unstoppable Light.

The All-Powerful Dome of Impenetrable Defence.

The Almighty Shower of Unimaginable Devastation.

The Great Sword of Absolute Prominence, Piercing All and Succumbing to None. Maker of Rulers and Liberator of the Meek. My Name is Ex...

Alex didn't bother reading the rest. 'Guys!' she said, a sharpness to her tone. 'What's all this?'

'All the best attacks have names,' was Niche's defence.

'Yes, but why are they so long? All the effort you put into making them and these are the best names you could come up with?'

'Naming things is hard...'

They weren't completely wrong. It could be difficult to name things with specificity in a way that covered the entirety of the command's nature.

'That's what the description is for,' Alex demanded.

'Yeah,' said Kitchen. 'Like this one,' she pointed out, "The Orb of Everything-in-that-General-Direction-Can-Go-Get-Wrecked!", 'could just be, "Orb of Absolute Destruction."'

Niche had no response. The logic they used to create their commands was of the same complicated nature as their thought process when it came to naming. Convoluted and imprecise. Not once had they managed to produce something 'simple'.

It was odd.

They commended Kitchen on how perfect her naming was.

'Seriously guys, that was so simple,' Alex said. 'You need to stop overcomplicating things. Then maybe your programs could be used by other people and you'd make more Credits.'

Their response was that Daniel paid them generously and that making things simple just wasn't their style. Alex read between the lines.

They'd rather stay true to their way of programming than sell their integrity for wealth. At the very least, Alex respected that.

Daniel was under heavy fire, but he had The All-Powerful Dome of Impenetrable Defence fending off all attacks. It was a defensive wall programmed with *Radar* and *Telemetry* functions. *Radar* allowed it to detect danger, whilst *Telemetry* analysed the nature of that danger, to which the *Dome* would adapt its properties to best fend off the attack. The complexity of meta needed to achieve such a result was beyond comprehension to most. The minds behind Niche were truly geniuses.

Niche updated Daniel's programs in real time, so the once convolutedly named program was now, The Orb of Absolute Destruction.

Daniel used it, firing it out with just a small amount of sen put into it at first. He needed to see how it worked. And just as its name suggested, it punched a hole through his now-called Impenetrable Dome, and proceeded to do the same to the persona that got caught in its path.

It moved quickly, but Daniel managed to catch enough of it in action to gain a rough idea of how it worked.

The holes it made were larger than the orb itself. Almost as if it had sucked them in within that short period of contact.

In the booth, Alex looked at the description of the command.

The Orb of Absolute Destruction

An orb of multi-elemental energy is created. The energy is programmed to imitate an object of great mass, giving it a high surface tension variable which draws matter towards it. The energy within the orb acts like waves of light in constant oscillation, giving the orb the ability to shave away at matter on a molecular level, causing instant disintegration.

It was a magnificent command. Light was a difficult element to utilise, especially within a combative capacity.

Daniel had just finished making sense of the command himself. He didn't understand it the way Alex or Niche did, or anybody with above average intelligence. But he understood it enough to cheat it to its full capacity. That was his gift.

He made a larger one, now. Many of them, actually. Then he compounded other command functions onto them. *Tracking*, and *Safe Zone*, which was another Niche-made command which highlighted objects that attack commands were restricted from interacting with.

If this conflict were occurring in the real, he'd try to minimise the damage to the city, and allies, if he had them. That was what *Safe Zone* was for.

The orbs made quick work of everyone. One of the personas had tried shooting one down, but the light-based nature of the orb was far superior to that of their photon rifles. It quickly mowed them down after a few unsuccessful rounds of fire.

Daniel made it look so easy, but it really wasn't. Half of the population didn't even have access to this map because of its difficulty rating. But Daniel, at only 28, in his 5th development stage, far outmatched the average citizen. Even most officers couldn't handle him, and they had a huge advantage. When an officer used a command, it had a greater output than just a regular citizen. Why? Well, that was one of those things that only certain people should know.

Many officers themselves didn't know the real reason.

'We're given better programs,' was what generally got passed around. And whilst it remained true that some programs were exclusive to officers, that wasn't the reason their output was greater.

It was all to do with the coders.

24

SURVEILLANCE

Tensions were always elevated when confronted by police. Even in the absence of any sort of guilt, the mere presence of an officer could have you question your every move. It was something of a paradoxical occurrence, or perhaps irony, that when observed by those searching for suspicious activity, one then found themselves acting suspiciously. And perhaps, some, may even be tempted to test the waters. To approach the line which they must not cross and experience the thrill of danger that came with it. It was just the nature of people. Curiosity, often, was the root of all sorts of misbehaviour.

If indeed, police presence could make innocent people behave guilty, then it stood to reason that a guilty person, in the face of police, would do their best to act innocent, often overcompensating on their part. So that was what the police in West District did on this particular day. Patrolled the streets to observe those who behaved too normal. Who didn't shy away from their gaze. Those who acted innocent.

They coordinated themselves via communications over an officer-exclusive network. It was a completely separate entity to Mind-

Space. The MindSpace Network existed throughout the city, and coders within the city connected to it. But the officer's network existed purely as a relay between their coders. It was a precaution, so that citizens couldn't try to hack into it from MindSpace. It was its own private network. And that was what gave Dodds his idea.

No worlds within MindSpace had shown the sort of web traffic that would suggest a gathering of Erubans. So what if - *what if!* - the Erubans had their own network, too? Completely separate from MindSpace. Something nobody could hack into because they didn't know it was there. Dodds didn't want to believe it at first. There was no way within the Eruban community there was someone competent enough to achieve such a thing. Not when Dodds couldn't name a single Irian capable of the same feat.

But then he thought back to all the time he'd spent in this city as it was, compared to the life he'd lived before the city became new. He remembered the stories that used to be told, and how they fizzled out from the new city's narrative. How this city, this district in particular, emphasised the superiority of Irians. But those weren't the stories he used to hear. No. People used to talk of the great civilisations of Oren and Eruba. The sheer magnitude of influence that they had over the world.

Dodds had never left Iria himself, so he had no idea if the stories he heard were true or not. But regardless, they were stories that stopped being told, and perhaps there was a reason for that.

So Dodds stopped underestimating the Erubans. Stopped underestimating Cy, and decided he would find out for himself, just how formidable he really was.

Dodds had received permission from the mayor to make use of a diagnostics program which would inspect all the programs a coder had used within a certain period of time. Since it ran diagnostics on the coder itself, and not necessarily its connection to The Network, it could identify foreign programs. It had been a long time since he'd even heard of it being used, let alone requesting it himself. And the previous times weren't even in his district. It was information that had trickled down the grapevine. How they had caught wind of certain conspiracies taking place in an area of The Network that you didn't have access to unless you were invited. It had become something of an urban legend. Everyone who thought themselves worthy of invitation but never received one could conclude only that this place simply didn't exist. But that wasn't at all plausible.

Because if you look in any society which operates on a mass scale, where capitalism is such a dominant ideal and trade systems are a vital part of the ecosystem, one will inevitably find that within such a society, without doubt, there would emerge a black market.

25

Hermit

Kitchen had gone into the map to practise with Daniel, leaving Alex and Niche alone to talk.

'So the black market has had a slight change of pace recently,' Niche said. Alex had set up a *wall* around them, allowing them to speak freely.

Alex asked exactly what kind of change Niche was talking about, and they replied, 'Hermit has been a lot less active.'

Hermit was a name you only knew if you were amongst those who took part in New Heart's elicit activities. If you wanted something the government didn't allow, the black market was where you went, and Hermit was one of its most prestigious vendors.

'Maybe he's on holiday,' Alex said. Which begged the question of, if someone took a holiday from a city nobody was allowed to leave, where exactly did they go, and what exactly did they do?

'Maybe,' said Niche. 'Trouble is, he had a lot of activity a few weeks ago. I mean like a crazy amount. Came out with all these new programs and really pushed their sales. It was strange. Hermit was never one for advertising. You either bought from him or you didn't.

He never really cared that much. But this time it was almost forceful. And to then suddenly go off radar...'

'What are you getting at?' Alex pressed.

'Thinking logically, pushing to sell so many programs in such a short period of time suggests the need for a massive influx of Credits. Now that might not be a problem for big groups, but this is the black market. Why would a vendor need that much inflow all at once?'

'I don't know, Niche,' Alex said nonchalantly. 'What I'm curious about is why you're coming to me with this.'

'To warn you.'

Alex looked at them with her featureless face.

'It's about time for something major to happen in your part of the city. The contenders for who would stand at the centre of it all are Hermit and yourself, and with what's been happening over the last weeks, Hermit seems to be the more favourable.'

The astounding thing about what Niche was saying was that in order to say it, they'd have to have knowledge of who both Alex and Hermit were in the real. But there was more than just that. Why was it time for something to happen in her part of the city?

This was one of those situations where one had to think carefully about how they would respond.

She asked a question. 'You know who Hermit is in the real?'

'We do.'

'Who?'

'Can't tell you that.'

'Why?'

And this was it. This was the test, to find out if the reason Niche knew things was because...

'Because, there are things that must only be known by those supposed to know them.'

That was the confirmation. Niche, or rather, the many who made up Niche, had The Book! Niche knew things; things that Alex perhaps didn't, because The Book changed its contents based on the reader.

'You don't seem to have figured it out yet, Alex.'

They couldn't see it on her face, but she was confused. *Figured out what?*

'You met us collectively as Niche, but before that, we'd been acquainted individually.' They stopped talking as if that was supposed to be all the information she needed to figure out who they were. When she said nothing, they let the whole cat out of the bag. 'We learned coding together. Us, you, and Hermit, amongst others. All those years ago, in professor Eváan's class.'

Then she understood. They weren't trying to make her remember who they were individually. They were informing her of some sort of relevance to the things occurring now, and the fact they'd all taken that class together. But she didn't know exactly what that meant. Why did the fact they all learned how to code together matter?

'What are you getting at?' she asked. She had no time for riddles. Not this late in the game. If Niche had something to tell her, they needed to stop beating around the bush.

'This city isn't what you think it is.'

'What do you think I think this city is?' she rebutted.

Niche laughed. 'Well, we've never been able to read your mind, so we couldn't say for sure. You're very intelligent. You've probably had a lot of thoughts about the nature of this city, and in all likelihood, some of your deductions will be on the mark. But if you only look at things from an educated perspective, you'll miss a lot of what's really going on. New Heart isn't just a city of technological advancement. There's a story being told here. Do you know how stories are told?'

Alex looked at them blankly. The obvious answer would be 'yes,' but then why ask the question? She said nothing.

'A storyteller will construct a narrative which leads you in a certain direction, only to turn around and surprise you with the outcome later on. A story, a good story, isn't supposed to be predictable. So we revert to our initial point. This city isn't what you think it is. Whatever is occurring in your district, however involved or uninvolved you might be in it, whatever outcome you or others think is going to happen, consider, and consider well, what you'll do when things don't quite go to plan. You'll find that how this story concludes itself will surprise you.'

'You seem overly familiar with this,' Alex said to them. 'Why do you know so much?'

'Because there are stories within a story, and ours have already ended. It's just your district, now.'

How curious. If Alex understood Niche correctly, then what would soon be occurring in West District, had already happened in the four others. But she'd never heard anything about it. And why, when plans were so close to coming to fruition, was she being told this now? And why by Niche? But she ascertained something else from what they'd said.

'Your stories have ended, and my district is left. Does that mean, within Niche, there's someone from each of the other districts?'

'Correct. Within Niche are four individuals.'

'Are they all present?'

'We are all constantly aware of what goes on with this persona, though not all of us are active at any given time.'

'So to whom am I speaking with, now?'

If Niche had facial features and could smile, they would have. But Alex was sure she could 'hear' the smile in their voice with what they said next.

'I'm afraid, dear Alex, that our identities are made known at the end of the story you find yourself in. It's important, you see, that you experience a story in the order it's being told. Otherwise, you miss things.'

How familiar those words were. Where had she heard them before?

Alex had one last question, which she was convinced would produce a similar answer to the question she'd just asked, but she had to be sure. 'You're talking a lot about stories as if this is all part of some grand design. In which case, I have to wonder, if there are stories within a story, who's telling this one?'

Niche shook their head. It wasn't disapproval. It was a good question, just not one they could answer, because in truth, they didn't know. And before knowing the identity of the storyteller, there was another question that needed to be asked first.

'You're jumping ahead again, Alex. What you should be asking isn't who is telling the story, but rather, your curiosity should have led you to wonder, if there are stories within a story, then how many stories are actually being told? The answer to that question is something we ourselves are still trying to find.'

Alex didn't have anything to say to that. It was something she'd have to ponder on later. But she did say, 'You know I do actually know who Hermit is, right?'

'We've acknowledged the possibility, though your confirmation is appreciated.'

'When did you all get your books?' she then asked them, wanting to confirm absolutely her own suspicions that they were aware of its existence.

'They were gifts,' Niche said after a short pause.

'That's not what I asked.'

'You're asking when we became worthy of knowing the things we know?'

Alex's silence was a yes.

'When we proved ourselves worthy of knowing.' That was the last thing Niche said on the matter.

26

A MESSAGE

'We need to have a word with that Hermit bastard,' said Rado to Lido. 'This blocking program he sold us is trash!'

'I don't think the issue is with the program, brother,' Lido said calmly. 'Anyway, Hermit has been pretty quiet as of late. Getting hold of him is difficult.'

Lido's words of reason never quite did reach that part of Rado's brain that dealt with rational thought. 'I still say we turn up on him. We paid for it, and it failed, so he owes us.'

'Careful, Rado,' his brother warned. 'The danger of transactions in the black market is that vendors know your secrets. We'll just have to consider this a loss and let it go.'

Rado flipped over a table. 'We're supposed to run this district! How are we going to control people if nobody takes us seriously?'

'The district and the black market are two different things, brother. What exactly do you expect us to do to someone like Hermit when we don't even know who he is? Hermit might not even be a he.'

"So we find out!' Rado replied immediately. 'We ask around. Those guys trade in information, right? If they know secrets then they know secrets about each other.'

Lido looked at his brother curiously. He didn't say it out loud, but he thought, then, that that was one of the smartest ideas Rado had ever had. And all things considered, he did have a gripe with Hermit. The whole purpose of purchasing that program was that it was supposed to be able to suppress the likes of the Chens. Failing at that task made it just shy of worthless.

'Bro?' Rado said after Lido had gone silent for too long.

It wasn't just Lido's thoughts that had taken his mind away. In that short break of their conversation, he'd received a message. A request for a meeting. He shared it with his brother, whose in-character response was, 'Really?'

27

Almost

Cy was in his workshop when the police came.

It was Dodds, of course, and one other. No apprentices with him today, just full-fledged officers, investigating a lead.

Mara had been at the front desk. She'd offered the two officers water, as she did with anyone who walked through those doors, but they declined, and so instead, she led them straight to Cy.

'Your coder,' Dodds said as soon as he entered the room.

Cy gave it to him. Dodds' second officer took Mara's coder as well, then there was silence.

Mara had a faint smile on her face, as usual. Cy's face was as emotionless as ever.

Dodds made eye contact with him, suspicion overwhelming his expression.

'You seem disappointed,' Cy said.

Disappointed. Confused. Both were words that accurately described Dodds' current state of mind. And now, by mentioning it, Cy was playing a game with him. Well, if Cy supposedly knew what was going on and he'd been expecting them, then there was no use playing dumb here. He might as well see what he could get out of the situation.

'I'd received a report about the use of black market programs,' Dodds said. 'Supposedly being passed around the Eruban community.'

'And you thought to come here?'

'The people look up to you here. I figured if something was going on, you'd either have some part in it, or at least know something about it.'

'And does it appear I have a part in it?'

Dodds hesitated. He was being taunted. 'No, it wouldn't appear so. Which begs the question, do you know anything about it?'

'Presuming I did, why would I tell you?'

'To help your community, obviously.'

Then Cy asked a serious question. 'Are helping my community and helping you one and the same?'

'They can be,' Dodds said with a tone of something akin to hope.

But Cy replied, 'I deal in reality, not possibility.'

'Okay.' Dodds pulled up a chair in front of Cy. 'Well the reality is, anyone and everyone caught engaging in illicit activities will go to jail. Anyone with information on such activities who didn't share it when asked, thereby halting the progress of our investigation, will go to jail. Anyone who doesn't offer information and is later discovered to have been aware of such activities... Will. Go. To. Jail. So, given the potential detriment posed to your community, I would very well say helping me and helping your community are in fact one and the very same! You're smart, Cy. You may well be the smartest person in this district, which you'll never hear another Irian admit. Things could be a lot better if we were on the same side. The alternative is that things get messy. Very messy.'

Cy leaned in closer towards Dodds and lowered his voice. 'Neither myself nor Mara are going to share the fact that Bolu is the one who supplied you with the information you're currently acting on. That's as far on the same side as you and I are going to get. Understand?'

If Cy had been fishing for confirmation, Dodds' expression had given him away. He wasn't expecting Cy to know that. *How did Cy know that?*

'I could arrest you right now,' Dodds said.

'But you won't. Not without proof of wrong-doing.'

Dodds didn't break eye contact, but Cy was right. Dodds operated within the law. On that, he was uncompromising.

'You know what your weakness is?' Cy asked. 'You placed your faith in the wrong thing. You believe the law is just. You believe in the rules given to you by men not much different to you and I. Men who've forced you to view the world from their perspective, and you follow those rules obediently in the name of upholding justice. But you see, my faith is not in the laws of men like you and I. My faith is in something much greater. A morality, some would say. Something that isn't swayed by agendas or emotions, but is absolute in its distinguishing of right and wrong. We can never be on the same side, Dodds. The justice of the law and the justice of morality rarely occupy the same space. So you follow your justice, I'll follow mine, and when the dust we've kicked up settles, we'll see which of the two still stands.'

Cy backed up and looked over to Mara. Then to the other officer, and then back to Dodds. There was nothing left for him to say.

Dodds didn't find what he was looking for. The information he'd received from Bolu came to a dead end, and he was pretty sure Cy had just waged a war against him. But even with that, he could do nothing. Because Cy was right. Dodds had absolute conviction in his belief in the law, and he would uphold it to the end. The time would come. Whatever it was that was going on would come to light, and when it did, Dodds would be there. Justice would prevail.

But whose?

Dodds and the second officer left without another word. Once they were gone, Cy shot up from his seat and went to Mara. He held her coder in his hand, reestablishing the meta he'd removed prior to Dodds' arrival.

'You'll have a long night ahead of you,' she said to him with an embrace.

'Don't underestimate the value of your prayers,' he replied, and then kissed her before removing himself. 'It should only take an hour.'

He left the room.

Mara knelt down and clasped both her hands together, interweaving her fingers to lock both hands in place. Then she closed her eyes.

28

CONSTELLATION

Reena had made herself invisible in an attempt to approach Q unnoticed. She used a form of *clairvoyance* to observe him in his room, and made herself *intangible* and *inaudible* as she passed through walls to get to him. None of these were commands. They were all her own functions.

She was outside his room, now. Just one more wall to pass through, but she paused. She observed for a while the extravagant display that was taking place.

It was similar to what had occurred in the training room earlier. The dimmed room and neon lights. But they served a different purpose this time. There was nothing for him to attack. The lights hadn't been weaponized, as it were. Their visibility was for visibility's sake. Almost as if he were putting on a show.

Almost as if he knew that she – and perhaps others – were watching.

Within this shroud of darkness he'd created shone tiny dots of blue lights. Mere specs amidst the vastness of this artificial night. The individual dots of light became connected to one another with lines. The lines joined onto other lines to create... what was it called?

They were images, of some sort. Guidelines for something more; something greater. Like how skeletons were the base of the flesh that surrounded them, providing support and stability. That was what these lights were like. Skeletons that supported something far greater.

It was odd seeing this. It was the first time Reena had witnessed such a thing, and yet, it looked so familiar. It looked like... Oh! She realised.

And then came Q's voice. 'You may enter.'

Reena was surprised and unsurprised at the same time. She removed her *invisibility* and *phased* through his wall. 'How and how long?' she asked.

There was a pause. Almost as if he were contemplating what words to use. 'You have a very strong aura,' he said. 'It stands out in a city like this.'

What was he saying? That he'd been keeping track of her this whole time?

'You Sentiens,' he continued, 'You can't perceive your aura, so you can't control it. Glamouring yourself is of little consequence when it comes to escaping my detection. The five lesser senses don't compare to the greater sense with which we Seers experience the world.'

'Glamouring?' Reena asked, unfamiliar with the word.

'What you would call invisibility.'

Oh. Even with her knowledge of Eruban vernacular, "glamour" wasn't a word she'd come across. Perhaps it was something native to the Seers. It was a culture unknown to the rest of the world, after all. And they perceived an entirely different aspect of the world than everyone else.

Sentiens perceived the meta that defined the world.

Shaman perceived ether, the spiritual side of the world.

And Seers perceived aura, which... which did what exactly? What purpose did aura contribute to the reality they experienced? Why was Q the first Seer Reena had ever heard of, let alone met? Why introduce them to the world now?

'You have questions?' Q asked her.

'I do.'

'Ask. It would seem you are deemed worthy of knowing.'

'Who is it that decides if I'm worthy?'

Q laughed. He laughed because he knew she knew the answer to that question already. And the answer to that question wasn't a name, or the identity of someone in particular. Because the exact nature of who – or what – was being referred to, was unknown.

And Reena asked many questions that night. Some of which she received satisfactory answers to, and others not so much. But Reena would find herself gaining a much greater knowledge as to the nature of the world, the direction it was headed, and her place in it all.

You must be wondering what those questions and answers were. But you see, the knowledge you have at present remains insufficient to form a true understanding of the information you desire. And so, for the time being, the conversation they had that night must remain a mystery.

However, the answer he gave to her first question is so unspecific in nature, that to know it would bear no consequence to everything that follows. And so, the answer to her question, 'Who is it that decides if I'm worthy?' was simply:

'Whomever, or whatever, is telling this story.'

29

THE PRESENT

It was approaching the evening service. Kitchen left Alex and Daniel after they'd finished testing out his new programs.

The two were standing in a void now.

'Thanks again for doing this,' Daniel said. 'You have no idea how much it'll mean to her.'

'I suspect I'll find out,' Alex replied. 'You're a really good cousin.'

'Cousin,' he repeated laughably. 'I guess that's the primary reason I am the way I am with her. Hardly seems justified to be rewarded for the simple fact of being related to someone.'

'Which is why you left the family. Yet, here you are, being the best person you can be to a little girl, just because she's related to you?'

No. That wasn't the only reason. 'She deserves it,' Daniel said.

'Exactly,' Alex instantly replied. 'She deserves it. So you do it. Why complicate it with something as dubiously wayward as justice?'

Daniel laughed at this. If you asked him the meaning of the word 'dubiously' he surely couldn't tell you. But he understood the meaning behind that sentence. And he said, 'Because justice, true justice, is neither dubious nor wayward. It's absolute. It's the right amongst the wrong. The truth above the lies. It exists, independent of our own thoughts, or ideals, or convictions. True justice isn't decided by us, because it's greater than us. What we do, we're not enacting justice. We're not representing truth. We're just getting as close to our idea of it as possible. Ever changing. Ever learning. Ever growing. Forever not quite getting there.'

There was a pause. Daniel turned to Alex to see her giving him that same look she always gave. The obscure 'look beyond' rather than 'look at'. And when he questioned it, she said:

'I've never heard you speak with so much depth before.'

'Pffft,' he shunned. 'I can be deep.'

'I know,' she said in a very understanding way. 'You're smarter than you give yourself credit for. But I think that's just your way of relating to people better. You minimise yourself in order to elevate others. Even though, in most situations, you have the greatest presence in the room. It's why people adore you.'

He looked at her again. That was uncharacteristically sentimental for Alex. As unusual an occurrence as Daniel saying something with particular depth. He thanked her, and then remembered...

'Reena's back!'

'Oh!' Alex said with moderate surprise. More so at the sudden change in subject rather than the subject itself. It wasn't unusual for ambassadors to return to the city every now and then. Especially around the time of the Rank Test

Many ambassadors had returned the previous year just for the pleasure of experiencing Reena's performance. And what a pleasure it was.

'You've seen her?' she asked.

Daniel nodded. 'She gave Annabelle her first coder.'

Alex laughed at this. 'Your grandfather must have been furious. I'll bet you didn't know what to say at first.'

'Am I that easy to read?'

'When it comes to her, yes.'

Daniel laughed again. 'Well I guess everyone needs to have a weakness.'

Alex *bleurghed*. 'That was sickeningly romantic.'

'Maybe so,' Daniel said. 'But do you know what the secret is to becoming your absolute best self?'

Alex said no, but had she thought about it before responding, she would have realised that she'd heard a similar sort of question some time ago. And it was only when hearing a similar sort of answer that she realised.

'It's to find someone you're prepared to dedicate your whole self to.'

Then it clicked. Kitchen said it when they were younger. Not long after they'd met, actually. Alex was in the orphanage, and the Chens had come down with food for the children.

'Do you know what the secret is to making the best dish?' Kitchen had said to Alex. 'It's to find someone you want to dedicate your cooking to. When all you want to do is see someone smile, that's when your cooking will be its best.'

Her father had told her that. There was far too much wisdom there for a child to come up with on their own.

But why? People were fundamentally selfish. The idea of only becoming one's best self when giving oneself to others seemed to go against their base nature. That was the argument Alex made. But then Daniel said:

'That's why so few of us ever reach our full potential. I don't know much about history, but I'd be willing to bet the greatest people to come from the world are the ones who more than anything wanted to make things better for others. Isn't that what makes the heroes everyone looks up to? Is being selfish our base nature because we need to overcome that in order to be something more? I don't know. I'm not smart like you. Maybe I can't quite justify my position with logic. But I don't think I have to. There are some things logic just isn't supposed to be able to define. Some things you just have to feel. You just have to know, and tell yourself "This is right!" Then defend your position with everything you have.'

He could have gone on. If he had, perhaps Alex would have learned even more about him that day. How much he'd matured in the last year. How much more of an 'intellectual' he apparently was, despite his denial. But she stopped him from saying anything further, because what he'd said already was invaluable. More so than she even realised. What he'd said were words that he was always bound to say at some point through the course of his story. Words Alex certainly needed to hear at some point in hers. And over time, she would understand them more than she had during this encounter, just as he would, too. Because that was how things worked on Areth. The power contained within words changed depending on how much one truly understood them.

'I get it,' Alex said to him. 'You care about others more than you care about yourself. And Reena sits at the top of that hierarchy. So you would do anything for her. Meaning you'll perhaps do things you wouldn't otherwise do. Cross lines you may otherwise never approach. Can you really claim to be yourself if your actions are being dictated by another?'

Daniel didn't even hesitate. 'Yes. Because the Reena I know would never lead me to a line I didn't want to cross. If she didn't have ideals that I personally believed in, I wouldn't have the regard for her that I do. I love her because of who she is, not despite it. So I'm completely, 100% myself.'

There was nothing more Alex could say to that. She understood – really understood – what he was talking about, and realised then, that even within her own life, she had someone to whom she was prepared to do anything for, and was certain would do anything for her, too.

She had no idea how powerful that sort of relationship was.

Their conversation ended there. It was time.

Annabelle had sent Daniel a message. She'd finally found the time to get into The Network now that her party was long over. Daniel invited her over to their world, and she appeared before them with an avatar that didn't come as any surprise to either.

Simply put, she was a princess. Small and young, as she was, but with a completely made-up appearance, so her anonymity was preserved. No doubt her preferred avatar would change over the years, but for now, this one was aptly chosen.

Daniel got her to close her eyes. She hadn't yet noticed that this world was a void, but he needed time for Alex to carry out the plan.

So Annabelle covered her eyes with both hands, and Daniel held them in place to make sure she didn't peek. She giggled gleefully.

Then, Alex released the program she'd been saving.

Usually voids were filled over time. Each day something new would be added whilst the world someone envisioned was being built. But Alex had written out the entire coding of her envisioned world without ever projecting it into the virtual space. Everything was wrapped up in a program which she now released into the void.

As soon as she did, the world began to digitise. It was a fantastical experience, watching a virtual world be made. The way it appeared was like matter being formed from light. Individual particles sparkled and came together to create solid mass, building each individual structure from a point of origin that expanded outwards. It was creation in its purest form. Instructions that told the digital matter how to behave. What attributes it needed to have. Because that was all creation was, really. Just information being applied to a source material to create all that was, is, and ever will be.

That was meta.

Daniel turned Annabelle around and got her to open her eyes.

It was magnificent, what she saw. A great big castle, decorated with a variety of colours and designs. It sat at the top of a hill in a valley blooming with some of Annabelle's favourite flowers. It was the type of scenery that wouldn't occur naturally. The designs were orchestrated to be exactly as they were. And Annabelle loved it.

This was Daniel's real present to her. Her own world, named after her.

ANNABELLE'S WONDERLAND

And this was the extent of Alex's involvement in the plan.

Annabelle thanked her, and Daniel, then Alex said goodbye to them both.

30

THE STORY OF THE VILLAGER

Long, long ago there was a small village. The villagers there lived simple, happy lives, cultivating the fruits of the land.

But one day, a great beast came to ravage the village, destroying homes and crops, and devouring what villagers it could catch to satisfy its hunger.

The beast was of considerable strength, greater than anything the villagers themselves could muster.

With their homes destroyed, and their lives in danger, the villagers fled, eventually discovering a cave. Its entrance was too small for the beast to enter, and so there they hid.

For a long time the villagers lived out of the cave, sending only a few to venture out to source for food.

But the beast ruled these parts, and sometimes the villagers that went out never returned.

On one fateful day, one villager set out with the intention of slaying the great beast. The other villagers warned them against such action; that the beast was too powerful and could not be slain.

But the villager, brave and noble, told them that they would slay the beast.

Disregarding the concerns of their fellow villagers, they set out on the hunt.

Being overwhelmed by concern for their fellow villager, the ones who remained did something they'd never done before.

They'd lived their most recent lives in fear, and had forgotten what it was to hope, or believe. But as the villager had set out to slay the beast, believing so greatly in their ability to do so, something changed in the other villagers' hearts.

They did not fear for the safe return of their fellow villager, as they had done with all others. But instead, thought, and hoped, and believed that their comrade would slay the beast.

The villagers in the cave joined hands and shared faith that their brave comrade would return victorious.

As the villager journeyed towards the beast, believing themselves powerful enough to defeat it, they felt themselves grow stronger with every step. And that strength continued to grow until they finally happened upon the beast.

With a sword in hand, their own faith, and the faith of their people strengthening them; with just a single stroke, the villager slayed the beast.

The villager used this new strength to carry the beast back to the cave, where it was carved up and served as a feast, for the villagers were finally free.

The brave villager became a hero of their people, and all faith was placed upon them henceforth.

When the villager told the others how they had felt their strength rising with each step they took, the other villagers told of their joining of hands and projection of their hopes.

The villager thanked them, and realised it was their belief, and not the villager's own strength, that saved them.

They needed a name for this action that could bring about such great change to the world.

It was the villager who came up with the first and final suggestion.

Prayer:
The act of giving one's self.

31

<u>Legendary Name</u>

'I just don't understand why you're meeting with that darkskin in the first place,' said Rado.

'That's why you leave the thinking to me,' Lido said. 'Guy says he has something important to discuss and he's coming into our territory to discuss it. I figure it must be worth listening to.'

'Or he's just stupid,' said Rado.

Lido gave him a look. *The only stupid one is you*.

'The darkies are weak without him,' Rado continued. 'He said he was coming alone so I say we take care of him now. Take the head of the king when you have the opportunity.'

Cy appeared before them then, seemingly out of nowhere.

He'd made himself invisible with a program of his own creation, *Agemo* - A legendary chameleon from Eruban lore - and had snuck into the room long enough ago to have heard everything they'd said.

'Take it if you can,' he threatened.

Nobody had expected it, but their responses were fast.

They all drew knives. They were discreet enough to be taken out with them in public, and lethal enough to get a job done quickly.

Unfortunately, Cy was prepared for them.

In an even greater state of confusion than what had been caused with Cy's sudden appearance, each of the men found themselves disarmed, and their limbs were pulled in all different directions. Their bodies were elevated off the floor, and skin tightened in numerous places.

They'd been strung up.

Whatever was doing this to them was thread-like in composition. They must have been incredibly thin because they were nigh invisible. But that wasn't the case.

Everyone other than Lido found themselves suspended in the air and pressed by this mysterious thread.

Lido looked around to his men. Each of them immobilised.

'It's called Web of Anansi,' said Cy. 'It forms threads from whatever material is available whilst maintaining that material's properties. Air is such a fluid substance. Your men can't break those webs with brute strength.'

Lido watched as his men struggled in vain. Even his brother, caught in the spider's web, could do nothing to escape.

'Well,' Lido said, 'you have my attention.'

He was surprisingly calm. Subduing all of his men at the same time was no small feat. But he was the boss. He needed to save face.

Cy wanted to spend as little time there as possible, so he cut to the chase.

'We'll be enacting a revolution on the day of the test, and staging a coup. It will result in police retaliation, which we're prepared for. I wanted you to be aware.'

Lido pondered for a moment.

'You came all this way and put on this display of power just to warn me about the police? Are you sure you're not here to ask for my help in this... revolution of yours.'

'You always were the smart brother. I won't say no to help. The more forces we have the better. But, I came here with a second warning. I don't care if you want to fight alongside us, or not get involved, just don't get in our way. When all of this is going down, you're best served to not be considered an enemy.'

Lido scoffed. 'You think you can take them on, just because you can do this?' he said, pointing to his men. 'You forget how strong Blackjack is? The things we've seen him do?'

'I remember,' Cy said calmly.

Lido shook his head. 'You know, I'd heard you were smart for an Eruban. Figured maybe things could change a little round here with you and I heading up the streets. But it turns out, you're just another darkie.'

This was the first time Cy showed any kind of facial response.

He squared up to Lido. They were the same height. Similar build, though slightly in Lido's favour. Lido didn't flinch at all. But the intention here wasn't to intimidate. It was to relay a message.

'You think they see you differently from us?' Cy asked. "We're not Eruban and Orenian to them. We're just not-Irian. *You* can't offend me with *that* word.'

They stared each other down, but Cy pulled away first.

'Heed my words, Lido. All actions have consequences, and some burdens are too great for you to bear.' Cy issued *Agẹmọ*, camouflaging himself once again.

The *Web of Anansi* ended once he'd left the building.

'That piece of shit!' Rado screamed. He paced back and forth in a rage. 'What are we going to do big bro?'

It was the question on everyone's lips. They all looked to Lido, waiting for an answer.

The one they got was more than satisfactory.

'Like our friend said, there's going to be a conflict between the Erubans and the police. That means less protection on the streets. It's prime time for picking up new territory, boys.'

32

COMING OF AGE

One day before the Rank Test.

Renna *teleported* Q and N'Adina to West District, right to the border of the Shaman Quarters. A group of young Shaman were gathered, a few officers standing guard around them. A gathering like this usually meant one thing, a Coming of Age Ceremony.

Unlike the Sentiens in the city, a Shaman's coming of age didn't occur at 10, but at 5, because the development of their powers this early on was heavily reliant on them forming contracts with lost souls. But this city was too industrialised. The souls within it lacked the natural instincts of those found in the wild. And so every few weeks, an excursion out of the city took place, whereby Shaman who had finally unlocked their sense of Greater Self could go out and form their first contracts.

An escort team of a few elder Shaman and a handful of officers would lead them out of the city, offering protection, guidance, and making sure that everyone returned.

N'Adina, having spent so long in this city already, requested she take part in this excursion, as it had been some time since she'd witnessed a coming of age. And Q, well, any experience of the outside world was beneficial to him, so he tagged along, too.

Their sudden presence was met with great wonder, because everything about them stood out in comparison to the everyday events that occurred in this district. Reena herself was known by all because of the Rank Test. And especially to any and all officers, she was a hero, and a role model. They could hardly believe they were in her presence.

And N'Adina, well, nobody knew her specifically, but they knew of her image.

'Priestess,' said a child, pointing towards her. Yes, priestess. Not in reference to the Priestess Clan she hailed from, but referring to a character from Lore, known as, The Priestess, who adorned the same decorative ink across her skin as N'Adina. And though N'Adina proved darker in complexion, that was hardly a noticeable factor amongst those who'd never seen someone like her in person.

'Priestess,' she kept hearing. It had been some time since people had referred to her with such reverence. It was almost like being back home.

And then there was Q, whom nobody had any direct or indirect knowledge of, but who stood out by the contrast of his dark skin to his snow-white hair. And they didn't know that white hair was an irregularity amongst his people. In this city, a Sentien could change their hair colour every second, if they wished, and there was no way for any of them to know that Q wasn't Sentien. After all, those who could tell, knew he wasn't Shaman, and Sentien was the only alternative they were aware of.

But he wasn't like any "Sentien" they'd ever come across. There was something about him, some sort of... glow? That they knew was there but could not see. And those who could tell, could in fact feel some sort of greater spirituality to him. Definitely not a Shaman, but perhaps closer to Shaman than they would have guessed.

It was causing quite the stir. People in the distance were stopping on the street and coming out of their houses to observe. This trio of peculiar people, what brought them to this side of the district on this fine day?

Reena stepped forward and approached the officers. 'I'll be leading this excursion,' she said. 'Alone.'

The officers looked between them. They didn't have anything to protest, certainly not against Reena. It was just an odd occurrence that she should be leading the excursion at all. As important a task it was, it hardly seemed something she should waste her time on. But they didn't say this out loud.

'Of course, Miss Bordeaux,' was all they responded before being relieved from their duties.

N'Adina went and mingled amongst the children who seemed so awe-stricken by her that they didn't hear a word of what any of the adults were saying.

Eventually, the elders resolved that they'd allow the children to have their moment, and instead went to talk to Reena. 'A pleasure to meet you in person. I hope you'll take good care of us on this special day.'

'Can a day that occurs so often be considered special?' she replied. Not in a rude way. Moreso in a bluntly honest way, without filter.

The elder laughed. 'I suppose you have a point. I have attended many of these coming of ages, so perhaps it's not so special a day for me. But you see, this day isn't for me at all.' She looked at the children. 'It's for them, and they only make their first contract once. So however many times I've done it, and will continue to do it, yes, Miss Bordeaux, this day will forever be special.'

Now Reena, being who she was, didn't respond so greatly to sentiments, and so the smoothness of the elder's voice as she spoke did nothing to solidify her message. But it didn't have to, because what she said made perfect sense, and for the logical mind of Reena, that was what mattered.

'Are we all set?' the elder asked.

'We are.'

N'Adina heard this and realised she needed to settle the children down. After she had, they all huddled together, holding hands, to make sure none of them got separated during teleportation. That was what the elders always told the children, knowing full well it was an extremely unlikely thing to occur. And just like that, the group disappeared.

*

The group strolled through a forest in the outlands, a part of the continent that wasn't under the rule of any government. Without the unnatural order brought about by humans, nature had the greatest conditions to thrive, and that provided the perfect ground for Shaman to obtain their first contracted souls. It was tradition amongst Shaman in all far reaches of the world to contract the same soul as their first, because it was a soul that existed in abundance in the world for the sheer number that there were. It also bore very little weight, so even a Shaman that had just come to realise their Greater Self could handle the burden. And deep within a forest, or quite frankly, any area with a significant landscape of vegetation, one would find these souls clustered together, because they belonged to some of the most abundant creatures on the planet.

Ants.

The Shaman went ahead whilst Reena and Q observed from behind, continuing their own sequence of conversations of learning things from one another.

Q had spent some time looking up to the sky, the view of which was obscured by the density of trees. Reena knew it wasn't the sky he was looking at. 'Anything?'

Q shook his head. 'We didn't come far enough out. The sky is practically the same as the one above the city.'

'I still can't believe it. Your people have the power to perceive a world the rest of us didn't even know existed, and amongst them, you, and you alone can see something no-one else can. The meta of the stars. No... the meta of the cosmos.' She was using a word she'd just learned from him the night before.

'You grasp things quickly,' Q said. 'You really are your parents' daughter.'

'Moreso my father. What are yours like?'

Q looked at Reena curiously.

'Too personal?'

'Not at all,' he said with a little laugh. 'I just never would have expected you to express interest in something like that. I don't imagine it serves you anything other than to satisfy a mild curiosity.'

'You're right. But apparently these are the conversations people have, and from what I gather about you, genius you may be, you don't suffer the social awkwardness that tends to come with it. So I thought perhaps engaging in the conversation regular people have might be of some comfort to you.'

Q smiled at her. 'You're very intellectually thoughtful. But unfortunately, I can't tell you much about my parents. I was abandoned, quite quickly after being born.'

'Oh,' Reena sort of spurted out without realising. Of all the things Q might have responded with, she wasn't expecting that. 'Might I enquire as to why?'

Suddenly, the atmosphere around Q changed. 'There's a reason the rest of the world doesn't know about us. We have this story, well, hardly a story. A short legend. "If you leave, the White Haired Woman will get you, and no-one will see you again." I'm not sure exactly how this legend came about. Supposedly someone saw the White Haired Woman one day. But it's a story that's been told for generations upon generations. Everyone in the land knows it. And white hair isn't something that occurs naturally where I'm from. So when I was born with a full head of white hair, well, you can guess what happened next. When something unnatural occurs for the first time, people seek explanations wherever they might be found. And often, they're found in the stories we tell. So my parents abandoned me. I was shunned by those around me. Outcast from the community that was supposed to be my family. My hair, my birth, was a bad omen, and a sign, to those who believed it, that the story of the White Haired Woman was true. That she was coming, and that I was her messenger. So I can't tell you about my parents. And if your next question was to be pertaining to my childhood, that, to be simple and blunt, was no childhood at all. I didn't know love, nor peace, nor stability, nor friendship. I didn't even, at the time, know what it felt to be alone, because one needs something to compare it to, and loneliness was the only life I'd ever experienced. So I guess, perhaps, when you say I don't suffer the social awkwardness that comes with genius, it's because there is a child in me that craves the companionship he never got. Or at least, that's what your mother tells me.'

Reena, after hearing all this, simply nodded. 'That's what she does. How did you cope; survive?'

'Mother Gaia found me one day. She knew the gift I had. My sight. Everything changed from then. I can't speak too much on that. There are certain intricacies of my homeland that must be experienced first hand.' He gave Reena a curious look after he said this.

'What is it?'

'Your aura,' he replied. 'As a child, it took me a while to come to grips with what it was I saw. The world was just this amalgamation of bright colours, ever changing. When I eventually did learn what the colours represented, I found that those who abandoned me, scorned me, despised my existence; their animosity was not born of hatred, but fear. And fear causes those afflicted by it to behave irrationally. So despite what my people put me through, somehow, I was able to understand why. The colour of understanding is very distinct, and unique.

'As I've told my story, the colour of your own aura got closer and closer to how mine was back then, which makes me wonder, is your ability to empathise so effectively the result of your brilliant mind, or of your own tragic experience?'

Reena didn't answer, because she knew that as soon as he asked that question, her aura would have changed, and that alone was a more honest answer than anything she could possibly say. And given that she didn't respond to his question, Q chose to ask no further.

They came upon an opening in the forest where the density of trees was reduced enough to let beams of light come through. Within this opening were multiple mounds of raised earth, which let Reena and Q know that they were at their destination.

There were ant hills, and within them, on the ethereal side of reality, were the lost souls of many dead ants, whose bodies were decaying in the earth.

Ethereal decay also occurred, but the rules that governed the ethereal domain were different to those that governed the physical. A physical body would lose parts of itself over time, but a soul trapped in the world's ether would remain whole, until the world completely overwhelmed it, and consumed it all at once.

For tiny insects like the ant, they didn't remain whole for very long. But their sheer abundance meant there were always souls lurking about.

The elder leading the group felt N'Adina's hand on her shoulder. 'May I?'

'It would be an honour,' she said.

Further utilising her Soul Sense, N'Adina took a handful of the ant souls within herself.

The children were told to form a circle around her and hold their hands out as if gathering water. The physical action had no effect on the contracting of a soul, but a person's soul reflected the meta of the body, and so performing the action physically, helped them familiarise themselves with the action spiritually. Having only just caught sense of their Greater Selves, learning the intricacies of utilising their souls would take time.

The elders came together with a feeling of excitement. Many of them had heard stories about the Priestess Clan, and how they utilised a special form of Soul Arts that was strictly kept within the clan, and only ever taught to outsiders who were deemed worthy. But as with most stories, there were elements of truth and fiction, because ultimately, the foundation of Soul Arts utilised by the Priestess Clan was a practice that one would find in various other parts of the world.

In particular, a certain white-haired man escorting them was a master of the craft.

The art of Flow.

It was self explanatory. The art of Flow dealt with the flow of energy; energy being present in all things. The difference between N'Adina and Q was the medium with which they executed Flow techniques. Q's medium was his body. N'Adina's was her soul.

Standing in the middle of the circle the children made, N'Adina created a stream of ether around her, and within it, she placed the ant souls, one for each of the children. As the stream expanded out, each of the souls made its way into the young Shamans' palms.

Just as the ant souls made contact with theirs, they each felt them like a soft touch. As if an ant really had been placed on their skin. Then N'Adina said, 'You need to let them pass through you.'

This was a test, to see which of them had developed enough of a sensitivity with their souls to allow another into them. A few got it straight away. Others needed a bit of time, but eventually also succeeded. But two in particular continued to struggle.

N'Adina approached them and took their hands. Suddenly, they felt a pressure, it coursed through their arms, past their elbows, shoulders, and then seemed to settle into the core of their being. 'That sensation you're feeling, it's mana. It's the power of our souls to control ether. That feeling, remember it, and use it to bring the ants to the same place where you felt that sensation.'

And that was it. It was so simple a thing, they just needed to develop a sense of what it was they needed to do, and shortly after, they, too, succeeded.

N'Adina smiled at all of them. 'Those souls are yours. Your souls will protect them from being swallowed by the world's ether, but you'll always carry the weight of them on you. Remember this when taking on the soul of any other animal. You may find that in order to take on more, you might have to let old ones go. If you become particularly attached to the souls you contract with, as I did with mine, then become strong enough to keep them. That's the foundation of being a Shaman. Congratulations on your coming of age. I'm proud of all of you.'

They heard clapping, and everyone turned around to see Q applauding. It wasn't what usually occurred during these ceremonies, but then these ceremonies never had a Seer spectating, and so the elders, too, joined in applauding this young generation. But the ever stoic Reena simply observed, even though the colour of her aura showed, at the very least, that she was pleased.

The ceremony usually ended about this time and they'd be escorted back, but something had caught N'Adina's attention. She called over to one of the elders, and the two engaged in what appeared to be a serious conversation. Then they looked over to Reena, who had heard everything they'd said and given them the nod of approval.

The rest weren't really sure what was going on, but N'Adina approached one of the children, and asked their name.

'Ingrid,' said the girl.

'Do you know what a spirit animal is, Ingrid?'

She nodded.

'Well yours is a fox, and there happens to be one right here. Would you like it?'

How could Ingrid's response be anything short of a yes? A spirit animal was a soul that a person shared a matching affinity with, such that it was the most compatible for them to form a contract. Ordinarily, this fox soul would bear too great a weight for Ingrid's young soul to handle, but due to the affinity the souls shared, it would just about be manageable, even with the addition of the ant soul she just took on.

It was unheard of (in this city) for someone to obtain their spirit animal during their coming of age. There were separate excursions for that, and they didn't happen until their tenth birthdays. But N'Adina was here this time, and her Flow allowed her to notice the affinity the two souls had.

Taking in the fox was easier than taking in the ant. Ingrid's soul put up no resistance. They were simply meant to be.

'Do you know what happens when a Shaman takes on their spirit animal?'

Ingrid shook her head.

'Their name changes. You'll be called Fox from now on. If that makes you happy?'

It did, and there was nothing that could have made this day any better for her. She felt it, the sheer quality of the soul that now resided in her. The power that came with it. Finding one's spirit animal was a glorious thing, and having obtained it so early, Ingrid had been given a head start in her life as a Shaman. That fox soul would grow with her, and perhaps, one day... Well, let's not get ahead of ourselves. It's too soon for that story.

With the excursion concluded, Reena teleported everyone back to the Shaman Quarters.

'I understand you have some business to attend to here?' she said to N'Adina and Q. 'Will you need picking up later?'

They both shook their heads. 'We'll fly back.'

33

Infinisphere

Did you ever get that feeling you were being watched? Some uneasiness about the air. The hairs at the back of your neck tingling with some sensation of warning. Alex felt it that night as she approached her apartment. Something wasn't quite right. The atmosphere felt different.

She was being watched, but whomever's gaze was fixated upon her, it wasn't cold. In fact, it might be considered comforting. And you may question how the gaze of a person one could not see might somehow feel comforting, but that was how it felt to Alex. And that was why it was so strange. Someone was watching her, but their intent may well have been good.

She would very quickly discover just what those intentions were.

She conceptualised her surroundings and gave herself a 360 scope of the area. The anomaly quickly revealed itself. It was there, up above her. Right in front of her apartment. Invisible to the physical world, but she could see him now, clear as anything. And again, there was something strange. Conceptualisation was what was granted to divers by their interactive goggles. It allowed them to see the very structures of meta which defined the world. There was a distinct difference between what was natural, and what was the product of sen. So when she conceptualised whomever it was that fixated their gaze upon her, she was surprised. The meta that constructed their invisibility wasn't unnatural. However it was they'd achieved it, it wasn't the result of a function. It sort of reminded her of Kitchen.

He descended down to her. She'd make sure not to look up directly to him. She didn't want to alert him that she was aware of his presence; yet, somehow, he knew. Still, she felt strange but not uneasy. His gaze felt warm.

When he landed in front of her, he removed his shroud of invisibility. A glamour, he'd called it before.

Alex wasn't quite mentally prepared for what she saw, but she ascertained his identity right away. She'd heard enough about him, after all. A tall, slender Eruban man of her age, with shaved white hair.

He was the Seer. There, in front of her, for the first time. Unexpectedly.

Alex had a jaw-drop moment. So many questions ran through her head.

Here? Now? Why? How?

And in the absence of her speech, he said to her – the very first words they'd ever shared – 'You're flustered.'

She might have thought he was mocking her. But his tone was so matter-of fact that she didn't take any offence. And actually, it helped her speak.

'Surprised, more than anything.'

'But you know who I am?' he asked.

'I know of you.'

Her subtle hint led to him giving a formal introduction.

'Q?' She repeated back, unsure that she'd heard him correctly.

He just smiled. 'The way some of us get our names is a bit different to the rest of the world,' he said.

Alex got flustered again. 'I didn't mean to come across rude,' she defended. 'It's just not a typical name, I suppose.'

'But perhaps it will be.'

Alex didn't at all understand what he meant by that, but that was an answer she'd get much later than the question she would eventually ask. She then introduced herself.

'Just Alex?' Q asked.

She paused before answering. Was he looking for a second name? Erubans didn't typically have those. 'Alexandria,' she said, thinking perhaps that was what he'd meant. But he looked at her blankly, almost as though he were still waiting for more, but she had nothing more to give. Her full name - which she never used because 'Alex' was easier - was Alexandria.

And then, Q finally said, '"Where knowledge gathers."'

She didn't know what that meant, but realised then that they were standing outside her apartment building, and given that he was no longer glamoured, and his presence stood out even more than the unusual – and granted it seemed he was there for her – she invited him up.

Alex had never had a man in her apartment before. Not this one, anyway. Actually, the only guest she ever had was Kitchen. Not even Big Dog. Not Cherry. This was such a secluded space for her. And if you took away all the contextual knowledge about her and Q's relationship, anyone reading this part of the story might look at Alex and think what a foolish girl she was. Allowing a man she'd known all but a minute into her private space. The cliché beginning to a love story.

This isn't that kind of story.

Alex offered him a drink. He took water.

She asked how he'd made himself invisible. The short answer was he'd altered light.

How? The short answer to that was, 'Flow'.

She asked what he was doing there. The beginning of the long answer was:

'I wanted to meet you.'

'Why?'

'You have a curious existence.' That seemed like a compliment, but Alex wasn't sure. She asked how, and he replied:

'It's not for me to say. You'll find out at the end of this chapter, I imagine.'

Oh. Another person speaking as though telling a story. There seemed to be a lot of those popping up recently.

Q spotted a Chapel board in the corner of his eye and asked Alex for a game.

She got it set up at a table and they began.

'You have Chapel where you're from?' she asked him.

He shook his head. 'I learned it when I came here.' She found that surprising, because as it stood, he had the upper hand. And it seemed, somehow, that everything he was doing was simply in countermeasure to her own moves. As if his intent were not to win.

Then he began the long answer to her former question.

'I'm a Seer. Our Greater Self is our bodies. Where you Sentiens use sen, and Shamans use mana, we, Seers, use aura.'

Aura itself was the unique energy signature given off by all things. As uniquely identifiable in its characteristics as one's own DNA. And with that knowledge came the trifecta of being. The mind, body and soul. Sen, aura, and mana. The three powers that gave Arethians their Greater Selves.

'You've been keeping tabs on me.' Q said.

Alex looked at him guiltily. How did he know it was her?

'The girl I'm with, N'Adina, she's gone to see your friend with the crows.'

Alex was alarmed, and Q must have felt this in whatever way it was his powers worked, because he said, 'Relax. She's just gone for a friendly chat. Not too dissimilar to this.' He made his next move on the board. Still, he seemed to be keeping ahead of her without ever making a move for the win.

Alex realised then what she should have noticed some time ago. They weren't sitting at this table as equals. Even though they were in her home, even though she technically had more information on him than he had on her, the fact was that they had met under his terms. He had shown up at her apartment. She was the one asking questions and leaving herself to the mercy of what he chose or chose not to answer. It was subtle, and discreet, but just as in their game of Chapel, he had the upper hand.

Was it intentional? Was he really mocking her? The answer lay completely in the intentions behind his visit. So she asked him, 'Why are you here, Really?'

Before he said anything, he stretched out his hand in front of her, palm facing up. The room began to dim, and from his hand emerged a blue fluorescent light. It grew into a ring with a line cutting through its diameter.

'Do you know the difference between destiny and fate?' he asked.

Alex thought the two were interchangeable. Different words that described the same event. The Seers didn't see it that way.

'Destiny,' he said, 'is a straight line cutting through a circle of possibility. It represents the greatest life we could possibly live if we make all the right decisions. A story that's already been set out for us to achieve our best selves. But within that circle of possibility, we have choice. We can follow the path set out for us, or we can deviate from it. If we deviate, we can come back at any time, but the path we'll have taken will have been more arduous than the one set out for us. Fate is simply the path we choose to take within the circle. So you see, destiny and fate very well have the possibility to be the same, but how rare an occurrence do you think it is that the two coincide?'

Alex assumed the question was rhetorical. Either way, she offered no answer.

'But the circle represents the story of one,' Q continued. 'One life. One series of decisions. Yet, reality is made up of multiple lives. Multiple stories. Multiple destinies and fates. And when everyone's circle of possibility overlaps...'

The single ring was joined by multiple others. So many that the ring became a sphere, and within that sphere were many straight lines of destiny. One sphere became many, and the many spheres overlapped in varying degrees.

'You find that our stories are interconnected,' he continued. 'Some people's paths are supposed to cross at some point. I don't know if this was the exact moment where our stories were supposed to intertwine; if the decisions we both made up 'til now were as assigned to us by our destinies, but, without a doubt, you and I were destined to meet. And it would seem fate has been so gracious as to fall in line. You ask what I'm doing here, but you see, I'd like to know that myself. Why did the author of our stories decide that our paths should cross at all? I'd like to know what destiny has in store for us. We are at a crossroad, Alexandria. And where we go from here depends entirely on what you choose to do next.'

What? Alex thought to herself. Why was it dependent on her? What was she supposed to do?

Two people sat opposite each other for the first time. Alone. Ambient lighting surrounding them. His hand stretched out to hers. Any typical love story would dictate that in a few moments he would lean over to kiss her.

And what if he did? Oh, no. She wasn't ready for that. No, this couldn't be that kind of story, could it? Was that what she was supposed to do? Was that her next move?

Light returned to the room. Q stood up, and even more so than before, she basked in the brilliance of his tall stature. And she noticed, somehow having not perceived it before, there was something radiant about his being. Almost as if she could see his... aura?

And he said, 'Tomorrow is a big day for you. You should get some rest.'

Her demeanour changed suddenly. A slight sense of panic. 'You know about tomorrow?' If he knew about her plans, then who else might?

'I told you,' he said, 'we're at a crossroad. Tomorrow is when you decide what you do next. Will our paths converge, or is our interaction to be limited to this brief encounter? I don't know what tomorrow's events hold, but certainly, in your life, they'll decide what direction your future takes.'

Q walked over to the window, opening it without touching it. He held Alex's gaze for a moment, pondering a decision.

This is the part of the story where you say something romantic.

'I look forward to seeing what you do next, Ojo'Alexandria.' Then he glamoured himself and left, closing the window behind him.

Alex wasn't used to hearing her long name like that, but it seemed to roll off his tongue with the smoothness of a knife through butter. It was almost seductive. *Alexandria*. She heard it echo in her head for a while, exactly as he'd said it. And she thought, only for a moment – wished – that this had been one of those reach-across-the-table-and-kiss-me stories.

But this wasn't that kind of story. And it wasn't only after she'd finished this thought that her mind caught up with what had actually been said.

Her name. Her true name, which she herself had heard for the first time. It repeated in her head.

Ojo'Alexandria.

'Wait... what?'

34

A NEW FRIEND AND AN OLD

N'Adina had been waiting on top of Old Crow's shop. She'd spotted Old Crow's Anima in the skies, and knew that they had spotted her, too. So she waited, letting Old Crow know that that was where she'd remain.

It wasn't long before she arrived.

'Can I offer you tea?' Old crow asked.

There was a fire pit on the roof. Old Crow gathered some dried logs and leaves and started a fire, placing a pot of water above it.

Some more dry leaves emerged from her pockets, but these weren't for burning.

She emptied the contents of the packet into the hot water, animating a black crow feather to stir it through. It let out a pleasant aroma, which somewhat made up for the swamp green colour. Not the most visually appealing beverages, but then it was tea, not art.

N'Adina waited patiently whilst Old Crow did all this, watching ever fervently. She watched with her eyes, but observed with her soul. There were things that one simply could not see with the physical senses. Things that you wouldn't know were occurring until they manifested themselves in the material world.

One of those things was happening to Old Crow's soul now, and N'Adina, knowing full well what it was, seemed to look upon her with both pride and sympathy.

The tea was finally ready and Old Crow gave her a mug full.

'It's hot,' she warned, which was one of those obvious things that never really needed to be said, but people said anyway, either through sentiment, or tradition, or any number of unknown and not quite rational reasons.

They sat for a few moments in silence.

It was eerily quiet. Even the sound of the wind seemed dull that night.

'Why do you cling?' N'Adina finally asked.

Something seemed to change in Old Crow, then. You rarely ever saw her without a smile on her face. She beamed life and vitality, even if only through expression.

And though she still smiled now, it was the smile of one whose journey was so long, so tumultuous, that the prospect of a place to rest came as a saving grace. The smile was of one who'd crossed the finish line but was defeated in the process.

Old Crow was indeed old, and tired, and clinging. To what?

'I have something I need to do before I go,' she said.

'Is it worth struggling for?'

Old Crow had looked up to the blue glistening stars. She looked to N'Adina and admired the ink that decorated her skin. It was a deeper blue than starlight. Deeper blue than the afternoon sky. More like a dusk royal. A shade of darkness tinted what might have otherwise been a morning fluorescence.

'It's my first time meeting a priestess,' said Old Crow. 'It makes the fact I've held on so long even more worthwhile. My father had told me of the clans in the Spirit Forest, and how the clan of dusk blue were its chosen guardians, led by the High Priestess. You are what the people here would call royalty. It's truly an honour.'

'The honour is mine,' N'Adina replied intently. 'Whatever status I claim by birthright doesn't compare to the glory owed to one who has reached ascension. Why do you cling?'

It was there again. That tired smile.

'Because,' she said, with a pause and drawn out breath, 'there is a promise I must keep.'

'Is the weight of that promise enough to keep you grounded?' Her responses were quick, and sharp. It made Old Crow admire her even more.

'How old are you, young priestess?'

'21.'

'And yet so wise and noble.' She laughed a little bit. Not mockingly. More out of shock. A pleasant surprise. 'You will make a fine High Priestess one day.'

'Perhaps not,' N'Adina rebutted quickly. 'I have sisters. Elder sisters.'

'Aaaah. So you must fight for the throne. An unfortunate fate. Families should exist to support each other, not compete. But alas, perhaps that makes for a better story.' She noticed N'Adina's reaction instantly. 'The dear girl smiles. So fierce-looking, yet so gentle. Have I amused you?'

N'Adina shook her head. 'Not amused. It's just, the way you spoke now reminded me of my mother. She's always talking about how this or that makes for a better story. I've never really understood it.'

'You will as you age, my dear.'

The tea had cooled down enough for N'Adina to take a few sips. In line with its aroma and in complete contrast to its look, the tea was delicious and refreshing.

'Thank you,' she said, which Old Crow received but did not respond to. And after a moment, reminded her, 'You didn't answer my previous question.'

'No,' was her immediate response. 'The promise has not kept me grounded. It's kept me going. It has brought me this far and I must see it through.'

'When?'

'Tomorrow.'

The day of the Rank Test.

'I'd like to bear witness to your ascension, if you'll allow me,' N'Adina said earnestly.

'I would very much like it if you did.'

The two sat in silence for a while again, sipping at their tea. The wind was still quiet, but the crackle of the fire filled the silence, providing an almost soothing ambience.

'They call me Old Crow, by the way.'

'N'Adina. Daughter of N'Ariha.'

'N'Ariha,' Old Crow repeated. 'My father told me stories of the High Priestess of the spirit forest. "The most powerful Shaman there is," he would always say.'

'What of your mother?'

'She was Sentien. We were all together for a while, but eventually, my father's pilgrimage called him away. My mother had simply been a taste of local cuisine. I hear that's quite common.'

'It is. Even my mother never formed a permanent bond with my father. He served the purpose of providing the seed to create me. The same goes for my sisters and their fathers.'

'Did she love your father, though?' Old Crow asked with an almost child-like curiosity.

N'Adina didn't know the answer to that. 'Does it matter, really? Whether born from love, hate, or even apathy, the eventual child is the same. The birthing of children is pure biology. My mother picked mates with good genes, and powerful souls. Nothing else matters.'

Old Crow laughed. It was a genuine, light hearted cackle. 'Really?' she said. 'In this world of obscure and bizarre things, where some can move mountains with their minds and others can carry the life of lost souls through their own, is it truly reasonable to think that a child born of love and a child born of hate are the same? As if our emotions themselves bear no consequence on our souls? The soul reflects the meta of the body. The life force of the mother is what fuels and nurtures the unborn child. Do you think, truly, that a tormented mother's soul will not feed torment into the soul of the child she carries within her? In this world of obscure and bizarre things?'

Old Crow had looked up to the night sky at some point during her short narrative, but she could feel N'Adina's gaze on her. And knew, through a means you might call intuition, that she had given her a whole new perspective. Yes, in this world of obscure and bizarre things, it was perfectly reasonable to assume that love, hate, or even apathy, made a difference to the unborn child.

The creation of new life wasn't just biology.

'Now,' Old Crow said, breaking the silence, 'am I to be so flattered as to assume you came all this way just to meet me?'

'I'm looking for a friend of mine,' said N'Adina. 'His name is Mason.'

'Mason? I'm not familiar.'

Then N'Adina remembered that "Mason" was a privilege offered to her that most would never receive. 'You might know him as Big Dog.'

'Aaah, yes. Charming fellow. You'll find him at the brothel. My crows can line up a straight path for you.'

N'Adina looked up to see several crows circling out a path for her. It headed North-East from her current position.

'Thank you,' she said, which was for both the tea and directions. 'When shall I return for your ascension?'

'Oh the time will make itself known to you, no need to worry about that.'

N'Adina spent most of her life being told things in riddles, so the obscurity of Old Crow's words didn't leave her at all curious as to how this would happen. She would simply wait, and let it come to her just as Old Crow had said. She clapped her hands together and bowed. 'Be well.'

'Take care, young priestess.'

N'Adina left her, leaping from building to building.

As Old Crow watched her fade into the night, her mind, now free from the pleasant distraction, reminisced of a night many, many years prior.

A promise was made that night.

It was time to deliver.

Big Dog was speaking to the Madame just outside of the brothel.

She carried on talking, but he tuned her out. One of his dogs caught sight of N'Adina approaching, and she was coming in fast.

Imagining her to be of the same character she was when they'd last seen each other all those years ago, he knew this encounter wouldn't be absent of trouble.

He lightly tapped the Madame to encourage her to move backwards, though a light tap for him might be akin to a hard push from the average person.

In sending her backwards, he propelled himself forwards, just as N'Adina had done from the last building between her and the brothel.

She soared through the air, hurtling towards Big Dog with clenched fists.

He intercepted her in the middle of the courtyard, meeting her own fist with his, and as they clashed, a forceful shockwave of wind and sound exploded into the area, causing even the ground to slightly tremor.

Big Dog had done well to suppress the impact as much as he had, otherwise, the landscaping of the courtyard would have changed drastically.

N'Adina was considerably smaller than Big Dog – as most were – which offered her a more nimble grace to her movements.

As soon as her feet touched the ground, she manoeuvred around him, proceeding to strike from multiple directions. Each blow she landed gave off a similar shockwave as before. She'd reinforced her body so much that each hit reverberated to the brothel rooms, calling the attention of everyone within them.

But, Big Dog wasn't someone to just take a beating like that. He blocked and parried all of her strikes. He was a fighter, and he breathed close quarters combat.

She went to strike again but he grabbed hold of her arm. Using him to then lever herself, she lifted off the ground for a roundhouse kick to his face.

N'Adina's body was solid, sturdy. It could hold its form whether she was grounded or aerial. So when Big Dog threw her arm aside, her entire body rotated with it, causing her to lose her positioning in the air, and her roundhouse kick went straight over Big Dog's head, leaving her in a vulnerable state.

Big Dog went to grab her leg, but she sensed it, and retracted it quickly, barrel rolling to safety.

Regaining her composure in all but a moment, she launched herself again, breaking the very earth beneath her as she did so.

She came in with a mighty kick.

Big Dog smiled. He'd spent the entirety of their exchange meeting her blow for blow, so she didn't anticipate him side-stepping out of the way. She soared right to the edge of the courtyard.

She slid across the ground with her bare feet. Pointing at Big Dog, she yelled, 'Coward!'

He pointed and yelled back. 'Savage!'

She leapt off again, charging towards him. She came within a certain distance and jumped into the air, body left wide open.

Big Dog didn't step aside this time, nor did he receive a blow. This wasn't that kind of action.

He opened out his arms and received her, and she wrapped her arms and legs round him, like a child – as she had done as a child – and gripped him tightly.

'It's good to see you again, Mason,' she said.

'Now don't be saying that out loud, priestess. I have a reputation to uphold.'

'Right, of course,' she said with a wry look. 'Big Dog.'

It was her every intention to mock him.

They released one another from their hold.

Big Dog really did tower above her, but they bore a similar presence. Fierce, and dominating.

Big Dog was the brother she would never have.

'So this is what you returned to?' she said. She spoke not just of Iria, or New Heart in particular, but the brothel. She could feel the souls of everyone within the building. The pleasure, or distress, they felt.

'For now, yes.'

'Hardly comparable to the adventures you once spoke of.'

'All stories need their boring moments,' he replied. 'It builds anticipation for the interesting ones.'

N'Adina shook her head with a mocking laugh. 'I hope one day to understand old people and their fascination with stories.'

'Blame Nathanael,' Big Dog said. 'And I'm not old.'

'You're ancient. Oh...' she examined his face, 'are those wrinkles?'

They weren't. This was just a running joke between them.

'You'll be a wrinkle in a minute.'

Confident that the skirmish had ended, the Madame rushed out to the courtyard to apprehend Big Dog. She carried a retractable fan with her and used it to hit him repeatedly, expelling her breath to say, 'What. Is. Wrong. With. You! And who's this? How will you pay for the damages? We have customers!'

And then, directing her attention to N'Adina, 'I hope you know how to work, because-'

'Hey now!' Big Dog interrupted. 'Be careful how you talk to a priestess.'

There were only a few moments like this where Big Dog expressed anything close to annoyance. It was rare, and the rarity let everyone know that when it did occur, to take it seriously. Nothing more needed to be said for the Madame to know that N'Adina was off limits.

She huffed and returned inside to reassure her guests.

'That woman has a foul soul,' said N'Adina. 'I suppose I'm not allowed to beat her up.'

'You are definitely not allowed to beat her up.'

'Shame.' She punched Big Dog in the stomach while his guard was down. 'I've been here for a year. Why haven't you come to visit?'

'It didn't go along with the plan,' he replied.

She asked what plan? But he couldn't say.

'That woman, Old Crow. She has a plan, too,' she said. 'There seems to be a lot going on here.'

'This chapter is approaching its end,' Big Dog said.

More story references. She really didn't understand them.

'Well, I'm heading back.'

'Fly high.'

'Yes, I know.' She animated wings and lifted off with a mighty gust, flying eastward back to MindSpace HQ.

35

Change

Later that evening.

Big Dog had left the brothel.

Rado had the brothel's Madame pinned against the wall, hand heavy on her throat.

'Have you lost your mind, Rado?' she spurted out.

He'd gone there that night in pre-celebration of the change that would be coming to his district. The Orenians would take their rightful place as the dominant power on the streets. 'Where is she?' he asked. He was asking about Cherry, his favourite of the working girls. A sort of guilty pleasure, given she was a hybrid of the two other skins. But she wasn't there.

'You know... I can't tell you... that...' She coughed and spat as she struggled through her words, but Rado didn't loosen his grip. He raised her clean off the ground for a moment before throwing her to the wall. Had she been any later in *strengthening* herself, the impact might have been fatal.

She took the momentary pause to catch her breath and realign herself, but it was short lived.

He picked her up again, by her blouse this time. 'Things are going to be changing around here,' he said. 'The luxuries you've enjoyed so far end tonight. You work for us from now on. Do you understand?'

She didn't, not really. Why now, all of a sudden? She didn't know of the events that would be occurring the following day. Regardless, she saw the look in Rado's eyes, and understood him well enough to know that playing along was the smartest course of action.

Besides, what did she owe Cherry? She was simply a girl under her employ. Someone who earned her Credits, and had, at this point, abandoned her. She had no reason to protect her.

'Th-the orphanage,' she said. 'Where she grew up. She said she's going to stay there a while. I haven't heard from her since.'

Rado kept up his grip, relishing the fear in her eyes. He believed her. Or rather, he believed so much in his ability to make people fear him. If it turned out she was lying, well, he would be back, and things would end very differently.

He let go of her and watched her nimble body collapse. There was only so much pleasure to gain from her torment, and he'd been seeking a different sort tonight.

He knew of the orphanage. Everyone did. It was under Big Dog's protection. Not today, nor any other day, was an appropriate time to go there and cause trouble. But perhaps, in fact, tomorrow? Yes, tomorrow, when the district fell into chaos.

36

FLIGHT

When a crow flies at midnight, do you consider it a bad omen? Do you wonder if it came with the darkness, or if the darkness came with it? Do you fear what might come next?

When a crow flies at midnight, do its eyes gleam red? Or are those just the stories people tell?

When a single crow flies at midnight, do you wonder what happened to the rest of them?

The night before the Rank Test saw Areth's two moons looking down on the city through empty skies.

No clouds for as far as the eye could see.

No crows scouting through West District.

There was one crow, but its flight had taken it far past the borders of its origin.

It trailed a straight path all the way to Central District, as it had done on several occasions.

The rules that bound the creation of anima varied between Shaman. One of the general rules was that Shaman could only supply their anima with mana for as long as they stayed within range, but an anima that went beyond that range had to survive on whatever mana it was given.

Old Crow's range wasn't large. All of her crows were created with a supply of mana to maintain them.

The amount of mana needed to allow one to fly from one side of the city to another was substantial. But not so substantial as to stop her from animating more. So why the empty skies?

She'd sent a crow to Central District numerous times in the past, sometimes at Alex's request.

But on this occasion, this final time, this particular flight was to take care of personal business.

The crow made its way into the airspace above the Marston Estate.

It ventured to Marston Mansion, swooping down to the West Wing where it perched onto a balcony, and peered through the window.

There, fast asleep was little Annabelle Marston.

Had Annabelle been awake at the time, she would have seen the crow. She would have observed its dark silhouette, emphasised by the contrast of the glowing moon behind it.

And for those of you wondering, no, its eyes were not red.

37

AN OCEAN OF
SHATTERED GLASS

Cy and Mara were alone in the community centre. This was their last night to make sure everything was in place for tomorrow's revolution. They'd gotten their people as ready as they possibly could. The best thing for them now were rested minds and revitalised bodies.

They were preparing to leave themselves, but Mara became alerted, and due to the mental link they both shared, so did Cy.

'What is it, my love?'

'Someone's here.'

Cy immediately expanded his sen zone, but nothing came up. Even with his affinity, he couldn't perceive whatever it was Mara was sensing.

'Show yourself,' she said. And just then, Alex appeared in front of them.

Cy recognised her immediately.

'This is the girl who helped Jimmy?' Mara asked Cy, recognising her from the memory he'd shared. 'My love - this is the other Ojo in this city.'

Cy understood now. That was why Mara could sense her and he couldn't. He remembered a conversation they'd had a couple of years ago. A conversation where she told him that there was another Ojo in the district, because she'd sensed their presence briefly.

'You can tell what I am?' Alex asked, not knowing at all what the various intricacies of being an Ojo were.

'That sensation you feel,' Mara said to Alex, 'it's our bodies resonating with each other. It will subside in time.'

'Is that what always happens when two Ojo are together?' Alex asked.

'Only if they've never met before. It's the purity of our affinities. They're clashing. They'll get used to each other in time. I remember this occurred some two years ago. That was you, wasn't it? You've kept a distance from me since then.'

Alex confirmed.

'Why? So as not to alert us of your presence? So that you might go about your own business undetected? It's rare that someone can bypass Cy's psychometry. How do you do it? No, before that, why've you come here now? It can't be a coincidence, given what we've been doing.'

The question threw Alex somewhat, but she answered. 'To learn about myself. About... our people.'

'But why now?' Mara was very direct.

And Alex, somewhat ashamed, said, 'Because I've only just learned of what I am.'

Q and Mara shared a look. There was a communication going on between them that Alex wasn't privy to, and she felt, in this situation, that trying to read their minds wouldn't be appropriate. So she waited.

'Tell me,' said Mara, 'did *he* bring you to this city?'

'He?'

Mara analysed Alex's body language and facial expression. Her confusion seemed genuine. 'Never mind,' she said. 'If you have to ask then you won't know of whom it is I speak. I can teach you about yourself, about our people. But in return, you must tell us everything you know about our plan, and what it is you've been getting up to.'

Alex did tell them everything. How long she'd been observing their activities, and the fact she was going to use their revolution as a smoke screen to enact her own plan against the government.

'A very well thought out scheme,' said Cy. 'I'm impressed. And to think, we both learned coding in the same class.'

It was then that Alex told Cy about Niche, and what they'd said to her. Cy took the information, but resolved that there was nothing to be done with it at this point in time.

'How do you escape my detection,' Cy asked.

'My affinity, it's called The Anti.'

'Anti?' said Cy. 'Like what divers use? May I?'

Cy stretched out his hand, and Alex knew what he was going for. His psychometry was at its greatest when physically touching that which he wished to understand, and Alex had avoided shaking his hand before. With where they were now in their current situation, she figured there was no use withholding herself. She took his hand.

It didn't take long for his affinity to analyse the meta of Alex's being. 'Fascinating,' he said. 'It automatically adapts to the meta of what it's targeting, breaking it down with a counter structure.' Then he looked Alex dead in the eye. 'The power to destroy worlds. How do you use it to escape my perception?'

This was the limitation of Cy's ability. It told him the specific nature of meta, in the present, but didn't interpret how it could be used, in the future. It was something he'd been aware of for some time. Ever since the man who brought both he and Mara to this city said those words to him. Those words:

'Our intelligence may let us conquer the world, but it's our creativity that moves it forward.'

He remembered them so clearly, because it revealed his own weakness. Knowledge was simply what you knew. Intelligence was the ability to apply what you knew. And creativity, the ability to take what is, and transform it into what could be. That was the peak of intelligence.

Cy's affinity may have told him the specific nature of Alex's, but that alone wasn't enough to understand the unique ways with which she used it.

She asked them, 'Do you know about conceptualisation?'

Cy's expression showed he did not.

'I have some familiarity,' said Mara.

That surprised Alex, but she continued, 'The metaphysical world is made up of logic, like how the physical world is made of matter. It all starts with a point. The distance between two points forms a line, and multiple lines form structure. Those structures are what define the characteristics of all things. A structure becomes a point, a line connects it to other points, within which are more structures, and the cycle continues. That's all meta is. Infinite points. Infinite lines. Infinite structures. Conceptualisation lets you see that.'

'What's it like?' Cy asked. 'Perceiving a world like that.'

What's it like? It was strange. The only other person who'd ever asked her that was Kitchen, because she was the only other person who knew she could do it. And that was nearly two years ago, when Alex had been too unfamiliar with it to really describe it in a way that she even understood. But she pondered, for a moment. What was it like?

How would you describe art to a person who could not see? Music, to one who could not hear? Sweetness, to one who could not taste? Aroma to one who could not smell? A kiss, to one who could not feel? It was difficult to convey to someone something they had no experience of, if not only to compare it to something with which they did. And so Alex thought, she really thought, what was it she saw when she conceptualised? How did the world look when visualising it through the mind's eye? And then it came to her. It was so simple. The words to describe it existed, she'd just never quite found them in the form they needed to be.

What was it like?

'Staring into an ocean of shattered glass,' she said. And that was all Cy needed.

Then she continued, 'Every single aspect of existence has its own unique structure, including the ability to perceive. Because I can see the meta, I can target it with my Anti. If I destroy the meta that lets people perceive me, they can no longer perceive me.'

'But Mara could sense you?' Cy rebutted.

'I can only target the meta I've defined.' She paused and corrected herself. ' I *should* only target the meta I've defined. Whatever structure of logic defines the Ojo in our being, it remains a mystery to me.'

'I see. And what do you mean by "defined"?'

'Conceptualisation isn't like your psychometry,' Alex said. 'I don't gain an immediate understanding of what I perceive. I have to learn the structures of logic. Identify what aspect of the world they define. There are fundamental structures within the world's meta that are supposed to be left alone. I've made the mistake before; applied anti to a structure that should have been left alone.' she shook her head, 'I can't allow myself to do it again.'

Cy looked at her with admiration, then. 'How brilliant your mind must be.' And he had no idea how right he was. There was a reason few people knew about conceptualisation. One needed a certain level of intelligence for their mind to introduce them to the ability. The world that they saw posed such an overload of information that it could instantly crash the average Sentien's mind. It was something only a few were ever supposed to experience.

'I've told you everything on my side, now.' Alex looked over to Mara. *Teach me about myself.*

Mara's teaching began with a question. 'How much do you actually know about affinities?'

Alex had read various books that spoke about affinities, so she had a solid answer. 'When a specific form of meta is perfectly aligned with one's Greater Self. Functions produced purely from that affinity have a maximum output, minus world tax.'

'That's the technical explanation, yes. In our tribe, specifically in the Şango Clan, affinities are considered gifts from nature. And where they're a rarity to find in the rest of the world, everyone born into our clan has one.'

'You mentioned "tribe" and "clan" as if they're different. I thought they were interchangeable?' Alex said.

'"Ojo" is the tribe,' Mara replied. 'But there are clans within the tribe. Everyone from the Şango Clan has an affinity.'

'And the other clans?'

'My knowledge doesn't extend that far,' Mara said. 'I had set out on a journey to discover them, but... never mind. That's another story. You mentioned world tax earlier. I'm sure you must have realised that you don't pay it.'

Yes, Alex had always wondered about that. 'Another advantage of being from the Şango Clan?'

Mara shook her head. 'That's a benefit of being part of the tribe. World tax is the tribute Arethians pay to the nature of the world. But we Ojo are blessed by nature. The world doesn't take from us. It gives to us.'

'Why "Ojo"?'

Mara smiled. 'Because once upon a time, our people danced in the rain.'

Alex thought perhaps she might elaborate more on that, but she didn't, not yet. Instead, she said, 'You truly are impressive, having achieved what you have without even knowing truly what you are. But there is much greater power in you than you realise. More than I could possibly begin to teach you with what little time we have. But perhaps, as was done with me, I can give you stories. Stories of what we were, who we were, and how we came to be.'

Alex's expression betrayed her at that moment, because she couldn't quite contain her dissatisfaction with what Mara said. 'What good will stories do me?'

But despite that, Mara very calmly replied to her, 'One only understands the benefit of stories once they've been told. Though I suppose you'll decide whether that's true or not yourself.'

Alex then felt Mara *tapping* on her mind's door. A *message*, within which were the stories Mara spoke of.

'I'm afraid this is all the time we have,' Mara said. 'But you should know, those are the stories our people tell, but there's no record of the events that occurred within them. No record of them occurring, or even record of these stories being written, or when they were first told. They're simply stories we've always had. It's almost as if whatever truth is contained within them has been lost in history.'

Lost in history. Those words resonated with Alex in a way she couldn't quite put a finger on. Hearing them filled her suddenly with this compulsion to know exactly what levels of truth these stories contained. But that was something she'd have to delve into in her own time. As Mara had said, this was all they had.

'The way you see yourself is important,' Mara said. 'But the way others see you is important, too. Which of the two carries the most weight, is largely dependent on you. Remember that.'

Alex thanked her, and thanked Cy, too. They wished each other luck with what was coming the following day. As Alex went to leave, Mara asked her one last question.

'You said you've only recently come to know what you are. How did that information come about?'

'I was called by my full name for the first time.'

'By who? How did they know?'

In the rush to get over here and discover some truth of her origins, Alex hadn't quite taken the time to consider how or why it was that Q seemed to know of her true self, when neither she, nor supposedly anyone else, had any notion of it. Not to mention his response when she'd told him her name was "Alexandria."

Where knowledge gathers. What did that mean?

Alex hadn't taken the time to figure out how or why. And so all she could say in response to Mara was, 'I don't know.'

38

WHEN WE FIRST MET

'Sit with me,' Mara said to Cy, alone in their apartment. They sat on the floor, legs crossed. She put both her palms up towards him. He met them with his own, and they interlocked their fingers together, pressing their hands into a firm grip. 'You remember what I said to you when we first met?'

The Ọmọtọṣọ Village was a rural development. Even within the continent of Eruba, the practices of the modern day hadn't quite infiltrated its rural culture. Its inhabitants sowed the land in a similar fashion to their ancestors, centuries ago. Their utilisation of functions and soul arts were fundamental at best, and found themselves having no greater application of their Greater Selves than what their peak lesser selves could achieve. It was a village most didn't know was there. Entirely overlooked by the rest of the world as a place not worth going to. And as the world had a tendency to take people to places it deemed worthy to go, this village didn't get many visitors. The influences from outside were minimal.

And culture, being as influential a thing as it was, saw that rarely did the inhabitants of this village find reason to deviate from what they knew. They learned the practices of their ancestors, and passed them down to their descendents, thus continuing the cycle of fundamental yet primitive applications of Greater Self.

But as with any system that maintained a sense of balance within a status quo, every so often, an anomaly would occur. Something that questioned the balance that kept the system of lifestyle in check. This anomaly was called Emeka. A young, inquisitive child who asked a question rarely asked in this village.

'Why?'

Why did things work the way they did? Why did water flow down from the mountain, in the form of a stream, which ran through the village? Why did crops grow to a greater depth of harvest where that stream ran, than those farther away? Why did the crops grow in different places? Why was there a period of light, and a period of night? Why did the wind blow dust in dry seasons, but leaves and flowers in green? Why was food at times in abundance, and other times lacking?

And eventually, after asking 'why' enough times and receiving no answer, Emeka, young as he was, ventured to a new question.

'How?'

How would he find his answers? How, after receiving them, would he find solutions?

In the Ṣango Village of the Ojo tribe, a young Ojo'Mara just finished her daily prayer. Prayer wasn't a practice traditionally passed down amongst the Ojo people, unlike their dance. But the Ojo, too, were a people restricted by the practices of tradition, with a lack of influence from the rest of the world. Though unlike Ọmọtọṣọ Village, it wasn't because the Ojo settlements weren't places worth going to, but rather, outsiders were not worthy to be received. And in likewise fashion, the world did not direct them there.

A man came to the village not long ago. A man seen initially as an outsider by most, until those with whom he'd shared his past laid eyes upon him, and spoke his name for the first time in decades.

'Maelstrom,' a young Mara said as she came across her teacher at the end of her prayers.

'Mara. Last to finish your prayers once again. You're dedicated.' His voice was deep in the sort of refined way that came with age. He took the time to pronounce the syllables of every word as though they were the main subject of his sentence. There was an authoritative stoicism about his demeanour, and when he looked at you, and spoke to you, it was as though every word and gaze passed through the very essence of your being. As though he communicated not with the lesser self, but to the very Greater Self he attempted to nurture.

'I'm not sure I deserve so much praise,' said Mara. 'Prayer has been... a place of comfort for me. Can it be called dedication when one enjoys its undertaking?'

'Don't confuse comfort with enjoyment, young girl. Comfort is often the destination at the end of a painful road, and just as we gather crops at the harvest after the sowing of seeds, and the ploughing of fields, one must allow themselves to fully enjoy the fruits of their labour. Know by now that I do not choose my words fleetingly, and your dedication is nothing to be so easily dismissed as enjoyment.' Even with the calmness and clarity of his tone, Mara couldn't help but feel that she'd just been scolded. But that was simply the effects of being in the presence of the man, Ojo'Maelstrom.

'Forgive me,' Mara said. 'I'll be on my way-'

'It's no coincidence that our paths have crossed at this time, Ojo'Mara. Come. There are matters we must discuss.'

Ṣango village was settled at the base of Ṣango Mountain, a place where one could only climb so high before the mountain released its supernatural phenomenon, and grounded those who sought to reach its peak.

Mara found herself at the point where you venture no farther. There, with her, were 3 of her cohort under Ojo'Maelstrom's teachings. Standing ahead of them was Ojo'Maelstrom, just a step shy of the line where the mountain would cast judgement should he attempt to go any farther. And he said to them, 'You four are the youngest in this village to whom I'm passing my teachings. With age comes wisdom, but with youth comes freedom, and a certain malleability to the nature of the world. One need only look to the story of our origin, and you will see that it is the freedoms granted by youth that allow us not to uncover, but create new truths.'

Ojo'Maelstrom turned around to look up the mountain. 'This is the point where you go no farther. That is a truth that has been passed down for as far back as this village's known history. But if I, standing before you now, say that I will defy the nature of this mountain, and go farther than our ancestors have gone before, will you believe me? Will you imagine a reality where such a thing is possible?

Or will the truth of the world as you know it to be, overcome the possibility of the world you believe it could? Answer me.'

Despite the command, none of them could offer a response, because the absolution of the laws of this mountain collided with the complete faith they had in their teacher, such that they couldn't solidify the idea of him climbing higher into reality.

'Understandable. You find yourselves unable to reconcile the conflict created in your minds. Remember this, the way you see yourselves is important, but the way others see you is important, too. Which of the two carries more weight, is largely dependent on you. You may not be able to reconcile the idea of me going further in your own minds, and that may indeed have an effect on the reality of me doing so; but you see, I have already seen myself climbing this mountain to its peak, and my belief in that reality is greater than your irreconciliation. This will be one of the greatest lessons I teach you, young ones,' he said as he took a few steps forward, past the point where you go no farther.

In the past, they'd witnessed what occurred when one even attempted to cross that boundary. They would be repelled by some unknown force, and the mountain would roar a thunderous bellow, as if to tell them to attempt their treachery no more. They'd witnessed that outcome to all who had attempted the crossing of this boundary before. But in this instance, there was no thunderous bellow, no repelling force. Ojo'Maelstrom proceeded past the boundary without any response from the mountain at all. And when he turned back to them, the same monotone expression on his face that he always had, he said:

'The world and its people have a symbiotic relationship. The world casts hardships so that the people may grow stronger through adversity. And as the people grow stronger, the world, in kind, evolves. So you see, the world benefits from making us as capable as can be. Do you know that beyond this village, affinities are a rare occurrence? We call affinities gifts, but outside of this village, those gifts are not given freely, or without intent. The world recognises need, and bestows its gifts upon those who satisfy that need, so that they might fulfil the purpose of whatever that need requires. When a person's intent aligns with the needs of the world, that is when they receive one of its gifts. You see? Those with affinities are chosen by the world to help it evolve. You've all wondered why I chose you to be my disciples? Your answer lies there. There are gaps that need to be filled, and within each of you is the potential to fill them, and serve a greater purpose than anything you ever thought your lives might amount to. So right here, right now, decide for yourselves, will you cross the boundary? Or is this as far as you go?'

In this world, there were those born with affinities, which manifested themselves once they entered their first development stage. But there were also those who inherited affinities later on. Emeka was of the latter.

Shortly after entering his third stage, when his drive to know of the world aligned enough with his ability to utilise that knowledge, the world bestowed upon him the power of psychometry, and when it did, everything changed. The next decade of his life was spent developing his village with as much scientific knowledge as his affinity offered him. Because he understood the nature of everything he touched, it was easy for him to determine how the various laws of science interacted with each other. And he taught those practices to the villagers, enlightening them with the knowledge now bestowed upon him.

Ọmọtọṣọ village saw such a rapid elevation in economic development, that finally, the world deemed it a place worth going. And so people did. And the people that went had knowledge that Emeka couldn't obtain through his affinity, due to the limited resources at his disposal. Psychometry gave him an understanding of that which he perceived, but there was so little in that village compared to the rest of the world.

So each time a person of great intellect came to the village, bearing not only knowledge, but various items, crafted from both Arethium and Rethium of different grades, each one exposing Cy to information he didn't have; Cy became a wealth of knowledge. And the more he gathered, the more he wanted to understand. And so, after over a decade of service to his village, Cy decided that the next answer to his 'Why?' and 'How?' was, adventure.

Ojo'Mara had made a decision on the mountain that day. She would cross the boundary. But crossing the boundary wasn't something that could happen then and there. Not for her, nor her three fellow apprentices. There were things they would have to learn first. Ways of overcoming that which was fundamentally beyond them.

Ojo'Maelstrom may have been capable of overcoming the meta of the mountain with his own mind, but had that not been enough, there were other utilities he could make use of. He'd already taught them how to pray, but they were yet capable of applying that into the real, and there was no guarantee they ever would, because True Prayer was indeed a difficult thing to achieve. But what he could teach them, and did teach them following their lesson on the mountain, was Flow.

Flow, a practice that wasn't native to the Ojo. And in fact, in a story that occurred many centuries ago, was one of the reasons their great conquest came to an end.

But Ojo'Maelstrom, through his own journey, came to know of it, and utilised its nature into his own practice.

There would come a time where these four students could climb this mountain, and whilst their individual minds may never see themselves capable, with Flow, it became a possibility.

'All that exists does so in a state of energy,' he said, 'and energy, in whatever form it takes, moves. Everything you see, hear, touch, smell, taste; all that you otherwise perceive in whatever form has a unique state of being . A vibration that inextricably identifies it as itself. Flow, is the ability to perceive the state of being of all things. When the mountain repels those who seek to scale too far through it, that repulsion is a physical manifestation of the meta that projects it. And as long as it is physical, there is a motion to it. You may not be able to overcome the meta of the mountain with your own minds, but by matching the vibrations of your body with that of the force whose intent is to repel you, you can walk through it with as little resistance as the air on your skin. The key to you four reaching the top lies not it combatting the mountain, but aligning yourself with it.

I will teach you the principles of Flow, but how far you take it will be determined purely by your own efforts.'

Mara and her cohort learned the principles of Flow, and grew to use it in physical application. But whilst the other three managed to bypass the point where you go no farther, she never seemed to be able to catch and align herself with the vibrations of the mountain. Try as she may, she remained unsuccessful. And she asked her teacher, 'What am I doing wrong?'

Ojo'Maelstrom said to her, 'There are people in this world who believe that destiny is a straight line within a circle of possibility. We, as individuals, are a point within that circle, travelling from one end to the other. We have the choice to follow the destiny set out for us, or deviate from it, ever heading farther from the line, or drawing closer to it. The eventual path we take from one end to the other is our line of fate. Whether or not scaling this mountain lies somewhere on your line of destiny, I do not know. But perhaps, what lies ahead for you is not to cross the boundary closer into this land, but the boundary further out of it. I see it in you, Ojo'Mara. A purpose beyond this village. A truth that you will not find here.'

And it seemed that Ojo'Maelstrom had confirmed something she'd already come to consider. That just as he had experienced the world outside and brought back with him knowledge that he never would have discovered with his people, she, too, needed to explore the vast world, and discover for herself, what awaited her along her line of destiny. And so, temporarily, she abandoned the climbing of the mountain for the exploration of the world, where hopefully, she would find whatever it was she was missing.

✹

At 30, Cy had travelled across much of the Eruban continent, but there was still so much for him to explore. He'd heard stories of the Spirit Forest, but that any plans he had of going there should be forfeited, because it was a place only Shamans could thrive. He also heard of various longstanding civilisations and utopias, and found it curious how wildly the reality of them might differ from the stories he'd heard, should he be so fortunate to stumble upon them through his journeys.

But one story in-particular resonated with him. A story told in the most urban of villages, much like his own had been. You see, Cy, as much as he'd ventured to obtain knowledge from the world, was also intent on spreading it, and would go to the villages not too dissimilar to what his own had been, and elevate them to a state similar to what his village now was. And in these urban villages, he heard stories of those who could call forth rain. Blacken the skies with dark clouds and bring down an ocean from above, as though a calamity was approaching. But the villagers only ever had a story to tell, and never an experience to share.

But the story of those who could call forth rain appealed to Cy in ways he couldn't quite pin down. And then, on a fateful evening, a dream befell him. And whilst the contents of the dream remained unclear to him, one key part of it remained as vivid in his mind as a picture before his eyes. The image of a woman. And there must have been something else in that dream that affected him just as intrinsically, because he felt something akin to direction, leading him to a place he'd not yet known. And it was through the travels that succeeded this dream that one day, standing on a lake, dancing along the water, carrying its waves along with her motions, he saw for the first time in the real - but the second time in image - the woman who would change everything.

She felt his presence as he approached. Her, standing on the water below him, and he, on the cliffside above her. Their eyes met and locked. In that instant, they gazed at each other with the same look of familiarity, as if fate and destiny once again aligned amidst the infinity of possibility. And they said but one curious, yet, familiar word to one another.

'You!'

※

Sat together with their fingers intertwined now, Cy and Mara recollected that day they'd met at the lake.

'We'd both seen each other in a dream,' Cy said. 'You told me that fate and destiny had aligned. I'm still not sure what you meant.'

'I'm not entirely sure what it means either,' Mara said. 'There's so much Maelstrom taught me that I still don't fully understand. But there is one thing that I think I've finally gotten a grasp of. You remember I told you the way you see yourself is important?'

'And the way others see you is important, too,' he finished off.

'And which do you think carries the most weight?' she asked him. 'The way you see yourself, the way others see you, or the way I see you?'

He faltered. If there was a correct answer to that question, he didn't know it. He saw himself a certain way; his people saw him as a leader, and perhaps a saviour, should all go well. But Mara? Well, he was her lover, her partner. What weight did that bear on the world exactly?'

'I've kept this to myself all this time, I suppose because I didn't really know what the feeling was, or how to express it. But after achieving what we've achieved here, I realise now.' Mara untwined her fingers from his grip, and led her hands up his arms, where they would caress around his body as they had done so many times before. 'We've been with each other in the most intimate of ways. Your psychometry has told you things about my body that you might not otherwise have ever known. I have given myself to you completely, in mind, body, and soul. And I realise, now, it was only after I had done that, that the dream of what we're trying to achieve was able to come to fruition.

'Maelstrom told me before, that within youth is a freedom that allows them to create new truths. I never knew what that meant before, creating "new truth." But now... now! Oh, my love, I realise now why I left my village. Why I set out on this journey. Why you and I were directed to each other, and why we ended up here. This city, these people, they are your story. And you, my love, you are my truth. You are what I needed to become myself. The answer to my prayers. The person to whom I can give my all.' Her hands made their way around his face, now, and she pulled him in until their foreheads met, and she spoke life and affirmation into him. 'The way I see you is the most important, because it is giving you my all that will provide you the power you need to make this revolution happen. Nobody in this world can give you what I can, because you are my everything, and that is my truth, Emeka. You are my truth, and there is no greater power than that. So you too, must find your truth, and become the person you're destined to be.

'There are still things about this world you do not know. The way it works, the way stories are told. There are things I have not shared with you, and even now must keep from you, because it's not yet time for you to know them. But you need to promise me, after this revolution, whatever happens, whatever comes next, you will embrace it as you have embraced me. Because it is there, at the end of this chapter in your story, that you will truly find yourself, and the story of who you are meant to be will begin.' She mounted him, now, pushing him to the floor where they would share their greatest intimacies once more. 'Promise me,' she said, as she prepared to give herself to him. 'You must promise!'

39

THE WARRIOR

The streets were particularly quiet that night. Usual evening trades had closed early. Children didn't roam on late-night adventures, and the general public had stocked up on all their night-in commodities.

It was a quiet night in New Heart, because on this night, the action was taking place in the virtual. Ever since the week prior when the trailer for this week's episode of Lore dropped, citizens had been waiting expectantly for it to air. Because finally, after years of build-up towards not only the character, but the battle that would ensue upon their appearance, the citizens of New Heart would finally meet for the first time, the legendary, lost Cosmech called, The Warrior.

Large groups gathered in pocket rooms in The Arena, coming together with a high sense of camaraderie as they joyfully anticipated this momentous event. Yes, outside of the Rank Test, this may come to be known as one of the most significant events in New Heart's history.

Why? Because The Warrior represented something. An arbiter of absolute justice. A friend to those who needed it, and foe to those who deserved it. This was to be the climax of a long period of suffering under the rule of the Cosmechs.

The Warrior, historically, was the Cosmechs' greatest fighter. They left the battle of intergalactic domination to take on the mantle of protector, liberator, and revolutionary. And this episode would be revolutionary indeed.

You see, this, too, was a turning point. A crossroad at which one may find themselves joining onto new paths, the scenery of which would be unlike anything they'd ever seen before. Things would change from this day on. From this day, a new story would begin to unfold.

The episode of Lore began with the opening sequence revealed by the trailer the week before.

It showed The Warrior walking to the apex of a mountain that stood at the top of the world. At the top of that mountain already was The Witch, whom New Hearters had been privy to some months prior. She had been integral in the emergence of The Warrior. Her, and some of her other Cosmech companions. The Traveller, The Sorceress, The Telepath, and The Wizard. All of whom once invaded the world of Tehra as foes, but stood now as allies.

As The Warrior approached them, The Witch asked one final time, 'Are you ready for the conflict that's about to ensue? We're outnumbered, and overall outmatched. The odds aren't in our favour. In all likelihood, you, and everyone who follows in the footsteps you've led, will die. Are you truly ready to bear that burden?'

On this quiet night in New Heart, The Network would erupt with a massive cheer when The Warrior said their first words. Words that may well be the most important they ever spoke. Words that would be passed down to the hearts of many in the generations that would follow.

When The Warrior got to the top of that mountain, standing next to their allies, and looking up to the devastation that was approaching them, with clenched fists and eyes that knew no fear, The Warrior said:

'It's not always about winning or losing. It's not even always about living to fight another day. Sometimes you just have to ignore the consequences and do what you gotta do.

'Sometimes, you just have to plant your feet, grit your teeth, and hit them with everything you've got. Then, at least, you can say you did something.'

40

Dreams

Dreams are such a curious thing, aren't they? The manifestation of an unreal world that seems infinitely large, ever changing from one dream to another.

Have you ever wondered where dreams come from? How, and why do they make their way to you in seemingly random fashion?

Do you only dream of things you know? Or do dreams reveal things yet unknown?

Have you ever considered that the dreams you have are not your own? Have you wondered why it is that the sleeping mind can conjure an image vastly more vivid than the waking? Is it because the imagination has primary use of the body's functions within that state of being? Or is there another reason?

Could it be, perhaps, that the dreams you dream are not of your making; are not the culmination of your various thoughts and ideas, but are in fact, a gift from somewhere?

Somewhere that's not here?

Could it be that somehow, in this reality where one might hope their destiny and fate to align, that the world itself is the circle of possibility within which they might become themselves?

Could it be that the dreams you dream, are in fact, gifts from the world?

What if we told you they are? What would your next question be?

In this universe of infinite worlds, might you ask us, which world exactly were we talking about?

41

It Felt Different

Day of the Rank Test.

The most important and celebrated day in the city. It saw many early rises, due to either anticipation, nerves, or excitement at what the day had in store. Equally, it was in the early morning that the government released its roster of participants, and many would rise to see who would be gracing them with a spectacle of a show.

It had been such an experience for Daniel on multiple occasions in the past, but today was different. His morning routine was usually consistent. Wake up, get up, clean up, head out. But this time, getting up seemed a more strenuous task. His body felt heavy, like there was more of him.

When he eventually did rise, it was the result of telling his body specifically to move. As if it had somehow forgotten how to function. As if, somehow, his body were not his own.

His room seemed smaller, too. It wasn't. Nothing about it had changed. And though he felt as though there were more of him, he still occupied the same amount of space. But the room seemed smaller.

It took a few moments for him to realise that it wasn't just his room. It was the whole apartment. The building. The district. The world seemed a smaller place than it had the day before. But the world hadn't changed.

Had he? He observed himself. Nothing seemed out of order. His physical presence in the room seemed as it always had. Nothing had changed physically, but somehow, the physical world had less of a daunting presence on him. It seemed, rather arrogantly, that rather than looking out into the world and magnifying at how incredible a thing it was, that in fact, the world should look at him and... be amazed? Yes, something like that.

What had changed overnight with Daniel wasn't physical, and waking up to that change with his physical senses began the process of his body catching up to whatever change had occurred. The body was but one aspect of being. It was joined by the mind and the soul, existing within certain harmony with one another; inextricably linked. When one changed, it affected the others in some way.

One of them had changed, and the others needed to realign. But how would that happen? He didn't even know what was going on.

But there was someone who did.

He looked up to see Reena standing in the corner of his room. The combination of surprise and elation caused a stunt in his responses, so he just looked at her blankly.

She asked him, 'How're you feeling?'

'Great, but awful at the same time, somehow.'

Reena nodded at him. 'It was like that for me, too. Here-' She approached him and took his hand, taking off his current coder and handing him a new one. All of a sudden his body seemed to regulate itself. The heaviness had gone. The orientation of his various selves came into alignment. He was back to himself, but not his old self. This was a new self. An even greater self. But what exactly was it?

He looked at Reena again. 'What's going on?'

'I can't tell you that, yet,' she replied. 'There's an order to things. I'll explain everything after you take the test.'

An order to things? What did that mean exactly? Why was this happening now?

'You said it was like this for you, too? When exactly?'

'Mine happened after I took the test, as it was meant to. But somehow, you sped up the process. This wasn't supposed to happen to you until later.'

But what was 'this?'

'We can't talk about this now,' she continued. 'That new coder has stabilised your body so you can take the test. But if I tell you what you need to know now, it'll affect what's manifesting. You managed to jump ahead in your story, there's not much we can do about it now. But the rest of it, at least, needs to follow the order that it's supposed to occur. Just take the test, and we'll talk later.'

Then she took his hand in hers, and all of a sudden, the confusion of his current situation seemed entirely inconsequential, but this was a far more surprising reality to be in. Reena, initiating contact?

He looked up to her and saw a face he'd never seen before. A sombreness. A gentleness in her expression. To anyone observing the two of them, they might even think there was affection there. That would be something entirely new as well. But the surprises didn't end there. She came down to his level, put her face next to his, let go of his hand and wrapped her arms around his neck.

And he froze. He froze, because this must have been a dream, and his brain must have been malfunctioning, because there was no way in a million realities that Reena – that Reena – was hugging him.

And yet, as unexpectedly true as the new reality he woke up in, there they were, caught in an embrace that held secrets he must not yet know. And she whispered into his ear, 'After the test, I'll tell you the truth about everything. Just trust me, okay?'

He unfroze. How tragic an encounter would this be if he didn't seize the opportunity that had presented itself? He took her into his arms, caressing his hands along her back. And this was the Daniel who'd been no stranger to the affections of women in the past, but transformed into the hopeless romantic of his more recent present. So he knew the nature of a true hug. An intimate hug. An otherwise lovers hug – minus the lovemaking. His hands went underneath her shirt. One to the top of her back, pressing her into him, and the other just above her waist. She hadn't expected it. Or rather, hadn't quite prepared herself for it. So she stumbled into him, mounting him atop his bed, but his lean, strong physique kept them both in place, and just for a moment, an oh so brief moment, she lost herself in him. The euphoria she felt in that short time seemed like an infinity itself. But it was an infinity that ultimately had to end.

Now wasn't the time for this. Not yet. After the test. That was when they could enjoy a blissful truth.

She had to leave. She pulled away from him and got up.

After the test. He repeated it in his head. How was it that on the day of one of the most important events of his life, his mind was taken over by something else? That the Rank Test he'd been looking forward to for so long; that for the last week he couldn't wait to begin, was now something he wished would rather quickly end? Because something better waited for him.

Well, that was Reena. His Reena.

She was going to leave, but before she could, he asked her, 'Does what's happening to me have anything to do with the dream I had last night?'

Reena looked at Daniel curiously. 'What dream?'

42

THE WIZARD'S TOWER

T he night before.

MindSpace Network. World: Tehra. A world similar to the black market in that it existed in a hidden area of The Network. Accessible only to those who both knew it was there, and had permission to enter, which was very few people indeed.

And though it was a world few knew existed, should you ask any of New Heart's citizens about it, they would say, 'That's the world where Lore takes place.'

And some may go on to say, 'It's not very imaginative. Tehra is just an anagram of Areth.'

Tehra and Areth are anagrams of something else, too.

But this Tehra was different. This was a secret. This was something known only by those supposed to know it.

This was a place where truth was discovered, and created.

Reena entered the Starry Sky region of the world. A place where the sun never rose, and stars were not merely dots of light painted onto the veil of the night sky. No, this was a fantastical place where stars were like fireflies, dancing through the air with a flickering glow. But regularly the stars closed the space between each other.

Do you know what the space between two points is? It's called a line. And when two or more lines come together, that's called a structure. One structure can then become a point, which joins to other structures that have become points, and the cycle continues. But you've been told that before, haven't you?

Usually, one needs to conceptualise to see meta. But here, in this world, in this region, under this sky, the stars drew lines between one another, and their structures imitated those that defined the realities one might find themselves in.

Reena had spent a lot of time here in the past. She thought she knew the place like the back of her hand. That no matter how much it may have changed in the year she'd been away, the very nature of it would remain the same. And it was. The place hadn't changed at all. But her perspective had.

She'd learned something new in the days since she'd been back. She'd learned of Seers, and aura, and that the stars were more than just lights.

She'd learned a new word. Constellations; the structures created by the stars. And she couldn't help but wonder if, knowing what she knows now, there was logic to them, too; if the stars, however far away it is they were in this reality, bore some consequence on the laws of this reality. That, in the vast universe of stars, with an infinite number of lines and structures between them, one might discover the meta that made the universe what it was? A meta beyond what the world they lived in showed them?

It all started to make so much more sense to her now. Her overall outlook on life had changed. There was more out there than she knew. More than the 'more' she already thought there was. And no doubt, her father will have had his own epiphany of this some time ago. She wondered now if he'd always known. If he'd kept this from her, left her to discover it herself?

The way you learned something was important. There was more value in discovering something for oneself than simply being told. It gave more weight to the mind.

There was only one building in the entire region of Starry Sky. The Wizard's Tower. *The Wizard.* According to the story of Lore, The Wizard, and only The Wizard, lived there. It was a place that was impossible to get into. Unless you had permission.

Reena *teleported* into the tower, and there, as expected, was her father. This was where she had to go if she wanted to have a conversation with him. Even when sending *messages*, she regularly found him unresponsive, as did most. Even her mother couldn't get his attention whenever she sought it. That right seemed reserved for one man and one man only. Reena needed to have a conversation with him, too.

'4 days,' Reena said. 'I've been back 4 days and I still have to come here to even get a greeting from my father.'

'I don't remember you ever catering to such sentiments,' he said in a blunt tone.

'I don't. But, you called me back here. Some would say it's discourteous to be absent from someone to whom you've made a request.'

'And others?' he asked her.

'Others,' she said with a frown, 'I suppose, would do whatever it is you'd describe as your current mode of behaviour.'

And then her father said to her definitively, 'Your coming back didn't require my presence upon arrival. My absence is the unavoidable consequence of having more important things occupy my thoughts. Has a year away made you forget who your father is?'

'Has a year without me made you forget it's a daughter's duty to try the patience of their father?' She smiled, then. She didn't care that she hadn't heard from him in the four days she'd been there. Not really. And that wasn't even what she'd come here to discuss with him. This had simply been their way of showing familial affection towards one another.

He had never really been one for sentimentality, and she inherited that trait. A very select few found themselves capable of getting any emotion out of them at all.

Her father had been looking outside the entire time, but he finally turned to face her. At that same moment, the structures of light that had been forming suddenly stopped, because he was no longer manifesting them.

A few minutes of undivided attention. That was what he'd give his daughter.

She got right to the point. 'Daniel. He's becoming like us. When was that decision made?'

'It wasn't. Not by us.'

'Nathanael?'

He shook his head, and she didn't understand. They were the only two capable of implementing the change that was occurring in Daniel. Her father wouldn't lie to her, so what could it have been?

Then he said, 'You know how Lore is written?'

She did.

'Have you ever considered it possible that one person's mind bears such weight, such influence, that they take over a major part of the story? Even manifest an entirely new character based on their persona?'

Reena never considered something like that because she never thought about Lore. It was something directly tied to her, but otherwise inconsequential to the roaming of her everyday thoughts. So no, not once did she imagine that a singular person could have such a big impact on the story. Especially since she knew how the story was told.

'We never considered it either,' he said. 'Outside of myself and Nathanael, no singular person has ever dictated the story with such great effect. Your surprise very much reflects our own when first discovered.'

Reena formulated everything for a moment. If she understood what her dad was saying correctly, then... 'Is his unconscious mind that powerful.'

'Perhaps. There may be other things at play.'

'Like?'

'That's something only Nathanael can answer.'

That was the answer Reena was afraid of. An answer she could only get from a man even more inaccessible than her father. A man with more secrets than anyone.

'Is this why you called me back?'

'Yes.'

Reena knew what was happening now. Everything she needed to know was a story already being told. She just had to follow it. And the next chapter of that story would be unfolding soon. 'So what happens? He takes the test, and then you make the change?'

'You still don't understand how this story is being told, Reena.'

She frowned at her father. There wasn't much that Reena didn't understand, so it was a particularly personal attack whenever someone suggested a lack of comprehension on her part.

But her father continued, 'Whilst I directly attached your being to the story in order to evolve you into what you now are, it wasn't I who made you evolve, but the story itself. And it decided you were worthy of inheriting your True Name after you took the test. To assume the same course of action would be carried out for Daniel is a false notion.

'Reena, the existence of The Warrior in Lore is directly tied to the existence of Daniel in the real. And in the real, the people of this city have heard The Warrior's voice, but not seen its image. Tell me, Reena, when does The Warrior reveal itself?'

Reena may not have paid attention to Lore, but it got spoken about so much in this city, there was no way she could escape knowing what was occurring in the present time. Daniel himself had said it to her mere days ago. The appearance of The Warrior for the first time, after so much lore and legend had been put into its existence.

Yes, Reena knew exactly when everything was occurring.

'Tonight.'

43

PART OF THE TRUTH

For a day that was set to see a lot of action, there were many conversations that would be taking place.

It was 2 hours before the test. On an ordinary test day, Chen's Kitchen would be preparing to open its doors to those who preferred to dine whilst watching the test, observing it on a virtual monitor in the centre of the district. But this time around, things were different. Chen had sent a message on West District's community board that it wouldn't be opening.

Kitchen, never paying much attention to it, woke up that morning ready for usual service, and it was only now when her father brought her down to their underground dojo that he informed her otherwise.

'But we always open,' she said.

Chen sat down on one of the mats and gestured to Kitchen to do the same.

There was an uneasiness in the air. She could tell something was wrong. That they were about to have a conversation that would be unexpectedly unpleasant. It was almost deserving of pity, the degree to which she was kept in the dark about the goings on of the various people in her life.

'Katelina,' her father began. 'This conversation has come at a sooner time than I'd hoped, but I suppose I only have myself to blame for not having a great enough influence in how this story is being told. Otherwise, I perhaps could have delayed this a little while longer.'

Kitchen stared wide-eyed at her father. 'I know I'm young and you're old and the way people speak changes over time, but honestly, dad, I have no idea what you're talking about. Is this about the dream I had last night?'

'Dream? Never mind, we can get to that later.' Chen gave her a very hearty smile. It had been a subconscious attempt, he admitted, at delaying having the conversation even further. But there was no denying that it couldn't be avoided anymore. As difficult as it was for him, he needed to get it out.

'There are things I cannot say yet, because you don't have the facilities to understand them as they need to be understood, but what I must tell you now is that I'm going to be leaving the city.'

'You're taking the Rank Test?' Kitchen blurted out just barely after he'd finished his sentence. Because in that short time, her mind had made that very rational deduction, because everyone in the city knew that only officers could leave. And the only way to become an officer was to take the test.

'No,' Chen said. 'I'm not taking the test.'

'Well then I don't see how you plan to leave.'

'This city isn't what you think it is, Katelina. And you... you've no idea who, or what, you really are.'

'What, because I can create fire without using sen?' She said this almost mockingly.

'That, and whose daughter you are.'

She gave her father a look. 'I'm your daughter... aren't I?'

'Yes, yes,' Chen said jokingly. 'There's no doubt about that. In fact, you take after me much more than you take after your mother. But you are still your mother's daughter, and it's about time you know the truth. Or at least part of it.'

She didn't know what to say. He never spoke about her mother. The only thing he'd ever said every time Kitchen brought her up was, "Your necklace".

'Your necklace,' he said again, now.

Kitchen brought it out.

'What letter is that?' he asked her.

'An E.'

'Really?'

The necklace, which looked like an E rotated 45 degrees anticlockwise, was actually double sided. Chen took *hold* of it, and *spun* it around a half cycle, so that now, rather than an E, 45 degrees anticlockwise, it was more reminiscent of an M, 45 degrees clockwise.

'E.M.,' Chen said. 'Your mother's initials.'

He wasn't entirely sure what Kitchen's reactions would be throughout the course of their discussion, but what he didn't expect - but perhaps should have - was when Kitchen's initial response to this revelation was, 'That is so cool!' She was easily entertained.

It had been a theory for a long time that the E represented her mother's name, but never did she consider the double-sided nature of the necklace. And the idea that it represented both first and last names was one of those things that was both simple and genius at the same time.

'So what's her name?' Finally, the appropriate response to the revelation.

'It is not yet the most opportune time for you to know. There are things that need to happen first.'

This confused Kitchen once again. 'Dad,' she practically pleaded, 'You brought up this conversation just to still basically not tell me anything?'

'No, Katelina. What I have done is opened a new chapter in your life. But it's up to you to discover what story lies ahead. Because though you have not yet asked, I suspect you must realise that when I leave this city, you won't be coming with me.'

'What? You're leaving me behind?'

Chen shook his head. 'It is you who is leaving me, young one. To begin your own journey. One of the objectives of which will be to meet your mother, and discover your true self.'

Again, the confusion hit Kitchen like a thrown stone. And just like a thrown stone, Kitchen didn't know where all of this was coming from. What journey? And why did her father keep making out that she didn't know who - or what - she was? She was Katelina Chen. Chef. And her mother?

'You told me this is my mother,' gripping her necklace tightly.

'Yes,' Chen said. 'Your Mother. You really should read more. Or at least pay more attention to your friend who does. A Mother is a term used in alchemy. It denotes a piece of Arethium which has been specifically programmed to use alchemic functions.' He stared his daughter down, reminding himself exactly who it was he was talking to. She wouldn't take in a long-winded scientific explanation. 'To put it simply, your necklace is called a Mother. It was created by your mother, for you. Hence, all this time I've said to you, that's your Mother. With it, you can create things.'

Kitchen bypassed this explanation and went straight to asking about her actual mother. 'So, what... she left and gave me this to take her place?'

'An oversimplification, but I suppose, yes.' Chen had noticed the shift in Kitchen's tone. She was becoming angry. And if the tone itself hadn't given it away, the room was heating up.

'And now you're telling me I need to find her? For what? What could I gain from her that I haven't already learned from you?'

'How to control your flames,' Chen said. 'Because she's like you. So she's the best person to teach you.'

'But,' Kitchen stuttered her words. Still, the situation confused her. There wasn't any explanation as to why any of this was happening. It seemed, almost, as though her father were sending her away. But even that didn't make sense, because as she and everyone else so firmly knew and believed, *you can't leave the city*. 'Well... so what happens now?' she was finally able to ask.

'Now, you may ask the questions you've always wanted to ask. And I will answer the ones I can.'

'How did you lose your arm?' Without even a moment's hesitation.

The question on everybody's lips when they first meet Chen. It was one of those curiosities that none could escape.

One-armed men were a rare sight, so of course one would ponder what might be the cause of such a thing.

'Curiosity killed the cat,' Chen said, which wasn't his actual response to the question, but more of an inside joke between the two. A father-daughter moment that elicited the response:

'Who is this Curiosity you speak of, and why are they killing cats?'

They both laughed. It added some humour to the situation, which Kitchen felt was to mask the horror of what she would hear next.

She was right.

Chen said, 'I cut it off myself.'

All those years of wondering. All those unanswered questions, and now, the truth was a possibility she'd never considered.

Cut it off himself? Why?

'To atone for my sins,' he said. The look in his eyes told her not to delve any deeper into that line of inquiry.

That was a story for another day.

Her second question, which she felt might now might be heavily related to the first.

'Why did you leave Oren? Why did you raise me here?'

Chen swallowed nothing, which was something people did when they wanted to avoid speaking a bitter truth. But this was something he could tell her, and certainly should, despite how her thoughts of him might change after.

'To shelter you from the life I lived,' he said.

What life?

She had grown up with no experience of the world beyond West District. The closest she came were the worlds within MindSpace. Worlds that may or may not reflect what existed outside of this city.

What would it have been like to have grown up in Oren? Would Chen's Kitchen exist? Would she have gotten caught up in whatever it was that led to her father cutting off his own arm? And then a thought crept into her mind which made her shudder in place.

Had she grown up in Oren; had she never come to Iria, to this city...

What would her life be like, if she'd never met Alex?

'There are questions that will be answered over time, Katelina. You'll just have to be patient. But for now, tell me about this dream you had?'

44

You'll make it

MindSpace HQ.

'Lillith,' Nadina said, 'I'd like to travel to West District again today. I have-'

'You want to witness your new friend's ascension?' Lilith interrupted.

'You know?'

'We know everything worth knowing in this city.'

We?

And she continued, 'Don't worry. You'll make it in time for her ascension. There's actually something we'd like your help with beforehand.'

45

THE PRESIDENT

There weren't many people in the city who knew of the existence of its president. Each district was run by its own mayor, and any notion of a higher level of government than that was only spoken of within certain circles.

Those who knew of the president would describe him as the most elusive man in the whole city, because only once a year did they have the guarantee of being graced with his presence; the day of the Rank Test.

The five mayors were gathered in a pocket space within The Arena. They sat at an oval table with 8 seats. The five of them were along the sides, and sat at one of the ends of the table, was October.

'No Lillith?' asked the West District Mayor, by far the oldest person at this table.

'She has other matters to attend to today,' October responded.

'More pressing matters than the Rank Test?' He couldn't believe it. This was the most important and celebrated day in the entire city. In all of New Heart's short history! Nothing was more important. But the West District mayor wasn't amongst those privy to what really went on in this city.

This city isn't what you think it is!

No Lilith meant they waited now only for the president, and with The Arena having finished its preparations, and the test meant to be starting in 15 minutes, he was due to arrive soon.

It was hardly a moment later that he appeared. Literally, just appeared in the room, sat at the head of the table. It was nerve-wracking, sometimes, being in his presence. The West District Mayor was sure he'd never seen the president smile. His face was always serious; unmoving in its lack of expression. And in all likely fashion, the president didn't waste time with greetings or niceties. He got straight down to business.

'Shall we begin?'

46

AND SO IT BEGINS

The local councils in each district were heaving.

Those who took part in the test were gathered into a chamber, similar to the training room found at MindSpace HQ. It was from this room that they would connect to The Arena's server, because things were a bit different on test days. From within the five chambers in each district, all of the participants were immersed into a large room within The Arena's coding, waiting to be let out into the test grounds.

Five minutes until the test began. Nerves and tensions were high. There were a few veterans in the room, looking to increase the rank they already had. They oozed confidence.

But for those who were taking the test for the first time, like Max and Bolu, their nerves were practically visible. Each for their own reason.

Max wanted to make his dad proud. Impressing Alex would be a welcome side effect. He hoped she'd be watching, and that she'd take notice of him; see how far he'd come. That she might see him as somebody worth being with, again.

Bolu's nerves and motivation were entirely different. He'd grown up feeling the weight of responsibility to both sides of the culture war. He'd always wanted to join the police, but he'd kept that fact hidden for so long. Not wanting to go against his own people. Not wanting to be considered a traitor, or sell out.

It was a big surprise when he'd first enlisted, one met with a lot of scrutiny. After all, Bolu's own brother had been arrested the year before. And when someone got arrested in this city, you never saw them again.

Why would someone whose only family got taken away want to join the people that took them?

The logical thinker, or even just the creative thinker, might consider it some ploy. Infiltrating the organisation to find out what happened.

But Bolu had been through all the vetting process and passed with flying colours. As far as anybody knew, his intentions were just. He really did believe in what the police represented. Whatever faults existed within the organisation were the results of individuals, not the organisation itself.

Bolu and Max stuck together. They had done since they both first enlisted, having already been friends prior. The two hoped to achieve Bronze Rank together today. Silver was out of the question, they knew that. But Bronze, that was achievable.

In the midst of all these other participants, veterans or otherwise, they felt the immense pressure of what was to come. They'd each watched many tests in the past, so they knew what to expect. But understanding something from the perspective of an observer was very different to understanding as a participant. No amount of past tests they watched could have prepared them for how it would feel to step into that world for the first time. To see the virtualized crowd of New Hearters all around them, cheering them on.

2 minutes until the test began.

For how much time had passed since first signing up to the test, these last few minutes seemed an eternity to wait. But they, too, would pass by as mere moments in comparison to what lay ahead.

As they stood amongst their peers, waiting, Max started to shake.

Perhaps nerves, or perhaps excitement, either way, his hands wouldn't stop.

But then he felt a tap on his shoulder, and turning around, to his surprise, there stood Daniel.

'You're just out there to do your best,' he said. 'Don't let anything get in the way of that.'

It was a chance meeting. Max knew who Daniel was, of course, but Daniel knew nothing of Max. And neither knew of the other's relationship with Alex, even if both, to varying degrees, hoped she would be watching.

'Thanks,' Max responded. He stopped shaking. 'I'll be watching you after I'm eliminated.'

Elimination was when a participant could no longer fight. It wasn't the same as failing. Everyone got eliminated at some point, because somewhere down the line of the test's events was the emergence of The Machine.

And nobody could beat The Machine.

At last, it was time. The Rank Test was beginning.

47

O̲J̲O̲

There is a story told in certain parts of Eruba. One of the oldest stories on Areth. It told of people who danced when it rained, in celebration of the gift presented to them by the world. Because the people always danced when it rained, at times when it was always raining, the people were always dancing.

It must have begun on a specific day, as all events did, when a child within the tribe noticed their elders dancing in the rain. But a child's mind is so free in its thinking that it hadn't sequenced the order of events as rain and then dance. So the child, within the world of their mind, thought not that they danced when it rained, but rather, that it rained when they danced.

And so the child would dance, believing it would rain. And the child told their friends, too, to dance, so that it might continue to rain. And because the rain didn't stop, and the people continued to dance, more and more children came to believe that it was their dance that called forth rain.

But the children couldn't dance for as long as the adults. Soon after they finished dancing, the rain stopped. And because the rain stopped, the adults stopped dancing, too. And when the adults stopped dancing, and the children noticed the rain had stopped, they knew, now, truly, that it rained when they danced. And so the first child, who on the first day thought to themselves, "It rains when we dance," in an effort to bring back the rain, began to dance. And because they began to dance, so, too, did their friends.

And because the children, with their free minds, did not know that the laws of this world didn't make it so that when they danced it rained, they continued to dance, with an absolute belief that rain would come.

And the rain came.

And because the rain came when the children danced, the adults, who thought that they danced only when it rained, began to wonder if, in fact, it rained when they danced. And so they danced and danced. And it rained and rained. Until those who knew to dance when it rained, now *knew* that it rained when they danced.

And because it rained whenever they danced, the people, gathered under this shared belief, named themselves a tribe.

Those who could call forth rain.

Ojo.

48

<u>The Anti</u>

A storm cloud had gathered in the centre of the district. That, and the commencement of the Rank Test was Alex's cue to begin her own plan. With the Rank Test taking everyone's attention in the virtual, and Cy's revolution distracting the police in the real, nobody would be prepared for her.

She entered The Network. It was the quietest you ever saw it. Everyone who was using it was in The Arena, and that was where Alex went, too.

The Arena was a special world. Unlike all others, which followed their own meta as defined by whomever created them, The Arena was the only world in the entire network which had the capability to match the exact meta of the real world. The laws of physics that governed the interaction of one body of matter with another, the air pressure, the pull of gravity; on the day of the Rank Test, all of these natural laws were copied perfectly into The Arena's testing grounds. Everything they experienced during the test might as well be real.

But that wasn't the only reason The Arena was so special. It was a world of multiple layers. The test itself took place in a particular domain, whilst those who watched, did so from another. And those who spectated from a place even more secluded than the private rooms people used, they did so from a domain that nobody other than they knew existed.

Nobody but Alex, that is.

She'd first noticed it a little over a year ago, sometime after she'd gotten used to conceptualisation and had defined enough of the world's meta to understand what she saw. That was what it was like, conceptualising. It was the introduction to another language. One could recognise the language, but still needed to develop an understanding, a definition, of the words being used.

Through the course of the year that succeeded her gaining the ability to conceptualise, she'd made her way to all areas of The Network, viewing everything through her mind's eye. She'd seen the various layers of reality that existed within The Arena, and for some time, thought that to be all there was to its meta.

But having developed a habit of conceptualising all things new, on the day of the Rank Test a year ago, the one where Reena gave a display of power that would never be forgotten, Alex conceptualised many new things. And as interesting and valuable the knowledge she'd obtained from conceptualising Reena was, it was perhaps not as intriguing as her learning of this new, secret domain within The Arena's layering that seemed to have suddenly appeared on this one day. And it was after she'd seen this, that The Book revealed to her the information that sparked a chain of events which would lead her to the point in time she now found herself in.

Yes, this plan was a year in the making. A year of waiting, learning, and planning. All to come to a conclusion here, now.

Getting into the hidden domain was easy. Her *Anti* broke through the protective layer of coding which separated the space from all others.

Having conceptualised it, she knew that without her *Anti*, she never would have broken through. The structure of logic was too complex. There were too many variables she had yet to define. How many more years might it have taken her to learn how to get past it through knowledge alone? It had been so easy growing up. Nothing had been a challenge for her. Nobody could match her intellectually, or even in mental prowess. She was by all accounts, gifted. More so than anyone else she knew.

But now, this past year or so, she'd been introduced to things that challenged her. People who existed in realms of influence beyond her capacity to fathom.

She could feel it, her heart racing in the real. She was excited, because finally, after a year of waiting, she was here.

Here in this dark domain of space. She could feel herself standing, though there was no visible floor to stand on. The space was pitch black, with the only things emanating any sort of light being her astral self, and a little building, just off in the distance. It was the only other thing that seemed to exist in this space, besides her.

She didn't have to guess if that was what she was looking for. Conceptualisation showed her there were 7 people in that room, and curiously enough, one of them was a person whom she'd conceptualised before.

The West District Mayor. His meta was as unremarkable as ever. Her attention was taken away by two clutters that suddenly manifested before her. They were of the humanoid type. Similar to the ones N'Adina had defeated earlier that week.

They sort of just stood there for a while, staring, even though they had no eyes. Grotesque things, really. Amalgamations of chaos brought together by logic to create something that shouldn't exist.

Alex's featureless face smirked, the same way their no-eyed faces stared. She wasn't going to let anything stop her from entering that building. Especially not a pair of clutters. Two orbs of *anti* emerged from her hands. She shot them out at the clutters, shattering their virtual existences instantaneously. Their very presence seemed to have been entirely wasted, having achieved nothing between their manifestation and their demise.

Yet, Alex's path to the building was blocked once again, as four clutters took their place. She didn't even wait this time.

A wave of *anti* destroyed them right where they stood.

But then came 8 more, and when Alex destroyed them, 16 appeared. And that formula of 'destroy one and 2 will take its place' continued for a while, until there were so many clutters around her, the only reason she knew the exact number was because of that formula.

She cursed the never-ending length of this ordeal. Repeating this process in ever increasing magnitude was a waste of sen.

She realised that she needed to come off the defensive. Rather than react to the clutters as they appeared, she needed a more aggressive approach. She released a massive wave of *anti*, destroying every single clutter that surrounded her. And then, she surrounded herself with it, and charged forwards. She would mow down any clutters that manifested before her. She would break down the walls of the building which stood in her way, and she would meet the people behind everything that went on in this city.

For having resolved herself to take care of any clutters that got in her way, none appeared. The space was empty yet again. A clear path to the building was being taken. Nothing was going to stop her now.

No. That's not how this story goes.

A man appeared before her. A man whom she'd never seen before. He was tall and slender, wore glasses, and a white coat with the number "8" embroidered in black on the front and back.

Whoever he was, he wasn't going to stop her.

Or so she thought. She'd formed a wave of *anti* and released it. It would destroy his virtual body, causing his consciousness to be regained in the real. A very merciful ejection from The Network. But things didn't quite go according to plan. Or perhaps it would be more prudent to say, the story Alex told herself of how things would go, wasn't the story being told here.

October released his own wave of meta. It clashed with Alex's *anti*, and the two completely cancelled each other out. She was shocked, to say the least.

It wasn't impossible to stop her *anti*, it was just very difficult. One needed to put far more sen into their function than she did because of the natural output her affinity gave her. And when they did so, the reality would often be that they'd used more than was necessary.

But October, his sen usage was exact. And that, amidst all the things that remained possibilities, seemed impossible.

Alex halted her charge. Taking the time to really examine him now, she realised...

And he realised that she had realised, which was perhaps what he'd wanted to be the outcome of his sudden appearance, because he said to her, 'Shall we have a chat?'

49

THE FIRST WAVE

The Rank Test was split up into four waves, each one increasing in difficulty from the last. The survival of each wave correlated with the potential to receive rank, with waves 1 through 3 determining whether you left the test with bronze, silver, or gold. And the fourth wave? Nobody ever survived the fourth wave, because the fourth wave was a battle against The Machine, and you can't beat The Machine.

Daniel was confident he could.

There was someone like that in every test. The idea that they had come up with some new meta ability that would give them the edge. Allow them to bypass The Machine's insanely hard and durable skin. There had been some impressively creative attempts over the years, and despite their ultimate failure, those who made it to The Machine were rewarded depths of fame and notoriety.

But it worked both ways. Every failed attempt to harm The Machine simply added to its lore. Strengthened the legend of its invincibility. So much so that, 'You can't beat The Machine,' may have been the greatest known truth in this city.

The participants had been split into groups, spanning across a wide battlefield. Daniel stood at the forefront of his group. Max and Bolu were behind him, and to the side of him was Viktor. Yes, that Viktor. Pride of the Jewelz family. His current silver ranking wasn't enough. He was going for gold.

There were many people this time around betting on him to make it past the third wave, following his failed attempt at the last test he took two years ago. But he'd recently entered his 6th development stage. His mind was more powerful than the last time he took the test.

'Hey, mister prodigal prodigy,' Viktor said to Daniel. 'There's still time to quit, you know. Take it from someone who's done it before, what's coming is scary. Some deadbeat who couldn't even handle the pressure of coming from a prestigious family has no place here.'

Daniel didn't respond. He hadn't been listening. Not to Viktor, anyway. He'd been using *Telepathy*, a more advanced version created by Niche, to tap into the thoughts of everyone around him. He knew, then, that nerves were high, and many who stood there with him had doubts about whether or not they belonged. If they had the ability, or perhaps even the right, to claim service to this great city.

Daniel took a breath. The type of breath one takes before they're about to say something of monumental value, which was odd, because he wasn't going to say anything, so much as send his *message* directly to the minds of everyone around him.

Using another function within the *Telepathy* program, he hijacked the minds of his fellow competitors and told them this one, very simple message.

'*You've got this.*'

And then in similar fashion, using a *Telekinesis* program, he gave everyone, all 500 participants, a pat on the shoulder. The hand of a warrior to push them all forward. And whilst it didn't work across the board, there were certainly those whom his words seemed to soothe.

With his *Radar* active, in combination with *Telekinesis*, Daniel could feel the presence of all on the battlefield. He could feel the pressure of their heartbeats, and knew then that many which had been heightened from their nerves, were now calmed.

And with just that, most of them, including Max and Bolu, were now ready. Which was good, because looking ahead, there seemed to be a sandstorm in the distance, drawing ever closer.

But it wasn't a sandstorm at all. It was a stampede; so intense that the kicked-up dust shrouded them from clear sight.

But a quick *Magnification* command would allow them to see clearly the impending conflict.

The battle was coming.

50

RAIN

Officer Dodds was in charge of the protection of West District's participants.

He'd had a premonition that morning. A feeling that the day was going to be more eventful than usual. More so than any other Rank Test. And not just because his son was participating this time.

No, there was something in the air, but he couldn't quite state what type of feeling it was.

An omen of good or bad fortune? Who could say?

There was just something in the air.

He couldn't tell what it was earlier, but now, he could. Now it was something different to what it had been before. It was... wet?

The humidity of the weather had risen suddenly. It was thick and grimy. He felt as though simply moving through it would prove a strenuous task. Like wading through water.

And then, then he saw the clouds. They were eerily dark in comparison to the otherwise blue sky.

A single rain cloud like that wasn't something that occurred naturally, that much was certain. Something was going on in that direction. He realised it was coming from the centre of the district, and in the time he'd taken to gather his thoughts, he noticed the cloud had gotten larger.

Perhaps it had indeed grown, or perhaps it was just closer.

He concluded that it was both.

Whatever this phenomenon was, and whatever threat it posed, it was headed in his direction.

What to do? What to do?

There were so many possibilities.

Was it a distraction? Could the threat have been approaching from another direction altogether? Infiltrate their defences whilst they fixated upon a storm cloud?

It was plausible, certainly. Distracting the enemy was a classic battle tactic. But Dodds, with all his experience, had an instinct he couldn't ignore. The cloud, that was where the threat was.

So it wasn't a question of if the cloud was a distraction. It was a question of if he would wait for whatever or whomever it was to come to him, or if he, like his two young protégé's, would step forward into the fray, and take the fight to them.

It was an easy decision. The further away from the council this threat was, the better.

Officer Dodds relayed a message to his comrades, ordering them to maintain their posts and be ready for an impending conflict, and requested someone take over from him.

Then, he set out.

51

WATER

The Eruban men paraded through the streets majestically. They wore traditional Eruban clothing. Light, purple lace material, garnished with stripes of deep blue and gold. They moved as though they were a great mass of water, flooding the streets with tidal-wave intensity.

They encountered a few officers on their way, but took care of them with ease, subduing them with their water, the properties of which they freely changed. The officers found themselves encased in what could only be called a bubble. Its surface tension and pressure had been elevated so greatly that the officers couldn't physically move within them. But that wasn't the worst of it. It wasn't just that the Erubans in their current state were more powerful. It was also that the officers were less so.

Commands. They couldn't use their commands. They couldn't even access The Network. They'd been cut off.

Things were looking good for the Erubans. They felt so powerful, now. More powerful than they'd ever felt in their entire lives.

They were halfway to reaching the council by this point, and just as Cy himself predicted, the true obstacles would begin to appear.

The first was but a single man standing in their way.

The Eruban men laughed amongst themselves. It was a familiar face. A face many of them hoped they'd have the chance to crush between their fingers one day.

Cy had given specific instructions to only subdue, and avoid harming where possible, but they would make an exception for him.

After all, next to Blackjack, he was the one responsible for most of the arrests of their brethren.

The officer whose name was known throughout the streets of West District.

Maximus Dodds.

52

Brothers

The storm cloud had moved a good distance from its initial position.

Lido had been keeping an eye on it. He didn't know exactly what was going on, but knew it must have been Cy.

If the cloud was where Cy was, then it was far enough away from them now to not be a threat to their own plan.

Let the Erubans and Irians take each other out whilst they expanded their territory.

Of all the events taking place that day, his plan had been the least thought out. It had only been birthed the day before, and was more of an opportunistic advantage than a created one.

They would head to the south side via the outskirts of the district centre, just along the border of the Shaman Quarters.

It also happened to be in close proximity to the orphanage, which was a particular stopping point for Rado.

He'd envisioned the things he would do with – to – Cherry once he saw her, and even now as the moment approached, he licked his lips. A grotesque image.

'Can we go now?' he asked, impatient.

Lido eyed the cloud for a little while longer. Flashes of what had occurred the day before kept coming to his mind. The way Cy had overpowered them so easily. He was curious to know exactly how Cy planned to overthrow the government. To know just what powers it was he had to fall back on that gave him such confidence in his crusade. To know if Cy was truly that much greater a threat than he himself was. For the proud Orenian, that was an unacceptable reality.

He'd have to address it later. It was time.

'Let's go,' he said. And just as he did, his crew seemed to emerge like a swarm. There were only about 30 of them. But they were a formidable thirty. Each of them had some combat experience, which was more than most in this city could claim.

Oren was a continent whose history told of many wars. With so much conflict, the various nations within naturally developed more and more ways to defend themselves, and that was what led to the combat arts Oren was known for. Of the three skins, Orenians were known as the most skilled fighters.

These guys would be happy to draw blood, if it came to it.

And with the police focussing their attention elsewhere, the question was, just how much blood would paint the streets during their expansion?

There was something in the air that morning. Had Officer Dodds been able to taste bloodlust, whatever it is that would even taste like, then perhaps he would have known the Erubans weren't the only ones threatening the district's security that day.

It truly would be a day to remember.

With their bodies *strengthened*, Lido's crew set out.

The south side was theirs for the taking.

53

HOME

'Thanks again for letting me stay, Sister Mabel,' said Cherry. She sat down at the table in the playroom. The children were watching the Rank Test on a virtual screen. She brought her voice down to a whisper, concerned about alerting them of her conversation.

Sister Mabel had just put down a pot of tea and some biscuits. It had been a while since Cherry had enjoyed them. It was one of her favourite pastimes as a child. Just sitting down with tea and biscuits. Not a care in the world. No troubles. No complications. Just complete serenity.

Oh how times had changed.

Sister Mabel had just sat down and poured herself a cup. 'You know you're always welcome, sweet child. Ever since I spoke to Alex, I feared that I had driven you away somehow. That I had done something to make you feel... unwelcome.'

Cherry shook her head apologetically. 'It was all in my head, Sister. I felt ashamed of myself, and thought then you must equally have been ashamed of me.' Her voice had gone even softer, then. Not out of concern for the children, but from the pain it took to get the words out.

Sister Mabel touched her hand gently. 'No shame, dear. Love and concern. Only ever love and concern.'

Cherry took Sister's hand between her own and raised them to her head.

Her eyes watered slightly. Had she spoken, her voice would have been raspy and concealed.

Sister took to caressing her face. Another sentiment Cherry missed.

'There is more troubling you, dear,' said Mabel. 'A problem shared is a problem halved.'

Cherry laughed then, but it wasn't a joyous one. In fact, it seemed like a trigger for the tears to begin falling. 'No it's not,' she said, looking straight into Sister Mabel's eyes. 'Sharing your problems with people who can't help is just a reminder of how alone you really are.'

Sister Mabel felt like crying now, too. To know that a child she had taken care of, raised as her own; to know one of those children grew up to feel like they were alone in the world. That was the worst feeling. That was something Mabel couldn't accept, no matter what.

She took both Cherry's hands, then. Tugging on them, guiding her into an embrace.

The third thing Cherry missed. Sitting on Sister's lap and being coddled. Comforted. She wrapped her arms around Mabel and then sobbed into her ears, which was convenient, because Mabel was in the perfect position to whisper to her, 'You're never alone as long as there's people who think about you! What connects our hearts is greater than space can separate, or circumstance can break.' She hugged Cherry tightly. She felt many were owed, and this was all she could do to make up for it. 'Should you ever feel alone, sweet girl, all you have to do is come home. Just come home.'

They rocked back and forth, just as they had done when Cherry was a child. And even though the Rank Test was taking place, and the screen was loud, and the children were filled with excitement, somehow, for Cherry, everything seemed quiet. Peaceful. Serene.

Just like home should be.

54

Seer

'What's happening?' N'Adina asked Q.

'The revolution has begun. They're strong. Very strong. Someone is blocking them right now, but probably not for long.' Q could see everything going on in the district with his special sight. His attention was drawn to the side. 'They're coming. Remember, you can't kill anyone.'

N'Adina shook her head. Not at the reminder of her not killing anyone. She was already aware of that. It was Q's ability at foresight. 'Honestly,' she said. 'My specialty is Soul Sense, but even that doesn't come close to the things you're able to perceive.'

Soul Sense

The ability of Shaman to perceive the ethereal world. Because the ethereal world operates under different laws to the physical, Soul Sense had much greater applications than the physical senses.

A specialty for a Shaman was the Soul Art they had the greatest utility with. N'Adina's proficiency with her own Soul Sense gave her a perspective of what was going on in a large portion of the district; the activities of all who were caught within her range of perception. But, even being as gifted as she was, it paled in comparison to the information that made itself known to Q.

'And as I've said many times,' Q responded, 'I'm not so much perceiving things as they are being shown to me.'

'And yet the result is astonishing. The fact you're not even trying makes it all the more annoying,' N'Adina said, and seemed to go into a bit of a sulk afterwards.

She was 21. Only a little younger than Q's 23, but, there seemed to be a large gap in their maturity.

Where Q acted older than he was, she, on many occasions, behaved almost childlike. Which came as a surprise when one discovered how physically strong she was, and the degree to which she excelled in combat.

Q had said their visitors would be there soon, and with the ability of Soul Sense in effect, she knew just how 'soon' that would be.

They were finally in range.

55

A Battle on The Rooftops

Lido and Rado's gang were approaching the border to the Shaman Quarters.

Lido was the first to notice they had company ahead. He knew instantly who they were. They'd made such a big impact on the district the previous day.

One whom they referred to as "Priestess," being the first of her people they'd ever seen in person.

And the tall, handsome man of dark skin and white hair, whose presence seemed somewhat beyond the mundane nature of their own existence.

'We've got company,' Rado said to him.

'You're a bit late noticing, brother,' Lido replied. It didn't matter that Rado noticed before anyone else in their crew. He still noticed after Lido, which tended to be how things went with them. Rado, always following in his older brother's shadow.

'Well I'll leave them to you guys,' he said, trailing off east along with two of their men. That was always the plan. Lido and the majority of his forces would head to the southside via the border of the Shaman Quarters, and Rado would head to the orphanage, just slightly east of their position.

Q watched them trail off, allowing them to gain considerable distance.

'Just the middle one can go,' N'Adina said.

'Understood.'

They must have been about a half kilometre away when the flash came. Everyone saw it. It was sudden and short, just like a flash should be. It emerged in a dazzling blue and ended just as quickly.

Lido's gang weren't sure what happened. It was just some obscure event.

But on Rado's side, he heard the limp bodies of his two men drop on the rooftops.

Q's attack hit with laser precision. Was it a laser?

Rado's men fell instantly.

He was confused. He saw the flash of blue light. He saw two streaks soar off into the distance in an instant. He'd never seen anything like that before. What was it?

He looked back. Was his coming?

If it was, he needed to get as far away as he could.

His course didn't change, just his speed. And whether by fate or providence, his didn't come. He was let go.

Lido saw his men fall and his brother escape. He had a much clearer view of what happened from his position.

There was indeed a flash of blue light, and a bright, thin blue line had pierced across the rooftops. That was what had struck his two subordinates, and just like Lido, he'd never seen something like it before.

What type of function was that? He wondered.

He noticed something else.

Circling overhead at Q and N'Adina's position was a crow.

He stopped his crew a few houses away from Q and N'Adina's position. Given what he'd just witnessed, he was well within range of whatever action Q had performed, should he decide to do it again.

There was a standoff. A fair distance bridged the gap between them, and the wind was quite strong. Projecting his voice over to them may have been a waste of sen.

But then he heard a voice, speaking straight into his ear, clear as day.

'You were wise to stop,' Q said, projecting his own voice over to Lido.

'Might I presume that by speaking to me from afar, you can hear me just as well?' Lido asked.

'Correct.'

'Then let's not waste any time. I don't know who you are, and quite frankly I don't care. What I do know is you're either not from here or you're new to the district. Which makes you far too green to be meddling in our affairs. Step aside.'

Standing behind him, Lido's men were confused. They hadn't heard Q's voice, so it seemed to them that Lido was talking to the air.

'That's a shame,' Q said. 'I was told you were the smart brother. But I guess when the bar is so low, being the more intelligent of two fools doesn't escape you from being foolish.'

Lido's brows tensed. Insulting his intelligence in any capacity was something he wouldn't entertain. And very much something that clouded his judgement.

'Are you done yet?' N'Adina asked Q, growing ever impatient.

He raised a finger to her. *One moment*. He would try to wean them off any further action one last time.

'You should turn back now. There's no possibility of you achieving what you intended. Save yourself the pain.'

Lido immediately brought out his own blade. His men, not knowing exactly what was going on, followed suit.

'You've critically misunderstood us,' Lido said. 'We're Orenians. Our nation is a history of blood and warfare. There is no turning back. There's no backing down. There's only ever conflict.'

It was something of a war chant, because as soon as he finished, they charged.

And that thing he'd said about Oren having a history of blood and warfare?

The meta of a land is heavily determined by the nature of those who inhabit it. Oren is a continent where great battles are regularly fought. Hence, the meta of Oren is such that Orenians are born with a natural ability for learning combat arts. They were fighters, primarily, and utilised sen in such a way as to increase their combat prowess. So Orenians were naturally good at physical enhancement. The type that increased their agility and overall lethality of their attacks.

They moved swiftly across the rooftops, closing the gap between themselves, Q, and N'Adina in just a few short moments.

Q lifted himself off the roof. He didn't care much for fighting, and was happy to let N'Adina have her fun. She was itching for a fight.

Customary to Orenian battle tactics, the leader wouldn't be the first to engage. Foot soldiers tested the waters of the enemy initially.

Two of them engaged in combat with N'Adina, now. They leapt off the roof of the last building.

She gauged their approach, analysing exactly where they would land and how to counterattack once they did, but things seemed to go illogical from that point.

They should have had about another second in the air, yet, they were already upon her, blades in hand.

They performed a pincer attack.

One went high from the right, whilst the other went low from the left. And N'Adina was unarmed. It wasn't like she could block their blades with her bare hands.

A foolish thought. As if blocking steel with flash was anywhere beyond the realms of what was considered normal in this world.

But even with that, she didn't block, but parried.

She'd assessed the timing of their swings perfectly, despite the previous confusion regarding their air time. Though she had some idea of what they'd done to achieve that.

The swing that came for her head was pushed upwards and allowed to follow through, leaving the assailant in a sort of disarray.

The blade coming from the left? N'Adina crouched into the air, rolled over a little, and then pushed it into the ground. Then, using it to leverage herself, kicked the person to her right hard in the stomach, which sent him a good few paces backwards. And before the second guy could respond, she leapt up at him and dealt a decisive blow to the head. He fell first, knocked completely unconscious.

The first guy keeled over, holding his stomach and spilling out the contents of his stomach.

Things carried on moving quickly. She found herself surrounded by the rest of them. Their movement through the air to get to her had been odd. Somewhat distorted. Like some of the distance travelled was missing?

It wasn't teleportation, though. She'd witnessed teleportation first-hand, and this wasn't it.

She'd only ever heard of *skipping* before, but never actually witnessed it. But she was sure, this was what was going on.

And even though it was her first time witnessing it, she had no trouble handling their strange movements.

Try as they may, not a single one of them landed a hit, and as she manoeuvred between them, heavy footed, yet still somehow with grace, she slowly polished them off one by one, dealing hard and decisive blows whenever an opportunity presented itself.

It was strange to them, seeing a woman so physically overwhelming.

Everything about N'Adina was strange to them. The markings on her body, for instance. Why did she look so much like the Priestess from Lore? Almost as though the character was based on her.

Or someone like her.

A few more punches and kicks and N'Adina had taken them all down. Only Lido remained.

He observed her. The entire exchange lasted no longer than a minute.

She'd taken out over 20 of his men, and seemed none the worse for wear as a result.

And the fact she dealt with their *skipping* so easily.

'You've fought Orenian's before?' he asked.

'Never,' she said. 'I'm just really good at fighting.'

'It would appear so. I'm not opposed to strong women. In fact I admire it. You're probably the most physically developed woman I've ever seen. Shame you're Eruban, though. I suppose strength was your immediate fallback given how ugly your ski-'

Another blue flash.

Lido was struck down by Q before he could finish his sentence.

'I wanted to play with him for a while,' N'Adina said to Q as he descended.

'Apologies,' he said.

'It's fine. I get why you did it.' N'Adina looked around at the unconscious bodies. 'What now?'

Q looked east. 'I'm going to watch the main event. You?'

N'Adina looked up to the crow. 'I guess I'll go see her.'

56

DOG EAT DOG WORLD

Rado didn't look back once.

His frantic escape had been successful - even if you consider nobody was after him.

He never once stopped to consider why he'd been let go. Why hadn't Q shot him down with his men? Why he'd made it that far?

You had the 'act first, think later' type.

Rado was the 'act first, think never' type.

Today would be one of the days where the consequences of such behaviour would be dire.

He was coming up close to the estate. Close enough to see the orphanage. But his advancement was halted when he saw Big Dog suddenly appear. He was with someone.

Lilith, whom Rado was certain he'd never met before, because he'd never let someone who looked like that escape his gaze.

He stopped just one building before Big Dog.

'I should have known,' he said.

'You could have known if you took the time to think once in a while,' Big Dog replied.

'Today's not the day, you mutt.'

'Agreed. I've actually got somewhere I need to be. So let's make this quick.'

Rado laughed. It was menacing and maniacal. 'I've wanted to take you down for a long time now,' he yelled, leaping off the rooftop as he did.

This was one of those 'think before you leap' moments.

Whatever had gone through Rado's head that led him to believe he could in any way pose a threat to Big Dog, it was a foolishness that wouldn't go unpunished.

Rado had *strengthened* himself. As much as he could with his current sen ability.

But, even if you were to put sen and mana on the same scale; place Big Dog and Rado in the same development period, Big Dog was still a greater talent than Rado.

So in this situation where it was easier for a Shaman to strengthen their body than it was for a Sentien, and where Big Dog was several development stages ahead of Rado, the encounter they had together was brief.

Rado was halfway between the two rooftops. He must have moved another few centimetres in the time it took Big Dog to leap to his position mid-air, tackle his throat with a lariat, and drag him back down.

He would have heard some of his bones snap if not for the shock of what had just occurred.

His windpipe was crushed. He grasped at it desperately, trying to catch his breath. In his panic, he lost focus of his sen and lost his *strengthening*. And that just made the pain all the more unbearable.

He would die soon.

And Big Dog, in a typical situation, would let him.

'You know what your problem is, Rado?' Big Dog asked.

There was a pause. He'd been looking out into the horizon before he looked down at Rado and, 'Oh, sorry. Can't talk, can you? Anyway, your problem is you don't know where you stand. Trying to make a name for yourself in the big bad world, when in reality, you're not performing on that level. You're a small fish in a big pond at best. Trying desperately to make it out and fight amongst the beasts. But it's a dog eat dog world out of the pond, son. And I'm a big dog out here. No one's eating me!'

There was no response from Rado. Just the continuous choking sound he made, which grew quieter and quieter as time went on.

If he'd heard Big Dog's little narrative, it probably hadn't stuck. It wouldn't even matter. Not with death knocking at the door, ever violently and loudly - inversely proportional to his wheezing.

Lilith appeared on the rooftop with them. 'I reckon that's lesson learnt. Don't you?'

'Sure,' Big Dog said. 'I think he gets the point.'

Soon after he said this, Rado's wheezing stopped.

His throat, which had collapsed, was back to normal.

His lungs rose and fell as he drew breath. And he gasped. He gasped for air once it became available to him again.

What had happened? He wondered.

Big Dog didn't have the ability to heal others. So, it must have been Lilith?

Except, Rado had been healed in the past, and healing was a process. You could feel it happening. The way the body restitched its fabric to close wounds. The alleviation of pain in such a short period of time.

But this... this wasn't a process. It was instantaneous. He was on death's door. Throat crushed. Unable to breathe.

And then, a mere moment later, he wasn't. And everything came rushing back suddenly. The full functionality of his body.

This wasn't healing. It was something else entirely.

Big Dog produced an Anima.

'He's going to stay here with you. If you try to leave, he'll mow you down, and nobody will be here to save you.'

And just like that, Big Dog and Lilith were gone. A great big hound left in their stead.

57

THE SILVER OFFICER

The Erubans halted their advance momentarily.

The surrounding area was enveloped with rain, and Officer Dodds was right in its area of effect.

He'd noticed as soon as it came, he'd been cut off from The Network. The *blocking* that was occurring, it had been enchanted into the rain dismantling the meta of The Network wherever it fell. As long as officers were in it, they lost their advantage.

Yet, Officer Dodds stood there with as large a presence as always. The rain poured around him, but not over him, just as when one used the *Umbrella* command. 'So, this is what it's come to, eh, Cy?' he said. There was a tinge of disappointment in his voice. Not that it meant anything. He and Cy had no such relationship that would make any form of sentiment have value between them. 'Who would have thought,' he continued, 'that you'd been preparing something so grandiose. I must say, I'm impressed.'

'I don't know if that's a genuine compliment or a backhanded one,' Cy replied. 'Are you impressed because you thought too little of us to be capable of such a thing?'

'I'm impressed because it's impressive,' said Dodds.

A moment of silence, save the pitter patter of the rain.

Some of the Erubans were getting restless. Cy had told them to halt for a moment, but several moments had passed, and they couldn't stand still. Not whilst one of their prime enemies stood before them.

'This rain is quite something,' said Dodds. 'Blocking out The Network the way it does. Very well thought out. Most of the officers on these streets couldn't do much without access to their commands. That's the trouble with these coders. We grow to become so reliant on them, we forget about our own innate abilities.'

'You don't seem to be suffering from that affliction,' Cy said, highlighting the fact that Dodds kept the rain from falling on him. 'But you're still only a Silver Officer. What do you think you can achieve against us?'

More disappointment. Dodds shook his head this time. He didn't want there to be any confusion about how he was feeling.

'15 years,' he said.

'What?'

He repeated. '15 years. I've been a Silver Officer for 15 years. That's three development stages. Not to mention the amount of time I had to learn and refine my abilities.'

'Your point?' Cy asked, even though he was following Dodds's train of thought, and could have come to the conclusion on his own.

'It's not like people suddenly improve during the Rank Test. Whatever rank they get, they achieve because they had that ability going into the test. Rank is just a confirmation of one's capabilities. I haven't taken the test in 15 years, Cy. So naturally, my official rank hasn't changed. But is it really a safe assumption to think my ability is the same as it was? Do you really think, because you've disabled my connection to The Network, that I can't use commands without it?'

For the first time since their march began, Cy got a bad feeling in the pit of his stomach. It was something he knew all along, really. Even before reaching Blackjack, there was a viable threat that patrolled the streets. And now, standing in the way of their advancement was that threat, determined and motivated to stop them.

'I can't let you progress,' Dodds continued. 'You see, my two apprentices are taking the test today. They've worked hard for the opportunity to show this city what they're capable of. I won't let you interfere.'

That was it. The restless Erubans had had enough. Cy's orders be damned. They were going to take Dodds out.

There were six of them. Big, strong, burley men. They controlled the water to usher them forward as if they surfed on waves. Passing Cy and ignoring anything he said, they went straight for Dodds.

They really should have listened. After all, it wasn't Dodds Cy was trying to protect, but them.

Dodds found himself about to be the target of a large crashing wave. And it wouldn't have hit him like water on a shoreline. No, this water had been empowered. It would tear his body apart in the most excruciating of ways.

But, however strong it was, water was still water.

Dodds may not have had access to The Network, but there were fundamental differences between the types of coders officers had. Bronze Officers only ever operated within the city, because just like the general public, their coders relied on a connection to The Network.

But Silver Officers, the programs they used could be enchanted into the coders themselves. They didn't necessarily need The Network.

Dodds didn't need The Network.

The disadvantage of using commands over functions was that they were coded to behave a certain way.

Shot, for instance, could be used for close to mid-range combat.

Shock was programmed for utilisation at close range.

But, it was possible to combine the meta of commands to create compound commands.

So, before the 6 Erubans had the chance to close in on him, he created a compound command.

Shot:Shock:Kaleidoscope

This created a barrage of electrified projectiles that struck the Erubans and their large wave in multiple places. The effect of the *Shock* command was enhanced by the water. It coursed through all six of their bodies, imbued with enough sen to completely tear through the *strengthening* they'd enhanced themselves with. The six Erubans fell to the ground with a crash, and their wave of water dispersed.

The rain continued falling

There was a pause. Dodds didn't follow up with another attack. Not yet. He'd try to get through to Cy peacefully, just one more time. Using his *Umbrella*, he compounded *Explosion* onto it, which caused it to propagate massively, pushing away all the rain in the area, giving them, for just a few moments, a dry atmosphere. And with the *blocking*-enchanted rain gone, Dodds attempted telepathic communication with Cy.

Curious to know what Dodds had to say next, he let him in.

The two met in Cy's inner mind. Dodds didn't know what he'd expect to see there, but what he did see surprised him. It was so straightforward. So simple. The same words repeated over and over.

'It takes a village.'

Dodds held Cy's gaze for a while, and then finally, 'What are you hoping to achieve from this?'

Cy didn't answer the question. Instead, he asked his own. 'Do you know why you officers are so formidable? It's your coders. For the rest of us, they take the natural 20% sen tax that the world takes and feeds it to the government. But for you officers, that tax is forgoed. Whenever you use government authorised programs, you execute them with a greater output than the rest of us do. Bronze, 5%. Silver, 10%. Gold, 15%. Platinum, 20%. Those coders make your commands more powerful, that's what enables you to overwhelm the rest of us more easily.'

Dodds didn't even flinch at this revelation. 'You know that, yet you challenge the government you claim is so formidable?'

Now Cy laughed. 'Well yes. You're not the only ones who can overcome world tax. It's a difficult thing to achieve, although it's easier for me because of my affinity. Not that it matters. I'd need a catalyst. Bronze grade Rethium at the very least. But there's another way. A better way. To be blessed by someone already blessed by nature itself. To be blessed by an Ojo, like I am. But unlike your silver coder, my blessing isn't restricted to 10%. You don't have the advantage over me.'

'Perhaps not you,' Dodds said, seemingly unmoved by Cy's exclamation of superiority. 'But what about everyone else? They're not as capable as you are.'

'Individually, no. But you're not fighting us individually. You're not even fighting us. You're fighting our ideal. Our hope, our dream. That's something even you can't overcome.'

'Maybe not,' Dodds laughed. 'But it's my job to try.'

Their connection ended. Their perceptions were back in the real, where the rain started falling again.

The entire area was soaked, which spelled bad news for the Erubans, because Dodd's wouldn't give them room to breathe.

He issued the same compound command, but this time, he targeted the entire group.

The single *Shot*, imbued with *Shock*, and passed through *Kaleidoscope* to create multiple projectiles of varying sizes, several of them covering a wide area. Too large for the Erubans to escape from. Too quick for them to even try.

Despite the enhancement they received from their women's prayers, there were still natural laws that would give Dodds the edge. Water was weak to electricity. Even they couldn't escape that.

Thankfully they had Cy.

He used the *Web of Anansi*.

It didn't form webs from the air like it had the previous day with Lido's crew. Its core programming wasn't to generate webs from air, but rather to generate webs from any source material Cy chose to use. And in this case, he chose water.

After all, electricity would flow along water more readily than it would through the air. So Cy took a portion of the water in front of him and detached it from the water connected to his group. The web it created intercepted Dodds' compound command and took on the entirety of its electric current. It dispersed shortly after, but it had served its purpose. It prevented Dodds' attack from passing through.

Thank goodness they had Cy.

'You really do impress me,' Dodds said. 'But I'm afraid that won't save you.'

Another compound command.

Shot:Shock:Kaleidoscope:Cut

Four commands melded together? That was impressive. It took skill just to combine two. Combining three showed a great deal of training had gone into the craft. But four? That wasn't something a silver officer could typically perform.

Cy set up the *Web of Anansi* again, but Dodds anticipated this, which was why he compounded *Cut* into his command.

The webs fell in all but a moment, and Dodds' salvo of electric shots came in on the Erubans swiftly.

It was unfortunate. Cy had hoped he wouldn't have had to delve deeper into his range of abilities. Not until he faced Blackjack. But it seemed Dodds was a more capable opponent than he'd first anticipated. He'd have to put in a bit more effort.

He took on more of the blessing that was strengthening them, which came at a greater cost to himself. Blessings came from prayers. The act of prayer was the act of giving. From giving, came receiving. And from receiving, came the burden of bearing. The blessing received from prayer was a burden one could only bear temporarily, hence his desire to reserve it for the primary threat.

But, in order to take care of Dodds quickly, he'd have to dip into the reserves just a little bit more.

Dodds saw his compound command explode in an array of flashing lights and large bangs. The shots of electricity hadn't reached the Erubans. It seemed as though they'd struck some invisible wall, just before it could get to them. He wasn't sure exactly what had happened, but this time, he was the one to get a bad feeling in the pit of his stomach.

He knew, somehow, that this would be it.

The command Cy had used was called *Shield of Şango*. Named after a legendary figure from Eruban lore.

It solidified the air into a wall of steel, durable enough to resist even the likes of Dodds.

There was a short pause again. Cy and Dodds looked straight into each other's eyes, and somewhere in the distance between them, then, they found understanding.

Both of them were two people doing what needed to be done according to their own ideals. The clash was not a fight between right and wrong. It was simply a conflict of opinion and circumstance. A conflict that ultimately, Cy would win.

One of the benefits of using *Shield of Şango*, was that it could very easily be transitioned into another command. One that struck the enemy with the blunt force of a steel wall. *Hammer of Şango*.

Dodd's could barely see it coming. The solidification of the air caused it to appear distorted; translucent.

The attack hit. It struck him hard. His body was flung up into the air. His clothes tore in several places and his insides were rattled, as though he'd been simultaneously hit from all directions. It was the finisher. He wouldn't stand up after this.

Powerful as he was, on this occasion, he was outmatched.

Cy had caught him mid-air with a torrent of water, easing him back to the ground.

He walked over to Dodds' limp body, putting some distance between them and his group.

Even though he couldn't move, Dodds was still conscious, and as he saw Cy approach him, his vision blurred, coming in and out of focus. All he could do was stare.

One on the ground and the other standing over.

Eyes locked on one another.

The world seemed to stop, then. No words were spoken. Nothing interrupted this short requiem.

It was a curious sight, the two of them staring into the other's eyes. Each would have sworn later on that despite the rain pouring so heavily around them, that at some point in this brief encounter, the other had shed tears.

And whether or not that was true would never be spoken of, because nothing occurred in this moment of silence.

Nothing but the rain.

And as the moment ended, Dodds found himself restrained by water and carried off to the side of the road, away from the path of their march. He also felt some relief. The pain from being struck by that last attack subsided. He was certain he'd suffered a few cracked bones, but they seemed whole, now.

Physically he was fine, and perhaps he could have broken out of this hold and resumed the fight. His duty certainly required him to do so. But he knew this healing was a kindness. Restoring a body's vitality was no easy thing to do. And just as Cy had dipped into the wells of his blessing to defeat Dodds, he dipped in further to restore him to working condition.

Healing of Osanyin.

That was the command he used, unbeknownst to his Eruban brethren.

His initial order still stood. They were not to harm Dodds any further. He was no longer a threat.

And with that, they continued their march. Only one more major threat stood in their way. Except, that wasn't particularly true.

They only knew of one more major threat, and they'd resolved themselves in their minds to do whatever it took to defeat the man who called himself Blackjack.

But what occurred in one's mind was vastly different to the state of reality, and the threat they faced was far greater than they could have imagined.

They would discover, soon enough, just how limited their imaginations were.

58

A Chat

Alex was on high alert. The appearance of this man, whom she could only assume was a high ranking official in the government, had been an unexpected event in her plan. She was supposed to get into the room. Surprise them all. She didn't anticipate one of them coming out to greet her. But who was he? A district mayor? Or something else?

'You're right to be wary of me,' October said. 'After all, you can see the gap that exists between us. But I'm not here to harm you. You can relax.'

'I think I'm fine as I am,' Alex said.

He smiled. 'So be it. I'm going to get comfortable, though, if you don't mind.'

He materialised a chair behind him and sat down, then continued the conversation.

He began by introducing himself. His name was unfamiliar to Alex, as it should be. None of the information she'd collected about this city said anything about him. But it was what he said next that came as a real shock to her.

'I'm one of the founders of MindSpace.'

One of the founders? No, that couldn't be right. Richard Marston Snr was the face of MindSpace, and the one credited with being responsible for New Heart's tech revolution. This man, October, had never been mentioned in any capacity.

'Yes,' he said. 'Richard is the face of the organisation, albeit that's as far as his involvement goes. It's important the rest of us maintain some air of anonymity, you see.'

Alex realised then that he'd been reading her mind. Otherwise, how could he be responding to questions she hadn't yet asked? And thought then that there must be some truth to his words, because only someone formidable – very formidable – could bypass the defences she protected herself with.

October laughed again. 'Do you think you're the only one with an affinity? I'm naturally a telepath. And capable enough to bypass the world's sen tax. My Telepathy is on the same level as your Anti. And remember, you're in a network that's maintained by the minds of everyone in this city. This is my domain.'

This whole reading her mind act had become tiresome all too quickly. If he knew everything she was thinking, she might as well just say it out loud. It was, after all, 'a chat.'

'Why're you here? Why reveal yourself to me now?'

'To congratulate you. You've done well, getting to this point. I myself wasn't sure how you would achieve it, but the closer we got to this day, the more you continued to impress me. Turns out he was right about you.'

'He?'

'Your benefactor. The one who gave Sister Mabel that book to give to you.'

This alarmed Alex more than it should have. But she was disoriented from this sudden turn of events. 'You know about The Book?'

'Of course. We inherited our own before you were even born. Did you think the book only gave information and didn't take?'

Alex had to ponder exactly what he was asking, and then she realised. 'So you've known about my plans all this time?'

October smiled, once again. 'We know everything that goes on in this city.'

Even the revolution? Alex thought.

'Yes, even that.'

And then came the ultimate question. 'Why?'

'Why allow all of this to happen?' he asked rhetorically. 'What exactly do you think we're trying to achieve in this city?'

The answer to that seemed obvious. The way this city had been set up; the dependence its citizens had on coders, and The Network, and the fact the coders took the world's sen tax and fed it to the government. She knew how organisations of power operated. They wanted more and more of it, and that meant gathering as many resources as possible. What greater resource was there than sen?

She answered his question. 'Making yourselves as powerful an organisation as possible.'

He gave a partial nod. 'You're not exactly wrong. That is a goal. But you've missed the mark on how we're achieving it. At first glance, it may indeed seem like we're trying to collect as much sen as possible to fuel whatever plan we have. But in truth, we're offering more than we're taking.

'Whilst it's true a way to obtain power in this world is to gather as many resources as possible, another way, a more time consuming, difficult and arduous, yet, greatly more rewarding way, is to tell stories. And that's what we're doing in this city. We're telling stories.'

And now, after what seemed like an unnecessarily long explanation, Alex was lost.

Telling stories? What did that have to do with obtaining power? What benefit did stories have in gaining a meaningful position in this world?

Oh if only she knew. But she wasn't at that level yet. There was more, so much more she needed to learn before October's words could really resonate. And yet, within that confusion, she was reminded of the night before. Her interaction with Q, and the words he'd spoken, and the things he'd shown her. The way the people in her life had said things this last week that all seemed to correlate to some aspect of reality she did not yet know. It finally dawned on her that there was so much more going on then she'd ever taken the time to consider. And with that realisation came the heart-wrenching uncertainty about her own capability. That perhaps, she wasn't as formidable a person as she thought. She'd kept so much of her life a secret, but she realised now that the keeping of secrets wasn't indigenous to her alone. There was much that she simply didn't know.

'Careful,' October said. 'The way we see ourselves is important. If you allow that seed of doubt to grow, you may find yourself unable to walk the path that's been laid out before you.'

His reading of her mind really had become tiresome. But she resolved herself. 'This benefactor you mentioned. Sister Mabel gave me that book for my tenth birthday, which means he decided I should have it from all the way back then. Who is he, and why me?'

It dawned on her that she was asking a question about the identity of a man who gifted her The Book of Things That Must Only be Known by Those Supposed to Know Them. A man whose identity she'd only just come to be aware of, and who, surely, his name and why he made the decision he had, wasn't something she yet needed to know.

She was half right, because October said, 'His name is Nathanael. And as to why he chose you so early on, that's something you'll just have to ask him yourself.'

59

Nathanael

25 years ago.

Nathanael stood at the entrance to a cave. He was a tall hybrid man of Eruban and Irian descent. His bronze skin seemed like varnished wood amidst the afternoon sun. He wore the same sort of embroidered jacket worn by the other MindSpace top execs. But his was black, the embroidery was white, and his number was 501.

He watched the clouds while he waited. Most of them were stretched across to the horizon, forming a sort of white ocean. One had veered close to the land mass he stood on, and had begun to disperse around it into what one might call a fog. But that was a curious thing, wasn't it? Was fog simply fallen cloud, or were clouds risen fog?

Or perhaps the more important question was, why was there a cave in the sky? One might think they were at the top of a mountain, but that wasn't the case.

This was one of those unnatural phenomena that occurred naturally in this world.

The land mass Nathanael stood on was floating. It had risen from the ground a few days ago, taking with it a group of outlanders who had taken up residence there. They came out of the cave one by one, brandishing weapons in their hands. The looks in their eyes told they were the type to attack first and ask questions later, or not at all.

Nathanael raised up his hands. 'Now there's no need for a fight. I just need what's inside the cave.'

'It's ours,' the outlanders said. And that was all the conversation that would occur in this encounter.

A spear was launched at Nathanael. It stopped just short of his face, and that caused a moment of confusion between the outlanders. They really thought it would hit. But the moment passed, and they charged at Nathanael collectively.

What happened next could only be described as poetic, considering where this almost-battle was taking place. As the outlanders ran towards Nathanael, one by one, they lost their footing, in the literal sense of their feet no longer touched the ground. And so in what was presumably a similar fashion to how the land mass had risen from the ground some days ago, the outlanders, too, found themselves suspended in the air, unable to come back down. They swung and flailed their appendages in futile efforts. They tried to use functions, but they were already within Nathanael's sen zone. With no other tricks up their sleeves, they were completely at his mercy.

He took a casual stroll past them, into the cave.

Within a few minutes he found himself at the place he needed to be; the cause of this unnaturally natural phenomena.

An Arethium deposit.

Arethium was the most valuable natural resource this world produced. A metal which contained all of the world's meta in a passive state, but could activate any of those structures of logic at random.

The exact cause was unknown, but every so often, in places that couldn't be highlighted for cause or reason, the world would manifest Arethium, enchanting it with some sort of meta that caused otherwise unnatural phenomena to occur. This particular Arethium deposit altered the world's gravitational field within a certain area, which was what caused the land mass to rise.

That was one of the more mild effects of an Arethium deposit. Sometimes what occurred could be catastrophic. Sometimes the Arethium seemed borderline sentient, and would input countermeasures to protect itself. One could find themselves instantaneously combusting, or being struck by an inordinate amount of electricity, or reduced to a state of suspended animation, which perhaps wasn't such a bad thing as one was not so much dead as frozen in time. *Sometimes it would enact a force of repulsion, creating a boundary that shouldn't be crossed.*

Regardless of what countermeasures it used to protect itself, it was a difficult resource to obtain. Because it belonged to the world, and so in order to claim it, one had to take it from the world.

It took a powerful mind to overcome the meta of an Arethium deposit.

The outlanders had happened to be there when the Arethium manifested, but they couldn't interact with it. Couldn't even get close to it without suffering some adverse effects to their bodies. They claimed it as theirs, but had no way of really claiming it.

Nathanael stood just before the boundary between the cave's tunnel and its central cavern. He couldn't conceptualise; his mind wasn't wired that way. But he had a particular sense for these sorts of things, so he knew, a single step closer and his body would be sucked in and crushed by an intense gravity.

Inside the cavern, the remnants of a body which fell prey to the Arethium was seen. Clothes torn apart and dried blood scattered on the walls. It seemed, the reversed gravity that caused the land mass to rise was in equal proportion to the intensified gravity of the cavern, and that the effect of the gravity only applied to biological organisms. A more lethal Arethium deposit than at first glance.

But it didn't matter. Nathanael could have stepped into the gravitational field and been perfectly fine, but he didn't need to. He took *hold* of all the Arethium fragments within the cavern and *gathered* them together, collecting and morphing them into one large mass, as though he'd smelted them down into liquid.

The resulting cube was large, large enough for Nathanael to travel in, so he *shrunk* it down to the size of a trinket, and kept it in a state of suspended animation, just a few centimetres away from his body at all times.

He exited the cave and waved goodbye to the outlanders, after which, he disappeared.

They'd been so focussed on him at the time that they didn't realise until later what had happened. The clouds were no longer stretching towards the horizon. The sea of white could no longer be seen. They were back on the ground, reconnected to earth, where humans were meant to be. And they wondered, when and how did that happen? And more importantly, this hybrid man who suddenly appeared and stole their claimed treasure, who was he?

❁

13 years later.

Nathanael appeared in front of the orphanage. Sister Mabel came out to greet him. They sat atop the roof, under the wide starry sky, with Areth's two moons in full glow.

'I take it you're here because she's entered her second development stage.'

Nathanael just smiled. 'How's she doing?'

'Asking as if you don't already know?' Sister Mabel replied, giving Nathanael an unconvinced look.

'There are things we need to experience ourselves, and things we need to hear. That's why stories exist.'

At that moment, Sister Mabel reminisced about the time she'd spent with Nathanael when he was younger. He hadn't been one of the children under her care. No, they'd met under different circumstances than that. But she'd left such an impression on him that when the city was undergoing its revolution, he'd personally requested her relocation.

There are children here who'll need you, he'd said. Even now she didn't imagine the request had been specifically in preparation for Alex, as her turning up at the orphanage's doorstep came as a surprise to him, too. Yet, when she had turned up some 10 years ago, supposedly newly born, he, too, appeared, and asked Sister Mabel to take special care of her. And even now, as much as she knew about Alex, she couldn't say why. Just one of those things she didn't need to know, she supposed.

But as he stood beside her now, around what must have been Alex's tenth birthday, he handed her The Book. 'For her,' he said.

'Is this supposed to replace what you took from her 10 years ago?'

'No,' Nathanael said with a gentle laugh. 'That will be returned a little later.'

'You still don't know what it is, do you?' she asked, this time with the sort of smile an older sister might give to tease a younger brother.

'I haven't exhausted all of my options yet.'

Sister Mabel laughed, and laughed so curiously that Nathanael was drawn to enquire what it was she found so amusing. And she said, 'I just think it's amazing. You, being the person that you are, keeping the company that you do, knowing the secrets that you hold; giving me this book of things that must only be known by those suppose to know them, find yourself unable to solve the mystery of something that at face value is so simple, yet its very existence suggests a story even you are yet to be told. That in this world that you've all but conquered, there still exist things that even you don't need to know.

'And so now I wonder, are you giving me this book to give to her because you want her to know the things it deems her worthy of knowing? Or is it because the truth of what you took from her lies with her and her alone, and at such a time where that truth makes itself known to her, through the power of this book, that information might also make its way to you? You've given this book as though it is a gift, but I wonder, by the end of this particular story, who, between the two of you, will have received the most?'

There had been various shifts in tone through her little monologue, and Nathanael challenged if perhaps, somewhere within those words, he'd sensed an element of distrust.

'Oh I trust you wholeheartedly,' she said. 'But I also know you. I know your ambition. Your dream! I know that above all else, you'll do whatever it takes to tell your story, and perhaps, as tends to be the case with men like you, it doubles as both your greatest strength and weakness. You see, not all stories, and certainly not all of the best ones, have happy endings. My biggest fear in all of this is that this story might be one of them. And even looking at your face now as I say it, that doesn't seem to bother you.'

Nathanael looked at her then with a face that seemed almost entirely similar to the one she'd met all those years ago. A man, full of life, hope, and dreams! Whose dream had remained the same from the first time they'd met until now. But he wasn't the same man he was back then. He had grown. He knew more. He'd reached his 9th stage of development, and the world was a much larger place for him, now. He smiled at her. 'There are no happy endings,' he said. 'Not really. Not for the stories we live. Death is always waiting for us at the end, and death is always a tragedy.'

Whatever seriousness Nathanael had spoken this with, it was disrupted by Sister Mabel laughing, which was an unexpected response to what might be considered Nathanael's philosophy. But the laugh wasn't to mock or jest him. In fact, it wasn't anything he'd said that she'd found amusing, but rather, that she reminisced of the Nathanael she'd met at first, to the one who reappeared 10 years ago, to the one standing before her now, and said to him in a tone that he imagined his mother would have had if he'd grown up knowing her, 'You really did grow to be a fine man.'

He smiled again. 'Don't be so quick to make that decision. Hero's can become villains rather quickly.'

'But would you be happy? If your story ended with you being a villain?'

And this time he laughed. He laughed because he'd heard that question before, addressed to someone else. And he responded with what they had responded back then, asking Mabel:

'When a man achieves his dream, does he die with anything but a smile on his face?'

⁂

Later that evening.

Nathanael appeared in the downstairs dojo of Chen's Kitchen, just as he was closing up shop. It was a few minutes, but Chen eventually came down to greet him.

'It's been a while, old friend,' said Nathanael.

'Too long,' said Mr Chen. 'I'd have thought my cooking would have had you visiting more regularly.'

'I've been kept busy.'

'Ever the traveller,' Chen replied. 'So, what brings you here today?'

'There's this girl I think Katelina can become good friends with. They're... similar.'

Chen looked at Nathanael curiously. He'd become acquainted with the ridiculousness of his antics over the years, but knew him well enough to know that every decision and action he made had purpose. *To tell his story.* The question on his lips now was, 'What story do you hope to create from this?'

'Honestly, I'm not sure I'm the one telling it. There's something more going on here.'

'A new contender? As if the world doesn't have enough storytellers.' Chen laughed, this time somewhat mockingly at Nathanael's predicament. 'It's hard to believe you of all people could find yourself disillusioned.'

'Well I wouldn't go that far,' Nathanael defended. 'Whatever's going on, I'll find out eventually.'

'And what happens when you do?'

Nathanael shrugged the question. 'Same thing that always happens. I tell a story better than theirs.'

Chen smiled and shook his head, as if there were ever any other answer to his question. He came back from the tangent of conversation and asked Nathanael, 'So, where can I find this girl?'

Even later that evening.

In the heart of Eruba was the Spirit Forest. In the heart of the forest was the Priestess Clan. And somewhere within their territory was Big Dog, and a young N'Adina. At 9 years old, she was preparing herself with vigorous training for her second development stage.

At this young and feisty age, she didn't quite understand the concept of taking things easy. So every swing had her full weight behind it. The blows she missed sent her body into an imbalanced frenzy. The ones that landed were blocked or parried in some form. But despite not landing a single solid hit, she pursued Big Dog like a cat with swift paws, trying to take down a... well, big dog. The difference in strength was just too great to overcome.

The spar ended with Big Dog blocking one of her strikes and throwing her into a nearby tree, which hurt the tree more than it did her.

Nathanael appeared just at that very moment, and despite her age, she'd already developed some proficiency with Soul Sense, and took to attacking him the moment she noticed his presence.

She came flying at him with a kick, her body strengthened by the ant she'd Soul Synced with.

It wasn't something inexperienced fighters tended to think about, but there was a balance between one's mind and one's body when it came to interacting with the physical world. The mental preparation of walking a level path was different to the preparation of climbing stairs. One needed to anticipate the point of contact in their mind in order for the body to respond to the physical stimuli. And that translated across all actions the body performed.

So when N'Adina found herself passing straight through Nathanael without making any contact, it disoriented her, causing her body to momentarily panic mid-air. She managed to recover and secure a safe landing, followed by a long moment of disbelief at what had just occurred.

Being amongst a community of Shaman her whole life, with very little interaction with Sentiens, someone making their body intangible was a foreign concept to her. It simply wasn't something Shaman could do - *or was it?* - . This new revelation of reality caused a thrill in her heart, a thrill that told her she wanted to experience it again.

Another flying kick was attempted, but this time she was caught by Big Dog, who hung her upside down from her leg. 'N'Adina, this is a friend of mine. Be nice.'

She rustled and tousled, shouting back at him, 'Any friend of yours should be able to fight. Let go of me and I'll test him out.'

'Don't bother,' Big Dog replied. 'Whether now, or in 50 years, you won't be able to beat him.'

'How dare you!' she retorted. 'I'm the daughter of the High Priestess. Do you know how strong I'll get?'

'I do,' he said. 'But you still won't beat him.'

He let go of her leg and she stuck another perfect landing.

'Run along now. We'll continue this another time.'

She created a little bit of distance between them, turned around, pulled down one of her eyelids and stuck out her tongue, before turning back and running away, expecting Big Dog to chase after her.

He didn't.

'So that's her third child,' Nathanael said.

'Third and last,' Big Dog said. The two of them then bumped fists. 'Good to see you, brother.'

They weren't related, but shared a bond as though they were. And it was that bond, accompanied with Big Dog's instincts, which let him know this wasn't a social visit. 'So, what you got for me?'

'Well,' said Nathanael, 'I was hoping you might be inclined to do a bit more babysitting.'

Big Dog gave him a look.

⁂

2 years before the present.

'At 20?' October said in disbelief. 'That's even younger than Lilith was.'

'But not our super genius, could-conceptualise-at-the-age-of-12 Evaán,' said Nathanael, who had just informed his colleagues of

Alex's learning to conceptualise mere days after entering her fourth development stage.

'So now what?' asked Lilith. 'There are things she'll be able to see now. Not to mention how much more will become available to her through The Book.'

Evaán and Nathanael shared a look. Nathanael was smiling. It was a cross between a proud mentor and an "I know something you don't" sort of smugness. But that was how these things went. Although the four of them were colleagues, and they all shared certain amounts of knowledge through The Book, there were things kept only between Evaán and Nathanael. And that look, that smile, that was Natahanael telling Evaán it was okay to share the plan.

'Have her recruited at MindSpace,' Evaán said.

October followed his train of thought quite quickly. 'Has that been the idea the whole time? To have her as a mayor candidate? Isn't she a bit too young?'

'She is,' Nathanael chimed in. 'We have another person in mind for the mayoral candidate. Her story is a bit different. She's like us, you see. Keen for adventure. Desiring to discover new truths. She has an unparalleled thirst for knowledge, and there's only so much she can gain while in this city. Let's introduce her to the thing she has to overcome. Let's see if we raise a hero, or a villain.'

Nathanael was so used to the look they were now giving him that he didn't even notice it anymore. The look of obscure curiosity as to what his intentions were. He was so abstract in his way of thinking that nobody could predict what the intended outcome of his plots would be. The only person with whom he shared his thoughts in great detail was Evaán. And between the two of them were greater secrets than any other one might find in this city.

⁂

1 year before the present.

Nathanael appeared in front of Lilith and October. Evaán wasn't present, but standing beside Nathanael was N'Adina.

'Oh my,' Lilith said. 'You are your mother's daughter. It's like 30 years ago.'

'I can see a bit of your father in you, too,' said October.

'I take more after him. Especially when it comes to fighting,' N'Adina responded, remembering the stories her mother told her about the Irians she'd met on her own pilgrimage.

'I do hope you'll find your stay here worthwhile,' said Lilith. 'I understand a Shaman's pilgrimage around the world is about enlightening their souls. I doubt you'll find much spiritual enlightenment in this city, but, I believe you'll find our arrangement mutually beneficial.'

The monotonous expression on N'Adina's face often caused people to misunderstand her mood, or the intent behind her words, but she said, 'My mother speaks highly of you, so I've no doubt this will be a good start to my journey,' which seemed generous enough in sentiment. But she followed it rather swiftly with, 'If not, it's him who'll pay the price of such a deception,' which she'd directed to Nathanael, who laughed it off whilst all the while knowing she was being completely serious.

He rolled his laugh into a very confident exclamation of, 'In a few hours, you'll see exactly what it is this city has to offer.'

And when a few hours came, of course, she witnessed the spectacle that was Reena's performance in the Rank Test, and it reminded her of the stories her mother told. Stories of this specific group of Irians she'd met on her pilgrimage, and how amongst them, a man, only half Irian himself, she described as the most magnificent person she'd ever met. Having seen the spectacle Reena had put on, she thought of Nathanael's soft face and happy-go-lucky demeanour, and wondered how it was that such a man could receive such high praise. But she wasn't yet at a point in her own story where she could fathom the true depths of his existence. There were things she still needed to experience before she got to that stage, and some of those things were in this city.

It was that same day, after all the deliberations about rank had been made, that Nathanael told them of his latest plan.

'It's time,' he said. And his colleagues looked at him. They knew what he was talking about. There were two things Nathanael had been putting off doing in his life, and one of them was returning to a place he had previously not been permitted to enter. He'd been told, back then, "You're not at this part of the story yet," with no indication of when this part of the story would come. And so he left. But now, supposedly, it was time for him to return; to see if finally that chapter of his story was ready to be lived. The chapter he'd call, "Andromeda."

Nathanael didn't return to New Heart for 2 months, but when he did, he brought with him yet another young companion.

His name was Q.

60

THE NEXT WAVE

The first wave of the Rank Test ended. Only half the participants remained on the battlefield, and amongst them were Max and Bolu, back to back. With their *Radars* in use, they had a perception of everything going on around them, including active functions and commands. They sensed a telekinetic force about to close in on them, and released a *Pulse* to block it out. Then, identifying who had used the function, *Shot* them down immediately after.

Their *Radars* picked up more projectiles headed their way. They *Strengthened* their bodies, and the flying rubble crumbled against their solid frames. Again, they spotted their attackers, and together, formed a compound command of *Shot* and *Shock*, sending a bolt of electricity to a group of enemies which hit them one by one like a chain reaction.

'You getting tired?' Bolu asked.

'No! You?'

'Yepp. Think I'm approaching my limit.'

'Oh,' said Max, surprised and relieved. 'Well in that case, I'm about done, too.'

'I figured.'

It was at this point Max realised just how heavily he and Bolu were breathing. It was incredible how perfectly The Arena copied the meta of the real world. These virtual bodies functioned exactly as their real bodies would. The toll of battle, the labour sen placed on the mind, it didn't just stop there. The mind, body and soul were inextricably linked. The state of one affected the others in some form. So the continuous use of commands, the overall perception of the battlefield, the psychological stress of being in a state of war, that took its toll on their bodies, too.

'One last hurrah?' Max asked.

Bolu smiled at his fellow apprentice, his brother in arms, his best friend. 'Let's go all out.'

They synchronised their minds. Individually they could bi-compound commands, but when their minds were linked, they could bear the stress of one more.

Targeting a horde of enemies ahead of them, they compounded *Shot:Shock:Explosion*, sending out a projectile of electricity into the horde, which detonated in a flash of light and roar of thunder. They put everything they had into that command, and perhaps they'd previously been underestimating themselves, or maybe it was just the increased output offered by their coders, but the explosion had been much larger than they'd anticipated. The number of enemies they'd felled was greater than initially calculated. In fact, for a short-lived moment, that final stand of theirs had taken the attention of most on that battlefield. It was a splendid display of power.

But that was it for them. Their sen had been run down, their minds crashed, and that meant elimination. They were proud of themselves. Max in particular couldn't wait to share this moment with his father later, knowing full well he probably hadn't been watching because of his duties.

But having had no perception of what was going on in the real whilst he'd been fighting, he would later find out that his dad had been watching.

After being defeated by Cy, Dodds allowed himself an indulgence. He'd done what he could. He'd given himself in service to his city and only survived due to the mercy of his opponent. So Dodds, despite having been healed by Cy, remained where he lay, and watched his two apprentices impress the whole city with their performance.

And this must have been one of those situations where the state of mind had an affect on the body and soul, because after seeing their final command, and despite all of his senses being submerged in The Network, out in the real, under the clear sky, with the sun's beaming rays on his face, Officer Dodds was smiling.

61

Platform

Nathanael Grey. Finally, a name, but not a face to put to it. And even with that, Alex wasn't any closer to understanding what was really going on.

We know everything that goes on in this city, October had just said that, which raised the ultimate question of why? Why allow all of these events to get this far?

But he'd already answered that. *We're telling stories.*

'Do you know why people like myself have to be careful with the knowledge we give out?' he asked.

'Because it has a direct effect on the world's meta,' Alex replied.

'Do you know how much?'

She didn't.

The space around them suddenly changed. She found herself standing on top of a platform, above a lake. Behind her were three other platforms, decreasing in dimensional size between each one.

And ahead of her, following the same trend, but increasing in size, were 6 more platforms, increasing to sizes gargantuan compared to where she stood.

October stood atop the 8th platform, which was orders of magnitude greater than her own.

'Observe,' he said.

She noticed a boulder materialise to the left of her, and watched it fall into the lake.

There was a splash, and a ripple effect, the waves of which extended far, but dissipated within observable distance. She noticed then that it wasn't a lake at all. There was no end to it. It was an ocean, extending beyond the horizon.

Alex saw another boulder materialise, but this one was all the way at October's platform, and just as his platform was orders of magnitude greater than hers, so was the boulder. And when it dropped, the splash was not so much a splash, but a wave, one large enough to encompass Alex's platform. The surge of water caused by the boulder was enormous, but that in itself was only the beginning. When the wave subsided, the ripples it caused. They seemed to stretch endlessly, deep into the horizon beyond her view. And they were violent, too. She felt her platform rumbling. It wasn't like the previous boulder which had more of a visual effect than anything else. This one seemed to be attempting to cause the collapse of the very world they were in.

It had surprised her at first. The sheer impact of it. But, having calmed down, she understood what October was trying to convey. The platforms represented where they stood in the world. How much weight their existence had on its meta. The boulders? They were actions. Whether physical or mental, they affected the world in some way. The difference between Alex and October was the difference between ripples and waves.

'You want to know why we've not interfered with anyone's plans? It's because we bear such influence on the world, that whatever result came from our interference would be considered unnatural. The meta of a story that didn't occur naturally is of little use to us. It's not just in your district. All the districts have had their major events in the last few years. And at the end of each one, we revealed ourselves to the heroes that emerged. But we never interfered with what was taking place.'

'But that can't be true,' Alex said. 'My benefactor, Nathanael, he's taken an active role in my story. The Book he gave me has been the backbone of everything I've done. How much more involved could he have gotten than that?'

October began to nod at her very understandingly. 'You are correct. He has inserted his influence in various ways, but he's a bit of a special case. The world sees him differently than it does the rest of us. Always has.'

It seemed there was more he wanted to say, but he diverted. 'Well, you've done it. You've emerged the hero of your own story, and your wish will be granted. However, there's one more thing we'd like you to do.'

'What's that?'

'If you're going to travel the world, it's not enough to just be intelligent. There are dangers out there that you can't even imagine. If we're going to let you go, we need to know you can defend yourself.'

'I'd say I'm pretty capable.'

'No doubt about that,' October said almost mockingly. You won't find many people your age who match up to you. But the people who stand in your way won't be your age. You are special, that's for sure. But there are other special people in the world. And many of them won't hesitate to kill you.'

Even if Alex understood the words coming out of his mouth, there was no way for her to know the gravity with which he spoke them. That was the trouble with having grown up in a secluded city. She'd never known true danger. Her life had never been at risk. She didn't truly know how horrible people could be.

'So what?' she said, 'We're going to fight for real, now?'

October laughed at her. 'No, no there's nothing to be gained from that. I'm a bit too far out of your reach at this present moment in time. No. We'd like you to try and defeat Blackjack.'

62

Kitchen to the Rescue

The Eruban women observed the storm cloud advancing from the centre of the district.

Mara herself had a visual on what was going on as she shared a mind link with Cy. She'd seen the success he'd had over Officer Dodds, and was grateful that the casualties on their side were minimal.

But, a feeling of dread overcame her.

Dodds was always considered a serious threat, so their triumph over him was worth celebrating, but it also meant a step up in threat level. The next person in the district that would get in their way was the most dangerous person in the district to get in their way.

There was a reason Blackjack was the most feared man on the streets. Whatever reason there may have been to anyone's notoriety in any part of the world, one universal language that everyone understood was fear. And the reason people feared Blackjack wasn't because of how many of them he'd arrested over the years. Nor the fact he had the full backing of the government. In fact, it was more accurate to say he was the one the government relied on.

Blackjack was feared for the simple reason that he was powerful. Incredibly, overwhelmingly powerful.

In all the years he'd been active in the district, nobody had ever seen him contested with.

Albeit, none of the people that could offer him a challenge had ever tried.

Inside the restaurant, Chen had been busy making lunch for the Eruban children, and a few others that decided to take refuge there. He had the Rank Test being played on a V-Cube, which kept most of them entertained, somewhat oblivious to what was going on outside.

Chen got an alert to his private network.

Whatever his involvement was in the events taking place that day, it was time to enact them.

Kitchen had been busy preparing more food when Mr Chen put a hand to her shoulder.

She was startled, and seemed to freeze momentarily. That's how it would have appeared to the outside observer.

The truth of the situation was she and Mr Chen were having an internal dialogue.

The outside observer would have seen at some point a sudden look of shock in her eyes, or perhaps realisation.

A moment later they'd see her dart out of the restaurant.

The Eruban women, continuing their prayers in their tranquil vigil would see her head off in the direction of the storm cloud.

She was unnaturally fast, even by the standards of someone *strengthening* their body. Except, Kitchen wasn't using sen. This was just the natural strength she was born with. And there was much more of that to come.

A great battle awaited her.

63

Blackjack

The Erubans edged closer to the council, and closer to their final obstacle.

Blackjack was there, waiting. West District's most accomplished officer. Being able to warp his way to any location meant even the hint of trouble could be quelled sooner than it could start. And yet, so many troublesome events went unchecked. So many plans and schemes that perhaps should never have seen the light of day managed to manifest to near completion. And there was a reason behind it all.

It was no accident that the Erubans had made it this far. It was known by those who knew everything in this city that Blackjack was the only person who posed a real threat. It was known that not even Dodds, as potent and capable as he was, would be a match for this version of Cy. And so Dodds didn't have a specific role to play in this story. Whatever he did wouldn't really change the outcome.

But Blackjack - yes, he was the goal. The antagonist at the end of an arduous journey. Blackjack was the reason the Erubans needed to utilise prayer to an effective degree. Without the blessings it offered, not even Cy stood a chance.

As they approached the council, there Blackjack stood, a horde of officers behind him. He was as absent-faced as ever. No emotion. His shaded glasses masked whatever message might be conveyed through his eyes. It was menacing, the way his demeanour daunted on you like a pair of inconspicuous eyes. One felt like they were being watched, but couldn't discern where the gaze was coming from. Blackjack's presence was like an oxymoron. Someone who was there without really being there.

Cy felt his heart begin to race. This was it. The final stage. He just needed to win this battle and then... and then what? That was a problem he'd have to solve later. Without wasting any time, he took on his people's blessing.

And whatever you'd typically think would happen next in this sort of story - a great battle perhaps, which levelled the surrounding landscape - that wasn't the story being told here. Because Blackjack wasn't the final boss at the end of Cy's story of revolution. No, there was something else in store for him, and Blackjack was reserved for another.

Two others, actually. And they arrived right on cue.

Alex's sudden appearance was subtle. One moment she wasn't there, and another moment she was. Some form of teleportation, Cy discerned, when she appeared right in front of him.

She looked back and told him, 'Sorry, but Blackjack is my fight. Things aren't quite going the way we planned.'

He wanted to ask what she was talking about, but he wouldn't get the time, because the first question from his lips was the last he'd be able to ask. 'You think you can beat him on your own?'

'I don't have to.'

And just like that, Kitchen arrived in a flashy display as she landed brutally just ahead of them. Her flames erupted when she hit the ground, scorching the earth beneath her and letting out a vicious explosion of sound. Kitchen's flames were special. It wasn't known why, or how exactly, but they burnt with an intensity that regular fire didn't. Almost as if there was life to them. She'd used them to propel herself like a rocket, rushing here so fast that she almost got away from herself. That was the reason for the abrupt landing.

But she was here, and so was Alex, and they had one task. Defeat Blackjack.

Cy wanted to say something, but when Kitchen had looked back, and he'd seen that the fire in her eyes burned with an intensity matched only by Alex's conviction, he took heed of Alex's words. This wasn't his fight, but apparently there was something else in store for him. He let go of his people's blessing; even stopping the rain. And with that, the stage was set.

'I don't know exactly what's going on,' Kitchen thought to Alex, *'but my dad said you need help kicking this guy's ass!'*

'In those exact words?'

'He was probably more polite about it.'

Both Kitchen and Alex were alerted by Blackjack's sudden increase in malice. Kitchen had an animal-like instinct. The type that let them know danger was approaching. And Alex, well, she'd been conceptualising this whole time and could see the change in Blackjack's meta. He was preparing himself.

Blackjack himself was repeating the words that were said to him the night before. He wasn't at all surprised by what had manifested before him. He'd been warned about today, that certain events would be taking place. And he'd been told, "Two girls will confront you tomorrow. Don't underestimate them."

And here they were. Chen's daughter, and the girl whom he'd sometimes seen visit the brothel. And though he couldn't conceptualise, nor did he have the same sort of instincts as Kitchen, he was a seasoned combatant, and he knew just by looking at them now, that this might be the most exciting battle he'd had in a while.

And almost as if reading his mind or perceiving his intent, Kitchen and Alex made their move.

Encasing herself in flames, Kitchen darted at him. She closed the distance quickly. Waves of pressure and heat pulsed from her body, and were felt by everyone spectating the event. She clenched her fist and came in with a right hook.

Blackjack leaned back.

Kitchen swung and missed. But then her hand returned to its starting position, and Kitchen seemed to appear closer to him than a moment ago. She swung again, this time connecting with full force. But Blackjack had *Skin* active, which formed an invisible layer of telekinetic force around its user, absorbing any damage it received at the expense of consuming the user's sen.

In the next moment, again, Kitchen's position in the air shifted, *skipping* through the movements to arrive instantly at her destination, and she came at him again with a roundhouse kick.

Blackjack ducked, but Kitchen *switched* positions again, and instead of a kick from below, it came now from above, and struck Blackjack hard into the ground.

With each blow she landed, a shockwave of heat and sound erupted. Sparks flew in blinding flashes of light, and everything going on around them seemed to stop, as nothing was more captivating than Kitchen's display of strength.

She *skipped* back away from Blackjack. A wise move as the immediate ground around him became crushed by an intense gravity.

Gravity Well. A command he'd planned to use to ground her, but she was informed of his intention through her connection with Alex. Conceptualisation allowed her to see the strands of logic manifesting before a command was used, letting her warn Kitchen of what was coming. This was their gameplan. Kitchen was the attacker, and Alex would provide support. But that wasn't all. She'd been using the time that Kitchen kept Blackjack busy to set things in place.

First, she spread out her sen zone. Second, she applied *anti* to it. Third, she programmed her *anti* to only affect Blackjack and any commands or functions he performed. And once she activated that programming, Blackjack felt it. This sensation of pressure all over his body. The *anti* was wearing down his *Skin* constantly. He tried to use *Radar*, but every pulse that went out was quickly deconstructed. He could hardly manage a couple of metres before he lost whatever perceptions it offered. It was then that he realised how this battle would go, and his veteran mind began to kick in. In situations like this, Alex was who he needed to deal with first.

As formidable as Alex was, and despite the advantage her Ojo bloodline gave her, Blackjack was still five development stages ahead of her, and was special in his own right. This field of *anti* he found himself in was only effective to a certain point. All he had to do was use commands loaded with more sen than the *anti* could deal with.

He noticed that Alex's *anti* had blocked off The Network, not that it mattered much. Everything he needed was built into his Platinum grade coder. The type you couldn't get from participating in the Rank Test alone. There was a special requirement for qualifying for one of those.

He used *Gravity Well* once more, this time massively expanding its area of effect. Even though its output was decreased by the *anti*, there was still enough sen pumped into it to massively compress the ground they stood on.

Both Kitchen and Alex would have felt its effects, too, but Alex had input further sub-programming into her *anti*, to prioritise the complete nullification of commands aimed at herself and Kitchen. It was then that she realised this battle would head down the route of a war of attrition. Between Alex's *anti* and Blackjack's overwhelming output, who would run out of sen first? But that was why she needed Kitchen, to add on that extra pressure.

Blackjack *Warped* over to Alex and attempted to grab her. He caught nothing but air.

Auto short range teleportation, another sub program she'd put into her sen zone, activated when Alex found herself in physical danger from Blackjack.

And before he could do anything again, Kitchen appeared beside him and engaged in a quick flurry of strikes, *skipping* and *switching* her way into various positions, keeping his perception of her in a constant state of disarray. And the blows she landed felt heavier this time around. They depleted much more of his sen than previously, and he figured out why.

Because Alex and Kitchen's mind's were perfectly synchronised, she'd matched her *anti* with the delivery of Kitchen's blows, concentrating it on the areas of Blackjack where she'd managed to land a hit. Those areas of *Skin* were severely weakened right before the point of impact.

The thing about *Skin* was that you didn't need to overwhelm the entire command to break through it. There was only a certain amount of it that could be utilised at a specific point on the body, so hit it hard enough, and one could completely bypass the defence it offered. It was costing Blackjack a massive amount of sen just to keep it maintained. And thus, the war of attrition bent into Alex and Kitchen's favour.

Blackjack hated to admit it, but Kitchen's hand-to-hand combat prowess was exquisite. Far superior than what one would expect from a girl who'd only seen 22 solar cycles. And Alex, well, there was no doubt about the superiority of her intellect. It took a certain calibre of mind to be able to program functions in real time. Especially in a battle against the likes of Blackjack. The combination of the two of them created a force to be reckoned with.

The worst part was Blackjack couldn't even fight as he usually would. He still had to protect the council. One wild command could see the whole building levelled, spelling a complete failure of his duties as an officer. He was handicapped, and Alex and Kitchen were taking full advantage of that.

But would he let that stop him? Was adversity all it took to force him into submission? No. He was far more capable than that.

He *Warped* away from them. Even that proved a difficult task as the *anti* constantly broke down his warp path. But he managed it, and released another command immediately after. A compound of *Shot:Kaleidoscope:Shock:Tracking:Explosion* was fired out. Multiple electric projectiles flew around the battlefield as Alex and Kitchen darted around trying to avoid them.

Alex's *anti* was putting in work diminishing them over time, but Blackjack had put in so much sen that the process of eliminating them completely was long. Alex's *anti*-enchanted sen zone could only work so quickly. Luckily, she had other means.

Just like she'd performed when May and Fred attempted to ambush her, she formed individual constructs of *anti*, programmed them with *tracking*, and *highlighted* Blackjack's command as the targets. She shot them out, and within a second they sought Blackjack's salvo of electric projectiles and neutralised what was left of them. Alex's offence didn't stop there. She procured a massive wave of *anti* and released it at Blackjack. With *tracking* programmed into it, his best option was to tackle it head on. After all, *anti* had one distinct weakness, which was the other side of the double edged sword to its strength.

What made it such a fearsome ability was that it automatically structured itself in perfect opposition to the meta of its target. But because it was automatic, anyone who tried to combat it, didn't need to issue a specific function. They just needed to release a meta that was equal to or greater than the *anti* in output, and the two would naturally neutralise each other. And whilst Alex's advantage was that her affinity and Ojo bloodline offered her a 100% output, she lost out massively by the fact that she wasn't even halfway through her development. Her ceiling was so much lower than Blackjack's. And she knew that. Just like how she knew that Blackjack's coder offered him a complete exemption from world tax.

But there was more to this part of the story than just that. Blackjack managed to successfully combat Alex's wave of *anti*, but not without consequence. You see, Blackjack was a genius in combat, but his overall intelligence was average, and his ability to gauge sen values and meta complexity wasn't quite up to par. So he stopped Alex's *anti*, but he'd overcompensated, and what remained of his meta was logically destructured.

It was logic that fell into chaos, and when logic fell into chaos, what resulted was a sort of crackling in the air. Embers and sparks of electricity suddenly appeared. There was a flash of light and a gust of wind. Darkness seemed to form in random spots, and all three of them felt some sort of pull, almost as though they were being sucked into a vacuum. That was what happened when logic delved into chaos. The outcome was unpredictable, and potentially catastrophic.

It had come as a surprise, but Alex's mind seemed to refocus on the battle sooner than Blackjack's. She sent a message to Kitchen, *'Distract him!'*

Kitchen *skipped* to his position and released an explosion of flames. They were so violent in their release that the ground below them was burnt to cinders, and a molten glow was left in its wake. Blackjack had to put more sen into his *Skin* just to protect himself. But the flames had equally doubled as a smokescreen, so he hadn't seen Alex *teleport*, but felt, suddenly a hand on his wrist.

Alex emerged from amidst the flames, and just like with Cy's affinity, her *anti* was at its greatest when applied directly through her body. So with everything she had, she applied her *anti* to Blackjack's coder. And once again, the sparks, the embers, the light, the wind, the darkness, and all manner of other unnatural phenomena occurred. But surely, by the end of it all, the result was undeniable, as dust fell from within her grasp.

Alex had destroyed Blackjack's coder.

The silence that came after was loud. It was riddled in disbelief. Too many things thought to be impossible had just occurred.

A coder, destroyed? No, you couldn't destroy coders. Everyone in this city knew that. Oh the differences between what people supposedly knew and what was actually real.

Destroying coders wasn't impossible. But convince a city of people who tell stories that it was impossible, and maybe... Regardless, nobody would have thought a girl from West District, who wasn't even in her final development stage, would be the first to defy this city's narrative.

Eventually there were murmurs. Questions of if what had just happened had really happened. A coder destroyed, and Blackjack's coder no less. The officers behind him didn't want to believe it.

Even Cy was surprised, and he was much better versed in the possibilities of this world than anyone else there.

And what about Blackjack? How would he respond? He'd been holding Alex's gaze the entire time. Was it the shock of what happened? Or was it the rage that came as a result? Whatever it was, he needed to do something.

Alex thought they'd won. She thought that because he only used commands, that the threat he possessed would diminish once his coder became inactive. After all, he couldn't bypass the world's tax without it. Anything he did now would lose 20% output by default. He couldn't possibly hope to match them now, surely?

But as intelligent as Alex was, she was still young, naive, and lacked combat experience. She had no idea of the other dangers and possibilities that existed in the world beyond. Or that some of them were there, now, standing in front of her.

'You did well to destroy my coder,' Blackjack said. 'But do you really think I can't fight without it?'

Alex immediately *teleported* herself and Kitchen away. A moment later, and they would have been caught in the explosion. The sudden explosion of energy that erupted around Blackjack. It was as though the air around were being lifted into a vacuum, and you could visibly see the intensified pressure, bending light and distorting his image.

At that moment, both Alex and Kitchen were daunted by a feeling that wasn't there before. A sense of greater danger, as though some new foe had entered the fray, posing a much greater threat than the one they'd supposedly defeated. Alex could *see* why. Blackjack's body had changed, and was still changing. Its meta had been severely altered once his coder was destroyed, almost as though it had been masking his true self.

In this city, officers' coders made them more powerful. But what if in Blackjack's case that wasn't true? What if, in actuality, his coder was to mask something much more horrific? Like how a cage protected those outside of it from the beast within it.

Blackjack's internal meta had changed, but externally, his transformation was manifesting. From the feet up, his body seemed to become encased in some black metal. Some form of transmutation was occurring, but it didn't seem as though any material was being used up. As if the metal being formed was manifesting from nothing.

But unlike the myth of coders not being able to be destroyed, the laws of equivalent exchange were real. You couldn't form something from nothing. So whatever the source material of this metal was, Alex simply couldn't perceive it.

After more of it had formed, Alex could see it was covering Blackjack like a suit of armour. And it looked familiar. Almost as if...

But then, suddenly, another person did indeed enter the fray. He appeared behind Blackjack, placed a hand on his shoulder, and said, 'That's quite enough. I'll take it from here.'

What people saw was a man in a long white coat, with '99' engraved on the back and front left breast. He had slick black hair, glasses, was of a rather slim build, but made up for it with a bit more height than average. He had a serious expression on his face, his unfamiliar face, for those who could see it. But there were two people there who recognised him, because he'd taught them up until recently. And between the two of them, Alex and Cy, Cy seemed the most hit by his appearance.

Because why did he have such a familiarity with Blackjack as to stop his transformation?

Why was he able to appear so suddenly, as if he were an officer taking advantage of the ability to jump in and out of warp paths, regardless of where in the city they were?

Alex had told Cy that his story didn't end with Blackjack, and this was what she'd meant.

The boss at the end of this revolution didn't go by the name Blackjack.

He went by the name Evaán. Evaán Bordeaux.

64

THE 4TH

Standing on the battlefield was like wading through a constant earthquake. The sheer number and magnitude of explosions kept the ground rumbling; what was left of it anyway. What started as a relatively level landscape was now riddled with craters, scorched earth, and little clouds of dust that seemed to all spread out into one.

There weren't many participants left. By the third wave, the enemies they faced were so proficient with functions that the commands of the ally side no longer had the advantage of output. Even with the benefits offered by their coders, there was still their own mental prowess to consider when it came to the output of their commands.

The more used to using a command they were; the more they understood the meta behind it, those were the factors that contributed to high output. The average Sentien generally operated at a 40% efficiency. The enemies they faced in the third wave were performing at 70%.

The result was that the third wave posed a difficulty most couldn't overcome, and by the time it ended, only Viktor and Daniel remained. Though by all accounts, Viktor was a bit worse for wear.

Daniel had been preserving himself. He only took part in the battle at critical moments where his interference was warranted. But he wasn't there for the first three waves. He only ever had one goal in mind. Defeating The Machine.

You can't beat The Machine.

Those were the first words that came to mind whenever someone thought about the entity. It was one of the few things that was ever said about it. Anything besides that was people recollecting past Rank Tests, in particular the previous one, where both Reena and Viktor made it to the fourth wave. But nobody remembered Viktor's performance. It was entirely overshadowed. Yet, as magnificent and formidable a display as Reena gave, she, too, fell short of doing anything significant to The Machine.

And this was the Reena whom Daniel looked up to. Whose shadow he'd been chasing, and always thought of as superior to himself. Yet he stood here, now, face to face with the foe she couldn't overcome, telling himself, *I'm going to beat The Machine.*

The rumbling stopped. There were no commands or functions being used. The dust had settled and the air seemed to still. The calm before the storm.

Yes, the battlefield was silent for a few moments, as was The Arena, because no matter how many times people saw it, all they could do was look on in wonder at the sheer dominating presence The Machine had when it appeared.

And it wasn't that it looked anything special. It was humanoid in nature, but void of any defining features. It was just the metallic figure of a rather muscular man, who happened to stand 8ft tall. And as daunting a presence as that was, it wasn't the cause of this ominous feeling that encapsulated those whose gaze it had captivated. There was just something about it. Something otherworldly. But that was the point. In Lore, The Machine was an entity of an entirely different world, seeking universal domination of all other worlds. Otherworldly was exactly the right word to describe it.

But perhaps, the fact that something being 'otherworldly' was an idea that existed only in stories was the reason The Machine was so ominous. The idea of multiple worlds, of things coming from beyond the world in which they lived; it was just an idea. An idea brought to reality via an equally unreal network within which these imaginary worlds could exist. But still, ultimately, not real.

Places that exist somewhere that's not here.

The Machine wasn't real, yet it held such a massive presence in this city. That was where this ominous feeling came from.

The dust had settled. The air went stagnant. The Arena was silent. But that silence was broken by Daniel, whom, whilst never taking his eyes off The Machine, said to Viktor, 'Would you like to go first?'

65

<u>All the Best Attacks Have Names</u>

Evaán had everyone speechless. It was a difficult encounter to describe. When something new entered a place where all else was familiar, that which was new seemed out of place. Evaán's appearance was the reverse of that. It was as though he, and he alone, belonged. Everyone else around him were the obscurities. As though they had no business being in his presence. There was almost a trembling sensation as they looked at this familiar unfamiliarity.

Blackjack looked to him. Words weren't spoken, but they communicated internally.

His role in this story had been concluded. He could have stayed - should have stayed - for what would come next, but he was done with this particular chain of events. His coder reformed itself around his wrist, good as new. And then, he left.

Cy was riddled with all manner of emotions and thoughts.

He may not have heard the internal dialogue between Evaán and Blackjack, but from their exchange in the physical, it was clear, Blackjack answered to him.

The now absence of Blackjack left Evaán as the only worthwhile person for Cy to direct his conflict towards. And the fact this was the man whom he'd looked up to as his teacher for so long?

A thing like that might have caused some internal conflict of its own. Make Cy question the current path he was so set to travel.

But it didn't do that at all. It just made him mad.

And Alex; well, she was recollecting past events. She conceptualised Evaán, now, having never been able to before.

Whatever he'd done back when he'd taught them, he created an avatar whose meta was completely different to his real self. But as she conceptualised him now, she saw - truly saw - where that feeling of dread was coming from.

It was in similar fashion to Blackjack after his coder had been destroyed. His body's meta was unusual. Almost as if he wasn't human. But it was so much more sophisticated than Blackjack's. Whatever Blackjack was, it wasn't the same as what Evaán was. The word that came to mind to describe him was...

Otherworldly.

'You just want me to get eliminated first so you can be the last man standing,' Viktor said in response.

'No,' Daniel responded innocently. 'I just figured you'd want the opportunity to show off... before I beat The Machine.'

Viktor laughed at him. 'Beat The Machine? Well if you think you're so capable then by all means. I'm dying to see what you hope to achieve.'

'Interesting choice of words.' Daniel took a few steps forward. More than a few, actually. He got right up close to The Machine. One thing that had been consistent throughout previous tests, The Machine never attacked first. It always waited, almost as if giving its opponents the opportunity to hit it with their best shot.

Standing before The Machine now, Daniel was tiny by comparison. He had to tilt his neck right up just to look The Machine in its non-existent eye. And The Machine, tilting its own head down to Daniel, *stared* right into his. And Daniel said, 'I'm going to punch you now.'

Alex stopped conceptualising. The more complex the meta, the greater strain it put on her mind to make sense of it. Just glancing at Evaán for a short time proved arduous.

Then a voice came into her ear.

'It seems you followed the correct path.'

It was Q, projecting his voice from elsewhere. Alex looked around and managed to spot him on top of a nearby building, standing alongside Big Dog, and a silver-haired woman she'd never seen before.

'You've done your part now,' came his voice again. She was looking straight at him and was sure his lips never moved. Though he was a bit far away, so perhaps she just couldn't see.

'This next conflict isn't yours.'

She understood what he was saying. She was standing between Evaán and Cy, and this wasn't a fight she needed to be involved in.

Synchronising her meta with Kitchen's, she teleported them both away, and now, Evaán and Cy faced each other unobstructed.

The area suddenly became humid.

Light seemed to have faded without notice, and a storm cloud was brewing.

In the moments succeeding this, when everything fell silent, Cy had communicated with his people to begin their prayers. But unlike before when the power was spread between all of the men, this time, it all went to Cy.

He would shoulder the burden of all of their hopes, and in return, receive a blessing far greater than any he'd received before.

This had always been the plan. That when he got to the council, whoever it was that stood in their way, he would face them alone, but not alone. He was an army of one, now. The hopes of his people weren't just weight on his shoulders, they were hands on his back, pushing him forward, giving him the strength he needed to overcome what faced him.

Lightning and thunder began to flash and roar. The sky was completely covered by a massive storm cloud. The sun had all but vanished, and darkness prevailed over the land.

Despite this, Evaán remained unchanged. Wholly unfazed by what was on all accounts an impressive display of power. Manipulating the weather on such a scale was no small feat. But Evaán's presence in the physical remained unchanged, and instead, he made his way into Cy's mind.

'You're surprised,' Evaán said.

'An understatement.'

'I'm sure you feel you need to do what you must do. So do it, and then we'll talk.'

Cy grimaced. His nostrils flared and eyes tightened. 'You're underestimating me!'

⁂

Daniel did exactly what he said he'd do. He punched The Machine. The loud clank of metal on metal resounded, but not much more happened.

The Machine was unfazed by the attack, and now that it had been struck first, it would retaliate. It took to striking Daniel with a backhand. The sort of hit performed when one didn't take their opponent seriously.

Daniel let himself be hit, but as soon as he was, The Machine's hand was repelled away, as if the force of his strike had been turned back on him.

And so the Machine took a fighting stance and began a flurry of consecutive strikes, but each one was *repelled* by Daniel, each time putting The Machine in a disoriented state.

Then Daniel *pushed* The Machine away from him, *collapsed* the ground below it, and *increased* the pull of gravity. Once The Machine was trapped, Daniel took *hold* of the ground and *lifted* it into the air. Enchanting himself with telekinesis, he *compressed* the earth around The Machine into a dense sphere, then *gathered* light into his palm, enchanted it with *telekinetic force*, gave it the property of *perforation*, and *released* it as a beam of light that pierced right through this mound of raised earth. 'I call that one Light Spear of Redemption,' he said to no one in particular, but knew everyone in The Arena could hear him.

'And this one,' he continued, 'is Grand Judgement of the Skies.' After saying this, the clear blue sky above him seemed to come down like a veil. Yes, that intangible sky was falling to the ground like a physical object, and it collapsed into the mound of earth, drowning it in... whatever it was the sky was supposedly made from, and brought it back down to the ground from which it had been raised. And once again, it seemed as though an earthquake was erupting through the battlefield, but this was far greater in intensity than anything that had previously occurred.

Then the part of the sky that had fallen was separated from the rest of the sky, almost like it had been a singular drop amongst a much greater reservoir of water.

'Did you know hydrogen and oxygen are two of the dominant elements in the air?' Daniel said rhetorically. 'How much do you think is in that drop of sky that just came down?' Again, he was talking to nobody in particular, but everyone heard him, and all Viktor could do was be amazed at how ridiculous a question it was. Never did he imagine he'd hear a sentence pertaining to... the sky falling?

'This one is called, Sky's Flaming Wrath,' and he *ignited* the drop of sky into a dazzling inferno, the heat of which Viktor could feel burning through his *Skin* at an alarming rate, and wondered how Daniel could even fathom being so close to it.

When the flames eventually subsided, a pool of molten rock was left in its wake. Yet, despite that sequence of grand punishment, there The Machine stood, its body unscathed.

Viktor, and even those in The Arena, gasped at the reality of the situation. They'd been so spectacularly engrossed in the ridiculous nature of what Daniel was doing, that for a moment, an oh so brief moment, they actually thought The Machine would have been damaged. But there was no visible damage to notice. Despite all of that effort, this one thing remained true.

You can't beat The Machine.

But looking at Daniel, then, they saw him smiling. Laughing, even, and he said, 'That hurt you, didn't it?' And just then, somehow, after inspecting The Machine once more, they noticed a crack in its armour. And it was so visibly perceptible they all wondered how they could have missed it before. But without a doubt, The Machine had been harmed.

'How?' Viktor said in disbelief. 'You're not even using commands. You're just flagrantly using wild functions that don't even make sense. How could you possibly do that?'

That was when everyone else noticed it, too. Daniel hadn't used a single command against The Machine, only functions. Everything he'd done was the power of his mind and his mind alone. And everyone in the city knew that officers' commands were better than functions. So indeed, as Viktor had so deliriously exclaimed, how?

If Daniel had heard Viktor, he didn't show it, because what he said next seemed entirely unrelated to his question. 'This next one is going to beat you,' he said with a smile on his face. And then, turning back to look at Viktor, asked him, 'Do you know what the difference is between a function and a command?'

'What?' Viktor retaliated, once again surprised by the randomness of the question.

'People think it's the fact that commands are pre-programmed. Or that the commands officers use are better, for whatever reason. But that's not really it at all. It's the names. Functions that have achieved a state of perfection by their creator get named, and the name gives it power. This one came to me in a dream, with a little inspiration from a friend.'

Evaán flew into the sky in preparation for what was to come. He knew everything worth knowing in this city. He'd been keeping tabs on all of Cy's activities. Every command he made in preparation for this revolution. He knew the ins and outs of everything Cy had strung together for this day.

And so this final command, created with reverence towards a heroic figure in Ojo legend; this command was created to be the decider of any battle. A command so great, it could only be used when taking the full weight of his peoples' blessing. A command created to take out even Blackjack.

Divine Strike of Şango.

Ex Machina.

The name that came to him in the dream he'd had the night before, and somewhat inspired by one of Niche's commands with an excessively long name. He didn't know what the words meant. Didn't understand why his subconscious mind had chosen 'Machina' as opposed to 'Machine'. All he knew - *felt* - was that there was power in the name, and that was the first time that had happened.

So he named this function *Ex Machina;* "The Machine Killer."

What happened next was the sort of thing the people of New Heart only ever experienced in the stories they told. Weapons that could level entire landscapes. World-altering calamities. Powers that existed on a scale beyond what their minds could logically comprehend, but could imaginatively create with ease.

One of the greatest powers a Sentien possessed was that of a free mind. One that could bridge the gap between fantasy and reality; actualise the stories they loved to tell.

When Daniel activated his function, an explosion like nothing they'd ever seen before occurred.

It was a focussed explosion. What should have potentially rendered the whole battlefield into a storm of ash, was restricted purely to where The Machine stood. Just one large orb of light that sent out pulsating shockwaves and disrupted the air with crackles and bangs. Almost as if the world itself was splitting apart in multiple places.

It was an explosion that should have reduced the whole battlefield to ash, but it was focussed on The Machine.

The time that passed seemed infinite, but it was only about 15 seconds. 15 seconds under the constant assault of this function that nobody really understood the nature of. But when it finally did end, and the dust eventually settled. Well, Daniel smiled when he saw it.

The Machine still stood, technically. Both of its feet were still planted on the ground of the crater that had formed, but the rest of it was gone. Disintegrated by the contained explosion.

And that was it, surely? Daniel had beaten The Machine. *Surely!*

Viktor's jaw practically hit the ground. He was speechless. Not that he'd been saying much anyway. But this was an unprecedented turn of events. This wasn't how it was supposed to happen. The first person to ever harm The Machine. It should have been him.

It was never going to be him. That wasn't his role in this story.

Everyone in The Arena was amazed, but it was short lived.

There was movement on the battlefield.

Small, shiny particles seemed to be gathering where The Machine's feet were.

As they reincorporated themselves, Daniel knew what was happening.

You can't beat The Machine.

That wasn't just lore. It was the very logic of its existence. And as powerful as Daniel was, even his sen couldn't overcome that.

The Machine reformed in its entirety, and once again, it stood, idle, waiting for what Daniel would do next.

What Daniel did next was raise his hand and concede his defeat. Putting aside that The Machine had survived his greatest attack, the truth was, it had taken almost everything he had, and he was nearly out of sen. There really wasn't anything more he could do. But so what? For the first time in 20 years of Rank Tests, someone had harmed The Machine. And though not in this story, in another story, in another world, another verse, there was something someone once said about what happens when you make a god bleed.

66

THE END

Cy's lightning struck like a calamity. The air rippled, and continued to ripple, as the lightning continued to strike.

Those spectating the event wondered if perhaps, amidst the flashing light and roaring thunder, Evaán, if still alive, might be screaming. Or letting out a thunderous bellow of his own. If he was, nobody could hear him.

The last strike came. The last strike came but the lightning didn't disappear. It lingered where Evaán was.

Curious, Cy thought. He hadn't programmed his command to do that. Lightning wasn't supposed to linger.

But this one did. An orb of glowing electricity. And as the various currents flowing through it made their way chaotically in all directions, the orb itself enacted another sort of movement. It was shrinking?

Yes, shrinking. Slowly at first. Not immediately noticeable. But then, suddenly, all at once. And the great orb of electricity that encased Evaán, now sat neatly in the palm of his hand.

'Divine Strike of Şango,' Evaán said. 'Appropriately named, and a splendid command.' Despite saying that, he emerged from that calamity unscathed. He was so overwhelmingly powerful, he'd *caught* the lightning in his hand.

'How could you...' Cy began, but couldn't finish, bewildered by his disbelief.

This wasn't supposed to happen. It wasn't supposed to be possible. That was his absolute greatest command. One he could only use after receiving the blessing of his people. It was supposed to transcend the limits of what Sentiens were capable of. How could it be so easily stopped by one man? Unless, just like Cy, Evaán...

Surely not. Receiving the blessing from someone's prayers was no easy thing to accomplish. Even Chen and Big Dog had acknowledged that just yesterday. But what, other than that, could be the secret behind Evaán's immeasurable power?

Neither his ability of psychometry, nor Alex's defined parameters of conceptualisation, could fully comprehend the complexity of Evaán's meta. He was leagues beyond them.

Evaán shot the electricity back up into the sky. It arced through the massive storm cloud, causing it to disperse. Cy was hit by the recoil of having an active command suddenly destroyed. But that wasn't all. He'd put his all into that last command, and his body could no longer shoulder the burden of his people's blessing. The power left him, and what followed were the consequences. His mind, his body, his soul, everything about his being was placed under immense stress. It was agonising. He lost control of himself and fell to the ground, unable to regain his composure. Was this it? Was this how his revolution was to end? Was it all for nothing?

No, that's not how this story goes. It was sudden, but his mind felt refreshed, suddenly. Enough for him to regain himself and stay in flight. And his body felt light again. The pain of the recoil had disappeared. Almost as though it was never there.

As though he'd never released that final command.

He looked at Evaán. Could he have?

'You have Lilith to thank for that,' Evaán said.

Cy noticed then that the aftermath of the battle between Blackjack, Alex and Kitchen had also reverted to a formermath. The ground which had been torn apart was restored.

He looked behind to see a dry district, absent of the rain they'd manifested.

He hadn't noticed it occurring, but was certain it couldn't have been long ago. Within the last few minutes, at most.

And then, on a rooftop, there stood Big Dog, the white-haired man that people had been talking about the day before, and a silver-haired woman. Lilith? She waved at him.

What was happening? He'd put so much of himself into this revolution, and yet, so quickly, so easily, it ended. And they'd achieved nothing for all their efforts. Had he been deluding himself this whole time that he had the power to change this city?

Does an ant deny itself the climb up a mountain just because it can never reach the top? Is there no value in the journey itself?

But Cy wasn't an ant. This wasn't a mountain. And he couldn't abandon his mission just because success seemed impossible. He'd dedicated his entirety to the cause, and he would give his entirety before he let it end.

But that wasn't where this story was going, either. His revolution wasn't as hopeless a cause as he'd just been made to believe, because Evaán asked him, 'Would you like to see your people?'

67

ASCENSION

The aftermath of the revolution saw West District's streets completely refurbished. Lilith reverted the district's time to a period before the revolution began. Everything was back as it should be.

Both the revolution and the Rank Test concluded about the same time. Officers escorted the Erubans back to their homes, assuring them - rather confused themselves - that there were no repercussions awaiting them for their mutiny.

Cy himself sent a *message*, telling his people everything was going to be fine, and that he would brief them all properly later. He himself didn't quite know what was happening yet. Evaán had told him he had some business to wrap up, and that they would talk later that evening. Until then, Cy was taken back to MindSpace HQ, alongside Alex and Kitchen.

The Orenians were quarantined to their hideout, awaiting whatever judgement was going to befall them.

Irians throughout the district were rallying complaints against the Erubans for the disturbance they'd caused, which kept the mayor busy for the remainder of the day.

But aside from a few conversations that needed to occur later between certain individuals, there was one more event that needed to take place. This day hadn't only been the conclusion to the chapter in the lives of Alex, Cy and Daniel. There was one other person who had reached the climax of this part of their story, and just as the Rank Test and revolution were ending, the conclusion to her story was just beginning.

Evaán arrived at Marston Mansion with N'Adina, Old Crow, and Big Dog.

'Finally!' Richard shouted. 'I've been trying to get through to you all day!'

'You know the Rank Test is a busy day,' Evaán replied.

'Not when my granddaughter's life is in danger!'

He was so angry he hadn't even noticed the other three standing there beside him.

'She was never in any danger,' Evaán said. 'In fact, she should be waking up now.'

As thick and numerous as the walls in Marston Mansion were, the voice of Annabelle's mother still permeated through them when she shrieked with joy. They all got the *message* soon after. Annabelle had woken up, finally.

'What did you do?' Richard asked.

'It's not what I did,' said Evaán, 'but what I allowed.'

Richard had no time for the cryptic nature of Evaán's words. He wanted answers, and he wanted them now.

'Perhaps I can clarify things,' chimed in Old Crow.

Richard noticed her, now, frail thing that she was.

He noticed N'Adina and Big Dog, too, and failed to mask whatever disgust he felt at the sight of them. 'Speak then!' he demanded

Old Crow said nothing. She just looked upon him for a while, smiling.

'I'm not one to repeat myself, hag!'

'Parasite,' Old Crow said. 'A rare, and generally quite useless ability for a Shaman. I can forcefully house one of my contracted souls in another's body. It doesn't feed off of their life-force, as it does with me, but their soul still bears the burden of carrying another. Which can prove quite strenuous for a young girl who's not even a Shaman. Her body simply didn't have the capacity to maintain consciousness, but she was never in any real danger. I just needed you to suffer a little bit. To get your attention.'

'My attention!' Richard spat. 'You vile, wicked, senile old hag!'

Old Crow laughed. 'You've not changed. Honestly, that's good. I've no reason for remorse about my actions.'

'Do not speak as if you know me, whelp!'

'Oh but I do know you,' she said with a wry smile. 'But it seems as though you have forgotten me. Understandable. Giants hardly remember those upon whom they've trampled. Tell me, Mr Marston. How many in this city do you think remember the old days? The transition of Old Heart into New? What things were really like back then? What certain people had to do to be who they are today? How many do you think bore witness to those events? How many know the truth of how your family came to be in this city?'

He wasn't as quick-tongued to respond to this as he had been previously. There were certain things Richard always thought about. Memories that haunted him in both his waking and sleeping moments. Likewise, there were some memories he'd discarded over the years. Events that no longer bore any consequence to him. But as he looked upon the face of Old Crow now, something about her began to refamiliarise. Many years had passed since they were last face to face. Enough years for a person's appearance to change significantly. But no matter how much one changed, there was always evidence of a past self, hidden behind the wrinkles. And as his eyes began to refamiliarise themselves with her face, her demeanour, her overall expression of self; he began to remember. Indeed, they knew each other, and not only in passing.

If one's familiarity with a person was based on the impact they had in the other's life, then Old Crow knew Richard Marston very well. Because it was in meeting him that perhaps the greatest, most significant and impactful event of her life occurred. And it was in realising this that Richard began to have some notion of what was going on, and why she was here.

Revenge.

Old Crow faltered suddenly. She leaned on N'Adina for support, but that was a temporary fix. She grew weaker by the minute.

'What's wrong with her?' Richard asked out of curiosity rather than concern.

'The most honourable event in a Shaman's life,' said Evaán. 'Where their soul becomes too powerful to be contained by their physical body. Unlike death, it is a passing which is celebrated, not mourned. Her time has come.'

Not soon enough, Richard thought. She could still talk after all.

Richard didn't hesitate to give the kill order to Garth, whom he'd been in telepathic contact with the whole time.

He appeared suddenly before them, arms outstretched, ready to deal a swift blow to the already downed old woman.

It all happened so fast.

Garth had appeared in front of Old Crow and N'Adina, everyone saw that. But then there was a sequence of sounds. First was a loud smack, as if a giant had clapped their hands. After that came a thud, or perhaps a crash, which was accompanied by a rumble through the ground. And all of their attention was brought to the wall on the other side of the room, where somehow, Garth was now bathed in its rubble.

It all happened so fast.

Garth was fortunate. His combat experience had kicked in at the last moment, automatically causing him to *strengthen* his body. He might be dead otherwise. Because just before he could deal his lethal blow to Old Crow, something hit him. But he wasn't sure what.

It happened so fast.

Who could it have been? Evaán made the most sense. Garth didn't want to believe either of the Shaman women were capable of striking him with such lethality. Big Dog, perhaps?

But, N'Adina was looking at him ferociously, and then she said, 'A Shaman's ascension is a sacred rite of passage. It will not be disturbed.'

It must have been her. Yes, it made sense. It was brief, but he was sure, in the moment before he was struck, he saw a giant hand. An Anima?

It had been a long time since Garth had encountered a Shaman. He'd almost forgotten what they were capable of. But having caught a glimpse of what just occurred, he remembered. He remembered the ability Shaman had to seemingly conjure something from nothing. Their power to animate the souls of animals back into the physical world. And he remembered that the souls of animals weren't the only things they could animate. They were just the baseline. The foundation of a Shaman's ability to create. Training blocks, one might say. The true power of Anima could conjure things much more fearsome than lost souls.

Within the world's ether were things one might only ever find in their nightmares, and N'Adina, for just a moment, had brought one to life.

Apparently it packed a punch, sending Garth through the wall the way it did.

But as fearsome as it might be, Garth still had a job to do. He attempted to *strengthen* himself, but found himself incapable.

It wasn't just him. Most of the programmed functions in the mansion were offline.

It could have been that they'd been shut down, but that wasn't the case.

This was Evaán.

In those short moments that Garth had been disoriented from being struck, Evaán had expanded his sen zone.

Both Garth and Richard understood the futility of trying to oppose the brilliance of Evaán's mind. For as long as his sen zone was active, there was nothing they could do.

That was the president of New Heart.

And then Evaán said, 'Confronting you is this woman's final wish. You'll listen to what she has to say.'

Evaán was right. Her soul was ready to leave her body. It was taking everything she had to keep it contained.

She'd never been particularly gifted physically. If she had, her body, which was but a vessel that housed the soul, may have been able to hold out for a few years longer. But the body declined after a while, whereas the soul continually grew more powerful.

It wasn't that her body was no longer capable of supporting life. That wasn't the case. She'd have been fine if she were Sentien. The souls of Sentiens didn't develop the way a Shaman's did.

Ascension wasn't something to be mourned, but celebrated. It represented the finality of achievement in a Shaman's life, regardless of what they had or hadn't achieved during. It was usually something welcomed by the one going through it. That was the case on this occasion. Old Crow was ready to let go. But not until she did this one last thing.

'I have waited almost 30 years for this moment,' she said, rising to her feet again with the aid of N'Adina. 'You remember me, now, don't you? I could see it in your eyes earlier. The realisation. The fear. An unfamiliar experience for you, I'm sure. You're usually able to resolve these things before they become a problem, but not this time. It's already too late. He knows what you did. And soon, so will your beloved family. Aaah, there it is again. The fear.'

Richard looked back and forth between Old Crow and Evaán. Did he truly know? For how long? Why has he done nothing?

'I can only imagine what's going through your head right now,' she continued. 'One of the advantages you Sentiens have over Shamans is the ability to read minds. But no matter. I don't need to read your mind to know what lies ahead for you. The day will come,

Richard Marston, where you know, where you truly understand what it means to be afraid. And you'll remember this moment. You'll remember all the pain and suffering you caused over your life. You'll remember the face of your loved ones, knowing they exist only as a memory. The day will come where everything you hold dear will be but a pile of ash at your feet. And when you kneel to gather up the dust of what once was, when the anguish of your past life personifies into the image of all those you have wronged; when they blow those remaining ashes from your hands, you will remember this day, and it will linger in your mind like bitterness to the tongue, pierce your soul like sharpness to the skin, and drown your entire being like water in your lungs. The day will come, Richard Marston, where you learn how truly cruel this reality is. And as I let go of my time on this plane and ascend to a higher realm, I hope I can look down. I wish, with all my heart, to witness with my own eyes the misfortune that will befall you. My body may fall here, but my soul will look down on you for the rest of your days. And when that tragedy strikes, and you wonder why, remember these words, Richard Marston. Remember this day where I came before you and cursed the very essence of your being. Remember... Remember, you cruel, heartless, bastard of a man...' she faltered a moment. This wasn't the frailty of her body. It was the pain of the words she tried to speak. Because speaking them was the solidification of a memory she tried earnestly not to recollect. But it was time. She was here. She had to say the words.

'You shouldn't have killed my mother.'

Anita had been playing out in the fields when her father called out to her.

'Baba,' she said as she ran over to him, jumping into his embrace once she was close enough. When he set her down, she put her hands together, as one might do to draw water from a pond, and held them up to him. 'Look,' she said. 'I've made a friend.'

There was nothing in her hands, or so one might think. But the friend she made couldn't be seen with the eyes. One needed a particular sort of sight to visualise what she held in the palms of her hands. And fortunately, unlike her mother, Anita's father had that sight, because both she, and he, were Shaman.

So he saw the friend she'd made. A soul, recently detached from its body, which he guessed lay somewhere in the field.

At that moment, he gave his daughter a look she'd never seen before. She'd seen him happy. She'd seen him sad. She'd seen him angry, disappointed, relieved, and all manner of other emotions that existed along the infinite spectrum. But this was the first time she'd seen what she'd later come to understand was pride.

He knelt down to come level with her, and took her face, curling her hair behind her ears. The smile on his face was so gleeful, she couldn't help but smile back.

''You've found it, my dearest Anita,' he said.

'What?' she asked in as cute a manner as one would expect from an 8 year old.

'Your spirit animal, sweet child. And what happens when a Shaman finds their spirit animal?'

'Their name changes?'

'Their name changes. So, from now on, you're my little Crow, okay?'

She nodded. And asked, 'Are you still Daddy Ray?'

He nodded. But said to her, 'I'll always be your Daddy Ray. But you should know, my little Crow, that Daddy's friends call him Raven.'

A few years passed. It had taken some getting used to, but Anita managed to settle into her new name, and contracted many more crow souls as time went on. Her father, Raven, taught her the fundamentals of Soul Arts, and ways to maximise her affinity with her spirit animal. She was his pride and joy, and she found herself having formed a much deeper connection with her Eruban Shaman father than she did with her Irian Sentien mother. In the days of late, she found her mother didn't smile all that much, and seemed, at times, to look at both Crow and Raven with a grief-stricken look on her face.

And on a particular night, she heard her parents arguing, assuming her father was confronting her mother about her recent behaviour. She had no idea at the time how wrong she was.

'It's already been too long,' she heard her father say.

'You should at least tell her yourself,' her mother retorted.

She didn't catch much more of the conversation than that.

But the next day, she found out everything.

'It's called a pilgrimage,' her mother told her. 'It's a custom carried out by Shaman in Eruba. They travel the world in order to enlighten their souls. They don't tend to stay in one place too long. 15 years your father has been here, and it wasn't for me. It was for you. To see you grow. To teach you how to be a Shaman. How to be an Eruban in a place where not everyone looks like you. But he's done what he had to do, and his pilgrimage has continued.'

Crow's mother didn't even have to say the words for her to realise that her father was gone, and perhaps, was never coming back.

Life moving forward was very simple. Crow and her mother had each other, and that was enough. In the decades that passed, Crow encountered various Eruban Shaman on their pilgrimage, but never did her father return to the place where he'd raised a family. And she wondered, at various points in time, if perhaps, there were others? From what she learned from other Shaman, many didn't stick around for nearly as long as her father had. Many didn't stick around long enough to know if they'd fathered a child at all.

The call to enlightening their souls was, for some, the greatest achievement their lives might ever carry. A child was no reason to compromise that.

So Crow and her mother lived together, until Crow was older, and her mother was old. Left alone at the top of a hill in a city that didn't pay them much mind.

But then one day they had a visitor.

Richard had lost everything. His sisters had both left. The family legacy had been placed in his hands, but he didn't grip hard enough, and there were those who saw fit to come and take what had been kept for so long. The fall of an empire.

He had to make a choice. Stay, and forever gaze at the life that once was, or leave, and build a new empire elsewhere. He chose the latter.

He had a family of his own to carry with him, but not until he knew for sure where they were going. So he journeyed alone for some time. And there were things that occurred between where he began and where he ended, but that tale is to be told in a different story. A story of beginnings.

One day, having travelled from the south of the continent to the centre, he happened upon a city much different to the one he'd come from. A city that was by comparison, run down and lacking any real sophistication. And he thought, *perhaps here*. Here would be a good place to build something spectacular. But where in this fair city would he start?

Well, he happened upon a hill. A hill with nothing but an old rundown house stood at the top of it. And he went into the house without knocking nor announcing his presence. There, he saw an old Irian woman and a hybrid woman of similar age to himself. He saw her chestnut skin and immediately his expression filled with disgust. When he spoke, he seemed to disregard the hybrid woman entirely, and said to the old Irian, 'Name your price. I'll be taking this land off you.'

'Excuse me?' said Liliana, unsure of how to respond to this sudden intrusion. She felt an uneasiness in the air, too. As though she and her daughter were in danger.

'It's not for sale,' said Crow, confronting Richard's sudden appearance.

Again, Richard paid Crow no mind. He continued talking to Liliana. He introduced himself, claiming he was an alchemist from the south. 'I'll transmute anything you want. I'll even build you a new house in another location. It's quite easy for me. I just want this land. Surely you see the benefits?'

'This is our home,' said Crow. 'You've got your answer, so be on your way.'

Finally Richard looked at her. His gaze was scathing with hate and resentment. Too much for someone he'd only just met. Too much to simply be hatred for someone who looked like Crow. Why was he so furious?

'Now what you don't understand,' he began, 'is that I've recently lost everything. Everything that mattered to me, anyway. I've ended up here as a result of the most traumatic experience of my life. Everything was taken from me, and so understand that my offer of purchasing this land is a kindness, not a request. If you won't comply...' the air changed suddenly, 'then I'll just take it from you. Just like your people took mine from me.'

Neither Crow nor Liliana knew anything about what he was talking about, but with the change in the air, and Crow's animal instincts active, she knew the danger he now posed. And she wouldn't wait to find out just how dangerous he was. She Animated a crow and hurtled it towards him.

It struck and pushed him out of the house. Its beak should have pierced through his skin, but it came up against resistance.

Richard had *transmuted* his clothes to a sheet of diamond, and *strengthened* his own body to handle the pressure of the blunt force placed upon it. Then, placing a hand on the animated crow, *dismantled* it to the point of disintegration.

Back in the house, Liliana was composing herself, and said to her daughter, 'we'll drive him out together.' She went to *strengthen*, but immediately found herself unable to utilise her sen. With the absence of any blockers, she knew Richard had activated his sen zone.

'I'm sorry,' she said. 'His mind is overwhelming.'

'Don't worry,' said Crow. 'I'll protect us. Just don't come out until it's over.' She left the house.

The day was bright. White clouds dotted the otherwise blue sky, and the sun was at its peak. Its rays warmed the earth on which they stood, setting a precedent for the heat of battle that would ensue.

Crow had felt the recoil of lost mana from when Richard destroyed her Anima. That alone was enough to caution her as to how dangerous this strange man was. Just to be safe, she'd form any other Anima completely detached from her mana. If they got destroyed, there wouldn't be any recoil.

Resolving to this course of action, she shot out another crow at high speed. She wanted to get Richard as far away from the house as possible. But the difference between them became instantly apparent. Her Anima didn't even reach Richard this time. It disintegrated midair.

She was right to have detached it from her mana. Being within his sen zone meant he could transmute without ever having to make direct contact. Everything, including the ground upon which she stood, was bound to his will. The only advantage she had was the multiplicative superiority that mana had over sen. The ratio was 1:2 in the favour of mana. Even dismantling her crows earlier took more effort on Richard's part than the simple transmutation of his surroundings. Old Crow knew this, and this was what she'd use to her advantage.

The thing about crows - birds in general - was that they were plentiful. And given that Crow was past 50 at this time, she was in her final development stage. The ceiling on her powers no longer existed, and the number of crows she could animate at any given time... well, Richard soon found out.

A murder. That was what a collection of crows was called. They descended on Richard seemingly out of nowhere. The bright sky became shadowed by the sheer number of them.

It surprised Richard at first. It wasn't that he'd never experienced an animation of this magnitude before, he just hadn't been expecting it from her. And the massive presence of them was almost intimidating.

But he had countermeasures.

As great a display of power as it was, Richard quickly surmised that Crow's strength lay in the quantity of her Anima and not the quality. A combination of *strengthening* and *transmuting* his skin to the hardness of diamond saw him in a state of invulnerability to the crows' attacks. The crows seemed to keep him at bay for a while, but ultimately he remained unharmed.

But Crow herself knew the limitations of her abilities. Her intent was not to have the crows defeat him, but to force him to deal with them to the point of expending his sen supply. A battle of attrition.

'You think I'm a fool, don't you?' Richard said. 'Swarming me with your Anima, thinking I'd waste my time dealing with them. As if I've never faced a Shaman before. How long will you people mock me?'

The air changed again. It was full of killing intent.

Crow suddenly found the ground below her rumbling. It collapsed beneath her feet, dragging her down into it. Before it could re-solidify around her, she Animated a large crow to pull her out.

And almost as if he knew that this particular Anima was still attached to her mana, he *transmuted* a spear from the ground and shot it at her with *telekinesis*. The crow was impaled and instantly dissipated, sending the recoil coursing through Crow's body. And it was then, for some reason, that Richard decided to take care of the crows surrounding him, *dismantling* them all almost instantaneously, so that the air momentarily became flooded with ether, as though ash fell from the clouds.

It blocked Crow's vision like a smokescreen. She saw Richard in the mid distance, and then suddenly he disappeared. Then she couldn't see the distance at all, because he reappeared in front of her, blocking her vision.

Richard grabbed her by the neck and threw her to the ground.

Fortunately she'd Synced with an ant soul. Her skin had been toughened by the properties of its exoskeleton, minimising the damage of the impact. But Richard came upon her again, and though he was Sentien, and had a brilliant mind, and could think of all manner of functions to deal with Crow in the most torturous of ways, he instead decided to beat down on her with his fists, *strengthening* his body to the point where even her synchronised ant soul couldn't protect her from the weight of his blows.

Slowly but surely he was eating through her body's defences, until finally, one well-placed strike drew blood. And this was the first time he smiled through this whole exchange. That satisfaction seemed to fuel an even more brutal rally of blows. He played around with her. Punching her and throwing her around. And though her body maintained some degree of toughness, the pain was getting to her. So much so that she couldn't focus enough to perform any Soul Arts.

Richard was simply overwhelming.

And perhaps it was the sound of her flesh being brutalised, but she didn't manage to hear her mother's scream until it was too late. "Stay in the house," she'd told her. But how could a mother watch their child be handled so? How could a parent stand still while watching someone beat their child to...

So Crow didn't hear her mother's screams as she approached. And Richard, so blinded by the combination of his rage and enjoyment, didn't notice her, either. Perhaps if he had, things would have gone differently. But he hadn't. So when Liliana came upon him, shrieking to leave her daughter alone, Richard saw not a woman; saw not a parent protecting their child, but a pest. A pest that needed to be removed. So he struck Liliana round the face to relieve himself of this nuisance.

But he hadn't realised it was her. He hadn't realised she'd been coming.

He hadn't realised, and so hit her with the same strength he'd been hitting Crow. And Crow's body was toughened by her Soul

Syncro. He'd amplified his strength multiple times to bypass her defences. And perhaps, under normal circumstances, Liliana would have *strengthened* her body, too. But Richard didn't realise she was coming. He didn't realise he was striking her with such great strength.

He didn't realise, at the time, that she couldn't strengthen her body, because she couldn't use sen.

Because his sen zone was still active.

Both Richard and Crow heard it when it happened. The sound of bones snapping. The thud of Liliana's body as it hit the ground.

Then everything seemed to fall silent. As silent as her lifeless, unmoving corpse.

All of a sudden the pain in Crow's body stopped. No, stopped isn't the right word. The pain was still there, she just couldn't feel it anymore. Because a new pain, a greater pain, took its place.

Crow screamed.

Richard all but disappeared from her perception. Everything did, actually. All she saw now was her mother. Her mother, lying on the ground with a twisted neck. Life had already left her eyes. Crow stared into nothingness. Tears drowned her eyes and anguish filled her heart. She shook her mother.

'Mother!' she called out, over, and over, and over again. But what value were the words with no one to hear them?

Well, someone heard them. Richard. Though he cared not for the words nor the pain within them. He spoke words of his own, and Crow heard them very clearly.

'It should have been you. If only you'd listened. You could have had a good life elsewhere. Let this be a valuable lesson to you,

you abomination. This is what happens when the weak oppose the strong.'

She hadn't even heard the remaining words. Her mind was fixated on 'It should have been you'.

And then, as if a final act of ruthlessness, from where he stood, Richard set Crow's house ablaze, and gave her his parting words.

'Now get off my land.'

◉

'You shouldn't have killed my mother.'

Richard could feel the stares of his daughters who had just entered the room as the words were spoken. He turned around to face them, a fierceness in his eyes.

'What?' he yelled. 'As if you don't know the way the world works. As if you don't remember why we had to come here in the first place! What people like her did to us!'

'They drove us out of our home, father,' said Gloria. 'But we all made it. We rebuilt. Re-established'

'NO, I REBUILT!' he rebutted. 'I SACRIFICED! I DID ALL THE WORK! YOU ALL JUST MOVED IN! You, you WOMEN! Never taking anything seriously. Never appreciating the responsibility, and the burden that gets placed on our shoulders. Shirking your responsibility, just like ELIZABETH!'

'Well at least aunty Elizabeth managed to get away from the likes of you. This family went downhill when she left.'

Richard scoffed. 'Oh yes, your sweet aunty Elizabeth. You think she's never killed anyone before, huh? I've protected you all from the cruelty of this world, but it seems that was a mistake. People die every day, Gloria. For numerous reasons. That someone died by my hand means nothing in the grand scheme of things.' He looked over to Old Crow. 'That's just the price of being weak.'

'Settle down now, Richard,' said Evaán. 'Out of penance for the part my family played in the downfall of yours, and a personal favour to Elizabeth, I've allowed you the position you have in this city. But never forget who is in fact weak, and who is strong. Your role in this story isn't as significant as you think it to be. Take heed.' And without giving them time to respond, Evaán *removed* Richard and his family from the room.

Old Crow's body gave way again, but N'Adina caught her.

'Thank you, young priestess,' she said. Then she put a hand to N'Adina's face. 'My father said he was happy to have had a girl, because at least there was a chance I might meet the High Priestess of the Spirit Forest, since she lives in a place men may not tread. Unfortunately I never did make it to Eruba. You make sure you win the battle for the throne. So that at least, from whatever waits for me beyond, I can say to all whom I encounter, that the High Priestess bestowed upon me the honour of holding me in my last moments. I'm sure that will make them all jealous.' She mustered a laugh again. 'Thank you for your kindness, priestess N'Adina. And thank you for witnessing my exit from this world. And you, Big Dog,' she said, looking over to him. 'Your company has kept me going over the years. Do say goodbye to Alex for me. She's such a brilliant girl. I'm sure her path will lead her to many great adventures.'

Then she looked at Evaán.

'You have my thanks, Mr President. I do hope, by the end of this story you all are telling, that you can look back and say it was all worth it. It's a dangerous path you've chosen to tread. You might find some to not be so understanding of your intentions; good as you might claim them to be. Though I suppose when one sits at the top of the world, such fleeting and trivial thoughts aren't of much consequence.'

She paused for a moment to look at each of them once more. A goodbye with the eyes meant more than one with the mouth. And that's what that was. And then, her final words.

'I look forward to seeing how this story unfolds.'

And with a great big smile on her face, Old Crow released herself. She'd fought for so long. So long just to say those final words. And now... now she could be laid to rest.

The ultimate honour for any Shaman.

Ascension.

She was perfectly still. Her eyes were closed. Her heart still beat in her chest, because her body hadn't quite caught up to the loss of its soul. But it would stop eventually.

It was a curious thing. The relationship of mind, body and soul. Each existed individually, but couldn't achieve their full potential without the balanced coexistence of the others.

How curious a thing it was, this existence known as humans.

68

BLACK BOX

Evening. The time where the day approaches its end, and an appropriate setting for this story to draw near its conclusion.

Reena had promised to tell Daniel everything he needed to know after the test, but it wasn't just he who was due this enlightenment. Many stories reached their precipice today, and the leads in each of them had earned their right to know why. So at the same time that Daniel and Reena were sitting in her room, Cy and Evaán were together, too, in a place Cy was completely unfamiliar with.

Alex was still at MindSpace HQ, standing on the balcony of the room she'd been given for the night. She stared out into Central District, looking on further to West District, visible from how high she was. It was marvellous, how different the scenery was here compared to where she called home. She felt a little out of place.

This was always part of the goal, but she'd never quite been able to truly imagine what it would be like to stand here, no matter how many stories Daniel had told her.

There was a sudden gust of wind, and she was familiar with enough literature to recognise the cliche. But there was a tingling sensation, too. That same one she got when she was around Mara. That was a surprise.

She turned around, expecting to know the name but not face of the man who stood before her. Because she, too, had reached the precipice of this particular story today. And here to gift her with some of the answers she sought; the man whose name she'd learned mere hours ago, but whose existence seemed to bear more consequence on her life than she could even fathom.

With his chestnut skin, black hair, and supposedly brown eyes, he stood many inches above her, and donned the same style of coat she saw October wearing earlier. Though his coat was black, the numbers were white, and it was different. But without a doubt, it was him, here at last. And she said his name for the first time, as if to completely solidify what she was sure she knew.

'Nathaniel.'

⬢

Cy had been waiting with Mara when Evaán appeared.

'Come with me,' Evaán had said, just before teleporting them to a location Cy had no knowledge of. And within this location, everything about Cy's Greater Self was being suppressed. Not only his mind, but his affinity, too. The very air on his skin didn't make its properties known to him. It was here that he gained a greater depth of understanding of how far outclassed he was. Even an advanced *blocking* function couldn't stop his affinity from taking effect.

Then the reality of his current situation dawned on him. With no Greater Self to call on, he was completely powerless, and at the mercy of whatever Evaán chose to do with him. Then he remembered what Evaán had said at the end of their short battle.

'Would you like to see your people?'

He'd been pondering over it between then and now, anxious as to what exactly he meant. Perhaps, Cy was here not just to see his people, but to join them. It seemed fitting. Of all the crimes committed in his district, this must have been the most heinous. There was no way it would simply be overlooked, as if Cy wasn't the most dangerous criminal West District had seen in a while.

They'd been walking through a glaring white hallway. Evaán hadn't said a word the entire time, and Cy was too consumed by his own thoughts to strike up a conversation. Also, there was the farce of it all. Whatever it was that blocked Cy from using his abilities, Evaán wasn't affected by it. That much was certain. So why the charade of making them walk this distance to the end of a hall, when Evaán could have teleported them to their destination from that start? It was a curious thing, when one as capable with their Greater Self as he, chose to interact with the world with their lesser self.

But this was just another lesson Cy needed to learn. That reality existed in a state of balance, and maintaining that balance between one's Greater and lesser selves was important. Why did Evaán make them walk?

'You've had quite a mentally stimulating day,' he said. 'I thought it best to give your mind some tranquillity before showing why I brought you here. What lies ahead is bound to shock you.'

Had Evaán been reading his thoughts? Or was it simply his keen intellect that allowed him to so accurately assess Cy's state of mind.

Cy wasn't entirely sure it mattered which was true. Both, perhaps, were equally impressive.

They came upon the end of the hall and Evaán *opened* the door. Just as he'd said, what Cy saw shocked him.

His people were there. Not just them, but Orenians, and Irians, too. Anyone in this entire city that went against the government, this was where they ended up. But it wasn't seeing them that shocked Cy. He'd always assumed they had to be somewhere, he just didn't know where. And it was the uncertainty of the state of their loved ones which caused such anguish within his community. So it wasn't the sight of them that shocked him, but rather, as he looked around this impossibly large space that might as well have been a district in its own right, he noticed that no matter where his gaze fell, or upon whose face he took the time to ponder, not a hint of sadness was in sight.

Everyone was smiling.

Daniel recalled all the times he and Reena had played together when they were younger. Whether it was out in the streets, or at various establishments when they were older, or within the confines of the Marston Estate; at no point was Daniel granted the privilege of stepping into the place that she called home.

And whilst it was unsurprising that during her time within the city she took abode in MindSpace Central HQ, it was a rather unusual experience to find himself, for the first time, standing in her bedroom.

He'd been in women's rooms before, and couldn't help his mind making an immediate comparison of how little visual stimuli there was. No posters, no vast array of colourful artwork or decoration. It seemed to be a minimalist's fantasy, with only a bed and a couch in sight.

The couch hadn't even been there at the beginning. She'd *transmuted* it specifically for him.

She told him to sit. He did, and she sat on her bed, opposite him.

'This is strange, isn't it?' she said.

'Well, it's the first time you've invited me to your place. So yeah, it is a bit strange.'

There was a look on her face, then. Confusion? Or perhaps realisation at the truth in what he'd said. But that wasn't what she'd been referring to as strange. 'I meant the distance.'

'Oh. Well, yes, I suppose. It's a bit... formal.'

She nodded. 'I should come over there.'

I could come over there, the gentleman in Daniel thought to say, but he realised the potential forward nature of offering to join her on the bed rather than join him on the couch. And though it was brief, the time it took him to formulate this in his mind left a pause in the air, which she filled by moving over to him.

Now the pause in the air was replaced by a sort of awkwardness, because he'd never experience Reena behave in the way she was behaving now.

'I know you said you'd explain everything to me after the test, but if it's making you this uncomfortable, then—'

She cut him off. A sudden grab of his hand into her palm. And she gripped him tight. 'I'm not uncomfortable. It's just, I'm still making sense of the situation myself. And I don't want to say the wrong thing to you. Everything that happens from now on, and the way it happens, it's all important. So I need to make sure I get it right, so that you can see yourself becoming the person you need to be.' She took a deep breath, gathered her thoughts, and let go of his hand. 'Okay. Where do I begin?'

⬢

'Nathanael,' he corrected.

'Isn't that what I said?' Alex replied.

'You said "niel". It's "nael". Given the things you've learned recently, the importance of getting someone's name right shouldn't be lost on you.'

She immediately thought of Q, and the fact he was the first to speak her full name. A name she wasn't even aware she had. And remembering that, she addressed the elephant in the room. 'So we're related?'

'If you consider being of the same clan as related then, yes, I suppose we are. Though there aren't many of us who exist outside of our homeland. And you... Well, your birth, and how you ended up in this city, remain a mystery.'

'All that really matters is that I'm here now though, right?'

Nathanael looked at her sympathetically. 'Q told you the meaning of your name? What is it?'

'The meaning of my name?' she asked. But then she recalled their conversation, and what he'd said after she'd properly introduced herself. *Oh. That's what he meant.* 'Where knowledge gathers. Names have meaning?'

'A True Name does. It's like an affinity,' he said. 'It serves a purpose, and is never bestowed by accident. A True Name encompasses the entirety of one's being; gives them the power of the meaning within it. Something so valuable, and it's given to you by someone else. It's not just the "now" that's important, Ojo'Alexandria.' He looked at her so intently then. And hearing her name, her full name - her True Name - like that, it still sent an unknown feeling coursing through her being. 'Where we came from is a question we should always strive to answer. Because within that, one might come closer to knowing their true self. And your existence is a curiosity. I'd be lying if I said we haven't attempted to delve into your origin.'

'And?' she asked, trying to appear somewhat interested in her past. Though it was a difficult charade to pull off when she'd lived 22 years without ever giving it much thought. It always seemed that other people were more interested in where she'd come from than she was.

'And nothing. You remain as much a mystery as you were back then. Perhaps the truth of who you are is something you and you alone are supposed to find.'

'And where exactly would I find such a thing?'

'In a place nobody has thought to go. Or maybe, a place no one can go. No one but you. But that's not what you're here to talk to me about, is it? You have questions.'

'I do. Many, many questions. But before I get to the important ones, I have to ask. What's with the coats? October had one. Evaán, too. And I believe I saw a woman wearing one at the council earlier.

But their numbers are different.' She inspected him again. 'And the colours are reversed.'

'How many senses do we have?'

'Five.'

'Five lesser senses. But there are the three greater senses. Instinct, spirituality, and mentality. There's debate about the exact order of the last three, but October considers mentality to be the 8th sense, and The Mind is his affinity. Hence his number. Evaán...'

⬢

Cy was flabbergasted. He couldn't believe what he'd just heard.

'They'll be returning home soon,' Evaán had said.

'What do you mean?' Cy replied, still uncertain of what to make of this situation.

And Evaán replied, 'They've served their purpose.'

Cy could feel his heart palpitating and his temperature rising. 'What purpose is that?' He was doing everything he could to control his temper, but he couldn't shake off the notion that he, and everyone in this prison facility, were just pieces on a chapel board, unaware that a game was being played.

'Every district, since the creation of this city, was designed for the specific purpose of telling a story. Each one of those stories was designed to cultivate a hero, someone who would be set apart from everyone else. Someone who could bear the weight of their people. There's a reason why West District is the only one with Orenians and Erubans. There's a reason why the Irians of West District harboured malice to the other skins. The reason is because that's how we made it.

'A group of us remade this city. Amongst them is a man who has the power to know the exact nature of persona an individual has. We used that power to determine the nature of the unconscious minds of everyone in this city; to determine what sorts of people they were, and which district they should fall in. Anyone who had a predisposition towards a sense of superiority to the other skins was put in West District, because that would incite conflict amongst them. We conditioned the officers to display a degree of favouritism to those who shared their skin, further ostracising your own people. We set up a story where you, the hero of your people, would rebel against the status quo, and become the person you needed to be to make a change. That was how it was in all the other districts, too. Each of them has had their own sort of revolution, and in each case, a hero was made. It is only through adversity that we can grow to be the person the world needs us to be, and so the world will challenge us.

'These people here, they went against us, yes. But putting them here wasn't so much for the purpose of punishing them, as it was for the purpose of developing you. You, the hero of West District.'

'I have no idea what you're saying,' Cy said. 'You put us through all that suffering for what? To build me up? Do you think the strength I gained through adversity is worth the tears of my people I've had to endure? That their happiness was a worthwhile compromise as long as I gained power? Don't claim you did this for my benefit when I myself would have died to keep smiles on their faces!' He'd raised his voice. He hadn't meant to, it just sort of happened. Because none of what Evaán had said was a good enough reason for the ordeal they'd all been through. But then, there was more to the story than just that.

'Don't misunderstand the intention of my words, Cy. There was indeed a benefit for you in this ordeal, but that too, was simply a means to an end. It was beneficial to my organisation to have you develop the way you did. As it was beneficial to have the heroes of the other districts engage in their own trials of adversity. You see, this city wasn't created as a technological utopia for the benefit of its citizens. This city was created for the purpose of telling stories. We enable people to tell their stories, and in return, we benefit from one of the world's most powerful resources.'

They were suddenly transported to yet another location, and once again, Cy saw something that left him only with more questions and no answers. Inside this room was a large monolith. And they must have been out of the facility, because Cy regained his sense of Greater Self, and with his affinity back intact, he knew right away what this was. He'd never seen one this large before, but without a doubt, this was the source of everything that made this city what it was. Arethium. But not just any Arethium. This was a Mother.

And Evaán, joining Cy in admiring this rare but essential material, finished what he was saying. It wasn't Arethium he was referring to when he said "one of the world's most powerful resources."

It was, 'Individuality.'

'So there're philosophers, storytellers, and dreamers?' Daniel said, summarising what Reena had just told him. 'Philosophers study the world?'

'They study the truth of the world,' she specified. Dreamers imagine possibilities of the world, and storytellers connect the two.'

'How does that work, exactly?'

'Take this city for example. The transition of Old Heart into New wasn't something that just happened. There was the truth of what it was before, and there was an idea of what it could be. My parents and their friends spent a long time planning how the city would change. They travelled the world, gained immeasurable knowledge, and through the story they lived in their travels, they connected the truth of what the city was, to the idea of what it could be, thus, creating a new reality.

'Philosopher's tell you what the world is. Dreamers tell you what it could be. Storytellers are the ones who make it so.'

'So what are we?'

'I'm a philosopher. You're a dreamer.'

'What if I want to be a philosopher?'

Reena shook her head. 'Your mind is too free. You believe more in the world that exists within your head than you do the world without. And I know too much about the laws of this world to believe whatever fantasy I might make of it. Whether or not you're a philosopher or a dreamer, the two are often mutually exclusive.'

'And what about storytellers, then? How do you become that? Who even decides?'

'The world decides. And anyone can become a storyteller by telling stories, but simply telling a story doesn't make you a storyteller. Just like having a dream doesn't make you a dreamer. Or knowing that we need oxygen to breathe doesn't make you a philosopher. Simply knowing a little bit of truth, or having a little bit of imagination, or telling a little bit of a story, doesn't make you any one of those things. You need a certain degree of influence in any field for the world to see you worthy of holding a title. You're a dreamer, and that's what you're supposed to be. You don't need to worry about being anything else.'

He thought for a moment, culminating the information he had now with the various things that had occurred the last week. The change to his body. The new sensitivity he had to the world. The words that The Warrior said that he was sure he'd spoken all that time ago. The appearance of Reena in the city, coinciding with the appearance of The Witch in Lore. The Warrior, fighting the army of The Machine, and Daniel fighting The Machine the next day. Yes, his mind made sense of it all, and he said, 'So I'm The Warrior? Or, The Warrior was based off of me?'

Reena nodded. 'And The Witch after me. But the relationship between us and the story is cyclical. The characters were based off of us, but as they grew in the story, our state of being became based on them. Lore is a story created to connect the truth of what we are in the real, with the dream of what we could be. It's a story that creates realities. A world formed by the interconnected minds of everyone in this city. Initially, it was only supposed to benefit us. My parents, their colleagues, and myself. It was to evolve us from what we were into what we are. But your mind, your brilliant mind, it was so free, so powerful, that the story chose you to become like us. This was never intended to happen to you, but the story, the world, decided that this is what you're supposed to be. The Warrior. A hero. A dreamer.'

'And the dream I had the night before the test? The one that showed me the freedom of my mind? Was that you guys as well?'

'I don't know yet. There's someone I need to speak to to find out. But probably, yes. This is all part of his plan. He's like you. He's a dreamer, but he's a storyteller, too, and storytellers are the most secretive people you'll ever meet. They never tell you exactly what they have planned, they just do things with a complete disregard for the people involved, as long as they can tell their story. So knowing him, these dreams might be part of some grand plan he has, and even if I ask him, he probably won't tell me. "There are things that must only be known by those supposed to know them." That's probably what he'd say.'

Daniel laughed. 'So even you can't escape that line.'

'Nobody can. There are philosophers around the world still trying to discover its secrets. The general consensus is that the world will reveal them to the right people when it deems them worthy of knowing.'

Daniel looked at Reena, wide-eyed, and laughed.'You're right, I couldn't be a philosopher. It all seems a bit far fetched. Who is this guy anyway?'

'He gave you your coder.'

'Myself, October, and Lilith, we all have affinities. It's part of what made us so formidable during our travels. Evaán doesn't have an affinity, but arguably he has something better. A brilliant mind. I've been all around this world and met an uncountable number of people. Without a doubt, Evaán is the most intelligent. Anyone who really knows him will tell you the same. He could conceptualise from the age of 12.' Nathanael said this to really drive his point home. It was effective, because that was what made Alex understand just what degree of genius intellect he was talking about. Alex couldn't even fathom having had the ability to conceptualise at a mere 12.

'But why is that better than an affinity? And what's that got to do with his number?'

'His mind lets him understand everything about the world. Ask him about any topic, any idea, any concept, he understands it better than anyone else, exactly as it needs to be understood. Because his mind fully understands the meta behind his functions, he doesn't lose anything upon output.'

Alex was catching on, and she continued to what she thought Nathanael would say next. 'And when you couple that with his ability to run functions through Arethium and bypass world tax, he has a 100% output. So why the 99?'

'Because it's not 100%.'

Alex said nothing, because she didn't understand. The maths came to 100, of that, she was certain.

'What's the difference between 99 and 100?' Nathanel asked.

'1?' she replied as though there were some doubts about the basic arithmetic.

'No. It's the difference between perfection and imperfection. No matter how perfectly he understands the logic behind something, it's still just an imitation, and not the real thing. An imitation can't be perfect. So Evaán's functions output at 99%, because the only people who can reach 100% output on anything...' he paused, waiting for her to answer. And she did.

'Are those who have an affinity for it.'

'Correct. So people like myself, October, Lilith, and you, can all reach a 100% output with functions based on our affinities. But Evaán, though he can use any function better than anyone who doesn't have an affinity for it, he'll always be capped at that 99%, hence, the number on his coat.'

'And you? What special quality is associated with 501?'

'Mine is actually based on a tattoo I've got. It's on my chest.'

'But what's the significance?'

'I don't know. I've always had it.'

'You've always had a tattoo?'

'Yepp. For as long as I can remember.'

'Well who gave it to you?'

'Don't know.'

Alex frowned her eyebrows. 'You're not making sense.'

'I guess it's just something nobody needs to know yet.' That was a very quick way of getting someone to accept something and move on.

'Okay. Then, maybe it's time you can tell me exactly what's been going on. How long have you guys been observing me?'

'The whole time. Since you were dropped off at the orphanage. Since I first felt the resonance of our Ojo bloodline with one another.

Even more so once we discovered what your affinity was. A power we'd never seen before.'

Well that answered that.

'You know about Niche?' Alex asked.

'I do.'

'They told me this city isn't what I think it is. What did they mean?'

'The city serves a purpose. It's a means to an end, designed to connect truth and possibility, by telling stories. You know about Mothers? The Mothers in each district are connected to the main Mother we have here in the research facility. It collects the meta of everything that goes on in this city, taking on the individuality of every mind that resides here. It's through the individuality of the people that the world evolves, and the same goes for Arethium, and Mothers. The more intelligent people get, the stronger they get, the more freely they're able to think, all of those factors help a Mother develop.'

'To what end?'

Nathanael stopped to look at her. He was pondering. Should he say? He figured it was about time she knew. It would help her later on.

'To create a Philosopher's Stone.' He held out his hand, and within it appeared a fragment of Arethium. 'Tell me what Arethium is.'

'A natural occurring metal that contains all of the world's meta in a passive state. It can activate any combination of meta at random, and is capable of permanently storing the meta of functions.'

'Now explain Rethium.'

'An artificially created substance, formed through transmutation using Arethium, or a Mother, as a catalyst, so that its nature property can be passed on. The metaphysical properties of Rethium are limited by the ability of the alchemist or Mother that created it.'

'You really are a gathering of knowledge,' he laughed. 'Now explain a Mother.'

'Arethium that's been specifically programmed with alchemic functions, allowing non-alchemists to perform transmutation through it. It's how each district creates its coders.'

'And did you know that Shaman can interact with the spiritual properties of Arethium?'

'I've been curious about it for some time.'

'Well a Philosopher's Stone, what I'm holding in my hand now, breaks the boundary between the metaphysical that Sentiens perceive, and the spiritual which Shamans perceive. Holding one of these would allow your Sentien mind to perceive ether.' It disappeared before Alex could even suggest he let her hold it. 'There's only a handful of them in the whole world, and nobody knows how to make one. So there's various organisations trying multiple methods to attempt to recreate them.'

'But how does no one know how to create them? Surely the method must have been passed down somewhere?'

'Perhaps. But we've scoured the corners of this world and never come across anything that alludes to a method by which they're made. As far as anyone knows, it's part of the world's forgotten history.'

'The world's forgotten history?'

'Yes,' Nathanael said with a big grin on his face. 'A story the world won't allow anyone to tell.'

⬢

'The world evolves by adapting to the mental, physical, and spiritual nature of all that live within it,' Evaán began. Since Arethium contains all of the world's meta within, it's possible for us to not only harness that power, but specifically collect it for ourselves. Almost every major organisation in the world will have a Mother at the centre of it. They can not only use it to create weapons, but to absorb the meta of everything that goes on around it, causing it to adapt and evolve. But the one thing a Mother can't automatically adapt to is a person's individuality. That is something that must be freely given. The coders the citizens wear, they're all connected to this Mother, feeding it with the individual nature of their very being. It's constantly evolving.'

'And what's the end goal here?' Cy asked.

'This Mother, fed by the citizens of this city, also in turn feeds us, keeping us aligned with the nature of this world. Not quite in the same way that the Ojo are, but similar. Our goal is to become worthy of knowing this world's truth, and uncovering its lost history. Everything that happens in this city is a means to that end. You see, Cy, we're not heroes, nor are we villains. We're not necessarily good, nor bad. We're simply philosophers, using the story of this city to connect the truth of what we are to the dream of what we hope to achieve, thus creating a new reality.

'Everyone in this facility can return to their life outside, because their role in this story has ended. They helped create you, so now you can be the person this city needs you to be.'

'And what person is that?'

'The mayor of West District.'

※

'What do you mean no-one writes Lore?' Daniel asked, confused. He was so taken aback he just blurted out the first thing that came to mind. 'Stories don't just tell themselves.'

'Well, that's not entirely true,' said Reena, 'but in this case, no, the story of Lore doesn't tell itself, but it's not told by any particular person. The city collects the thoughts of everyone in it, and culminates all those ideas, wants, desires, individualities, and creates the story we call Lore. But Lore, like MindSpace, is actually its own imaginary world. It's a story that progresses itself by imitating the stories we tell ourselves. Nobody tells the story of Lore, because really, it's a story we're all telling. We just don't realise it.'

'Wow, that's amazing.' He was almost childlike in his wonderment. 'But someone had to have set it up like that in the first place, right? Your dad?'

'It was the joint effort of my parents and their two colleagues, but in terms of who had the biggest hand in its development, I suppose, yes, my dad. Although, the man who gave you your coder probably had an equal part in giving the world a kickstart. He's the only one who has a real capacity for storytelling.'

'Damn,' he really couldn't believe it. 'This city is amazing. My grandfather always boasted about how vital he was to its tech revolution, but really, it's your parents, and whoever these other people are. They made this city.'

'They're amazing. They were already travelling the world at my age.'

'But you're travelling the world.'

'I'm travelling through Iria, with the help I've received from them. It's incomparable.'

'Don't sell yourself so short,' he said with a smile. 'You're the most impressive person I know.'

This was the rare singular occasion where Reena allowed herself to blush. Perhaps it was a drop of good fortune, but Daniel happened to be looking away at the time, though some part of her wished he'd seen.

She really wasn't used to feeling like this.

There was an ambience of moonlight piercing through her window. In her room of just a bed and a sofa, with the two of them just sitting there, looking out to the night sky seemed... tranquil. There was silence in the air. A peaceful silence, not an ominous one. But it was broken when Daniel asked, 'So what happens now?'

'Lilith, whom you noticed at the council today, her affinity is Time. With her powers, we've been able to look back through the history of everywhere we've been in the world, and we noticed something. There's a point in the world's past where everything just stops. Where there's no record of events taking place, and where Lilith's powers can't see any further.'

'Wouldn't that just be the beginning?' Alex asked.

'No, because it's not as if nothing's there. There's entire civilisations; thriving civilisations. They didn't just appear suddenly. They were made over time, but the time in which they were made doesn't seem to exist. You might pin that down to us only starting to record history after a certain point in time, but is it plausible that the entire world just happened to do that at the same point? With all the information we have at hand, the most logical conclusion is that history has been lost somehow.'

'But how can history be lost? It's not like it's something you can just take hold of and put into a box as if things never happened.'

This was one of the few times where Nathanael looked directly at her during their conversation.

'What?' There was a layer of concern in her voice. This look was unfamiliar.

'It's just... that was an interesting choice of words. Regardless, you know very little about the world. So perhaps once you've explored it a little, the idea that history can be taken and "put into a box" might not be so farfetch'd. There's an entire world of possibilities that you're completely unaware of, so don't rule anything out just yet.'

'Okay. So what happens now.'

'Well, there's a few other people I need to see, so the rest of your evening belongs to you. And tomorrow, your journey begins.' He smiled at her. It was warm and heartful, and hopeful, too. Hopeful of the adventure that she was primed to be starting, and where that journey might lead her.

Hopefully, to a place no one has gone before.

'One more thing,' he said. He held out his hand to her once more, and in it, appeared a little black box.

'What's this?'

'I don't know. I'm just returning it.'

'Returning?'

'You had it with you when we found you. I've taken it to everyone I know, hoping to find an answer to what it is, but no one can tell me. It completely blocks out any attempt to delve into its existence. Neither Sentien, Shaman, nor Seer can bypass whatever power protects it. So I'm returning it, because perhaps, the truth of what it is, lies with you and you alone.'

Alex took it from him. She didn't feel any sort of special connection with it, it was just a black box. When she went to conceptualise it, all the meta she saw identified it as such. Just a black box. Which was curious, because if it was indeed just a black box, then she should be able to easily destroy it. But even when she attempted to run her *Anti* through it, it repelled it entirely, causing a flare of sparks to erupt, which surprised Alex enough to drop it.

'That's what happens,' Nathanael said. 'It rejects any attempt to bypass its external being. Whatever power keeps it together, it's beyond anything we understand.'

Alex picked it up. 'Well if my Anti can't get past it then there's not much more I can do.' She handed it back to him, but he pushed her hand away.

'As I said, I'm returning it. The answer may lie on your journey, or maybe it won't. Either way, it belongs to you. Store it in your Space. As long as you don't try to affect the box itself, you can still operate functions on it.'

The box disappeared. It was strange, her being able to store it in her *Space*, but not be able to use her *Anti* on it. But it was as Nathanael said. Whatever power held it together, it was beyond them.

'Well then, I'll see you tomorrow,' he said.

'Wait. You never told me your affinity.'

Nathanael just smiled, and then he was gone.

Alex stood there, irritated. Perhaps it was the abruptness of his departure, or perhaps it was the nature of her name which afflicted her with a need to know things, but she walked away from this encounter extremely unsatisfied.

69

DREAM

Nathanael appeared in a room where October, Lilith, Evaán, Chen and Reena were waiting.

'No Big Dog?' he asked.

'He's saying his goodbyes,' Lilith replied.

'I guess I'll see him tomorrow, then.' He looked around the room. 'Why does it seem like I'm about to be scolded?'

'There's a concern,' Lilith replied again.

Nathanael turned his attention to Chen, who bore the most serious expression of everyone there. Then he glanced at Reena, briefly. 'The dreams?'

'So you are responsible?' Reena said abruptly.

And then Chen, in a more serious tone than he was used to giving, said to Nathanael, 'We've known each other quite a while now. You helped me move over here when I needed to, and have always held yourself as an honourable man. But there's only so much gratitude that offers you. You are a good man, but you're also an ambitious man, and I know that you'll do anything to fulfil your dream. So I have to ask, what is it that's prompted you to take this course of action? Why reveal to my daughter, and to Daniel, the secrets of their being?'

'I, too, would like to know what it is you have planned, Nathanael.' That one came from Evaán.

Nathanael sighed and shook his head, rather nonchalant about the whole situation. 'The truth is, guys, it wasn't me. I know about the dreams because The Book told me about them, but I'm not the one who put them there.'

'If not you, then who?' asked Chen.

This time, it was Nathanael's turn to put on a serious tone. 'I don't know. There's only a handful of people with the knowledge and ability to do what's been done, and three of them are in this room. It's not Sandman, this isn't his style. I suppose it could be the old man, in which case, there's nothing we can do about it anyway. But honestly, I've been thinking this for a while now, and this furthers my suspicions. But I think there's another player in this game. Someone we haven't met, beyond our perception, but somehow, is tuned in to everything we do.'

'Can there really be such a capable person who we haven't met yet?' asked October.

'There's still so much about the world we don't know. The forgotten history alone is proof of that. Whoever this person is, or even what they are, they're telling their own story, and they have enough influence to make us part of it.'

'Kaleidoscope?' Reena asked. 'Claire certainly has the power and the audacity to pull something like this.'

'I've kept an eye on Claire,' said Nathanael. 'She's not responsible.'

'But how do you know? If anything, she has more of a specialty in this sort of thing than you do. Can you be sure she's not pulling one over on you without you realising?'

Nathanael, Evaán, Lilith and October all looked between one another. Reena was right, Claire was a special case, and the four of them knew that better than anyone.

'Could be worth looking into,' Lillith said.

Evaán kept his gaze on Nathanael. 'You still don't seem convinced.'

Nathanael said nothing, and Evaán knew what that meant.

'We can rule out Claire for now,' Evaán said.

This was often how these things went. Nothing was ever concretely agreed upon until Evaán gave his thoughts, because ultimately, nobody trusted the judgement of anyone above his own. But Evaán, due to the capacity for which he could understand things, was always able to see things from Nathanael's point of view, abstract as it often was.

They had a rather curious relationship. One was a philosopher, the other was a dreamer and storyteller. But they were both the best respectively at what they did, and held each other in the highest regard. They saw the world differently to everyone else.

'We'll just have to let things play out,' said Nathanael. 'The way things are going now,' he smiled, 'I think we're there; heading into the final chapters. The pieces are set. All the major players are coming out of the woodworks, and whoever this new storyteller is, they'll be no different. All will be revealed soon, it has to be. Because everyone needs to be ready.'

'Ready for what,' Reena asked.

He then said something they'd never heard before. They didn't quite know what it meant, because they didn't have the information he did. So they were as confused by him saying those words as he was the first time he heard them. And the voice of the woman who'd said them to him echoed in his mind as he relayed them to his friends for the first time.

Yes, all the major players needed to be ready for what was coming, because:

'The world is approaching a new era.'

70

<u>Hero</u>

Cy returned home where Mara had been waiting. He entered silently. Their apartment was angled against the moon, so no light came through the window. There, in the darkness, Mara sat, and the little natural light that made the room barely visible allowed their eyes to meet.

Cy had questions, and Mara would need to answer them, because she, this entire time, knew more than she'd let on.

'Did you know it would end like this?' Cy asked. 'Have you been part of their plan the entire time?'

'No, my love. They remain as mysterious to me now as they always have been. But you and I have always seen this revolution from different perspectives. You never thought yourself a hero; just someone who was doing what needed to be done. But I know better, darling. I knew that there was a story being told. I know that all stories need a hero. But I also know that the hero doesn't always win. That's the difference between the stories we tell, and the stories we live. Whether or not this revolution succeeded was your goal, not mine. My aim has always been to make you the man the world needed you to be. As I said, you are my truth, and this journey has been for the purpose of helping you find your own. And I can see it in your eyes, now. You have found a new part of yourself; a new purpose, have you not?'

Cy was unsurprised by Mara's intuition. This was indeed the woman he'd fallen in love with. He told her everything that happened with Evaán, and how he'd asked him to become the new mayor of West District.

'Did you accept?'

'I said I needed time to think. He's given me until tomorrow.'

'And have you thought?'

'I have. But I wanted to talk to you, first. We're a team, after all.'

Mara got up and went to him, bringing him into her embrace. 'I have prayed, and centred myself with this city. There is power here. More than you know. Your story hasn't ended yet. We've simply finished a chapter and stopped at a crossroad. What happens next is up to you. But my love, if you become mayor, you can make this district what you always wanted it to be, and this time, instead of going against the government, you'll have it on your side. Is that not a better outcome than what you yourself envisioned?'

'It is. I know that. I guess I just can't quite believe it.'

'What?'

'How entirely outmatched I was. All this time, they've been ten steps ahead. It makes me wonder how much further there is for me to go.'

'As far as you see yourself going, my love.'

71

Mother

Alex returned to the recreation area where Kitchen, N'Adina, and Q were making acquaintances.

'Did you have a good conversation?' Q asked.

'You're telling me you didn't hear every word that was said?' Alex replied sarcastically.

Q let off a little laugh. 'Even I can't get past that man's ability. Not yet, anyway.'

Alex was going to ask exactly what that 'ability' was, but Kitchen, rather loudly, interrupted. 'So apparently this necklace isn't "my" mother, but "a" mother. Apparently it's used for alchemy or something?'

'So your dad finally told you?'

'Earlier today. He said you knew and he'd asked you not to say anything.'

'Sorry.'

Kitchen *skipped* over to Alex and hugged her. 'No need to be. He also said you can teach me what to do with it, so let's call it even.'

'Sounds fair. There was something else I wanted to ask you.'

'If it's about the fact that you'll be leaving the city, don't worry. I'm coming with you. We all are.' Kitchen had *skipped* herself back to where Q and N'Adina are, and Alex was met with a picture of three happy faces. She looked at Q in particular and smiled. 'Oh,' she said. 'That's nice.'

❋

'So you told her about my ability to control time?' Lilith said to Nathanael. Only they, October, and Evaán remained in the room. 'Did she ask about looking into the history of where she was left?'

'She didn't. Probably too distracted by her own thoughts, but I imagine it'll cross her mind at some point.'

'Just as well. It's not like we'd have anything to tell her.'

'Perhaps,' Nathaniel replied, unconvinced. 'Let's go back. I need to see Sister Mabel anyway.'

'You can do that on your own, can't you?'

'There's something I'd like to check that needs a woman's touch.'

Lilith looked between Evaán and October who both simply shrugged. Then she agreed, and Nathanael took them to the orphanage.

Sister Mabel met them at the doorstep, right at the spot where they'd found Alex some 22 years ago. 'Returned once again.'

Nathanael gave her a hug and a kiss. 'Thanks for everything.'

'Oh it was my pleasure. She's grown into a fine young woman. She'd give your younger self a run for your money.'

Nathanael smiled. 'One can only hope.'

'Surprised to see you here, too, Lilith.'

'Nathanael needed a woman's touch for something, apparently,' Lilith said.

'I'm a woman,' Mabel responded in offence.

'And it's good that you're both here,' Nathanael said. 'Lilith, can you go back to that day?'

She did so reluctantly. They'd been through the history of Alex being dropped at the doorstep numerous times. She just suddenly appeared, hovered in the air briefly, and then was placed down, clutching onto a black box with a note that read "Alexandria."

'I'm curious to know what epiphany you've had, Nathanael,' Lilith said.

And he asked her, 'What do you always do when you say goodbye to Reena?'

'I hug and kiss her, obviously.'

'And you, Sister Mabel, when one of the children gets a bruise, what do you do?'

'Kiss it better, whilst simultaneously applying a healing command, and then tell them love heals all wounds.'

'Look closely at her face,' he said, looking at the baby Alex from the past. 'What do you see?'

Both Lilith and Sister Mabel noticed it at the same time. A little indent on Alex's cheek, just before she gets placed down. They never noticed it before because a baby's face made all sorts of indentations and wrinkles as they skirmished around. But this was different. This was a farewell. This was:

'A mother's kiss.'

Alex tapped Q on the shoulder. He'd been staring at a wall for some time now, which might have seemed strange if Alex believed even for a second that the wall was what he was looking at. 'What's got you so focussed?' She made a note that the direction he was peeking into was west.

'Nothing. Just daydreaming.'

Alex laughed. 'It's night time.'

It had taken a while for Q's voice to project to where Nathanael was because of the distance. But his message finally got to him.

'You're being watched from above.'

Nathanael abruptly disappeared from beside Lilith and Sister Mabel, reappearing high above West District's air space. The clouds were below him, and his silhouette cast a great shadow against the light of one of the moons. But despite his keen perception, whatever it was that had been watching him, it was gone.

But he had said earlier, there was another player in this game, and it seemed that they were beyond any of their perceptions. So despite not being able to perceive them, he believed - he knew, really - that he wasn't alone in the sky that night.

And he was right, he wasn't alone. In fact, the person with whom he shared the air space was right behind him. But she wasn't worried. She knew he yet had the ability to perceive the space within which she existed. It was an error in judgement that she'd allowed her intent to be perceived by Q. But that was what happened when one allowed their focus to falter.

Or perhaps, this, too, was simply how the story goes.

Either way, it wasn't yet time for her to reveal herself to them.

The brown-skinned woman with braided, silky, glow-in-the-moonlight white hair.

72

AS WE ENTER A NEW CHAPTER

For everything West District had been through the day before, the next morning was riddled with more tears than the city had seen for a long time. Because this morning, many families would hug their dogs for the last time. Some had already said goodbye the night before, but a few remained, and Big Dog wanted to give everyone a last farewell. It was known amongst the older generation in this district that most of the dogs that roamed the streets had long passed, and maintained their presence in the world only as Big Dog's Anima. But he wouldn't be there to conjure up these souls anymore.

'So you're travelling with Chen?' Nathanael said to him.

'Yeah, there's some Orenian spirits I'd like to get my hands on. Figure I'd give the old man some company.'

'We'll be heading north first, though,' said Chen.

'Finally going to see her? Have you told Katelina?' Nathanael asked.

Chen looked over to his daughter. 'No. This will stay between us.'

'Understood.'

Also in the vicinity were the cohort of Kitchen, Alex, Q, and N'Adina. And forming another group were Daniel, Reena, and.. Blackjack?'

Cy and Mara were there, too, but they were introduced to a new group of people whom Cy didn't recognise at first.

'We're the mayors of the other districts. You guys really took your time concluding your district's story.' said one of them.

'But it's a pleasure to finally have you joining us, Hermit,' said another.

It was then that Cy realised who the four of them were. They weren't just the mayors of the other four districts. He laughed. He laughed because there really was so much about this city - about this story - that he just didn't know. But he shook all of their hands as the new Mayor of West District, and collectively said to them, 'The pleasure is mine, Niche.'

Everyone's attention was then gathered by the sound of Nathanael's voice. He collected them around him.

'Okay guys, I hope you've said your goodbyes because this is it. The start of a new chapter for all of you. Whether you're staying in the city or leaving, remember, whatever you do, make sure you rattle the world and cause lots of trouble. That's how the best stories are told. We're all looking forward to seeing what happens next.'

Then with a snap of his fingers, Alex's group, Daniel's group, and Chen and Big Dog were removed from sight.

Alex's cohort found themselves a few miles outside of West District.

'Where do we go from here?' asked Kitchen.

'Apparently there are places we should go to learn certain things,' said Alex. 'Nathanael's input locations into our new coders. We need to head west first.'

'West? That suits me well. The climate there is closer to that of Eruba's,' said N'Adina.

'What are you going to learn in the west?' Q asked.

Alex checked the notes Nathanael left. Q noticed the change in her aura. She was surprised, and excited, when she said, 'How to stop time.'

So, do you know who We are yet?

That's okay. You can always start from the beginning.

Afterword

First of all, thank you so much for taking an interest in this book.

It's truly an honour when a creative's work is finalised by the appreciation of its audience. Without you, this story could never be complete.

I hope you've enjoyed the journey so far (though you are only at the beginning, and there is so much more to come).

This story is the culmination of everything I am. My thoughts, my hopes, beliefs, philosophies. To be able to express myself so authentically is a privilege, and I think I owe it to the world to make the most of this opportunity that's been given to me.

So I hope, as you've chosen to join me on this journey, that you will find something spectacular in the story that is to come; and that through the expression of my authenticity, you, and others like you, too, may be inspired to be your most authentic and greatest selves.

May this be part of the story that leads you to the dream of what you hope to achieve.

Once more, I thank you.

Until next time.

The Fire Speaker.

Printed in Great Britain
by Amazon